D0174023

LAURA SCOTT

HER MISTLETOE PROTECTOR
&
IDENTITY CRISIS

HARLEQUIN® LOVE INSPIRED®CLASSICS

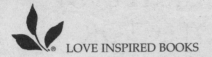

LOVE INSPIRED BOOKS

PLEASE RECYCLE · THIS PRODUCT IS RECYCLABLE

Recycling programs for this product may not exist in your area.

ISBN-13: 978-0-373-20865-4

Her Mistletoe Protector & Identity Crisis

Copyright © 2017 by Harlequin Books S.A.

The publisher acknowledges the copyright holder of the individual works as follows:

Her Mistletoe Protector
Copyright © 2013 by Laura Iding

Identity Crisis
Copyright © 2012 by Laura Iding

www.Harlequin.com

Printed in U.S.A.

CONTENTS

Laura Scott is a nurse by day and an author by night. She has always loved romance and read faith-based books by Grace Livingston Hill in her teenage years. She's thrilled to have published over twelve books for Love Inspired Suspense. She has two adult children and lives in Milwaukee, Wisconsin, with her husband of thirty years. Please visit Laura at laurascottbooks.com, as she loves to hear from her readers.

Books by Laura Scott

Love Inspired Suspense

Callahan Confidential

Shielding His Christmas Witness
The Only Witness
Christmas Amnesia

Classified K-9 Unit

Sheriff

SWAT: Top Cops

Wrongly Accused
Down to the Wire
Under the Lawman's Protection
Forgotten Memories
Holiday on the Run
Mirror Image

Visit the Author Profile page at Harlequin.com for more titles.

HER MISTLETOE PROTECTOR

Rejoice in the Lord always. I will say it again: rejoice!
—*Philippians* 4:4

This book is dedicated to my sister, Michele Glynn.
I know Madison is only an hour away,
but I still miss you so much. I love you!

ONE

"Ms. Simon, wait! I have a letter for you."

Rachel Simon, CEO of Simon Inc., froze, despite the fact that she was running late for her nine-o'clock meeting. The sick feeling in her stomach swelled with dread as she forced herself to turn and face the receptionist.

"Here you go," Carrie Freeman said with a wide smile.

Rachel stared at the thin envelope with her name typed neatly on the front, the dread congealing into a mass of fear. The letter looked exactly like the one she'd received in her mailbox at home last night, and she instinctively knew there was another threat inside. She swallowed hard and took the envelope from the receptionist, being careful to hold it along the edges. Then she cleared her throat. "Who dropped this off for me, Carrie?"

"I don't know… It was sitting on my desk chair when I came back from the restroom. There was a sticky note, telling me to deliver it to you first thing."

Rachel tried hard to keep her fear from showing as she cast a worried gaze around the lobby. Was the person who had left the note watching her right now? "Do you still have the sticky note?" she asked.

Carrie's expression turned perplexed. "I tossed it in

the trash bin." Rachel glanced over the receptionist's shoulder at the large stainless-steel trash container standing near the lobby door. "Do you want me to go through the garbage to find it?" Carrie's tone indicated she wasn't thrilled with the idea of pawing in the trash although Rachel knew she would if asked.

As much as she wanted to see the note, she shook her head. Asking Carrie to search through the bin would only bring unwanted attention to herself. She wasn't ready to go public with the weird phone calls and the threatening letter she'd received. The last thing she needed was some sort of leak to the media, as if her company hadn't been through the wringer already.

"No thanks, just curious to see if I recognized the handwriting, that's all. Thanks again, Carrie."

Rachel turned back toward the elevators, her mind focused on the contents of the letter rather than on her upcoming meeting with the two top research scientists in her pharmaceutical company.

The ride to the tenth floor, where her office suite was located, seemed to take forever. She smiled and chatted with various employees as if the envelope in her hand didn't matter.

"Good morning, Rachel," her senior administrative assistant, Edith Goodman, said as she entered through the glass doors. "Dr. Gardener and Dr. Errol are waiting for you in the conference room."

"I'm sorry, but please tell Josie and Karl that I'll need to reschedule our meeting."

Surprise flashed in Edith's eyes, but she quickly nodded and crossed over to the conference room next to Rachel's office. As her assistant delivered the news to the two researchers, Rachel ducked inside her office and closed the door, dropping the envelope on her desk as if it might burn her fingers.

She didn't have any gloves, so she put another piece of paper over the envelope and used her letter opener to slice beneath the flap. Inside was a single piece of paper with a computer-printed message, exactly like the one she'd received at home. Her stomach knotted with anxiety as she carefully opened the paper and read the short message.

"You will scream in agony, suffering for your past mistakes."

She shivered, the words searing into her mind. She opened her purse and drew out the letter she'd received last night, when she and her son, Joey, had come home from basketball practice. The wording was similar, yet different.

"You will repay your debt of betrayal."

The two letters, spread out side by side on her desk, seemed to mock her. She couldn't ignore the threat any longer, not when she knew, with grim certainty, the source of the veiled threat.

The only person she'd ever betrayed was her ex-husband, former State Senator Anthony Caruso. A few months after they were married, the joy of discovering she was pregnant was marred by learning Anthony had ties to organized crime. At first she couldn't believe he was involved in anything illegal. She was embarrassed that the man she'd fallen in love with was nothing more than an illusion. His fake charm covered a black soul.

All too soon, Anthony was openly talking about his Mafia association as if nothing she did could touch him.

But he'd been wrong. She'd lived in fear for months, but one night, he'd lost control and hit her hard enough to give her a black eye and a minor concussion. The evidence of physical abuse, along with her father's money—and the fact that her father's best friend was a judge—helped her buy her freedom.

And Joey's, too. She received sole custody of their son and a no-contact order. Joey was nine years old now, and she was eternally grateful Anthony hadn't seen his son since Joey's first birthday.

But since Anthony's untimely death last year during a crime bust, it was obvious he couldn't have sent these letters. So who had? She could only assume they'd come from someone inside the Chicago Mafia. Most likely from Anthony's uncle, Frankie Caruso.

She buried her face in her hands and fought the rising wave of helplessness. How long would she continue to pay for her naive mistake of marrying Anthony? This past year, since her ex-husband's death, she'd thought she was finally safe. But now it seemed the Mafia wasn't going to leave her alone.

Ever.

Taking several deep breaths, she did her best to control her fear. When she raised her head, she knew she had to take action. With trembling fingers, she went through her files to find the business card of a Chicago police detective who'd questioned her about Anthony last year. She needed to talk to someone who knew the truth about Anthony. Someone who understood how deeply infiltrated the Mafia was in this city.

Someone who would believe her—like Detective Nick Butler. They'd only met a few times, but she remembered him well. He was tall, broad shouldered with light brown hair and amazing blue eyes. In so many ways, Nick was the complete opposite of her ex-husband.

To be honest, Detective Butler hadn't been very happy with her last year during his investigation of Anthony, but that knowledge wasn't enough to stop her from picking up her phone and making the call.

If there was one thing she knew about Detective Butler, it was that he sincerely cared about justice. He'd worked against the Mafia before. She could only hope that he wouldn't turn his back on her now.

Nick stared at the various reports spread over his desk as he tried to figure out a way to breathe new life into his dead-end cases. With his partner out on medical leave and the upcoming holidays, he hadn't been assigned anything new. But working their old cases felt pretty much like beating his head against a brick wall.

When his phone rang, he answered it absently. "Detective Butler."

"Good morning, Detective. I don't know if you remember me, but my name is Rachel Simon."

Nick straightened in his chair, his instincts on full alert. "Of course, I remember you, Ms. Simon. How are you and your son, Joey, doing?"

"Fine. Well, sort of fine. I, uh, have a problem I'd like to discuss with you. I think it's linked to your past investigation...."

The subtle reference to the Mafia wasn't lost on him. He was surprised to hear from Rachel after all this time, yet he couldn't ignore the underlying hint of fear in her tone. He rose to his feet and glanced at his watch. "I can meet you now, if that works."

"That would be great. Do you remember where my office is located?"

"Yes. I can be there in fifteen minutes."

"Thank you."

After ending the call, Nick slid his cell phone into his pocket and strode to the door. He remembered Rachel Simon very well, as he'd questioned her last year related to a missing-person's case. Her ex-husband had been the prime suspect in the twenty-two-year-old model's disappearance.

Rachel hadn't been much help to his investigation, because she claimed she hadn't seen or spoken to her husband in seven years. Which, based on the divorce settlement and the no-contact order he'd uncovered, was likely true. But at the time he'd felt certain she was holding back on him, that she knew far more about her ex-husband's connection to the Mafia than she'd let on. And even then, her fear of her ex had been palpable.

Ironic how she'd contacted him now that she needed his assistance. And he couldn't deny being curious as to what was going on.

The ride to the office building of Simon Inc. took less than his allotted fifteen minutes. He walked into the lobby and smiled at the perky redhead sitting behind the receptionist desk. "Good morning, I'm here to see Ms. Simon."

"Yes, she mentioned you were coming." The redhead wore a name tag that identified her as Carrie Freeman and she was young enough to make him feel ancient at thirty-seven. "Just take these elevators here to the tenth floor."

"Thanks." He pushed the elevator button, already knowing Rachel's office was on the tenth floor. Once he arrived up there, he was greeted warmly by Rachel's assistant, Edith Goodman. A far cry from the last time he'd been here, when the sixty-something-year-old had protected her boss like a mama bear hovering over her cub.

"Rachel's waiting for you in her office," Edith said. "Is there something I can get for you, Detective? Coffee? Soft drink?"

"Coffee would be great."

"Black, no sugar, correct?"

He shouldn't have been surprised she remembered, considering Edith Goodman ruled Rachel's office with an iron fist. "That's right."

Rachel's office door was open, and she met him halfway, offering her hand as he strolled toward her. "Detective, thanks for coming on such short notice."

Her slender fingers were firm as they gripped his. She was as beautiful as he remembered, with her sleek blond hair framing her face and distinctive green eyes. But despite her smile, dark shadows hovered in her eyes. "I have to admit, I was intrigued by your call."

Her smile faded, and she waited until Edith had handed him a mug of coffee, before inviting him inside her office. "Please, have a seat."

He sat in the chair facing hers, and his gaze immediately landed on the two pieces of paper lying on her desk. They'd been turned toward him. He took a sip from the steaming mug before setting his coffee aside. He leaned forward and read the messages.

"You will repay your debt of betrayal."

"You will scream in agony, suffering for your past mistakes."

The threats were all too real and his protective instincts jumped to the forefront. He was angry at the idea of Rachel being stalked by some lunatic. He lifted his gaze to meet hers. "Who sent these to you?" he demanded roughly.

"Isn't it obvious?" Rachel scowled and crossed her arms protectively across her chest.

"Not to me," he said, striving for patience. "An ex-boyfriend? A disgruntled employee? You must have some idea."

Her scowl deepened. "I don't have a boyfriend, ex or otherwise, and a disgruntled employee would more likely try to sue me rather than send threats. I've received a few phone calls, too. The caller never speaks, but I can hear heavy breathing on the other end of the phone. Don't you see?" She spread her hands over the letters. "These have to be from someone within the Mafia."

He stared at her for a long moment, trying to figure out what was going on in her mind. Their last interaction hadn't been entirely cordial, since she'd avoided discussing anything related to her husband's ties to the Mafia. He sat back and reached for his coffee mug. "So you're admitting that Anthony Caruso was involved with the Mafia?"

Her cheeks turned pink and she avoided his gaze as if embarrassed. "I told you that much a year ago," she said defensively.

"But you claimed you didn't know any details," he reminded her.

"Look, Detective, my goal last year was to do whatever was necessary to protect my son. And I never lied to you about that missing woman. At the time we spoke I hadn't seen Anthony in seven years, so I had no idea who he was seeing or who he was associating with."

"But you knew what he was capable of," Nick said, capturing her gaze with his.

She stared at him for a long moment before breaking the connection. And when she spoke, her voice was so soft he could barely hear her. "Yes. I knew exactly what he was capable of. I believe he murdered that woman. But my belief is a far cry from actual hard-core evidence. There was nothing that I knew that would have helped your case."

The simple admission helped squelch his lingering anger. He was a bit ashamed that he'd spent time rehashing the past instead of moving forward. He caught sight of the photo of her son, Joey, that was displayed proudly on her desk. The kid had blond hair, green eyes and a smile that matched his mother's. Nick could understand her need to keep silent if it meant protecting her child.

For a moment, he thought about how much he missed his wife and daughter. He would have done anything to protect them, too. But unfortunately, they both died in a terrible car accident two years ago. And while he knew they were in a much better place in heaven, he still missed them every day.

He pushed the painful memories aside. "Okay, maybe someone within the Mafia sent them, but at this point, we don't have any proof. We can't go after anyone in the syndicate without evidence. I'll take these notes and have them dusted for prints. Maybe that'll give us a place to start."

She grimaced. "Well, to be perfectly honest, the first one probably won't help much. I treated it normally since I had no idea that it was a threat. The second letter I was very careful with, although the envelope was handled by my receptionist." She went on to describe in detail how she'd received the letters.

He made notes in his notebook. "Do you remember when the phone calls came in?" he asked. "Was there a common number?"

"The calls came from a blocked number, and they started three days ago."

Three phone calls and two written threats in the past three days. Hard to tell if the danger was escalating. He'd known some stalkers who called their victims twenty or thirty times a day. These messages seemed to be aimed at keeping Rachel off balance and afraid. "You haven't noticed anyone following you? Or watching you?"

"No. Nothing like that." Her gaze rested on her son's photograph. "Right now, the threats are centered on me, but I called you because I need to be sure Joey is safe."

"I understand. I'll see what we can get from these letters, but at this point, our hands are tied." As much as he wanted to order protection for her, they needed more than just her suspicion that the Mafia was behind the threats. He took out his business card and slid it across the desk. "I want you to be extra vigilant. If you see anything suspicious, please call me on my personal phone regardless of the time of day or night."

She took the card and nodded. "Thank you."

He rose to his feet, wishing there was more that could be done. After donning a pair of gloves, he placed both notes and the envelopes in a plastic evidence bag, even though he knew the odds of getting a decent set of prints were slim. And they'd have to get Rachel's fingerprints as well as the receptionist's on file to cross match them.

Having a new case to work on would help keep him busy. But first he needed to see what the forensic team came up with. Otherwise, he'd have nothing to go on, which wouldn't help keep Rachel and her son safe.

And he wasn't about to lose another mother and child on his watch.

Rachel managed to get some work done before heading out to take Joey to his last basketball game before the

Christmas holiday. The drive to the school, located on the outskirts of town, was uneventful. The game turned out to be a lot of fun and her son scored four points, edging their team to a ten to eight victory. Joey and his teammates were loud and rambunctious as they celebrated, and Rachel felt more at ease as the night unfolded. But as she and Joey headed home, she noticed a big black truck keeping pace behind her. No matter what speed she chose to go, the truck remained right behind her.

Detective Butler had warned her to be on the lookout for anything suspicious. At the moment, the truck certainly seemed suspicious, but maybe she was letting her imagination get the better of her. She didn't recall seeing a truck behind her on the way to the basketball game or parked anywhere along the long country road outside the school.

So how would the driver of the black truck know where to find her? How would anyone have access to Joey's basketball schedule? Maybe this was nothing more than a coincidence.

She did her best to keep her expression neutral as Joey relived every moment of winning the basketball game.

"Did you see my last basket? The coach said it was amazing and that without my score we might not have won the game. Isn't that awesome, Mom?" he asked for the third time. "I can't wait until our next tournament. Coach said I can be in the starting lineup!"

"The game was awesome," she agreed, looking once again in her rearview mirror. Was the truck gaining on them? Darkness came early in December so it was hard to gauge the distance. She tightened her grip on the steering wheel and pressed down on the accelerator. For the first time she bemoaned the fact she'd traded in her high-powered sports car for a four-cylinder eco-friendly hybrid last year. The hybrid's engine chugged as she fought to increase her speed.

The truck edged closer, and she glanced helplessly around at the winding country road she'd taken to avoid the traffic on the interstate. Was the driver of the truck behind her the same person who'd sent her the threatening letters? Was he working for someone linked to the Mafia?

Swallowing hard, she drew her cell phone out of the front pocket of her sweatshirt and pushed the preprogrammed number for Nick Butler. He'd told her to call day or night and, thankfully, seven-thirty in the evening wasn't too late. She held her breath until he answered.

"Butler."

"It's Rachel. We're being followed by a black truck license plate number TYG-555. We're on Handover Road, just past Highway 12."

"Mom? What's going on?" Joey swiveled in his seat, finally realizing that something was wrong.

"Hang tight, I'm not far away. I'll be right there," Nick said in a calm, reassuring tone.

"Hurry," she urged, before sliding the phone back into her pocket and returning both hands to the wheel. She increased her speed more, wondering why Nick would be so close, when suddenly, the truck rammed into her from behind, causing the steering wheel to jerk in her hands as the car swerved dangerously. She and Joey were wearing their seat belts, but she wasn't sure the restraint would be enough to prevent them from being harmed. "Hang on, Joey!" she shouted as she fought to stay in control.

"Mom!" Joey screamed as the truck rammed into them again, and this time, she couldn't prevent the car from slamming into the guardrail with a sickening lurch. She tried to ride against the rail, but the car spun out of control, doing a complete three-sixty before hitting the side rail again, thankfully on the driver's side.

The impact caused the airbags to explode in their faces. Pain radiated through her face and chest. "Joey!" she shrieked, frantic to know her son was all right.

The car came to an abrupt halt, but the driver's side door was bent inward to the point of pinning her left foot. She batted away the air bags as she frantically reached over for her son. "Joey? Are you all right?"

"Yeah," he said, between hiccuping sobs. "I think so."

Coughing as air bag dust filled her lungs, she tried again to get her foot out from the twisted hunk of metal. When that didn't work, she reached over to help Joey get out of his seat belt. "I need you to get out of the car, Joey. Run away and get help. Find Detective Butler. Do you understand me? You need to get away from here and find Detective Nick Butler."

"Not without you," he cried.

"I'll be right behind you," she said, even though she wasn't sure she'd be able to wrench herself free. "Now go. *Hurry!*"

Somehow, Joey managed to crawl out of the passenger-side window, which was completely busted open. She pulled, gritting her teeth against the pain as she tried to yank out her pinned foot.

Through the open window she saw Joey stagger a bit before he managed to pick up his pace enough to run. She heard the distant wailing of a police siren and hoped that was Nick, as she shifted in her seat again, determined to find a way to get free.

But then she saw a large man dressed completely in

dark clothing, recognizing him as the driver of the big black truck that had caused her to crash. Through the glow of her headlights, she saw him take off running after her son. "No! Joey!" she screamed, ripping her foot out of her shoe, finally gaining freedom. *"No!"*

Too late. The tall stranger easily scooped up her son and dropped a black hood over Joey's head before taking off with him thrown over his shoulder like a sack of potatoes. Joey struggled against him, but the guy never hesitated, ignoring her son's kicks and punches.

"No!" she wailed, scrambling to get out of the crushed car. She threw herself across to the passenger seat and wiggled her way through the broken window. "Stop! Joey!"

But the moment she fell from the window onto the paved road, the big black truck engine rumbled to life and pulled away, tires screeching, with her son trapped inside.

TWO

Nick slammed his foot down hard on the accelerator, racing to Rachel's location, his heart pounding in his chest. Earlier that day, he hadn't been entirely convinced her stalker was really someone from the Mafia. But the threats had been enough that he couldn't bear to leave her totally on her own, so he'd followed Rachel to her son's basketball game without telling her he was nearby.

Now he realized his instincts had been right on. The panic in her tone gripped him by the throat and he couldn't help feeling that this was his fault for not doing more to keep her safe. He saw Rachel and Joey leaving the school after the game, but at that moment he'd taken a call from his boss, questioning why he'd taken on Rachel's stalker case. He'd explained about the possible mob connection, which had eased his captain's concern. But in the time it had taken him to placate his boss, Rachel and Joey had disappeared from sight.

His fault for not telling her he was there. And if something bad happened to Rachel and Joey, he'd never forgive himself. As he drove, he silently prayed for their well-being.

Please, Lord, keep Rachel and Joey safe in Your care. Amen.

The closer he got to the location she'd given him, the more his gut tightened with fear and worry. And when he saw her mangled car wedged against the guardrail, his stomach dropped. He was surprised to see there weren't any police cars or ambulances at the scene. As he pulled over, Rachel was there, limping and crying, making her way down the road. He bolted from his car and ran toward her. "Rachel, what is it? What's wrong?"

"He took Joey!" She grabbed his arm in a tight grip. "You have to do something! Right now!"

"Which way did they go?"

"N-north."

"All right, let's go." He took her arm since she was shaking so badly he was afraid she wouldn't be able to stay upright. She managed to hang on long enough to climb into his car. He slid quickly into the driver's seat.

As he drove he reached for the radio. "I have to call my boss, tell him to send a chopper. The truck will be easier to find from the air at night."

"Wait! I have a text message."

He froze, watching as she pulled her cell phone from the pocket of her pink hoodie sweatshirt.

"Oh, no," she whispered.

"What is it?"

"Don't call the police or I'll kill him." She lifted her tortured gaze to his. "I knew it! I knew the mob was after me. And now they've kidnapped Joey!"

Every instinct he possessed told him to radio for backup, but Rachel had grabbed his arm again, squeezing so tight he winced as her nails dug painfully into his skin. "We have to find him. We have to get to Joey!" she sobbed.

"Rachel, I know you're scared, but let's calm down

and think this through. We need to get the helicopters to go after that black truck."

"If that guy sees the police he'll kill Joey. You don't know how ruthless the Mafia can be. Please don't do anything that will hurt my son. *Please!*" Her green eyes implored him to listen.

He pressed harder on the accelerator, going well above the speed limit. He wished a cop would try to pull him over, because then they'd have their badly needed backup.

"This is all my fault. They have Joey and it's all my fault," Rachel moaned.

He glanced over at her, wishing there was something he could say to make her feel better. But he knew only too well what it was like to lose a child.

"There!" Rachel's excited shout drew him out of his depressing thoughts. "That's the black truck that hit me."

He couldn't believe they'd found the black truck here, on the side of the road. But as they came closer, it was clear that the vehicle had been abandoned. Was it possibly a different truck? No, the damage to the front bumper convinced him they had the right vehicle. The passenger-side door was left hanging wide open, as if someone had grabbed Joey and taken off running without bothering to shut the door behind him.

He scanned the area, but there wasn't much he could see in the darkness outside the glow from his headlights. He could tell that beyond the open cornfield was a subdivision full of houses, many of them twinkling with various holiday lights. The kidnapper could be anywhere. Either on foot or—if he wasn't working alone—in another vehicle.

"Where are they? Where's Joey?" Rachel barely

waited for him to stop the car before she was out and racing over to see for herself.

He followed hot on her heels, ready to prevent her from disturbing any evidence. But he needn't have worried.

She simply stood there, staring inside the empty truck, her eyes welling with tears. "They're gone," she whispered.

He curled his fingers into helpless fists, knowing there wasn't any way to put a positive spin on this latest turn of events.

Joey was gone and Nick didn't have a clue as to where he might be.

Rachel shivered, ice creeping slowly through her bloodstream like a glacier. She'd been so certain they'd find the black truck. Find Joey.

But her son was still missing.

"Come on, Rachel. I have to call my boss," Nick urged, putting a hand beneath her elbow to nudge her away from the truck.

She didn't move, couldn't seem to tear her gaze from the empty truck. Joey had been in there, with a hood over his face. She couldn't bear to think of how frightened her son must be. "Hang in there, Joey," she whispered, as if he could hear her. "I'm coming to get you."

"Rachel, there's nothing more we can do here. Not until we get a forensic team to go through the truck to pick up trace evidence."

"No cops," she said weakly, even though she knew it was too late. Nick was a cop and she'd called him right before the crash. And obviously they needed all the help they could get to find Joey. Her frozen brain cells finally put a few pieces of the puzzle together. "How did you get to me so quickly?" she asked with a frown.

He shrugged and ducked his head before he abruptly turned away, heading back to his vehicle. She forced her legs to follow him, wincing as she stepped on a stone with her foot that didn't have a shoe.

"Wait," she said, stopping him once again as he reached for the radio. "Can you call this incident in as a hit-and-run? Without mentioning Joey?"

"Rachel, you know that's not smart," he said with a heavy sigh. "I get that they have you running scared, but the more people searching for your son, the better."

Logically, she could agree, but there was nothing logical about her feelings regarding the mob. And she was convinced that her husband's uncle, Frankie Caruso, was the mastermind behind Joey's kidnapping. "You don't understand," she said brokenly, wishing she could convince him. "If they get any sense that the police are involved there's nothing to stop them from killing him."

"Why would they kidnap your son in the first place?" he asked. "You have to admit, kidnapping is a huge leap from stalking."

She drew her arms across her jacket, trying to maintain some warmth in the cold December night. Her left ankle throbbed, but she shoved the pain aside. No matter how much she hurt, she wouldn't allow anything to stop her from finding her son. "Maybe the Mafia is looking for money from my company? Money that will help them rebuild their organization?"

"It's possible, since the Mafia has taken several big hits lately," Nick mused. "And you think they targeted you because of your marriage to Anthony?"

"Yes. Don't you see? It all fits! My father's money

helped me escape Anthony all those years ago, so now they want me to pay them back. That's basically what those threatening notes said, right?"

Grimacing, Nick nodded slowly. "I guess in a twisted way, that makes sense."

She was dizzy with relief, knowing she'd finally managed to convince him of the Mafia link. "The mob fights dirty and plays for keeps," she murmured. "If you call in reinforcements, the dirty cops might find out and let Joey's captors know. I just can't take that chance."

"Not all cops are dirty, Rachel," Nick said, a hard edge to his tone.

She sensed she was losing the battle. "During my brief marriage to Anthony, I knew of several Chicago cops who were on his payroll. None of them would lift a finger to help me. Can you honestly say that there isn't the possibility of dirty cops still on the force?"

He scowled as he twisted the key in the ignition. "No, I can't tell you that as much as I wish I could. I hate knowing that some of the very men and women who are supposed to put criminals away actually join forces with them, instead. Kidnapping is a federal offense, so we could call in the FBI."

Fear tightened her chest to the point she felt she couldn't breathe. "Are you sure there isn't any possibility of someone linked to the Mafia working inside the FBI, too?"

Nick let the car idle as he scrubbed his hands over his face. "No, I can't tell you that, either. Because there was a dirty FBI agent involved in a case I worked on last summer. We arrested him, but I always wondered if there weren't others, too. Others that we missed."

The thought of losing her son was making bile rise

to her throat. "Please, Nick. All I'm asking for is a little time. Please keep Joey's involvement out of this for now."

He turned his head and stared at her for a long moment. "I'm going to at least let my boss know what's going on. I know he's not dirty and we need someone to trust." She wanted to protest but knew that he had a job to do. Nodding stiffly, she dropped her hand from his arm so that he could call in a crime team to investigate the crash scene and the abandoned truck.

She didn't relax a single muscle until he disconnected the call, without once mentioning Joey. Unfortunately, her relief was short-lived when Nick punched in another number.

"Hey, I think we have another link to the Mafia angle," he said into the phone.

She strained to hear the other side of the conversation, which she assumed was with Nick's boss. "Yeah? Like what?"

Her heart squeezed when Nick briefly explained what had transpired. "I'd like to keep this quiet for now, while we wait for some more evidence. If the Mafia is behind this, there isn't much to stop them from doing something drastic if they sense we're onto them."

"I'm not sure I like that plan, Butler." She could hear Nick's boss's weary tone. "The feds won't be happy if we don't follow protocol."

"Yeah, but you and I both know that there have been far too many dirty cops, both locally and at the federal level. Just give me a little time to see what we can shake out, okay?"

"All right. But keep me posted."

"Will do." Nick hung up the phone and then put the car in gear.

"Thank you, Nick," she murmured softly.

"Don't thank me," he said in a harsh tone. "We don't have Joey back yet. And you need to know this may not turn out the way you want it to."

"We'll get him back." She wasn't even going to consider the possibility of failure.

He let out an exasperated sigh. "I hope so, but you have to understand that we don't have a lot of time. If we don't hear from the kidnappers soon, I won't give you a choice. We will call in the FBI."

She wanted to argue, feeling deep down that calling in the FBI would be the worst thing they could do. After all, she knew from personal experience how the Mafia worked. The members of the mob were cruel and ruthless and wouldn't hesitate to kill her son just to prove their point.

The threatening notes she'd received were right. She had screamed in agony when they'd kidnapped her son. And if they demanded a ransom, she would repay her debts in order to get him back.

Panic bubbled in her throat and she had to swallow the urge to start screaming all over again. She needed to stay calm, to think this through logically, if she was going to have any chance in finding Joey.

After several long deep breaths, she felt somewhat calm. "You never did mention how you reached me so quickly," she said, glancing over at Nick.

There was a long silence before he admitted, "I followed you and Joey. I guess I was hoping to catch the guy in the act of leaving another note for you."

He'd been sitting in the parking lot of the elementary school? She tried to grapple with that revelation.

"I didn't see you," she said. "And believe me, I was on alert, searching for signs of Frankie or one of his thugs."

Nick shifted in his seat. "I stayed in my car, a little ways down the road, just close enough to watch your vehicle."

She wasn't sure that news was reassuring. If she hadn't seen Nick, maybe she'd missed the driver of the black truck, too? She couldn't bear the thought that she may have led the kidnapper straight to her son's location.

More deep breaths helped rein in her fear. She tried to find comfort in the fact that Nick had cared enough to try to protect her, but the image of her son being kidnapped by the driver of the truck was seared in her mind.

Helplessly, she gazed down at her phone, looking at the text message again. Don't call the police or I'll kill him.

Why hadn't they already demanded money? That had to be the reason they'd kidnapped Joey. Nothing else made sense.

"We should probably stay in a hotel tonight," Nick said, breaking into her grim thoughts. "Especially because you received those threats at both your office and your home."

She pressed her fingertips against her aching temples, trying to think. "I guess a motel would be okay."

"It's our best option. For now."

She understood the warning implication in his tone. This was a temporary plan at best. She stared down at her cell phone for another long moment, willing the kidnapper to contact her again. The sooner they told her how much money they wanted, the sooner she could get her son back, safe and sound.

"Tell me what you know about Frankie Caruso," Nick said quietly.

Her stomach twisted into painful knots. "I'm afraid I don't know much. I only met him for the first time at our engagement party and then again at our wedding. I knew he'd raised Anthony after his parents died, but I didn't know about their link to the Mafia. Not until after we were married."

Nick glanced at her, and she wondered if he thought she was an idiot for not figuring out what was going on sooner. She'd often asked herself the same thing. She didn't like to think about how naive she was back then. She graduated college early and by twenty-five had worked her way up in her father's company to vice president. Hours of studying meant she hadn't dated much. Anthony had swept her off her feet with his dashing good looks and his charm.

It was only after they were married for a few months that she caught a glimpse of his dark side. But by then she'd discovered she was pregnant and tried to make the marriage work.

Until she was on the receiving end of his violent temper.

"Has Frankie been living here in Chicago?" Nick pressed.

"Early on, he did, but after Anthony won his second term as state senator, Frankie moved down to Phoenix. Anthony told me that his uncle was tired of the brutal Chicago winters."

"But you think Frankie's back in the area?"

She lifted her shoulders in a helpless shrug. "Honestly, I haven't kept track of Anthony's uncle in the years since our divorce. I was lucky to get away from Anthony early in our marriage, shortly after Joey's first birthday." Two years of marriage that had seemed like a lifetime. "I suspect that since Anthony is dead, Frankie might have come back to take his place within the Mafia."

"Rachel, there isn't much of the Mafia left for him to return to," he said. "I happen to know that Bernardo Salvatore and his right-hand man, Russo, are both dead."

The news surprised her. "Really? How?"

He pressed his lips into a grim line. "I can't go into details other than to tell you that I was there when they were killed. You have to consider there might be someone else besides Frankie Caruso after you."

"I'm telling you there's no one else I can think of," she said, wishing he would believe her. "Besides, if Salvatore and this Russo guy are dead, then it makes even more sense to me that Frankie came back to Chicago. Clearly he wants to pick up the crime syndicate where Salvatore left off."

"Maybe. I'll try running a search on him," Nick murmured. "It's possible we'll get lucky."

She didn't bother to tell Nick that she didn't feel lucky. The thought of her son being held by the Mafia, alone and afraid, made fear clog her throat to the point she could barely breathe. Outside the passenger-side window, she stared at the holiday decorations lighting up people's houses. Would Joey be back in time for Christmas? She couldn't even imagine the possibility that he wouldn't be.

Nick pulled up to a low-budget motel and secured two connecting rooms. She reluctantly took her room key from his hand, knowing she couldn't relax, couldn't rest.

Not until she found her son.

"Rachel?" She glanced up when she heard Nick call her name from the open doorway between their rooms.

"What is it?" she asked, rising to her feet and crossing over to meet him in the doorway.

"Are you hungry?"

She grimaced and shook her head. "No." The mere thought of food made her nauseous. "You mentioned doing a search on Frankie Caruso. Do you have a laptop with you?"

"Yeah, I have my laptop," Nick replied. "So far, I haven't found much."

Frankie Caruso was too smart to leave an obvious trail. She kept her phone gripped in her hand, unable to bear the thought of losing the small link that she had with Joey's kidnapper. She hated to think of what her son might be suffering through right now. Why hadn't they contacted her again? What were they waiting for? "We have to keep searching. We have to find something!"

"Rachel, I know you're upset, but there isn't much more I can do. If we don't hear something soon, we'll have no choice but to pull in the FBI."

"No. We can't." The very thought of bringing in the authorities nearly made her double over in pain. "Your boss promised us some time, right? I'm sure the kidnappers will contact me soon."

"All right." There was a hint of disappointment in his gaze. She told herself she didn't care what Nick thought of her. He couldn't possibly imagine what she was going through. Or what she'd already suffered at the hands of the Mafia. She'd lived with Anthony for two long terrible years and had learned early on that confronting the Mafia directly only made them angry.

She didn't want the man who'd kidnapped Joey to take his anger out on her son.

"I'm going to get something to eat," Nick said over

his shoulder. "Stay here and don't let anyone in except for me."

"Can I use your laptop while you're gone?" she asked.

He shrugged. "Sure, why not?"

She waited for him in the doorway, gratefully taking the computer from his hands. "Thank you."

"I'll be back soon," he said huskily, and he closed the connecting door on his side.

She opened the computer and tried to think of what little she remembered from those early days with Anthony—the places he went, the people he considered friends. She'd purposefully pushed all those bad memories out of her mind after she escaped, so dredging them up again wasn't easy.

Typing Frank Caruso's name into the search engine didn't bring up many hits. She tried using Luigi Gagliano's name too, as he was a distant cousin to Anthony.

Still nothing. And as she stared blankly at the computer, a terrible thought occurred to her.

Here she was, waiting for Joey's kidnappers to call with some sort of ransom demand, but what if she was on the wrong track? What if Frankie didn't want her money, but simply wanted her son?

Frankie had raised Anthony, bringing him into the world of crime at a young age. Was it possible he wanted to use Joey as a surrogate for Anthony?

Was it possible that Frankie was, right now, driving far away with her son?

Rachel's heart rate soared as she surged to her feet. Nick had been right! They should have called the police and the FBI right away! If Frankie had kidnapped Joey for personal reasons then he already had a head start on them.

She grabbed her phone, intending to call Nick, but then forced herself to stop and think. Why would Frankie send her threatening letters, saying she would repay her debts, if he didn't want money?

Pacing the length of the small motel room helped calm her ragged nerves. Her ankle throbbed, but she ignored it. She'd never had a panic attack like this before, not even in the dark days after Anthony had beaten her. She had to stop overreacting to every thought. Every remote possibility.

Somehow she had to be smarter than Frankie Caruso or Luigi Gagliano.

She sat down at the small desk and clicked on the mouse to reactivate Nick's computer. There was one angle she hadn't considered, and that was Frankie's ex-wife, Margie Caruso. Frankie and Margie had divorced the year Rachel was pregnant with Joey, but, surprisingly, they'd stayed on friendly terms. She'd often wondered if Margie had also been involved in illegal activities; otherwise, why wouldn't Frankie have tried to silence his ex-wife? After all, Anthony had often threatened to kill Rachel if she ratted him out.

Anthony's threats hadn't been empty ones, either.

And if Margie was part of the Mafia, it wasn't a stretch to think that she could be in cahoots with Frankie on this kidnapping scheme.

A quick search revealed that Margie was still living in the Chicago area. She wrote down the address, determined to convince Nick that they needed to pay the woman a surprise visit.

THREE

Nick couldn't stop thinking about Rachel and Joey as he ran a few errands. He understood what Rachel was going through—he'd been inconsolable after his wife and daughter went missing, too. He knew he shouldn't let his emotions get in the way of doing what was right, but seeing the pain etched on Rachel's face was impossible to ignore.

After picking up some new clothes he'd put a call in to his FBI buddy, Logan Quail, only to find out his friend was out of the country on his honeymoon. No wonder Logan hadn't returned his calls. The timing was unfortunate, since Logan's expertise would have been perfect for Rachel's situation.

But he'd just have to use another way to help Rachel find her son.

As he was picking up some fast food, his phone rang and he was surprised to discover that the caller was his boss, Ryan Walsh. "Hi, Captain."

"Butler. We have some news from the crash scene you called in earlier."

"You do?" He juggled the phone as he handed over cash and accepted the bag of food from the bored teen at the window. "What do you have?"

"We got a hit on one of the fingerprints. Perp's name is Ricky Morales and he's got a rap sheet, largely for drug busts, but, most recently, he was arrested for armed robbery. He just got out on bail about six months ago."

Nick pulled away from the drive-through window and parked in the first open slot he saw. "Do you think Morales has found a home working as a thug for the Mafia?"

His boss grunted. "Don't see why not. It's a lead worth following since the truck is registered in his name, too. Explains why he dumped his ride as soon as he did. I'll send his last-known address to you in an email. Where are you right now?"

"Getting something to eat." Nick didn't want to say too much. "We also have a possible suspect in Frankie Caruso, who happens to be Anthony Caruso's uncle. Ms. Simon is convinced that Frankie is back to take over the Mafia."

"What do you think?" Walsh asked.

"I think she could be right. You might want to see what you can find out about Caruso's activities. In the meantime, we'll start looking for leads related to Ricky Morales."

"Sounds like a plan." He could hear his boss scribbling notes. "Good work so far, Butler. Keep in touch."

"I will." Nick disconnected from the call and stared at his phone for a moment. He debated searching for Morales right now, but then decided he needed to get back to the motel. At least he had some positive news to give Rachel.

The drive didn't take long. He grabbed the clothes and the bag of food, his mouth watering at the aroma of burgers and fries, and swiped his key card. The moment he closed the motel door behind him, he heard Rachel knocking on the connecting door.

"Coming," he called as he reached for the door. He smiled at her. "Don't argue, but I brought food for the both of us."

"There's no time to eat," Rachel said in a rush. "Look what I've discovered." She gestured to the computer screen. "Margie Caruso, Frankie's ex-wife still lives outside of Chicago. We have to get over there right away."

Her excitement was palpable. "Good news, but I have something to follow up on, too." He pushed the laptop out of the way so he could haul the food out of the bag. "I'll search while we eat."

Rachel frowned, but he noticed she was staring at the burgers and fries as if her appetite may have returned. He bowed his head and gave a quick prayer of thanks. Rachel didn't say anything, respecting his silent prayer, until he finished and dug into his food. "What are you following up on?" she asked.

"Sit down and eat," he suggested.

She grimaced, but came over to sit beside him. As if she couldn't help herself, she popped a French fry into her mouth. He waited until she surrendered to her inevitable hunger by unwrapping the second sandwich and taking a bite before telling her what his boss had uncovered.

"You think this Ricky Morales is the guy who kidnapped Joey?" she asked, her green eyes filled with hope. "I mean, that seems to be the most logical conclusion. And we should be able to find him, right?"

He nodded, even though he knew tracking Morales down wouldn't be quite that easy. As he ate, he pulled up his email and jotted down the information his boss had sent. "Here's his last-known address. It's on the opposite side of town from Margie Caruso's place."

"It's only eight-thirty…there's plenty of time yet to head over to see what we can find. I need to keep busy, searching for Joey. We have to find him as soon as possible!"

"We'll check both addresses out tonight," he assured her.

"Thank you," she murmured.

He shook his head, not wanting her gratitude. He was beginning to identify with Rachel on a personal level. Her fear tugged at his heart. He knew, only too well, what she was going through. Those hours his wife and daughter were missing had been the longest, darkest hours of his life. And when the news came in that they were both found dead in their mangled SUV at the bottom of a ravine, his grief had been overwhelming. Without his faith, he never would have survived the dark days following their deaths.

Grimly, he hoped and prayed that Rachel's outcome would be different. *Please, Lord, keep Joey safe in Your care and guide us in finding him. Amen.*

Rachel pushed away her half-eaten sandwich and the remaining cold French fries, her patience wearing thin. She couldn't bear the thought of sitting here another minute. If she didn't take some sort of action to help find her son, she'd go stark, raving mad.

She tapped her fingers impatiently on the table, as Nick finished his meal. "I bought a dark sweatshirt for you, since that pink one is too easily seen at night, and a new pair of athletic shoes," he said between bites. "Also hats and gloves. Why don't you change while I finish up?"

"Okay, thanks," she said, reaching down for the bag of clothes. The shoes were a welcome sight, and while she loved her pink sweatshirt, she realized Nick was right about how it stood out. The black sweatshirt beneath her jacket would blend far better with the night.

She disappeared into the bathroom and quickly changed. Her left ankle was swollen, but she managed to get that shoe on by loosening the laces. The pain in her foot was nothing compared to the gaping hole in her heart.

When she emerged from the bathroom, she was grateful to see that Nick had finished his meal, disposing of all the garbage in the trash can by the door. He'd pulled on the matching black sweatshirt, too, before zipping up his jacket. He shut down the computer and then turned to her. "Ready?" he asked, rising to his feet.

"Yes." She was more than ready. She tucked her room key into her back pocket and followed Nick out to the car. Once she was buckled in, he set his phone in the cradle where he could easily read the GPS directions.

"Where are we going first?" she asked.

"Morales lives closer," he said, glancing over his shoulder as he backed out of the driveway. "We'll go there, first."

She didn't argue with his logic. Granted, it wasn't likely that Morales would abandon his truck and take Joey to his home address listed on the registration, but, then again, criminals weren't always known for being smart.

The minutes ticked by with agonizing slowness as Nick drove through the night. She tensed when she noticed they were heading straight into a seedy part of town. Her stomach roiled at the thought of Joey being kept in a place where he was likely to be assaulted, or worse even, if he managed to escape.

"There it is," Nick murmured. "Second apartment building on the right."

"Do we know which apartment might be his?" she asked, leaning forward to see better. The dilapidated building sure wasn't comforting. "Do you really think he would have brought a kidnapping victim here to his place?"

"Doubtful, especially if he's working for someone else," Nick said. "I'm going to get out here to see if I can find out if he's still living here. Slide into the driver's seat and head around the block. This won't take long."

"All right." As soon as Nick pulled over and climbed from the vehicle, she slipped over the console and adjusted the seat so she could drive. "Be careful," she added before he shut the door.

He nodded and then pulled his sweatshirt hood over his head and hunched his shoulders as he loped across the street to the apartment building. As much as she wanted to watch, she forced herself to put the car in gear. At the end of the block was a stop sign and she turned right. There was a small group of tough-looking kids smoking cigarettes as they gathered at the street corner, beneath a streetlight where a small Christmas wreath was hanging. As she watched them she saw the gleam of silver. A knife? Or a gun? Several of them hid their hands in their pockets as she went past, giving her the distinct impression they were hiding something. Drugs? Maybe. Swallowing hard, she made sure the doors were locked before she gripped the steering wheel tightly.

As she came around the last corner to the street where Morales's apartment building was located, her heart sank when she saw the group of teens had moved down closer to the apartment building. Had they noticed Nick getting out of the car and going inside? What if they planned to rob him when he came out? This was a bad neighborhood, where crime ran rampant. She knew Nick carried his service weapon, but the odds were still stacked against him, especially since all six of them were likely armed, too.

She was fumbling with her cell phone, intending to call Nick to warn him, when he slipped out of the apartment building and headed down the steps. Her heart hammered in her chest as the group of kids stepped forward, cutting him off.

Nick kept his hand in the pocket of his jacket and she assumed he had his gun ready. He sidestepped the kids, but they crowded closer and once again, she caught sight of a flash of silver.

Rachel unlocked the car and leaned on the horn. The group of kids swung around in surprise, and in that split second, Nick ran around them and jumped into the car. "Go!" he shouted as he slammed the door shut.

She stomped on the accelerator and the car leaped forward. In her rearview mirror she saw the group of kids begin running after them. Did they still intend to rob them? Or worse? As she approached the stop sign up ahead, she glanced frantically both ways before ignoring the sign and going straight through the intersection without stopping.

"Take it easy," Nick said, putting a hand on her arm as she took another turn a little too fast. "They flashed a few knives and demanded money, but we're safe now."

She couldn't speak, could barely calm her racing heart

enough to take a deep breath. Her entire body was shaking in the aftermath of their close call.

"Pull over up ahead," Nick instructed.

She knew he wanted to drive and couldn't blame him. She did as he requested, trying to hold herself together. She dragged herself out of the driver's seat as Nick came around to meet her. He lightly clasped her shoulders, peering down at her. From the streetlight behind her, she could see the concern etched on his handsome face.

"Are you all right?" he asked.

She tried to speak, but her throat felt frozen. It abruptly hit her how much she was depending on Nick to help find her son. If anything had happened to him, she'd be lost.

As much as she longed to lean against his strength, she forced herself to step back, putting distance between them. "I'm fine, but I was afraid they were going to hurt you," she confessed softly.

"Me, too, and I didn't really want to shoot any of them. Thanks to your quick thinking, I didn't have to. Now let's get going, okay?"

She nodded and went around to the passenger side of his car. "Did you find anything?" she asked, hoping the stop at the apartment building hadn't been in vain.

"Yeah. Morales still has a place there, apartment number 210 according to the mailbox. I spoke to the manager, but he claims he hasn't seen Ricky in weeks."

She tried not to be too discouraged by the lack of information. Truthfully, he'd found out more than she'd hoped. "I guess that means he's not likely keeping Joey there."

"I doubt it. There are too many nosey people around, like those thugs back there."

"I hardly think they'd be the types to turn Ricky in to the police," she said with a sigh.

Nick didn't say anything to the contrary, which only made her more depressed. "Are you still up for heading over to the ex-wife's place?" he asked, changing the subject.

"Yes." Granted she'd been terrified back there at the apartment building, but nothing was going to stop her from searching for Joey.

Nick glanced over at Rachel, marveling at the depth of her strength. Granted, she'd been scared to death back there at the apartment building, but that hadn't stopped her from doing what needed to be done.

He used his radio to request a search on the Morales apartment related to the hit-and-run case. The dispatcher agreed to send a couple of uniforms over. He didn't really think they'd find anything useful, especially since the manager had been all too willing to talk once he'd seen Nick's badge.

If Morales had been around, the manager would have told him so.

The trip to Margie Caruso's house took about twenty minutes. Her neighborhood was several steps up from where Morales lived. At least the houses were neat and clean for the most part, several decorated with Christmas lights.

The address indicated the house they were looking for was the third one on the right. Nick slowed down as he drove past the modest red brick home with the tan trim and black shutters. The entire place was dark, not a single light on inside the place that he could see.

"What do you think? Is anyone home?" Rachel asked.

"I don't know. It's about nine-fifteen, so I suppose Margie could already be asleep…." But it wasn't likely.

Maybe they were on the wrong track? Could be that Margie Caruso was living a normal peaceful life that had nothing to do with the Mafia or kidnapping Rachel's son.

"What's the plan?" she asked, keeping the house in sight as he drove by.

"Don't have one yet. It's not as if we can simply walk up and demand to search the place, even if someone answers the door."

"Why not? I could try talking to her," Rachel said impulsively. "We're both ex-Carusos and I can use that connection to feel her out."

He wasn't sure he liked the idea, but couldn't come up with anything better so he reluctantly nodded. "All right. I'll park on the street, in front of the neighbor's house. If anything seems off, you need to get out of there right away."

"I will." She hesitated for a moment before reaching for the door handle. Extremely bright lights bloomed in his rearview mirror as a car headed straight for them.

"Wait!" Nick shouted, reaching out to grab her arm. She paused, half in and half out of the car, so he yanked her back inside at the same time gunfire echoed through the night.

FOUR

"Get down!" he yelled, stomping on the gas and peeling away from the curb. He kept a hold on Rachel while she managed to get her legs tucked inside the car. He let go long enough to take a sharp right-hand turn, which caused the half-open passenger-side door to slam shut.

"What's going on?" Rachel asked.

"Stay down," he barked. Glancing at the rearview mirror, he could see the vehicle was keeping pace behind them. He could tell by the high yet narrow set to the headlights that it was a Jeep.

He had to figure out a way to lose it and fast.

"Why is he shooting at us?" Rachel gasped, her eyes wide with fear.

He shook his head, unable to answer as he concentrated on losing the gunman. He took several more turns, dodging around various vehicles in his way. Thankfully, traffic was relatively light this far outside the city, or escaping the shooter would have been impossible.

When there was a gap in traffic, he jerked the steering wheel to the left, taking the car up and over the curb, making an illegal U-turn. It wasn't easy keeping his eyes on the road while watching the Jeep behind him. The other car didn't make the turn right away, which was reassuring.

He immediately took another right-hand turn, putting even more distance between them. When he found an on-ramp for the interstate, he took it and pushed the speed limit as hard as he dared until he found the next exit. On that road, he switched directions, heading left.

Fifteen minutes later, he was convinced he'd lost the Jeep. "Are you all right?" he asked, as Rachel eased upright and reached for her seat belt. "He didn't hit you, did he?"

"I don't think so," she said, patting her arms and legs as if she wasn't entirely sure. "Did you get the license plate number? Do you think that was Joey's kidnapper?"

"I didn't get the plate number because I was blinded by his high-beam lights." He tried to figure out what had just happened. The whole event was weird. "Don't you think it's odd that he took a shot at us, but didn't keep firing? And that he didn't target anything important?"

"What do you mean nothing important? He almost hit us!" Rachel protested.

"Not even close," he argued mildly. "We were practically sitting ducks and he didn't hit either of us, or any significant parts of the car, like the gas tank or wheels. It's almost as if he wanted to scare us more than kill us."

"So it must have been Joey's kidnapper!" Rachel's tone had a note of excitement. "He didn't want to kill us, because he still wants the money."

"Maybe," he agreed, although the scenario didn't quite feel right. This entire case wasn't like anything he'd experienced before. He knew crooks, had investigated them for years and they always had a reason for what they did.

Only this time, nothing made sense.

He took the next exit off the freeway, slowing his speed to the posted limit.

"We have to go back there," Rachel said urgently, interrupting his train of thought. "To see if we can find Joey. We must have been close if they were so desperate to scare us away."

"Rachel, calm down for a minute and think this through. How did they find us outside of Margie Caruso's house in the first place? I made sure no one followed us when we left Morales's apartment building."

"I don't know, maybe it was all just a big coincidence? Morales could be working for Margie Caruso, and maybe he just pulled up as we got there."

"I don't think so." Nick hated to burst her bubble, but she wasn't thinking rationally. He pulled off onto the side of the road and turned in his seat to face her. "Even if he saw us there, how could he know we were the ones in the car?"

"Maybe he recognized your car from the crash site?"

"I came in from the south and you said he went north," he reminded her gently. "Rachel, they have your cell phone number. They sent you a text, threatening to kill Joey if you called the police. Don't you see? The only thing that makes sense is that they've tracked us through the GPS in your cell phone."

Rachel swallowed hard as she stared down at her cell phone. Was Nick right? Had they really tracked them through her phone? She wasn't a techno-geek so she had no clue how to even do something like that.

But she knew the possibility existed.

And if Nick's hunch was correct, then Joey's kidnapper already knew she wasn't alone.

Fear swelled in her throat, choking her as tiny red dots swam before her eyes.

"Breathe," Nick commanded, giving her shoulder a shake.

She didn't even realize she was holding her breath. She took a shaky gasp of air and lifted her tortured gaze to his. "They're always going to know where we are, aren't they? We're never going to be able to escape."

"Not unless we ditch your phone," he said grimly.

She clenched the phone so hard she was surprised she didn't break it in half. "No. No way. This is the only connection I have to Joey. This is the number they're going to use in order to contact me for the ransom demand. I'm not giving it up, Nick. I'm not! *I can't!*"

He stared at her for a long moment before releasing a heavy sigh. "Okay, if you're not getting rid of it, then we need to figure out our next steps. Because the kidnappers are going to be able to find us, no matter what we do or where we go."

"What if we buy a new phone, but keep the same number?" she asked suddenly. "Wouldn't that work? I mean, the GPS is linked to the device, not to the actual phone number…right?"

Perking up, Nick flashed her a smile. "You're brilliant, Rachel. That's exactly right. Now we have options."

"Do you think the stores are still open?" she asked.

"There are plenty of twenty-four-hour superstores. Here, use my smartphone to find the nearest one.…"

"Okay." She took the phone and used the search engine to find the closest superstore. "There's one about seven miles away," she told him.

"Perfect."

They arrived at the superstore and quickly made their

way over to the electronics section. She stayed back as Nick purchased the phone, along with a car charger, explaining to the clerk how they wanted to keep the same number.

"We can do that," the clerk said. "But it can sometimes take up to twelve hours to get the number transferred over."

"Twelve hours?" she echoed in shock.

The clerk shrugged. "It might be quicker, but I can't say for sure when."

Nick's expression was grim but he purchased the new phone and car charger, paying for a full year so that there wasn't any way to trace the contract fee. He gave her the phone and she stared down at it.

Twelve hours. She had to hang on to her old phone and evade the kidnappers for the next twelve hours.

And they were no closer to finding Joey.

She wanted to scream in frustration but forced herself to take several deep breaths to fight off her rising panic instead. She had to believe the kidnappers would keep Joey alive in order to get the payout. They had to.

She followed Nick to the car. When he started the car and pulled out of the parking lot, back onto the road, she plugged the new phone into the charger and then glanced at him. "Where are we going?"

He shrugged. "I think it's better to stay in the car and keep moving for now. We'd only be sitting ducks in a motel."

She couldn't argue his logic. "Would you be willing to split up so one of us could go and check out Margie's house? I need to know for sure Joey's not in there."

Nick was silent for so long she thought he was ignoring her. "Rachel, you're not a cop…so no, I'm not willing to split up. Let's just worry about staying alive tonight, okay? Unless you're having second thoughts about going to the FBI?"

She shivered. "No, I'm not having second thoughts. I heard what you told your boss about dirty cops at the local and federal level. I can't risk losing my son, Nick. I just can't."

He sighed. "I know what I said, but I can't help wondering if God isn't trying to tell us something the way these obstacles keep getting thrown in our way."

She was a little uncomfortable by his reference to God, but just the thought of calling in the police made her sick. "Your boss is willing to give us some time, so why are you still pushing the authorities on me?" When he opened his mouth to protest, she held up her hand. "I trust you, Nick, and I don't have much choice but to trust your boss, too. But I can't take the chance of trusting the wrong person. It could end up costing my little boy his life."

Truthfully, it was hard enough to trust Nick. But the fact that he'd been so angry with her for not giving him details about Anthony's involvement with the Mafia a year ago had gone a long way in convincing her that he was one of the good guys.

However, that didn't mean she wanted to open the circle of trust to include anyone else. Not unless there was no other choice.

Nick pulled into a mall parking lot, and she wasn't surprised when he positioned the car in a way that they'd be able to escape in a hurry if need be. She shivered a little, burying her face in the collar of the dark sweatshirt beneath her jacket. Her jean-clad legs were cold, and she rubbed her hands on her thighs to try and warm up.

"I have a blanket in the trunk," Nick said gruffly, before sliding out of the driver's seat. He returned a few minutes later with a wool blanket. "Why don't you stretch out in the backseat?"

"I won't be able to sleep," she protested. "Besides, we should take turns keeping watch."

"I'll keep watch first while you try to get some rest." His tone indicated there was no point in arguing.

Resigned, she opened the passenger door, pausing for a moment as she realized there was a bullet hole near the bottom of the window. The reminder of being used for target practice made her shiver again. Clutching the blanket, she climbed into the backseat and huddled down, grateful for the added warmth from Nick's blanket. She vowed to give him the blanket when it was her turn to keep watch.

The backseat was hardly comfortable, but that wasn't the reason she couldn't sleep. Images of Joey kept flashing through her mind, haunting her to the point where she almost couldn't stand it another moment.

"Nick?" she said softly, breaking the silence. "You don't think the kidnappers will hurt Joey, do you?"

"Try not to torture yourself thinking the worst, Rachel."

"I'm not trying to torture myself, but every time I close my eyes I picture that man grabbing Joey and slinging him over his shoulder. Don't you see? I'm the one who told Joey to get out of the car and run. It's my fault he was kidnapped."

There was a long pause, then Nick said, "Rachel, it's not your fault. I'm sure he would have gotten Joey even if you hadn't told him to run."

"Stop trying to placate me," she said sharply.

There was another brief silence. "Look, Rachel, I don't know if you believe in God, but if you do, praying can help you get through this."

She remembered how Nick had prayed before eating their fast-food dinner. Maybe he believed but she wasn't sure she did. "My parents weren't very religious. When I was growing up the only time we went to church was at Christmas and Easter." She hadn't thought about church or God in a long time. "I'm not sure I believe there really is a God, or that He cares anything about me or Joey."

"There is." Nick's voice exuded confidence. "And He does care about you and Joey. If you keep an open mind and an open heart, you'll be rewarded."

"Rewarded?" She couldn't hide the sarcasm in her tone. "I hardly think having my son kidnapped is anything close to rewarding."

"You're twisting my words, Rachel," he said quietly. "I meant that God can help you through difficult times."

"There's nothing more difficult than having your child in danger." She fought the rising anger. Who was he to preach to her at a time like this? Her son was missing and he wanted her to pray?

"I do know a little about what you're going through, Rachel. Two years ago, I lost my wife and my daughter in a terrible car crash. I nearly went crazy during the hours they were missing, before they were found dead in the bottom of a ravine. And trust me, I wouldn't have made it through those dark days without God's strength and the power of prayer."

His blunt statement surprised her and caused her to feel ashamed. Why was she taking her anger out on Nick? None of this was his fault. Clearly, he knew what it was like to lose someone he loved. Losing his wife and a daughter had to have been horrible. But prayer? She wasn't sure she was buying that idea.

She couldn't remember the last time she'd prayed, if ever. And she wasn't sure that prayer alone would make her feel better about losing her son.

She wouldn't survive if Joey died. Everything inside her would die right along with him.

"I've been praying for Joey's safety," Nick went on in a low voice. "And I want you to know, I'll keep on praying for Joey and for you."

Tears pricked her eyes and her throat swelled, making it hard to speak. Knowing that he would pray for her son brought a surprising level of comfort. And she suddenly realized that he was right. She did need to keep an open mind. Because if Nick's prayers could really help, she would gladly take them. She would take anything she could get if it meant keeping Joey safe.

She cleared her throat, trying to hide the evidence of her tears. "Thank you, Nick. And I'm sorry I snapped at you. I didn't know you lost your wife and daughter. I guess you really do know what I'm going through."

"For a long time I wanted to join them up in heaven," he admitted. "But God chose another path for me, so I've decided to dedicate my life to putting bad guys away and leading a Christian life, until God calls me home to be with my family."

She wasn't sure what to say in response to that, since truthfully, his plan sounded a bit lonely. Although who was she to argue about being alone? She wasn't interested in having a relationship again, either, especially not while she was raising her son. She was too afraid to trust her instincts about men after the way she'd messed up with Anthony.

Was Nick subtly warning her that he wasn't interested in being anything more than friends? If so, she was happy to oblige.

Right now, she didn't care about anything except getting her son back safe and sound.

As the minutes passed slowly, she stared out through the car window at the stars scattered across the night sky. And suddenly, she found herself uttering a simple prayer to a God she wasn't even sure existed.

Please keep my son safe.

FIVE

Rachel must have dozed in spite of herself, because, when she opened her eyes, dawn was breaking over the horizon and she didn't recognize the area. She assumed Nick had driven somewhere else at some point in the middle of the night. It took a moment for her to realize the beeping noise that woke her up came from a phone. She scrambled around, searching for her phone as Nick twisted in the driver's seat to look at back at her.

"Another text message?" he asked.

She pushed the button on her old phone and her heart leaped into her throat at the message that bloomed on the screen.

Ten million dollars will buy your son's freedom. Details on the exchange to follow. Remember, no police or your son will pay the price.

She tore her gaze from the message and held up the phone to show Nick. "It's the ransom demand," she said in a choked voice. She wasn't sure if she should be relieved or worried that the message had come so early in the morning.

She stared at the phone, wanting desperately to believe that some sort of contact from the kidnappers was better than nothing.

"Text them back that you need proof that Joey is still alive," Nick ordered, starting the car and driving out of the parking lot. "Tell them you want to talk to your son."

She hesitated, afraid that if she made the kidnappers mad they might hurt Joey.

"Rachel, you have to know Joey is alive, or there's no point in agreeing to the demand."

Although she hated to admit it, she knew he was right. She took a deep breath and texted back, No money until I speak to my son.

The moment she pressed Send, she wanted to call the message back. She stared at her old phone for several long moments, hoping the kidnapper would respond. With every minute that ticked by, raw fear rose in the back of her throat, suffocating her.

"What if they don't let me talk to him?" she asked, unable to hide the quiver in her voice. "What if they hurt him, instead?"

"You have to insist on it," Nick said, a hard edge of steel lining his tone. "Please trust me on this, Rachel."

"I do, it's just that I don't care about the money," she whispered in agony. "I just want them to give me Joey."

"I know that, and believe me, they know that, too. They're playing on your fear, Rachel. They're doing this to keep you off balance. You have to be strong. For Joey."

She nodded, but the vise grip around her heart wouldn't loosen. She wanted to talk to Joey. Desperately needed to hear his voice.

Please, God, please keep Joey safe.

Just when she was about to give up all hope, her old

phone rang, from another blocked number. She pushed the button and lifted the device to her ear. "Hello? Joey?"

"Mommy? Are you there?"

Hearing her son's voice made her eyes well up with tears. "Yes, Joey, I'm here. Are you okay? They didn't hurt you, did they?"

"No, but I'm scared," Joey said, and she could tell he was crying, too.

"Ask him something that only he knows," Nick whispered from the front seat. Belatedly, she realized he'd pulled off to the side of the road. "To prove it's him and not some other kid playing the part."

She nodded, indicating she'd heard him. "Joey, sweetheart, listen to me. Everything's going to be okay. But I need you to tell me who your favorite basketball player is. Can you do that for me?"

"K-Kirk Hinrich."

Yes! The starting point guard for the Chicago Bulls was Joey's favorite player. "That's good, Joey. I love you. I'm going to get you out of there soon, okay?"

"That's enough." A mechanically distorted voice broke into her conversation with her son. "We will give you details about the exchange soon."

"Wait!" she shouted, but nothing but silence was on the other end. She stabbed the button on her phone to call the blocked number back, but all she heard was a weird click then nothing. It took every ounce of willpower she possessed not to scream in frustration. But nothing could stop her tears.

"Don't cry, Rachel," Nick said in a low, soothing voice. "We're better off now than we were a few minutes ago. At least we know Joey's alive and that they're going to set up the exchange."

Nick was right, but she couldn't seem to stem the flowing tears. Just hearing Joey's voice made her furious with the kidnappers all over again. Her son was alone and afraid. "We have to find him," she sobbed.

He reached over the back of the seat to gently squeeze her shoulder. "We will. Remember God is watching over him, too."

Despite how she'd already prayed twice for her son's safety, Nick's words were far from reassuring. Because suddenly she couldn't understand why, if there really was a God, He would put an innocent nine-year-old boy in this kind of danger.

"I don't believe that," she said abruptly, pulling away from his reassuring touch. She used the bottom of her sweatshirt to mop her face. "I don't trust a God who allows my son to be in danger. And I can't understand how you could believe that, either."

Nick stared at her for a long minute, his gaze shadowed by a deep sorrow, before he wordlessly turned away and began driving again.

She ducked her head, swiping away the moisture from her cheeks. She shouldn't feel guilty for hurting him, but she did. Yet, at the same time, she couldn't bring herself to apologize, either.

Right now, nothing mattered except Joey. That was how she'd lived her life since leaving Anthony. A woman on a mission to provide a normal life for her son, keeping him safe from harm.

This wasn't the time to allow herself to get distracted. By Nick or by the God he believed in.

Nick drove to the truck stop he'd passed earlier, so they could use the restrooms and get something to eat.

He tried not to be hurt by Rachel's anger as he understood, better than most, what she was going through. He'd been angry with God, too, at first when he'd discovered his wife and child had died. Anger was a normal part of the grief process, but that didn't mean he was giving up on her.

He'd continue praying for both Joey and Rachel.

Besides, she needed to cling to the knowledge of her son being safe and sound. There was still hope that they could figure out a way to get him back.

Rachel didn't say anything when he pulled into the truck stop parking lot, bringing the car to a halt between a pair of twin semitrailers. He climbed out of the driver's seat and then glanced back at her. "I thought we'd clean up in the restrooms first. I'll meet you in the diner in about fifteen minutes or so, okay?"

She nodded and pushed her way out of the car to join him. Wordlessly, they walked inside together before splitting up.

His stomach growled and the scent of bacon and eggs caused him to hurry. He scrubbed his hands over his rough stubble, wishing he had a razor. When he finished up in the restroom, he slid into a booth next to the door and perused the menu while he waited for Rachel.

She joined him a few minutes later and he didn't waste any time in placing their orders. Once they were alone with their coffee, he leaned forward and said firmly, "We need to figure out what to do from here, Rachel. Ten million is a lot of money."

"I know." She stared at her coffee, her hands huddled around it for warmth, but she didn't drink any.

"I know you're the CEO and president of your company, but are you really going to be able to get that much together?"

Slowly, she shook her head. "The economy has been tough, and we've had a large class-action lawsuit that has eaten away a significant portion of our profits."

Lawsuit? How come she hadn't mentioned this earlier? "What was the lawsuit about?"

She grimaced before answering. "We put a new diabetes medication on the market about two years ago. In clinical trials it was superior in performance to the medication that almost two-thirds of the diabetes patients are currently taking." She hesitated for a moment. "But something went wrong, and several people suffered very bad side effects and two patients died. The FDA mandated that we pull the drug off the market, and the lawsuit was filed shortly thereafter."

He stared at her in shock, mentally kicking himself for not investigating this angle earlier. "Rachel, isn't it possible that Joey's disappearance could be linked to this lawsuit rather than the Mafia?"

She sighed and lifted her gaze to his. "I don't see how the lawsuit could be related. I authorized a large settlement for those patients and their families. They deserve to be compensated for our mistake. What reason would they have to come after me now?" She gripped the mug tighter in her hands. "Besides, does it really matter who took Joey? All we need to do is to figure out a way to get him back."

It did matter, but he didn't say anything as the waitress headed their way with two plates of food. She plopped them down on the table, and then glanced at the two of them. "Need anything else?"

He forced a smile. "No thanks, we're fine."

The waitress turned on her rubber-soled heel and strode away. He bowed his head and prayed. *Thank You, Lord, for this food we are about to eat, and please keep Joey safe in Your care. Guide us in our journey to find him and help Rachel open her heart and her mind to Your peace and Your glory. Amen.*

When he opened his eyes, he realized Rachel had her head down, waiting for him to finish before eating her breakfast. She didn't join him in prayer, but she didn't lash out against God again, either, which he chose to believe was a good sign.

He dug into his bacon and eggs, savoring every bite. When the knot of hunger in his stomach had eased, he glanced up at Rachel again, noting with satisfaction that she was doing a good job of demolishing her own meal. "Tell me more about this lawsuit."

She lifted one shoulder. "There's nothing to tell."

"How is it that you didn't find the side effects of the medication during the clinical trials?" He didn't know much about the pharmaceutical industry, but surely there would have been an indication of the dangerous side effects long before the medication was released to the public.

Rachel tapped her fork on the edge of her plate. "That's one of the things I've been working on with my research team. We don't know why the blood clots only showed up after the medication was approved. The FDA wants a full investigation, and we're actually in the middle of pulling everything together." She sighed, and then added, "At least we were. Until all this happened."

The timing couldn't be a coincidence. "Who benefits if your company goes out of business?"

"No one." She set her fork down and pushed her half-eaten plate away. "My company employs well over three thousand people, who would all be out of a job if something happened. I can't see how this could be connected to Joey in any way."

He found it impossible to ignore the sliver of unease. "Rachel, be honest with me. Is your company in danger of going under?"

"Not yet, but we can't afford to take another hit like the one we took earlier this year. So far, we've managed to weather the storm."

Relieved by that news, he continued to finish his breakfast. "What about your competition? Wouldn't they benefit if you went belly-up?"

"I can't imagine any company going to these lengths to get rid of the competition. You're on the wrong track, Nick. Those threatening notes have the Mafia written all over them."

She could be right. "You better eat," he advised. "There's no telling when we'll get our next meal."

She picked up her fork. "As soon as we're finished here, I need to call Gerry Ashton, my vice president of Operations."

"Why?"

"Because he's my second in command and owns forty percent of the company stock. I'm fairly certain he'll be willing to buy my shares. And I know his wife has a significant amount of money."

His stomach clenched at hearing her plan. "Do you think something that drastic is really necessary?"

She shrugged and toyed with her food. "Yeah, I do. Besides, I'd give up my company in a heartbeat if it meant getting Joey back safe and sound."

As Nick finished up and paid their bill, he couldn't

help wondering if this was exactly what the lawsuit victims had planned all along. Forcing Rachel to give up everything she owned in order to save her son.

Rachel glanced at the clock, wondering if she dared call Gerry this early on a Thursday morning. They were both generally early risers, but it was barely seven-fifteen. She couldn't deny the deep sense of urgency. What if the kidnappers called right away, wanting the exchange? What if she didn't have enough time to pull the money together?

Logically, she knew that they would give her some time—after all getting the money was the end goal. Wasn't it?

She wished Nick hadn't questioned her about the lawsuit, because now uncertainty gnawed away at her. But those messages *had* to be from Anthony's uncle Frank, or from someone else within the Mafia. Nothing else made sense. Once they were back in Nick's car, she scrolled through her old phone's list of contacts until she found Gerry's cell number. Just as she pushed the button to call him, another text message came through. Another message from the kidnappers?

No, it was the text message stating that her phone number had been successfully transferred to her new phone. "Finally," she muttered.

"What?" Nick asked.

After she filled him in, Rachel got busy activating the new device. She had to click on a link first and then wait another few minutes for the phone number to be registered before she could use her new phone. When that was finished, she typed in Gerry's number and waited anxiously for him to pick up.

There was no answer, so she left a message. "Gerry, it's Rachel. Call me as soon as you get this. It's urgent."

Nick filled up the gas tank at the truck stop and dumped her old phone in the garbage before he slid behind the wheel and drove back out toward the highway. "Where does Gerry live?"

"About fifteen miles west of our corporate offices," she answered.

Nick glanced her way. "Okay, we're a good hour away, so I'm going to head in that general direction."

She nodded, hoping Gerry would call her back soon.

Forty-five minutes passed before her new phone rang, and she pounced on it when she saw Gerry's number come across the screen. "Hello?"

"Hi, Rachel, what's going on? What's so urgent?"

She relaxed a bit, hearing the sound of his voice. "Gerry, I'm so glad you called me back. I need your help. Would you mind meeting with me right away?"

"Of course, but why? What's wrong?"

"I'd, uh, rather explain in person."

"Okay, well then why don't you come to my house? We'll have plenty of privacy as Nancy is out visiting her mother, helping her recover from her hip surgery."

Nancy was Gerry's wife and she vaguely remembered that he'd mentioned Nancy's mother needing surgery. "That sounds perfect," she said, feeling relieved to know that Nancy wouldn't be there. "I'll see you in about fifteen minutes or so."

Asking Gerry for money wouldn't be easy—he'd been like a father figure to her since her own father had passed away from a sudden heart attack. She didn't like the thought of selling off her company, but she didn't have a choice. She'd give up everything she owned if it meant getting her son back safe and sound.

"You're not going to see him alone," Nick said, breaking into her thoughts.

She glanced at him in surprise. "I wasn't planning to."

He scowled as he navigated the streets heading toward Gerry's house. "But you didn't mention that you'd be coming with someone," he muttered.

"I didn't want to put him on guard," she admitted. "I'm not sure how much I should tell him."

"As little as possible," Nick responded. "No sense in dragging him into this mess."

"You're right. It's bad enough that I'm asking him to bail me out by buying my shares of company stock. And we still have to find a way to convince the bank to bypass their normal requirements to give me the cash immediately."

"One step at a time," he advised.

Gerry's house was much grander than hers, but then again, she preferred the family-friendly neighborhood she'd chosen to raise Joey in. There was nothing better than watching the neighborhood kids get together to play a quick game of soccer or baseball in the park across the street.

She had to shove the poignant memories aside. She needed to believe Joey would play again in the park, as soon as they got him away from the kidnappers.

"This is it," Nick said, as he pulled up into the driveway. There was a large wreath on the door and she could see the twinkling lights of a Christmas tree through the window. "Are you ready?"

She nodded and slowly climbed out of the car. She rang the doorbell and braced herself as Gerry swung open the door. He looked surprised to see Nick standing beside her. "Hi, Rachel, come on in."

She stepped across the threshold and then turned to make introductions. But before she could speak, Nick thrust his hand out. "Gerry, my name is Nick and I'm a good friend of Rachel's. I'm so glad we finally have a chance to meet in person, after all I've heard about you."

Her mouth dropped open, and she quickly closed it again. Nick's message was clear—he did not want to be introduced as a detective.

Gerry accepted Nick's handshake. "Nice to meet you, too," he said, throwing a suspicious gaze at Rachel. "I have to say, Nick, you have the advantage here, because Rachel hasn't mentioned you to me at all."

The reproach in his tone was obvious and she swallowed hard, already hating the way she wasn't being completely up-front and honest with Gerry.

"Gerry, I'm sorry to bother you," Rachel said abruptly. "I'm in trouble. Financial trouble."

His eyebrows furrowed together as he gestured for them to come in and sit down in the living room. "What do you mean by financial trouble?"

She twisted her hands in her lap, unable to hide her nervousness. This was extremely important and she couldn't afford to have Gerry refuse her request. "I can't tell you, so please don't ask. I need a lot of money, and I'm hoping you'll be willing to buy my shares of stock in the company."

The stunned expression on Gerry's face would have been comical if the situation wasn't so grim. "Rachel, I'm happy to loan you whatever you need. There's no reason to sell your stock."

His offer was humbling, but she knew she couldn't

take him up on it. Gerry was in his late forties and his two sons were currently enrolled in college. She couldn't take advantage of his generosity. "I insist on selling them to you. That way, if anything happens…" She couldn't bring herself to finish her thought. "It's just better this way, because I need ten million dollars."

"Are you kidding me?" Gerry leaped to his feet and began to pace. "Rachel, that just about covers all your stock! And how are you going to get the bank to give you that much money?"

"I'm hoping Edward Callahan, the bank manager, will bend a few rules for me," she said. "He knows the company is worth far more than that."

Gerry let out his breath in a huff and then turned to glare at Nick. "Can't you talk her out of this nonsense?" he demanded.

"I'm afraid not. Rachel is the one in charge here. I'm just helping her out as a good friend."

Gerry's gaze narrowed and he threw up his hands. "All right, fine. I'll help you. But, Rachel, please reconsider taking a simple loan. There's no reason to sell off your stock from your father's company."

His offer was generous, but she shook her head stubbornly. She'd never sleep at night with that heavy a debt hanging over her head. "I need you to buy the stock, Gerry. I want everything legal. Please don't fight me on this."

She couldn't explain that the likelihood of getting the money back was slim to none. And besides, if something happened to her during the exchange, she wanted the company to be in good hands. Gerry would be able to pick up where she'd left off without any trouble.

And even if she did survive, she knew full well that,

after this was all said and done, she and Joey would have to start over, with a new job and maybe even a new house.

A price she was willing to pay if it meant getting her son back safe.

SIX

Nick watched the interchange between Gerald Ashton and Rachel with interest. There was no denying the gentleman, who he guessed was roughly ten years their senior, seemed to care about Rachel. There was a casual familiarity between them as they ironed out the details of obtaining the money. While they worked, he swept a curious gaze around the room.

Family photos featuring Gerald, his wife, Nancy, and their two grown sons were proudly displayed. The furnishings in the room, including the holiday decorations, were expensive and fancy—not to his taste at all but not awful, either. The place looked like something out of a fashion magazine, and he didn't doubt for a moment that a professional decorator had had a hand in the outcome.

He'd never been to Rachel's house and wondered if her style was similar to Gerry's. Not that he should care one way or the other. But somehow, he couldn't imagine Rachel raising Joey in a fancy, formal place like this.

Or maybe that was wishful thinking on his part.

He had to admit there was nothing to make him think Gerry was anything but what he seemed—a wealthy businessman who cared about his family and about Rachel. He told himself to relax and tuned back into the conversation.

"I'll call Edward," Gerry told Rachel, putting a reassuring arm around her shoulder. Nick had to grit his teeth to stop from going over to forcibly remove it, even though the gesture was clearly intended to be reassuring and friendly. "I'm sure we can come up with some way to get you the cash you need. But the earlier I call him, the better."

"We appreciate your help, Gerry," Nick said, determined to make his presence known. He was more than willing to play the role of Rachel's boyfriend, if necessary. "Rachel said such kind things about you, I'm glad to see she was right."

Gerry actually looked flustered by the compliment. He removed his arm from Rachel's shoulders and pulled out his phone. "Give me a few minutes to talk this through with Edward, okay? We'll have to sign the paperwork in front of a notary, too, and he'll have someone at the bank we can work with, I'm sure."

"Thanks, Gerry."

While the older man was making the call, Nick crossed over to kneel by Rachel's side. "Are you okay?" he asked. As far as he could tell, she was holding up pretty well, considering.

"I will be once we have the cash," she murmured in a low voice. "At least we're one step closer to getting Joey back."

"Agreed. Just hang in there a little longer, okay?"

She nodded again but was still twisting her fingers together. He gently put his hand over hers, stilling her motions. "We'll get through this, Rachel," he said reassuringly. He wanted to invite her to pray with him but, after her outburst in the car earlier, settled instead on praying silently for her and Joey.

When Gerry returned, Nick rose to his feet. Rachel stood, too, and he stayed close by her side. Gerry's gaze was openly curious as it moved between the two of them, but he didn't comment. "Edward is going to do his best to pull the funds together. He's asked that you call him in two hours. We can meet him at the bank to finalize everything."

"Sounds good. Thanks again, Gerry." She set the drafted forms aside. "Bring these with you, okay? I'll see you in a little while."

Gerry hesitated before taking the documents she'd handed over. "I feel terrible about this, Rachel, and my offer still stands. If something changes, and you still have the money, I'd be more than happy to rip this agreement up as if it never happened."

"Thanks, Gerry." Rachel's smile was heartbreaking, and she reached up to kiss Gerry's cheek before turning away. Nick followed, as they made their way back outside.

In the car, he turned toward her, half expecting tears, but her eyes were dry and her expression was determined. "What now?" she asked, as if she hadn't just agreed to sign her life away. "We have two hours until we need to be at the bank."

"We'll find a coffee shop with free Wi-Fi so we can do some more research on Frankie Caruso. I also need to update my boss." He put the car in gear, backing carefully out of Gerald Ashton's driveway. At this moment, he didn't think he'd ever admired a woman more than he admired Rachel. She was beautiful, smart, sincere, and the one of the best mothers he'd ever known.

And the part of his heart that he'd sent into a deep freeze after Becky's and Sophie's deaths thawed just a little.

Rachel gratefully climbed out of the car at the coffee shop, hanging on to her new phone with a death grip. Nick purchased two large coffees and then found a small table near a gas fireplace. It was nice and cozy near the fire, and she sipped her coffee, gazing up at the wreath hanging above the mantel as he booted up the laptop.

"You can do some searching while I figure out a plan about handling the exchange," Nick said, turning the computer toward her. "Plus, I need to call a friend of mine to help with the exchange. Don't worry," he added, when he saw her dismay. "Jonah is someone I'd trust with my life. Unfortunately, we can't do this alone, Rachel. We need backup."

She nodded, her stomach twisting as she understood what he was saying. Getting the money from the bank was the easy part. Keeping her son alive during the exchange was going to be much tougher.

But failure was not an option.

As Nick made his calls, she sat there feeling numb. Even after he'd finished, she could only manage to stare blindly at the computer screen. For a moment she was tempted to start praying again. She regretted her harsh words to Nick earlier this morning. She'd been angry and had taken that anger out on him, wanting to hurt him the same way she was suffering.

Was she crazy to ask for God's help? Why would God listen to her? Her parents hadn't been religious, but she sensed they'd believed in God. At least they'd seemed to. Maybe she really was missing something important.

For a moment she bowed her head and opened her heart. *I'm sorry, Lord. I never should have said those hurtful things. Especially when they're not true. I know Nick believes in You and I want to believe, too. Please help show me the way. And please keep my son safe in Your care. Amen.*

As before, the moment she finished praying, a sense of peace settled over her. She looked up and caught Nick staring at her, and she forced herself to smile. "I'm sorry, Nick. I do want to believe in God. I want to believe He'll keep Joey safe."

"I'm so glad, Rachel," he murmured, reaching over to take her hand in his. "Looks as if my prayers have been answered. I've been praying that you'd allow the Lord to help carry your burden."

Nick's hand was warm on hers, and she found it odd that she didn't want to let go. Never before had she ever depended on a man to help her. Except for her father, especially when she'd needed to escape Anthony. She knew she was lucky to have Nick's help with this. She never would have been able to manage alone.

Her new phone rang, interrupting the peaceful silence. Startled, she glanced at the screen, half expecting to see the familiar blocked call.

But the call was from Edith Goodman, her assistant. She winced as she realized she had forgotten to let Edith know she wouldn't be in the office today. Or at all, considering she wouldn't be the owner of the company once she returned from the bank in a few hours. "Hi, Edith," she said to her assistant. "I'm sorry I forgot to let you know that I'm taking the rest of the week off."

"The rest of the week?" Edith's voice rose sharply.

"This isn't like you at all. What in the world is going on, Rachel?"

"I'm sorry, Edith, but there's something important I have to do." She wanted to reassure her assistant that Gerry would be there to take over the company, but Edith would find that out sooner or later. No need to spill the beans yet. "Just cancel my meetings and let everyone know I'm taking a personal leave of absence, okay?"

"If that's what you want," Edith replied slowly. "But that wasn't the reason I called. I just thought you should know what happened, before you read about it in the newspaper."

"Read what?" She had no idea what her assistant was talking about. She hadn't even thought about reading the newspaper since getting the threatening notes. Surely there wasn't another pending lawsuit? She'd feel guilty selling her shares of stock to Gerry if in fact they weren't worth the price.

"Dr. Josie Gardener is dead, Rachel," Edith said, her voice tinged with sorrow. "It looks like she may have committed suicide late last night."

Nick knew that, whatever the contents of the phone call between Rachel and Edith, it was bad news. Rachel went pale, her fingers gripping the phone tightly as she listened.

"Do you know anything else?" she asked. He couldn't hear Edith's response, but then Rachel said, "Okay, thanks for letting me know," and she disconnected from the call.

"Rachel? What happened?" He took her hand in his, trying to offer some sort of comfort.

"One of my top research scientists was found dead

in her home early this morning," she said in a whisper. "They think it might be a suicide."

Suicide? As before, the timing was too much of a coincidence. "Was this the same research scientist who was responsible for the new diabetes drug going to market and then being recalled by the FDA?" She nodded. "Josie Gardener wasn't the only one involved in creating the new medication. She worked with Dr. Karl Errol, too."

Nick glanced around, not wanting to discuss anything further in a public place. "Let's go out to the car," he murmured.

Rachel seemed to move in slow motion as they packed up and went back outside, carrying their coffee. He felt better once they were safely settled in the car. "Is there any reason to suspect she was involved in covering up the side effects of the medication?"

"Of course not!" Rachel's denial was swift. "Her reputation was on the line with this new medication. And even if it wasn't, why commit suicide now? Why not back when the lawsuits were initially filed?"

She had a point, but he found he couldn't let it go. "Maybe she was afraid you'd find out the truth and couldn't bear to face the consequences of her actions?"

Rachel frowned for a moment, as if considering his idea. "I don't know, Nick. We have been working on releasing our research documents to the FDA, but if there was something Josie was trying to cover up, I'm sure Karl would have told me."

Unless Karl was in on it, too, he thought. Was it possible that Karl was responsible for kidnapping Joey? Maybe Karl's goal was to keep Rachel preoccupied while he swept the truth about the diabetes drug under the rug?

Once he had the money, he could disappear out of the country without anyone being the wiser.

The more he thought about the theory, the more convinced he became that he was onto something. But he didn't think Rachel was going to go along with his idea—she was too loyal to her coworkers to think anything bad about them. "Where does Karl live?" he asked, trying to sound casual. "Maybe we should pay him a visit? See what he knows about Josie's death?"

"He lives in a small house not far from the company," Rachel said, her forehead wrinkled in a deep frown. "I would say he'd be at work, but, with Josie's death, I guess I'm not sure. They were close, but only in a professional way as far as I know. Neither one of them is married. Josie has a brother and a twin sister, but no children."

Nick felt bad for Josie's family, but he was more interested right now in where Karl Errol was. "Do you know Karl's home address?"

Rachel rattled it off as he entered it into his phone GPS. He pulled out of the coffee shop parking lot and followed the directions with a sense of grim determination. Hopefully, the good doctor would be at home, playing the role of grieving colleague.

When they pulled up in front of Karl Errol's house, the small, brick Tudor appeared to be deserted. There were no holiday decorations adorning the home, and the yard had a shaggy look of neglect beneath the light dusting of snow. "Stay here," he advised Rachel. "I'm going to take a look around outside."

"Should I call Edith and see if he's at the office?" she asked, as he slid out from behind the wheel.

"Sure." He flashed a reassuring smile before heading up the cracked sidewalk leading to the researcher's front door.

No response from inside the home, which was pretty much what he expected. He peered through the windows but couldn't see much—the sunlight outside caused a glare that made it difficult to see. He walked around the house, crunching on leaves as he made his way to the garage, which was closed and locked up tight. He strode over to the back door and checked it as well. The screen door opened, and his heart quickened as he tested the interior door.

Locked, but with a flimsy, old-fashioned type of lock. He considered trying to jimmy it with a credit card, but was loath to do anything illegal.

He hesitated on the cracked stoop. What if Joey was inside the old house? What if his theory about Dr. Errol was right? That he'd kidnapped Joey to keep Rachel from uncovering his mistakes?

Wrestling with his conscience, he turned away from the door, but then caught sight of one of those fake rocks that were sometimes used to hide keys. Why people bothered with that sort of thing, he had no clue. Talk about being obvious. He reached down, opened up the fake rock and removed the key.

He accessed the house, wrinkling his nose at the stale air. When was the last time the doctor had been home? Either the guy simply lived like this, or he was holed up somewhere else—with Joey—biding his time until he could get his hands on Rachel's cash.

He quickly swept through the house, including the upstairs bedrooms but didn't find anything suspicious. There were only three bedrooms, and they were all empty. He even went down in the basement, which was dark and dank, smelling strongly of mold.

Nothing. Which he found a bit odd. Usually people left a bit of themselves strewn around, at least a bill or a coupon or something. But the place was so void of anything personal that he couldn't help wondering if he was on the right track. Granted, he hadn't found Joey here, but he wasn't willing to give up his theory just yet.

Back up in the kitchen, he searched for notes or anything at all that might indicate where Dr. Errol had gone. The garbage can was empty and there wasn't a single stray note to be found. He even went back to the master bedroom, but still didn't find anything.

Dr. Errol was either innocent or smarter than he'd given the guy credit for. And he was leaning toward the latter.

He left the house the same way he'd come in, returning the key to its hiding place in the fake rock. He hurried back around to the front, where Rachel was waiting in the car.

"What took you so long?" she asked, when he slid in behind the wheel. "I was getting ready to come out and look for you."

"Sorry, I was poking around and lost track of time. Did you get in touch with Edith?"

"Yes, she said that Karl called in saying he was staying home today." She stared at the house through the windshield. "Maybe we should try knocking at the door again?"

Time to come clean. "Actually, I found the house key hidden in a rock near the back door. I went in and checked out the house. Believe me, no one is home. And from what I saw, I don't think he's been home in a couple of days, either."

"He hasn't been home?" She stared at him incredulously. "But that's crazy. I know for a fact that Karl was at work the day we met in my office. I had a meeting scheduled with both him and Josie that I canceled."

"That was on Wednesday," he said thoughtfully, going back through the timeline. It was Thursday and he found it hard to believe that only twenty-four hours had passed since he'd sat in Rachel's office looking at the threatening notes she'd received. "That means he must have been planning this for a while."

"You don't know what you're talking about," Rachel said, crossing her arms over her chest. "I saw the guy who kidnapped Joey, remember? He was young, in his late twenties or early thirties. I can guarantee he wasn't Karl Errol. Karl is a short, rather nerdy type of guy with glasses and a half-bald head, although I don't think he's hit the age of forty yet."

She was clearly exasperated with him, but he couldn't just let this go "Rachel, it's best if we keep all possibilities open, okay? Errol could have easily hired Morales to kidnap Joey."

"Believe what you want," she said with a disgusted sigh. "I know that Karl isn't capable of doing anything like this."

There was no point in continuing the argument, so he concentrated on backing out of the driveway and heading back toward the city. They still had a good hour and fifteen minutes before they were due at the bank.

However, Rachel wouldn't drop the subject, even though he hadn't said a word. "Obviously you've forgotten how we were shot at outside Margie Caruso's house, which implicates the Mafia, not one of my employees."

He hadn't forgotten, but that incident had been more of a warning rather than an attempt to kill them. "Maybe we should head back over there, then?" he asked. "We have time."

"Great idea," she agreed enthusiastically.

He stifled a sigh and headed toward the freeway. They'd driven about twenty minutes when Rachel's cell phone beeped. He tightened his grip on the steering wheel because so far the only person who'd texted Rachel since this nightmare began was the kidnapper.

"He wants to know if I have the money yet," Rachel said, glancing up nervously. "What should I tell him?"

"Tell him that we'll have the money by one o'clock this afternoon. That gives us a little bit of a buffer since we're hoping to have this settled by noon."

"I don't know if that's a good idea," she protested. "I don't want to make him angry."

Nick understood her concern, but he wanted some time to react to the kidnapper's exchange plan. Since Logan was out of the country, he'd had no choice but to call his friend and fellow cop, Jonah Stewart, for assistance. Jonah lived with his wife, Mallory, in Milwaukee, but once he'd heard the story, Jonah had readily agreed to drive up to Chicago. "If this guy understands anything about banks, he'll understand the time frame is more than reasonable."

Rachel swallowed hard and sent the message explaining they'd have the money by one o'clock in the afternoon.

There was a tense silence as she waited for the kidnapper's response. When her phone beeped again, she picked it up with shaking fingers.

"Well?" he asked. "What was his response?"

Rachel lifted her tormented gaze to his, her lower lip quivering with fear. "He said to text him the minute we get the money and not a second later. He also said he'd hurt Joey and keep on hurting him for every minute we're late."

SEVEN

Rachel shivered, despite the bright sunlight streaming in through the windshield keeping the interior of the car toasty warm. She couldn't bear the thought of the kidnapper hurting her son. She didn't even want to think about what Joey may have already suffered.

She forced her frozen fingers to text back. I promise I'll call as soon as I have the cash. Please don't harm my son.

"Rachel, try not to panic. I'm sure he's bluffing," Nick murmured, reaching over to squeeze her hand.

"I'm not willing to take that chance," she snapped.

Nick didn't seem a bit fazed by her anger. "Remember, we've just purchased a new phone. There's no way for him to track us from now on. And it could be that he isn't even aware of that fact, yet."

Suddenly, the idea of getting a new phone didn't seem like such a good one. Her heart lodged in her throat and she gripped his hand tightly. "What if he gets mad about the switch and hurts Joey?"

"Don't worry, Rachel," Nick said in a soothing tone. "The kidnapper has come too far to turn back now. He wants your money, remember?"

Nick's theory wasn't at all reassuring. Yes, the kidnapper wanted her money, but it could be that he also had a sadistic streak and took some kind of perverse pleasure from hurting young children, too. She was tempted to beg Nick to return to the truck stop, so she could grab her old phone out of the garbage.

But he was already heading down the highway toward Margie Caruso's house, so she bit her tongue and tried to relax. At least for now, the kidnapper couldn't track their movements, which was a good thing. She hoped and prayed that they'd find Joey there.

This time, Nick didn't pull up in front of the house, but drove around the block, parking on the opposite side of the house. It was broad daylight, so it wasn't exactly easy to hide from curious eyes.

"Remember, I'm the one who's going to do the talking here," she reminded Nick as they slid out of the car.

He grimaced and nodded, keeping a sharp eye out as they walked down the street. Margie Caruso's house was the third one in from the corner, so it didn't take long to get there.

She could hear the faint hint of Christmas music coming from one of the houses, and she couldn't help quickening her pace, eager to see if Margie was home. Nick hung back as she walked up the sidewalk and rang the doorbell.

The seconds passed with agonizing slowness, but soon the door opened, revealing a well-dressed and nicely groomed woman who didn't look anything close to her fifty-some years. But the moment Margie saw Rachel standing there, she frowned. "No soliciting," she said abruptly.

"Wait! My name is Rachel Caruso. I'm not selling anything, I just want to talk to you for a minute."

Margie paused in the act of closing the door, her gaze raking over Rachel from head to toe. "You're Anthony's wife?" she asked.

Hiding a wince, she nodded. She tried to think of a way to forge a bond with the woman. "We divorced a long time ago, but I was hoping you wouldn't mind talking to me for a few minutes."

The former Mrs. Frankie Caruso pursed her lips for a moment. "Who's he?" she asked, gesturing toward Nick.

"This is Nick, a good friend of mine." She twisted her hands together, hoping Margie wouldn't guess that he was a cop and refuse to see them. Rachel didn't exactly want to have this conversation outside. Not that she was even sure what she was going to say. The main reason they'd come to Margie's house was to make sure Joey wasn't being held here.

"I guess you'd better come in, then," Margie said, opening the screen door for them.

Nick held the door as she entered the house first. She glanced around curiously and was a little disheartened to find nothing unusual. There were some holiday decorations, including a small fake tabletop-size tree. Would Margie invite her in if she was hiding her son here? Somehow she doubted it. Yet she firmly believed Margie Caruso would be a link to her son. "You have a very nice home," she murmured as she stepped into the living room.

Margie let out a bark of laughter. "Yep. Bought and paid for by Frankie," she bragged. "Do you want something to drink? I have coffee and soft drinks."

"No thanks. I really hope you don't mind us just dropping in like this," she said, before Nick could respond.

"It's just I need to find Frankie and I was hoping you'd know where he was."

"Have a seat," Margie said, waving at them as she dropped into a recliner. "What do you want with Frankie?"

Rachel's mouth went dry and she wished she'd agreed to take something to drink. "It's nothing major, I just need to ask him a few questions."

"Ms. Caruso, do you mind if I use your bathroom?" Nick asked, interrupting them.

"No problem, it's down the hall to your right," Margie said, waving in the general direction.

Rachel figured Nick was trying to give them some time alone, most likely thinking that Margie might open up more if he wasn't sitting there. She stared down at her hands for a minute trying to figure out a way to get Margie to speak openly about Frankie. "Last I heard, Frankie was in Phoenix," she said in a low voice. "I should tell you that I've received some threatening letters and phone calls." She glanced up, trying to assess Margie's reaction. "I guess I couldn't help wondering if your ex might be involved."

Margie let out a sigh. "I highly doubt Frankie's entangled in something like that," she said without hesitation. "It's not really his style."

"What is his style?" Rachel pressed. "I divorced Anthony a long time ago, so how do I know Frankie's not holding some sort of grudge against me?"

Margie tapped one long, lacquered nail against the end table. "Frankie has been splitting his time between Phoenix and Chicago, but I can't imagine he's holding the divorce against you. Why would he? Our divorce wasn't that big of a deal."

The news that Frankie Caruso could be right now in Chicago made her pulse race with a mixture of dread and excitement. Frankie had to be the one behind Joey's kidnapping…it was the only thing that made sense. "I have to tell you, I admired how you and Frankie seemed to get along, even after your divorce," Rachel said.

"Yes, well, we had some business ventures together, which helped," Margie replied evasively. Rachel tried not to show her distaste—certainly, those business ventures were likely Mafia related.

"Like I said, it's just amazing that you both managed to stay friends," Rachel added. "Obviously, that wasn't exactly the case with me and Anthony."

"I know. Anthony wasn't shy about telling us how upset he was at how you managed to keep him from your son." Margie's gaze was challenging, as if daring Rachel to disagree.

The mention of Joey kicked her pulse into high gear. So Frankie and Margie knew about Joey. Knew that she'd kept Anthony away from his son. Was this the motive behind the kidnapping? A way to show her the power of the Caruso name?

"Me and Frankie didn't have kids," Margie continued, clearly oblivious to Rachel's spinning thoughts. "I guess it was a good thing, considering how we didn't stay together."

Rachel couldn't decide if Margie was putting on an act for her benefit or not. She didn't dare glance at her watch, even though Nick had been gone for what seemed like a really long time. She didn't want Margie to wonder where he was, either. "I guess maybe you're right," she murmured. "Divorce is much easier without fighting over kids." Before the other woman could ask anything more,

Rachel quickly changed the subject. "Are you going to see Frankie anytime soon?"

Margie's eyebrows lifted. "Maybe. Why?"

Flustered, Rachel strove to keep her tone light and casual. "I thought maybe you could just mention to him that I'd like to talk to him. If he has some time. Nothing urgent…"

Margie stared at her for a long moment, as if trying to gauge what Rachel really wanted. "Yeah, sure. I might see him. Maybe you should give me your phone number so that he has it if he wants to get in touch with you."

"Of course. Do you have a pen and paper handy?"

Margie rose to her feet at the same moment Nick walked back into the room. "Wait here for a minute."

After their hostess left the room, she looked at Nick. "Well?" she asked in a low voice.

"Nothing," he murmured with a slight shake of his head.

Nothing, as in he didn't get to search very much? Or nothing, as in he truly hadn't found anything?

Before she could ask anything more, Margie returned. Rachel hastily scribbled her number on the slip of paper the older woman handed her. "Thanks so much, Margie. I really appreciate you taking the time to talk to me."

"No problem." Margie walked them to the front door. "Take care."

"You, too," Rachel said, before slipping outside. Nick followed her, grabbing her hand as they strolled down the sidewalk to the street. "We probably shouldn't have parked far away," she murmured under her breath. "Margie will think it's odd that we didn't pull up right in front of her house."

"You might be right," Nick said. "But you did a good

job of convincing her that your reason for being there was related to Frankie. Maybe she'll think we're just paranoid."

Once they turned the corner, Rachel relaxed. "I *was* there because of Frankie. He's been here in Chicago, Nick. I think he must be involved in Joey's kidnapping."

Nick didn't say anything more until they were in the car. "Frankie might be involved, but as far as I could tell, Margie isn't. I looked around and didn't find anything. I even managed to sneak down the basement stairs. There weren't any hiding places down there that I could see, so I didn't spend a lot of time searching. I was afraid she'd hear me."

Rachel couldn't believe he'd managed to get all the way into the basement. "What would you have done if she had heard you?" she demanded.

He shrugged. "I would have claimed that I took a wrong turn."

She put a hand over her knotted stomach, glad she hadn't known what Nick was doing while she chatted with Margie. Her nerves were already at the breaking point. Time was running out; they were due to be at the bank in the next twenty minutes.

Soon, they'd be one step closer to getting Joey back, safe and sound.

Nick glanced at Rachel as he navigated the traffic, taking the fastest route to the bank. He couldn't say he was surprised that they hadn't found anything at Margie Caruso's house. He still believed that Dr. Karl Errol might be the missing link. But no matter what he thought, there wasn't enough time to keep searching for Joey. He knew that once they'd finished their transaction at the bank, Rachel would contact the kidnapper.

There was no way she'd risk anything happening to her son. Not that he could blame her. Easy for him to say the kidnapper was bluffing. If Rachel found a single mark on Joey, she'd never forgive him.

His phone rang and he picked it up, recognizing Jonah Stewart's number. "Hey, are you in town?"

"Yep, sitting in the parking lot of the hotel down the road from the bank."

Nick could feel Rachel's curious gaze on him. "Good. We'll be at the bank within the next ten minutes or so. I'll be in touch as soon as we're finished."

"Sounds good. I'll be waiting."

"Thanks, buddy." He disconnected from the call.

"Was that the cop buddy you told me about?" Rachel asked.

"Yeah, Jonah Stewart is a Milwaukee detective who helped build a case against your ex-husband. Anthony tried to kill him. Thankfully, Jonah and Mallory escaped, and Anthony was the one who'd died that night."

"So he was the one responsible for bringing down Anthony," Rachel mused. "I always wondered exactly what happened."

The last thing he wanted was for Rachel to hear the gory details. "None of that matters now. Just know that we really can trust Jonah."

Rachel nodded and looked away, staring out the window as if lost in thought.

He mentally kicked himself for reminding her of Anthony Caruso, especially at a time like this, when her son was still missing. Didn't she already have enough to worry about? Right now, she needed to stay focused on the task of getting the money together. That was the first step. The second was to exchange the money for her son.

With the kidnapper calling the shots, they'd be lucky to get Joey back without incident, even with Jonah's help. "Nick?"

He dragged his gaze to meet Rachel's. "Yes?"

"I want you to promise me something."

Uh-oh. He braced himself, certain he wasn't going to like this. "Promise you what?"

She locked eyes with him. "Promise me that you'll get Joey out of there safely. I don't want you to worry about me—I want you to focus on keeping my son safe."

Every instinct in his body protested, but he knew very well that if the situation was reversed, he'd ask the exact same thing. Children were a cherished gift from God and they deserved a chance to be protected. As much as he didn't want to lose Rachel, he knew he had to give her this much.

"I promise," he vowed, silently asking God to spare both Rachel and Joey so he wouldn't be forced to make an impossible choice.

Rachel rubbed her sweaty palms on the sides of her jeans before picking up the pen to sign over her shares of the company stock to Gerry Ashton. She couldn't help glancing at her watch, wondering if right now, the kidnapper was somewhere close watching them.

"Are you sure about this, Rachel?" Edward Callahan asked. The poor bank manager had been beside himself since they'd arrived. She wanted to believe he cared about her, but she suspected the large withdrawal of cash was the main source of his concern.

"Absolutely." She wasn't nervous about selling off her

company; she was worried about Joey. Because the moment Edward handed over the cash, she'd have to call the kidnappers.

Please, Lord, please don't let them hurt my son.

The transaction was completed with ridiculous simplicity—she was sure she'd completed far more paperwork when she'd bought her house eight years ago.

A house that she'd have to sell, once she had her son back. She shoved the thoughts away, refusing to dwell on her decision. She'd give up everything she owned to get Joey back.

"I have the cash pulled together in the vault," Edward said as Gerry finished his portion of the agreement. "It wasn't easy… I had to send couriers to several other branches to get what you needed. I—uh, put it all in a large duffel bag for you. I didn't want it to look too obvious as you left the building. A cashier's check would be much safer," he added, even though he'd already lectured her on the perils of walking around with so much money.

"I know, thanks, Edward." She forced a smile as she turned toward Gerry. "I haven't told anyone at the office yet, but I'd appreciate it if you'd tell Edith first, privately."

Gerry's forehead was puckered in a concerned frown. "I will. Rachel, I wish there was more I could do to help you…."

"You've helped more than you could ever know," she assured him. "Thanks again."

Gerry gave her a quick hug and then tucked his copy of the paperwork into his briefcase and made his way toward the door. She turned her attention toward the bank manager. "I'm ready."

Nick stayed close at her side as they walked into the bank vault. Edward used his ID to open the first door and then punched in a key to access the second door. Once inside the vault, she saw the duffel bag he'd mentioned, surprised to find that it was the size of a small suitcase.

"I promise it's all there," Edward said, as she opened the bag and went through the contents. She'd never seen so much money before, especially not such crisp one-thousand-dollar bills.

"I'm sure you'll understand Rachel's need to verify the amount," Nick said, standing over her as if worried the bank manager himself was in on the kidnapping.

"Of course," Edward agreed, discreetly wiping more sweat from his brow.

She focused on the task at hand. The thousand-dollar bills were bound in stacks of one hundred so it didn't take long to validate the amount was correct. "Thanks again, Edward," she said, as she rose to her feet, slinging the duffel bag strap over her shoulder.

"We'd like to leave through the back door," Nick announced.

Edward nodded and led the way back out the vault, pausing long enough to close and lock both doors before he took them to the back of the bank.

Nick stayed close to her side as they left the building and climbed back into the car. She crammed the duffel bag on the floor between her feet, too afraid to store it in the backseat. The minute they were settled, she pulled out her phone.

"Wait just a minute, okay?" Nick said, putting a hand on her arm. "Let me call Jonah first."

The image of her son being hurt was impossible to ignore. It took every ounce of willpower for her to wait for Nick to call Jonah. He hadn't even completed his call when she quickly texted the kidnapper, I have the money.

Within seconds, her phone rang. Before she could push the button to answer, Nick whispered, "Put the call on speaker."

With trembling fingers she did as he directed. "This is Rachel."

"Go to the abandoned barn located twenty miles outside the city near the intersection of Highway F and Highway 93 in exactly one hour," the mechanically distorted voice directed. "Come alone or your son will pay the price."

Rachel swallowed hard. "I'll be there," she whispered, never doubting for one moment the kidnapper would make good on his threat.

If he hadn't hurt Joey already.

EIGHT

Nick watched the blood drain from Rachel's face, leaving her pale and shaking. He wanted nothing more than to take her into his arms and offer comfort, but this wasn't the time or the place. Right now, they had to get to the abandoned barn as soon as possible, if they were going to be successful in getting Joey back.

He called Jonah, repeating the kidnapper's directives. "I'm not sure where this place is, but we need to take only one car, as it doesn't sound like there's a lot of cover," he told his friend. "And, if you don't mind, it might be best if we take your car to change it up a bit. Rachel and I have been driving around town in mine, and the kidnappers might recognize it. What do you think, buddy?"

"Sounds good." Jonah quickly gave him directions to where he was parked at his hotel on the edge of town and they agreed to meet there in less than ten minutes.

"It's almost over, Rachel," he said, reaching out to squeeze her hand before he put the car in gear and drove away from the bank. "We're going to get Joey back."

"I'm so scared," she whispered. "There are so many things that could go wrong."

"Try not to think of the worst-case scenario," he advised, knowing that was his job.

"I won't. But I'll be glad when this is over."

He didn't bother pointing out that even if they managed to get Joey back unharmed, the nightmare might not be over. There was no guarantee the kidnapper would simply disappear once this exchange was completed. Especially since Morales was nothing more than a hired thug, doing what he was told. Whether the source of the kidnapping was the Mafia or someone related to her company, Rachel and Joey could still be in danger.

And of the two scenarios, he still found himself leaning toward the possibility that this was all somehow connected to her company.

He slowly unclenched his hands from the steering wheel. He needed to keep a cool head. Right now, it was best to focus on the upcoming swap. Later, there would be plenty of time to think about who was behind this.

The moment he pulled into the hotel parking lot, they quickly switched vehicles. Rachel lugged the duffel bag of money and Jonah handed the keys to Nick, choosing to climb into the backseat.

Nick quickly introduced the two and then started the engine. "Pleased to meet you, Rachel," Jonah Stewart said as he buckled himself in.

Rachel tried to smile, but it wasn't much of one. "Thanks for helping us."

"I don't mind at all. We're going to get your son back, Ms. Simon," Jonah said reassuringly.

"Please, call me Rachel."

Nick listened to their brief conversation as he drove, pushing the speed limit as much as he dared while following the directions leading them to the designated meeting spot. The GPS took them directly out of town, into farm country. As the traffic thinned, he pushed his speed even further, wanting to make good time.

The kidnapper hadn't chosen the location or the tight timeline by accident. Clearly the guy didn't want to give them too much time to prepare. And Nick absolutely didn't want to get there after the kidnappers were already there. He was hoping that the perpetrators might have to pick up Joey first, before meeting them, which would give them the time they needed.

A half hour would be nice, but he'd take less time if he had to. They would need every second to get the lay of the land. And to get Jonah hidden someplace nearby where no one would see him.

"Dear Lord, please keep my son safe in Your care," Rachel whispered.

Her quiet prayer caught him off guard, but he quickly joined in. "And, Lord, please guide us and give us strength as we fight to get Joey back safe and sound."

"Amen," Jonah said from the backseat. Rachel glanced over her shoulder at Jonah in surprise.

Nick reached over and squeezed her hand. "Jonah is a believer, too."

"Good to know," she said in a soft voice. "I feel like I need all the help we can get." There was a slight pause before she asked, "Does praying always make you feel calmer?"

"Absolutely," he agreed. "Sharing my burdens with God always helps me feel better."

"I wish I knew more about God and faith and prayer," Rachel said. "I feel like I'm not worthy of His help."

"You are worthy, Rachel, and so is Joey. But if you'd

really like to learn more, I'd be honored to teach you." He didn't want to push her too hard, but he was thrilled that she had opened her heart and her soul to God and faith. "Once we have Joey back, I'll be happy to study the Bible with you."

"After we have Joey back," Rachel repeated. "I'm going to hold you to that, Nick." She was twisting her hands together in the way he knew meant she was worrying again.

"We're going to be okay, Rachel," Jonah chimed in from the backseat. "God will guide us through this. We've been in other tight spots before, right, Nick?"

"Right," Nick agreed drily.

There was so much more he wanted to say, but off in the distance he caught sight of an abandoned barn at the end of what looked to be a hard-packed dirt road. That must be the meeting place. His heart sank as he realized it was out in the middle of a wide-open space, where it would be difficult to hide any backup.

"Take a look, Jonah," he said, gesturing toward the barn. "They sure didn't leave us many options."

"We'll find something," Jonah replied with confidence. "I doubt they're going to take the time to search the entire barn. I suspect they'll make this a quick exchange and get out of Dodge."

"I hope you're right," Nick muttered, pushing down harder on the accelerator. He couldn't help constantly looking at the clock on Jonah's dashboard. It seemed that time was slipping away from them.

The kidnappers would be there in forty-two minutes. Unless, of course, they decided to show up early. In that case, there was no way to judge how much time they had to prepare.

* * *

Rachel's stomach hurt so badly she feared she might be sick. She took several deep breaths and wrapped her arms tightly across her middle. She could do this.

She had to do this.

The big dilapidated barn loomed ominously as they approached. This was it. The moment she'd been waiting for and dreading at the same time. In less than forty minutes the kidnappers would drive up with her son, demanding money in exchange for his freedom.

Please, Lord, please keep Joey safe!

The calm she'd felt before after praying seemed to have deserted her now. Maybe because her prayers betrayed the depth of her desperation. Despite Nick's reassurances that she was worthy, she couldn't help feeling that maybe God thought she was a big fraud. But she hoped He wouldn't punish her son for her previous lack of faith. She took another deep breath.

Nick backed up the dirt road so that the car was facing outward toward the road. The minute he shut off the car, he and Jonah jumped out to see what they had to work with.

She was still trying to pull herself together. But when she stared down at the duffel bag, she realized she couldn't sit here. She had to be in the driver's seat, as if she'd just driven here by herself. Swallowing hard, she shoved open the door, hauled the duffel bag up so that it was on the seat, and then slammed the door.

Nick had Jonah's car keys, so she went to find him. She needed the kidnappers to believe she'd followed their instructions to the letter.

The barn door was open only about a foot, so she turned sideways to slide inside. The interior was surprisingly dim. She's expected it to be brighter considering there were several missing boards and glassless windows. The place reeked of fertilizer mixed with musty old hay, thanks to the piles that looked as if they'd been there untouched for years.

Nick stood, looking up at the loft. She followed his gaze and gasped when she saw Jonah carefully going up a rickety old ladder that didn't look strong enough to hold his weight.

"Are you sure that's safe?" she whispered.

"Not really, but he insisted on giving it a try."

There was a loud noise as Jonah's foot broke through one of the rungs of the ladder. Her heart lodged in her throat as he hung there for a moment before he regained his balance. In a few minutes, Jonah was safely on the loft.

"Wouldn't he be better off down here?" She couldn't imagine the rotted wood that made up the loft floor would be any sturdier than the ladder.

"I'll be down on the ground level, and he's going to try and get some leverage from up above. See that window up there?" He indicated the open space in the wall of the barn located above the loft. "It overlooks the front of the barn, and that's our best option."

She felt dizzy watching Jonah ease his way into position, so she lowered her gaze and tried not to sneeze. Despite the cold December air, the moldy hay was making her eyes water. "Where are you planning to be?"

"Outside, as close to you as I can manage," he said grimly. "There are several stacks of hay outside along the north side of the barn. If I drag a few more out there, I should be fairly well hidden."

She helped Nick carry a couple of stacks of smelly,

musty hay outside. They had to open the barn door wider and it groaned loudly in protest. She froze, hoping it wouldn't fall off.

After two trips, they had a decent-size stack of hay along the side of the barn. Nick carefully closed the barn door and then used a bunch of hay like a broom to brush the dirt, covering up their footprints.

The north side of the barn seemed too far away for her piece of mind, but she bit her lip so that she wouldn't complain. After all, she couldn't very well expect Nick to hide in the backseat of Jonah's car. Truthfully, she was lucky to have any backup at all.

"You might want to give me the car keys, just in case they want me to go someplace else," she said.

Nick scowled and dug them out of the front pocket of his jeans. "Here you go. But don't follow those guys someplace else, Rachel. There would be nothing to prevent them from killing both you and Joey, while still taking off with the cash. Your best option is to stay right here, where Jonah and I can protect you."

"I know," she said, taking the keys from Nick. As much as she knew he was right, she wasn't sure she'd be able to say no if it came to the kidnappers giving her an ultimatum. Her greatest weakness was her son's safety. If they threatened to hurt him, she knew she'd go along with whatever they asked of her.

She turned to walk away, but suddenly Nick grabbed her hand to stop her. Glancing over her shoulder, she found him staring at her intently. "What's wrong?" she asked.

"Nothing. Just—be careful, okay?" he said gruffly. Then, before she could respond, he pulled her close and gave her a quick kiss.

The kiss was over before she had a chance to register what had happened. But she longed to throw herself into his arms, absorbing some of his strength. This wasn't the time or the place, though, so she said the first thing that came to mind. "Remember your promise," she blurted. "No matter what happens, save my son."

He stared at her for a long moment. "I won't forget my promise, Rachel. But my goal is to get both of you out of here safely." He turned away and began digging a hole for himself in the hay.

She turned and hurried back to the car. By the time she'd slid into the driver's seat, she couldn't hear him any longer. He must have gotten himself hidden very quickly.

Her lips tingled and she wondered if Nick had kissed her on purpose to distract her. If so, his ruse had worked. For a couple of minutes her stomach hadn't hurt, although now the pain was back with a vengeance. She took another deep breath and focused on the task at hand, anxious to be ready if the kidnappers showed up early.

The driver's seat was all wrong, so she scooted the seat up so that she could reach the pedals and adjusted the mirrors to accommodate her smaller frame. From the way Nick had parked the car, she couldn't see much of the north side of the barn, which was back and to her left. Using the rearview mirror, she could just barely catch a portion of the stacked hay.

Nick and Jonah were both armed and ready. She tried to find comfort in the fact that if she couldn't see Jonah or Nick, then the kidnappers couldn't see them, either.

The minutes ticked by with excruciating slowness, and she resisted the urge to turn on the car to warm up. If she was cold, surely Jonah and Nick were even more so.

Within five minutes of waiting, she spotted a black

Jeep coming down the highway from the same direction they'd come. With a frown, she followed the Jeep's progress. If this one belonged to the kidnappers, they were fifteen minutes early.

Rachel clutched the steering wheel and strained her eyes in an attempt to catch a glimpse of her son. She thought there might be someone in the passenger seat, but the Jeep was too far away to be certain.

At the last possible moment, the Jeep slowed and then turned onto the dirt road. She held her breath as the vehicle approached. The driver was the same big dark-haired man who'd snatched Joey out from the car crash. There was a smaller person in the passenger seat and when the Jeep came closer, she could tell the small person had a dark hood over his head. The Jeep pulled to a stop about thirty feet from her vehicle.

Panic threatened to overwhelm her. What if the person in the front seat really wasn't Joey? What if this was nothing more than a horrible trick? What if they planned to kill her and take the money, while keeping her son to sell him in the black market of human trafficking?

Her pulse thundered in her ears as she pushed open the car door. She grabbed the duffel bag of money and dragged it over the console so that it was right next to her, as she stepped out of the car.

"I want to see my son!" she said in a loud voice.

The driver, who had to be Morales, reached over and yanked the hood off her son's head. Joey squinted and ducked his head, shying away from the light. He reminded her of a prisoner who'd been locked in a cell for days, unable to bear normal daylight.

Cold fury swamped her. It was all she could do not

to rush over to grab Joey and yank him out of there. She narrowed her gaze and stared, waiting for direction.

Morales slowly and deliberately pushed open his door and stood. Her heart dropped to the soles of her feet when he leveled his gun directly at her son. "One wrong move, lady, and I'll shoot to kill."

"I have the money," she blurted out. "You can have it. All I want is my son."

"Hold on, now," he said, sweeping his gaze around the area. She never flinched, trusting the men behind her to stay well hidden. "You'll get your kid soon enough."

"I'm not armed and I'm here alone, just like you asked," she said, drawing his attention back to her. "Here's the money. If you'll just let Joey out of the car, we'll make the swap."

His expression turned ugly. "Listen here, lady, *I'm* the one who's in charge. The kid doesn't move until I say so."

Her fingers clenched on the duffel bag as the seconds drew out to a full minute. He approached her with slow, deliberate steps, rounding the front of the Jeep. With every step closer, she grew more nervous. She came out from behind the safety of the driver's door, lugging the duffel bag.

"Set it down, where I can see it," he said in a low, guttural voice. So far, his movements had been slow and cautious, but the glint of excitement in his eyes betrayed his greed.

Ironically, that glimpse was enough to make her relax. She was certain he wasn't going to do anything foolish if that meant risking the money. But she didn't set the duffel bag down the way he told her to. "I will, but only if you let Joey open his car door."

He glared at her for a minute before giving a little wave of the gun. "Open your door, kid, nice and easy."

She tried not to divert her attention from the gunman, but she couldn't help sneaking a sideways glance at Joey. He was still squinting, as if he couldn't see very well but managed to open his passenger-side door. She could see his feet dangling outside the car, in the familiar basketball shoes she'd bought for him earlier in the school year. They were bright orange, his favorite color, and her eyes stung with the memory of how excited he'd been when he'd worn them for the first time.

The Jeep was high off the ground, and she wanted to call out a warning to Joey to be careful. But with the gunman so close, she didn't dare. Instead, she opened the duffel bag, holding it awkwardly against her chest, to show him the cash inside.

The gleam in his eyes got brighter, and she was struck by the fact that this guy obviously wasn't very smart. Nick was right—there had to be someone else acting as the brains of this operation. Morales was nothing more than a pawn. Right now, though, all she cared about was her son.

"Get out of the car, kid," Morales shouted. When she glanced over at her son, the thug lunged forward in an attempt to grab the money, but Rachel was faster. She snatched the handles of the bag, whipped it around and threw it at Morales, hitting him directly in the chest. "Run, Joey!"

While Morales was grappling with the bag, trying to make sure he didn't lose any of the cash, she leaped forward and grabbed her son. With a herculean effort, she hauled him up and ran toward the car, using her body to protect him as best she could. "Get inside," she urged.

"Stop!" Morales shouted. The sound of gunfire erupted and she ducked behind the open driver's door and threw herself over Joey, squashing him against the front seat.

"Stay down!" Nick shouted, coming around the corner of the barn, looking like a madman with straw sticking out of his hair and clinging to his clothes.

Morales turned and fired again. Panic-stricken, she glanced sideways and caught a glimpse of Nick hitting the ground. "Nick!" she screamed.

More gunfire, this time from up above, but Morales had already thrown the duffel into his Jeep and taken off, his tires churning up clouds of dust as he barreled down the dirt road.

NINE

Nick ignored the burning pain in his left arm as he crawled across the ground to reach Rachel and Joey. She held her son in a tight hug as if she might never let him go. Every instinct in his body was clamoring for him to follow Morales, but he couldn't bring himself to leave Rachel and her son. Or take them along, putting them in more danger.

"Are you all right?" he asked, pulling himself upright and leaning against the car. "Any injuries?"

"No injuries," Rachel murmured as she lifted her tear-streaked face from her son's hair. She barely glanced at Nick, her attention focused solely on her son. She brushed his hair away from his forehead. "Joey? Are you sure you're not hurt anywhere?"

Joey shook his head but didn't say anything, burrowing his face once again against his mother. The boy's silence was a bit concerning, but not completely unexpected considering the trauma he'd been through.

"Nick, you're bleeding!" Rachel reached out to touch his arm. "He hit you?"

"Winged by a bullet, nothing serious," he said, glancing around for Jonah. His buddy shoved open the barn door and came out, limping.

"I tried to take out the Jeep, but I fell through a hole in the floor," Jonah said with disgust. "I'm sorry I let him get away."

"Nothing more you could have done, Jonah," Nick assured his friend. "And the way you shot at him from up in the loft obviously scared him off, which is probably a good thing. He was armed, and the way things were going down, I doubt he intended to leave any witnesses once he got the cash."

"Yeah, I got that same feeling," Jonah muttered. He looked at his car and scowled, fingering the bullet hole in the back door along the driver's side. "Now I know why you wanted me to take my car. Hope he didn't hit anything in the engine."

The bullet holes in the back door of the driver's side were sobering, proof of how lucky they were to get out of this with a gouge in his arm and nothing more serious. "I'll reimburse you, Jonah."

"No biggie," his friend said, waving him off. Joey lifted his head and gazed at both him and Jonah with suspicion. Nick belatedly realized they were both strangers to the child, so he dropped to his knees and smiled over at the boy. "Hi, Joey, my name is Nick Butler and I'm a detective with the Chicago Police Department. And that's my buddy Jonah Stewart, who is a police detective, too, from Milwaukee. We've been helping your mom find you."

"Thank you," Joey said in a wobbly voice, his curiosity apparently satisfied. "Can we go home now? I'm hungry."

Nick was trying to figure out a way to let the boy

know it wasn't safe to go home yet, when Rachel interrupted. "You're hungry? Did they give you anything to eat or drink?"

Joey shook his head. "No. They kept me in a room in the basement. It was dark and I think there were big hairy spiders, too. The door was locked and I had a mattress and a toilet but nothing else," he admitted, his lower lip trembling with the effort not to cry.

Rachel's eyes filled with tears. "I'm so sorry, Joey. So sorry…" Once again, she hugged him close as if she could erase the horrible memories by will alone.

"We'd better get out of here," Jonah said quietly. "In case they decide to come back."

Nick couldn't agree more. "Rachel, do you have the car keys?"

She sniffled and used the sleeve of her jacket to wipe away her tears. "Here you go," she said as she handed them over. "Joey and I will take the backseat."

He understood she couldn't bear to let go of her son. "You'd better drive," Nick told Jonah, as he loped around to the passenger side of the vehicle. "I'm going to call my boss and put an APB out on that Jeep. And I don't suppose you have a first-aid kit in here somewhere?"

"In the glove box," Jonah said. He slid behind the wheel and grunted as his knees hit the steering wheel. He adjusted the seat back and then started the car.

Nick called Ryan Walsh, quickly filling his captain in on the details. "I'm fairly certain the driver was Ricky Morales and the Jeep's tag number is JVW-555."

Walsh wasn't entirely thrilled to hear what had transpired. "I'm glad you got the kid back, but we need to keep looking for the link to the Mafia," he said. "When are you coming in to file your report?"

"Soon," Nick hedged. "Just let me know as soon as you hear anything about Morales or the Jeep, okay?" He disconnected from the call.

"Where to?" Jonah asked, as he turned off the dirt road and back onto the highway.

"That's a good question," Nick muttered, as he rummaged around for the first-aid kit. "We should probably pick up my car first."

"No, we need to stop for something to eat, first," Rachel said from the backseat. "Joey's hungry."

"Is he all right? Or should we get him checked out by a doctor?"

"Physically, he looks fine," Rachel said after a moment's pause.

He knew she was already worried about the emotional trauma Joey may have suffered. "You're right, eat first and then pick up my car."

From there, he wasn't sure, other than he wasn't going to take Rachel or Joey back to their home.

Not until he knew for sure they were safe.

Rachel knew she was smothering Joey, but she couldn't seem to stop touching him—his hair, his arm, his knee—to remind herself that he was actually sitting right here beside her.

Thank You, Lord, for keeping my son safe!

There was a tiny voice in the back of her mind telling her that there was a good chance God didn't have anything to do with getting Joey back safely, but she was too emotionally drained to listen. Right now, she found an odd comfort in believing God had been with them through those horrible moments when she'd faced Morales.

"Can we eat at Mr. Burger's?" Joey asked in a soft, hesitant voice. His lack of confidence broke her heart.

"Of course," she agreed, even though she normally avoided those types of fast-food joints like the plague. "Nick, let me know if you see a Mr. Burger's."

"There's one up ahead," Jonah pointed out. She wasn't surprised, as they were everywhere. A few minutes later, they pulled into the parking lot. Jonah swiveled in his seat. "Inside? Or drive-through?"

"Drive-through," Nick said, before she had a chance to respond. "All of us going inside would draw too much attention."

She belatedly remembered his bloodstained jacket. "The drive-through is fine."

Nick warned her to go light on Joey's food, as they placed their order. She went with both a chocolate shake and a soda for her son, along with chicken pieces. No one else ordered anything to eat, including Rachel. The nausea that she'd lived with for the past few hours had dissolved, but she still wasn't hungry.

Jonah kept driving as Joey ate. He only ate about half his food before declaring that he was full. The thought of her son going hungry gnawed away at her, although she was grateful he didn't appear to be physically abused. The only indication of what he'd suffered was the traumatized expression in his eyes.

"That's okay, we can save the rest for later," she said, bundling up the leftovers.

They reached the hotel parking lot where they'd left Nick's car, and there was a heated debate between Jonah and Nick about what to do next.

"Go home to your pregnant wife, Jonah," Nick said stubbornly. "If I need anything more, I'll let you know."

"I'm not leaving when you're wounded," Jonah argued. "Besides, where are you going to go?"

"My mother's uncle has a cabin in Wisconsin," Nick said. "I thought we'd go there for a while. I still have my laptop and we can maybe do some searching while we're there. Hopefully, we'll hear some good news from my boss soon."

"A cabin?" Joey echoed, his eyes wide with enthusiasm. "Can we go to the cabin, Mom? Can we?"

She couldn't bear to deny Joey anything. At least not now. Of course, they'd have to go back home, eventually, to figure out their next steps, now that she didn't have her company anymore. "If that's what Nick thinks is best," she murmured.

"I don't have enough cash to keep going to motels," he said, his tone apologetic. "Besides, Morales is going to report back to whoever hired him that you weren't there alone. I'm worried they might be able to spot my car if we stick around here. I think the cabin is the safest place for us to be right now."

Jonah didn't look convinced. "I still don't like leaving you alone," he grumbled. "But Mallory's due date is next week so I should head home. Promise you'll call if you need me?"

"Yes. And I'll give you the address to my uncle's cabin, too." Nick rattled off the address as Jonah punched it into his phone.

Soon, they were back on the road. Nick had managed to wrap gauze around his arm, which helped stop the bleeding. Jonah insisted on leaving the first-aid kit with them, and Rachel accepted it gratefully, knowing that as soon as they'd reached the cabin, she'd need to do a better job of cleaning up Nick's wound.

She stayed in the backseat with Joey, unwilling to leave him there alone. As Nick's car ate up the miles, crossing over the Illinois/Wisconsin state line, she closed her eyes and clutched her son's hand, wondering if their life would ever be normal again.

Nick glanced in the rearview mirror as he drove, noticing that Rachel had fallen asleep. He was glad she was getting some rest, but Joey, however, was still wide-awake. Dusk was already darkening the sky, and Nick's goal was to make it to the cabin well before nightfall.

"Are you doing okay back there?" he asked softly, trying not to disturb Rachel.

Joey nodded, although his gaze seemed troubled. "The bad man isn't going to come after me again, is he?"

Nick's heart lurched at the panic in Joey's young voice. No matter what happened, the poor kid was going to have nightmares about the kidnapping for a long time to come. He made a mental note to discuss with Rachel the need for Joey to get counseling.

He didn't want to lie to the boy, but he didn't want the child to live in fear, either. He chose his words carefully. "The reason I'm taking you and your mom to the cabin is to keep you safe from the bad man," he said finally. "I've already called my boss and asked him to put out an arrest warrant for the bad man, too. Once he's in jail he won't be able to hurt you or your mom any more."

Joey nodded and seemed to relax at that explanation. "I'm glad you're a police detective," he said.

Nick caught the boy's gaze in the rearview mirror and flashed him a warm smile. "Me, too." He paused, before asking, "Joey, you mentioned you were in a basement room with a mattress, a toilet and a locked door. Do you remember anything else? Anything that might help the police track down the bad man?"

Joey's lower lip trembled as if he might burst out sobbing. And as if she instinctively knew her son was upset, Rachel woke up. "Joey? What's wrong?"

"I c-can't remember anything else," he stuttered. "I couldn't see because the bad man put a black hood over my head!"

Nick winced when Rachel glared at him. "You don't have to remember anything, sweetie," she said gently, daring Nick to disagree. "I don't want you to worry about the bad man anymore. All that matters is that you're safe here with me. We're going to make sure nothing happens to you, okay?"

"Okay," Joey mumbled.

He sighed and dropped the touchy subject. He didn't want to upset Joey, but at the same time, they needed to know what, if anything, the boy remembered.

Maybe once they reached the cabin, Joey would relax enough to open up about his ordeal. Refusing to discuss what happened wasn't going to help Rachel's son get over what happened.

But talking through the events just might.

He didn't voice his opinion though. Instead, he concentrated on trying to remember the route to his uncle's cabin. The farther north he drove, the more the temperature dropped. There was evidence of a recent light snow, although nothing deep enough to worry about. He hadn't been to Uncle Wally's cabin in the past year, since his uncle had passed away, leaving the cabin to his mother. And since Nick's parents had chosen to retire in Florida last year, he doubted anyone had been up there since he and Wally had been there the summer before his uncle's passing.

Nick's wife and daughter had enjoyed spending time up there, too. He smiled remembering how Sophie had laughed as she played in the fallen leaves. For the first time, remembering his family didn't cause his heart to ache. He'd treasure every moment they had together.

He forced his attention on his surroundings. Twice he had to backtrack, because the area looked so different from what he remembered. But then he caught sight of the red fire sign with the numbers 472 and knew he'd found it. The gravel driveway was barely visible between towering evergreen trees, and so completely overgrown with brush and weeds that he only went far enough to make sure the car was out of sight from the road, before shutting off the engine.

"Sorry, but we'll have to walk in from here," he said, grabbing the bag of clothes in one hand while keeping his weapon ready with the other. Just in case. "I'm afraid we'll get stuck if we drive in any farther."

"That's okay," Rachel replied, opening her door and pushing it against the brush. Joey climbed out right behind her as if eager to be out of the car. He saw Rachel reach for Joey's hand, but when her son eagerly strode through the tall brown grass without so much as glancing at her, she let her hand drop back to her side.

"Be careful," he called to Joey as he came over to walk beside Rachel, their feet crunching against the half-frozen brush.

"I hope there aren't poisonous snakes around here," she said nervously, as she followed her son's progress down the driveway.

"December is too cold for snakes," he assured her.

He wanted to reach for her hand but sensed she was still angry with him. "I'm sorry, Rachel. I didn't mean to upset you or Joey."

"Then stop asking him questions about what happened," she said wearily. "Don't you think he's been through enough?"

"I think you've both been through more than enough," Nick said in a low voice. "But we can't afford to relax now. For one thing, Morales knows we saw him and that you didn't come to the barn alone."

"He has the money, what more could he want?" she asked.

"I don't know, but I'm pretty sure he planned to kill you both," he rasped out.

Before Rachel could respond, Joey shouted, "There's the cabin!"

Sure enough, Nick could make out the familiar log cabin through the bare tree branches. The place looked smaller than he remembered, but as long as the wood-burning stove worked, he thought they'd be fine.

"We'll need to discuss this more, later," he said quietly to Rachel. "For now, let's get settled, okay?"

When she nodded, he lengthened his stride to catch up to Joey. Rachel didn't want to believe she and Joey were still in danger, but he knew they were. And he vowed to do whatever it took to keep them safe.

Rachel explored the small kitchen area inside the cabin, relieved to note that there were plenty of canned goods, soups and stew for them to eat. Everything was coated in a thick layer of dust, but nothing was outdated or spoiled. She frowned, knowing that the place needed to be cleaned but that it would be impossible without water.

"First we'll build a fire to make it warm in here," Nick was telling Joey. "Then we're going to prime the pump outside."

"What does that mean?" Joey asked, hovering near Nick as he stacked wood in the large wood-burning stove in the center of the room. There were dried leaves and twigs, too, and soon he had a roaring fire going.

"The well has to be closed up in the winter, or else the pipes will freeze," Nick explained. "We'll prime the pump to get the water running again. I'll show you how it's done."

Rachel watched Joey and Nick interact with a distinct male camaraderie. She knew her son longed for a male role model, which was one of the reasons she'd gotten him involved in sports like basketball. At least his coach was a decent role model for her son.

But to see Joey bond with Nick like this was worrisome. What would happen once this nightmare was over? When Nick went back to his job, leaving her and Joey to make a new life for themselves? She and her son might even have to move in order for her to find work.

The last thing she wanted was for Joey to be hurt again. He'd already suffered so much. The image of the way he'd reacted when Morales ripped the hood off his head was seared into her memory.

Granted, Nick wasn't going to hurt her son on purpose, not the way Morales had. But she knew, with deep certainty, that her son would eventually be hurt just the same.

This was exactly why she hadn't dated or tried to form any relationships with men. And even though she knew most men weren't connected with the Mafia, she wasn't sure she was ready to think about a relationship of any sort. Friendship, yes. But she'd stayed alone because she knew Joey was at a vulnerable and impressionable age. Avoiding relationships was easier than allowing Joey to get close to someone, only to be hurt if the relationship didn't work out. When Nick and Joey went back outside to work on the pump, she grabbed several cans of stew and set them on the counter.

Nick wanted to talk later, and that was just fine with her. Because she wanted to talk to him, too. He had to understand that he needed to keep his distance from Joey.

For her son's sake.

The interior of the cabin warmed up to the point she could take off the bulky jacket and the dark sweatshirt, wearing just the long-sleeved crew neck T-shirt. She stripped off the sheets draping the furniture, sneezing as the dust ticked her nose.

When Nick and Joey returned a few minutes later, they were both grinning from ear to ear. "We did it, Mom!" Joey exclaimed as he and Nick stamped their feet on the mat inside the doorway. "We primed the pump and now we have water."

"Great," she said, forcing a smile when her son looked up at her. "I'm going to clean the place up a bit, and then I thought we'd have the canned beef stew for dinner." Lowering her voice, she slanted a quick glance Nick's way. "Don't forget, we need to change the bandage on your arm, too."

"Plenty of time for that… Let's eat first," Nick said. "We're lucky to have electricity. Apparently my parents are still paying the bills."

"The cabin belongs to your parents?" she asked, curious in spite of herself.

"To my mother," Nick corrected. "I'm going to hike back to the car to get my laptop."

"Can I come, too?" Joey asked.

She opened her mouth to protest but was interrupted by the sound of Nick's phone ringing. He scowled at the display and then walked down the hall, obviously seeking privacy as he answered. "Yeah?"

She couldn't hear much of the conversation and was still trying to figure out a way to prevent Joey from following Nick around like a lost puppy, when Nick came back to the main room, his expression grim.

She tensed, fearing more bad news. "What's wrong?"

"They found the Jeep and, Morales, uh, is no longer a threat," he said carefully, glancing at Joey in a way that told her the man who'd kidnapped her son was dead. "But I'm afraid there's no sign of the duffel bag or the cash."

Her heart squeezed painfully in her chest and she couldn't think of anything to say.

"Unfortunately," Nick continued, "whoever hired Morales appears to have gotten away with it."

TEN

Nick mentally kicked himself as Rachel's expression froze at the news. He felt helpless knowing that Morales had been killed and all of Rachel's money was gone. The chance of finding out who had set up the kidnapping was slim to none at this point, now that their best lead—Morales—had just become, literally, a dead end.

After a long moment, Rachel let out a sigh and shrugged, avoiding his direct gaze. He knew she had to be upset at losing her company like this, but if that was the case, she didn't let on. "I'm glad Morales won't be able to hurt anyone else ever again," she murmured. "Maybe it's wrong, but I can't help thinking he ended up getting exactly what he deserved."

It was on the tip of his tongue to explain how God expected them to forgive those who trespassed against them, but there was a tiny part of him that tended to agree with her. He could forgive Morales and even the guy who'd hired him, but he also knew that those who sinned often paid the price.

If they were alone, he'd go into more detail about the crime scene, but since Joey was listening, he chose his words carefully. "The man behind all this is a professional, but we can't give up. We'll figure out who it is sooner or later."

"I know," she agreed, although her expression didn't exactly radiate confidence.

"Do you want to come for a walk with us to the car?" he offered. Oddly enough, he didn't want to leave her here in the cabin alone, especially after giving her such depressing news. "Shouldn't take us more than fifteen minutes or so."

She hesitated but then nodded. She put both her sweatshirt and the jacket back on and crossed over to join them. He held the door as they trooped outside, and he sniffed, appreciating the woodsy scent intermingled with fireplace smoke that lingered in the air, bringing back fond memories of the good times he'd spent up here with Uncle Wally and with his family.

Joey grabbed a small branch that had fallen from one of the trees and swatted the brush as they walked. Rachel stayed next to Nick, and his hand accidently brushed hers, making him wonder what she would say if he took her hand in his. She'd never said a word about the kiss, although he hadn't mentioned it, either.

But he'd certainly thought about it. Too much. He wanted to kiss her again. But this wasn't the time or the place.

"Are you okay?" he asked under his breath when Joey had gotten far enough ahead of them that he couldn't hear them.

"Fine," she said, kicking a rock with the toe of her athletic shoe. "I knew the risk, right from the start. As I told you before, getting Joey back safe and sound was worth every penny."

Nick couldn't help playing the what-if game. What if

he'd insisted on getting the FBI involved? Would they have gotten Joey back and still have Rachel's cash, too? Would they have caught the guy who'd killed Morales? Would Rachel and Joey be safe at home where they belonged?

As much as he wanted Rachel and Joey to be okay, it bothered him to think about the fact that once this was over, he wouldn't be seeing either of them again. Immediately, he felt guilty for even considering replacing Becky and Sophie with Rachel and Joey.

No, he couldn't do it. As much as he cared about Rachel and her son, he and Rachel would be much better off if they simply remained friends once this was over. Maybe he could be sort of a big brother to Joey. Do things like taking him to ball games or just playing catch. Surely, Rachel wouldn't mind having some downtime— being a single mother couldn't be easy.

The more he thought about the possibility of staying in touch with Joey, the more he liked it.

But, first, he had to keep Rachel and Joey safe, while figuring out a way to get her company back.

"I'm going to need your help in order to keep investigating all the possibilities," he murmured.

"I'm not sure how much help I'll be," she protested wearily. "And what's the point of getting your computer? I can't imagine there's any internet available up here."

"The last time I came up with Uncle Wally, I was able to get a signal from someone else's internet tower as they didn't have it secured with a password." He caught her surprised gaze and shrugged. "Figured it was worth a shot to see if the signal is still available."

"There's the car," Joey shouted, running forward as if they were in a race. "Open the trunk, Nick!"

He caught a glimpse of annoyance in Rachel's gaze

and tried to figure out what he'd done to upset her as he pushed the button on his key fob, making the truck spring open. Joey grabbed his computer case and proudly brought it over to him. "Here you go," he announced.

"Thanks, Joey," he said, looping the strap over his shoulder. Before he could say anything more, the boy ran back to shut the trunk for him, too. Nick grabbed the first-aid kit from the front seat and then locked the car.

"We need to talk later," Rachel whispered as Joey made his way back over to where they waited.

"Okay," he agreed, even though deep down he could tell by her tone that, whatever she wanted to talk about, it wasn't going to be good.

Rachel knew she was overreacting to Joey's eagerness to assist Nick, but she couldn't seem to help herself. As they made their way back to the cabin, she quickened her pace to keep up with her son rather than lagging behind with Nick.

"Hey, stop here a minute and look up at the stars," she said to Joey. "Aren't they beautiful?"

"Wow, there's so many," Joey whispered in awe.

"Out here in the country it's easier to see them," she explained. "Back home, the lights from the city tend to get in the way."

Nick came up to stand beside them, tipping his head back to enjoy the view, as well. For a moment, she could almost pretend they were a family, rather than hiding up here fearing for their lives.

This was what Anthony had stolen from her all those years ago. And she hadn't even really understood how much she'd missed what she'd never had, until now.

A loud noise, like a tree branch snapping in two, made

her jump, and she instinctively reached out to grab Joey's hand. "Stay with me," she whispered, drawing him close.

"Rachel, take Joey and this stuff back to the cabin," Nick said in a low voice.

A shiver snaked down her spine and she glanced around warily. They were surrounded by trees, which wasn't reassuring, since she couldn't see much in the darkness. She took the computer case from him and slung it over her shoulder. She held the first-aid kit tight to her chest. Despite being irked with Nick earlier, she was loath to leave him now. "Come with us," she urged softly.

"Could be nothing more than a deer or some other animal," he assured her. "Go inside and lock the door. I'm going to take a look around."

Nick was armed and could probably take care of himself, yet it was still difficult to leave him alone. But now that she had her son back, she wasn't about to risk losing him again, so she gave a jerky nod.

"Come on, Joey," she whispered, shielding him as best as she could as they quickly ran in the direction of the cabin. Even after getting safely inside, she couldn't relax. She secured the dead bolt lock into place, set down the laptop and the first-aid kit on the rough-hewn kitchen table and then doused the lights. She hoped the darkness would shield them from anyone watching from outside, although there wasn't much she could do about the yellow glow of the fire.

"I thought the bad man was gone?" Joey asked fearfully.

"He is gone," she said, trying to smile. "You heard what Nick said—I'm sure the noise was probably from a deer. Nick is being extra careful because he's a police detective and that's what policemen do. Come sit on the sofa in front of the fire with me."

Joey went over to the sofa and she desperately searched for something to use as a weapon. A kitchen knife would only work if the thug came in close, so she bypassed that option. Her gaze fell on the trio of fireplace instruments Nick had used earlier to help start the fire. The poker was long, made of cast iron and was pointy on the end. Since the poker gave her the best chance to protect herself and Joey, she carried the stand of fireplace instruments to the right side of the sofa and set the poker so that it was well within reach, before she snuggled in next to her son.

"I'm scared," Joey whimpered beside her.

Her heart squeezed in her chest. "I'm not going to let anything happen to you, sweetie, and neither will Nick," she said. "You're not alone anymore. We're safe here inside the cabin with Nick protecting us."

He responded by burying his face against her arm, clinging tight. She hugged him close, a wave of helpless despair washing over her. How much more could the poor kid take? He'd already been through so much. More than any child should have to bear.

She'd thought that getting Joey back would solve all her problems, but she was wrong. Because they were here, cowering in the darkness of the cabin, fearing the worst.

Nick was right—they needed to keep investigating in order to find the person who'd set up the kidnapping. Because they wouldn't be safe until they knew the truth.

Tense with fear and worry, she stared at the front door of the cabin, hoping and praying Nick would return soon.

Nick melted into the trees, moving slowly and carefully, the way Uncle Wally had taught him all those years ago. He hadn't liked hunting deer the way Uncle Wally

had, but he'd learned enough from his uncle to move quietly through the woods. He held his gun ready, in case
he stumbled across a man or wild beast.

White-tailed deer tended to feed in the early morning
or early evening, so there was a good possibility that a
buck or a doe moving through the woods had made the
noise. There weren't bears in the area, at least not that he
knew about. The snapped branch had seemed too loud
for a small animal like a raccoon or a skunk, although
possums could grow to a fairly good size. Maybe one
had fallen out of a tree?

Nick was sure he hadn't been followed on the ride up
to the cabin, so he found it hard to believe the kidnapper
could have found them. Even if the kidnapper had the
brains and the means to track him here, it would take a
lot of expert digging to connect the cabin to him.

He made a slow, wide circle around the cabin. He
didn't see anything out of the ordinary, no signs of anyone lurking around. He came across a deer bed about
twenty yards behind the cabin, which made him relax.
Deer were close by, so it was likely that's what they'd
heard.

There was a small structure back there, too, and he
moved forward cautiously. When he got closer, he wrinkled his nose at the smell, realizing this was the old outhouse that Uncle Wally had used before installing the
well and the small but functional bathroom. He opened
the door and flashed his small penlight inside, to make
sure it was indeed empty. Then he made his way back
around to the front of the cabin.

The lights were off inside, although he could see the
flickering flames from the fireplace. He stood on the
porch for another few minutes, straining to listen. When

he didn't hear anything, he tapped lightly on the door. "Rachel? Open up, it's me, Nick."

After a few minutes, he heard her disengage the lock and open the door. "Did you find anything?" she asked.

"Just a deer bed in back of the cabin," he said cheerfully. He closed the door and relocked it. "Not only does that prove that deer are close by, but also that they've felt safe enough to make a bed here."

Rachel's smile was strained as she nodded and glanced over at her son, who was burrowed into a corner of the sofa. "Did you hear that, Joey? There's a deer bed behind the cabin."

"What kind of bed?" Joey asked, a puzzled frown furrowing his brow.

"Deer like to sleep in tall grass. Not only is the grass soft, but it also keeps the deer hidden during the day. In the early-evening hours they get up and move through the trees, looking for something to eat."

"What do they eat?" Joey asked.

"Speaking of eating, how about I heat up our supper?" Rachel suggested, heading over to the kitchen area.

He crossed over to sit beside Joey. "White-tailed deer are vegetarian, meaning they eat grass, leaves and berries. In the winter, when there aren't as many leaves, they eat the bark off the trees." He remembered his uncle Wally explaining that culling the herd of deer by hunting them in season was better than letting them starve to death. Logically he agreed, but that didn't make it any easier to kill the beautiful, graceful animals.

Joey continued to ask questions and he patiently answered them, figuring that the more they talked, the more the child would be able to relax and feel safe.

"Dinner's ready," Rachel called a few minutes later.

Joey crawled out from his spot on the sofa to cross over to the kitchen table. Nick threw another log on the fire and then joined them.

He clasped his hands together and bowed his head. "Heavenly Father, we thank You for providing us food and shelter tonight, and we ask that You continue to watch over us, keeping us safe from harm. Amen."

"Amen," Rachel echoed.

After a brief moment, Joey, too, said, "Amen."

Nick lifted his head and smiled at them both. "Thanks for praying with me. And this looks great, Rachel, I appreciate you cooking dinner."

"All I did was heat up the beef stew in a pot on the electric burner," she protested. "I don't think that counts as cooking."

"It does in my book," he said. The hearty beef stew hit the spot and Rachel and Joey must have been hungry too, because between the three of them, they finished every bite.

"I'll clean up," he said, carrying his and Joey's empty bowls over to the sink.

Rachel looked as if she might protest but then must have decided to take the opportunity to spend time with her son. He heard them exploring the cabin, although since it wasn't very big, it didn't take them long. Rachel brought a quilt with her from the back bedroom and covered them with it as they sat on the sofa, staring into the fire.

Seeing Rachel snuggled up next to Joey filled him with bittersweet longing. If he were alone, he'd probably think about Becky, but right now, he found himself captivated by the way the light from the fire flickered over Rachel's hair.

Washing the dishes didn't take long, and when he finished he pulled out the computer and tried to find the wireless signal that he'd used the last time he was here. Sure enough, the signal was weak but available, as it still wasn't password protected.

He searched for information on Dr. Karl Errol since he still thought that Josie Gardner's suicide wasn't just a coincidence. He soon discovered that Dr. Karl Errol had attended Johns Hopkins to earn his doctorate and had worked for a large international pharmaceutical company before coming to work for Rachel.

Sitting back in the chair, he tried to figure out why a highly respected research scientist from Johns Hopkins had left a large pharmaceutical corporation to work for Simon Inc.

"Joey's asleep," Rachel said, interrupting his thoughts. She came over to the table, pulled up a chair next to him and sat down. "You should let me take a look at your arm."

Nick grimaced and then nodded reluctantly. He worked his arm out of the sweatshirt sleeve while she jumped up and heated up water on the two-burner stove.

The angle was too awkward for him to see the extent of the injury and he was glad it didn't throb as much as it had at first. Rachel came over with the first-aid kit they'd brought in from the car, along with a small pan of hot water.

"This might hurt," she warned as she picked up a soft cloth and began cleaning the wound.

He didn't say anything, too distracted by her nearness as she fussed over him. He couldn't help remembering the kiss they'd shared and wondered if she'd let him kiss her again. Soon.

"Almost finished," she murmured, and he blinked, realizing she was putting antibiotic ointment over the flesh wound before wrapping it with gauze.

"Thanks," he murmured huskily. When she turned away to take the water back over to the sink, he carefully put his arm back into the sleeve of his sweatshirt.

Once she'd finished cleaning everything up, she came back to the table. It took all his willpower to turn his attention to the investigation at hand. "Tell me about Dr. Karl Errol. How long has he worked for you?"

Rachel frowned. "He's been working for me for about three years now," she said slowly.

"How did you come to hire him? Did he apply for a job? Or did you purposefully recruit him away from his other company?"

"Neither. Josie Gardner is actually the one who recommended him for the job. She apparently met him at a research convention and talked about some of the work we were doing. He was very interested and Josie convinced me to make him an offer. To be honest, I was surprised when he actually accepted it."

"Why do you think he did? Accept the job, I mean?"

Rachel shrugged. "During our interview, he mentioned that he liked the way I put so much time and effort into research and development for new medications. He claimed that his old company had gone stagnant and that he was looking for change."

Nick hesitated, knowing that she wasn't going to like his next question. "Could it be that he was searching for a place where no one was constantly looking over his shoulder? Because maybe he liked to cut corners? What if the problem with your new diabetes medication happened in the first place because he hid something important?"

"No way… Josie would have been all over that," she said.

"Maybe that's why she committed suicide."

She stared at him for a long moment. "It's possible, but why would Karl do something like that in the first place? Why bring forward a medication that has life-threatening side effects?" She blew out a breath. "Don't you see? There's no logical reason why anyone, especially a well-respected researcher, would risk ruining their reputation and their career by doing something so crazy."

He hated to admit she had a point. What could the motivation be? He shifted several scenarios through his mind. "What if he's doing it on purpose to sabotage your company?" he mused.

Rachel closed her eyes and rubbed them. "Again, Nick, for what purpose? What's the link between this and Joey's kidnapping? I keep telling you that none of this makes any sense. The only logical explanation is that someone within the Mafia needed cash and orchestrated Joey's kidnapping to get it." She sighed impatiently. "Sabotaging the company would only make it more difficult to come up with the money. Whatever is going on within the company probably isn't connected."

He understood why she chose to believe the Mafia was behind the kidnapping. For one thing, the threatening letters did seem to point to the crime syndicate. But what if someone inside her company had sent them, pretending to be with the Mafia? He thought she had blinders on when it came to thinking anything bad about the people who worked for her.

"Rachel, hear me out for a minute, okay?" he said,

leaning in toward her. "You said the lawsuit was filed last year and that you have already offered a generous settlement, right?"

"Yes, that's correct."

"Was your settlement accepted?"

She flushed and shook her head. "Not yet."

Interesting. "What if that was essentially the start of this mess? What if all of this—the failed medication, the lawsuit and now the kidnapping were just ways to put you out of business?"

"Who would want to put me out of business?"

"You tell me," he countered. "Which company is your biggest competition?"

"Global Pharmaceuticals," she answered automatically.

Global Pharmaceuticals. The same company where Karl Errol used to work. "That's it! The link we've been looking for. Don't you think it's possible that Karl Errol, who used to work for Global Pharmaceuticals, is actually doing corporate espionage for them? That he's sabotaging your company on purpose?"

The dawning horror in her eyes made him feel bad for shattering her trust, but, at the same time, he firmly believed they were finally onto something.

Now, all he needed was a way to prove it.

ELEVEN

Rachel didn't want to believe Nick's theory, but she couldn't deny that his idea had merit. "Seems odd that Global would go to such drastic lengths to put me under," she said softly. "But, okay, let's say they did convince Karl to sabotage my company. And that the failed diabetes medication was part of the master plan. How does kidnapping Joey fit into the picture? Removing me as the CEO isn't going to put the company under. Gerry Ashton has been working for the company over the past seventeen years and he's perfectly capable of running the company without me."

"Isn't there anything about your management styles that could make the difference between success and failure?" Nick pressed.

Rachel clenched her teeth in frustration. She didn't understand why he remained so focused on someone working against her from inside the company rather than the Mafia link.

Although now that Morales was dead, she was forced to admit they might never know for sure who was behind the kidnapping.

"The only difference between Gerry and me is that I

take more risks in research and development," she said. "Gerry tends to be more conservative."

"That's all? Nothing else?" Nick appeared disappointed by her response.

"The only other thing we disagreed about was settling the lawsuit," she admitted. She still remembered the heated argument they'd had. Gerry had pushed so hard she had been forced to take the issue to the board of directors. "He wanted to continue to fight, but I managed to convince the board that settling right away would be better for us in the long run. And there's still hope that the lawsuit will be settled soon."

"How long has Ashton worked for you?" he probed.

"I've only been in charge as the CEO for the past three years, since my father died. Gerry was a VP colleague during the years my father was in charge." Before he could ask another question, she quickly changed the subject. "I need to talk to you about Joey."

Nick's eyebrows lifted. "What about him?"

She took a deep breath and released it slowly, trying to figure out a way to articulate her concern without hurting his feelings. "Joey is at a vulnerable age, and I think it's clear he's looking for a father figure. I've noticed he's been following you around, and I'd appreciate it if you didn't encourage him. Please try to keep your distance."

He stared at her for a long moment. "I haven't encouraged him on purpose," he finally said. "Besides, I'm not sure I understand what your problem is. Showing your son how to build a fire and how to prime a well isn't a big deal."

"Maybe not, but can't you see that I don't want him to rely on you too much? Once this is over..." She trailed off, unable or maybe unwilling to put her deepest fears into words. "I just don't want him hurt," she repeated lamely.

"I'm sorry you feel that way, Rachel," Nick said with a frown. "I was hoping that Joey and I could hang out once in a while, even after this is over."

Her jaw dropped in surprise. It had never occurred to her that Nick would want to continue to see her son. And, for some reason, she found the idea disconcerting. "Well, uh, I guess I'll think about it," she said, unable to come up with a good reason for refusing him outright.

Nick's intense gaze bored into hers and she squirmed in her seat, feeling as if he was seeing right through her. She couldn't explain why the two of them forging a relationship after this was over bothered her so much, but it did. She glanced at her sleeping son and rose to her feet. "I'm going to take Joey to the back bedroom."

"Good idea," Nick agreed readily. "I'll stay out here, since I'll need to keep feeding wood into the fireplace, anyway."

She nodded, relieved to have an excuse to avoid Nick for the rest of the night. The way she'd warned Nick to stay away from her son was just as important for her to remember, as well. In all honesty, she was becoming far too dependent on Nick. She crossed over to lift her sleeping son into her arms. At nine years old, he was too big to carry, but she managed, staggering under his weight yet unwilling to ask Nick for help.

The bedroom was cool, being farther away from the fire. She set Joey on the bed and, amazingly, he didn't wake up. She shivered and searched for more blankets. Luckily, she'd found earlier a huge hope chest filled with handmade quilts. She retrieved several of them to use as covers and then stretched out on the bed next to Joey.

After everything they'd been through, she was physically exhausted. But her mind raced, replaying every moment of the past twenty-four hours. No matter what she tried, her mind wouldn't settle and it was only after she recited the Lord's Prayer, the only prayer she remembered from her childhood, that she finally managed to fall asleep.

Nick dozed, waking himself up every few hours to put more wood on the fire and to make sure everything was all right outside. He hadn't gotten much sleep the night before, when they'd spent the night in the car, so he had to depend on the deeply ingrained training his four years in the Marine Corps had given him in order to keep watch, despite his bone-deep exhaustion.

He tried to formulate a plan for the following day, but every time he closed his eyes, he fell asleep. When he dragged himself off the sofa at six in the morning, dawn had lightened the darkness and the fire had dwindled.

It didn't take long to bring the glowing embers back to life. Since it was too late to go back to sleep, he washed up in the small bathroom. He opened the medicine cabinet, thankful to find a somewhat rusty razor along with some ancient shaving cream. There were other items his uncle had left up there, too, but he limited himself to using the razor.

When he came out of the bathroom, he heard movement from the back bedroom. He wasn't surprised when Joey's head peeked out from behind the door. "Hi, Nick," he whispered.

"Good morning, Joey," he whispered back. Rachel must still be sleeping or he was sure she'd have already put an end to the brief conversation. At some point during the wee hours of the morning, he'd figured out that the main reason Rachel didn't want him spending time with her son was that she thought he might get too attached to Joey, after the way he'd lost his own child.

Still, he couldn't ignore the kid gazing at him with wide green eyes, so he gestured for Joey to come out of the bedroom. "Are you hungry?" he asked.

Joey nodded eagerly and slipped through the narrow opening, quietly closing the door behind him. The boy was wearing the same clothes as the day before, not that he seemed to mind. "What's for breakfast?"

Good question. "I don't know. Let's take a look, okay?" He put a hand behind Joey's back, urging him down the short hall to the main room. Rachel couldn't be too upset with him for not waking her up, he rationalized, since she obviously needed the rest. "I think I saw some oatmeal," he said to Joey. "Do you like oatmeal?"

"With brown sugar," the boy said excitedly.

"I'm not sure we have any brown sugar," he said cautiously. "But I think there's some regular sugar, which should work just as well."

Joey stopped in front of the fire, holding his hands toward the flames as if he were cold. "Did you keep the fire going all night, Nick?"

"Yep. It's our main source of heat for the cabin." He found a box of oatmeal, but it wasn't the instant kind, so he followed the cooking directions on the label.

Joey kept up a constant stream of chatter, and Nick couldn't help admiring the boy's quick mind. Rachel's son was interested in everything, from camping to sports. To help pass the time until breakfast was ready, he showed Joey how to carve small animals in pieces of wood with his penknife.

As they talked, he realized he couldn't have kept his distance from the boy if his life depended on it.

When the oatmeal was ready, he poured the steaming breakfast into two medium-size bowls. His uncle actually did have some brown sugar stored in an airtight container, so he liberally sprinkled their breakfast before taking Joey's hand in his.

"We have to pray before we eat," he said.

"Why?" Joey asked, his gaze curious.

Nick sensed he was heading down a path Rachel might not approve, but he wanted Joey to be given the option of believing in God. "Because we need to thank God for the food we're about to eat."

Joey pursed his lips. "Is God in heaven?" he asked.

"Yes, and He's always there for us, whenever we need Him."

Joey frowned for a moment. "You think God was with me when I was in the dark, stinky room?" he asked.

Nick's heart clenched and he nodded. "Yes, Joey, I do. Your mom and I were praying for God to watch over you the whole time you were gone."

"Really?" Joey brightened at the news. "I wish I would have known that," he confessed. "Maybe I wouldn't have been so scared."

Nick wished the same thing, but no sense in going back, trying to change the past. In his opinion, it was never too late to believe in the Lord.

He closed his eyes and bowed his head. "Heavenly Father, we thank You for the food and shelter You've provided for us, and we ask You again, to keep us safe from harm. Amen."

"Amen," Joey echoed.

Nick lifted his head and opened his eyes to find Rachel

standing behind Joey's chair. She'd approached so quietly he hadn't heard her. He tensed, expecting an argument, but she simply added "Amen" to his prayer.

He immediately pushed back from the table. "Here, take my bowl of oatmeal, I'll get more."

She hesitated for a moment but then accepted his hot cereal and took a seat next to her son. He was touched at how they both waited until he returned before eating.

They were too busy eating to talk much. He watched with amusement as Joey quickly emptied his bowl. "Can I have seconds?" he asked anxiously.

"Of course," Nick responded, exchanging a knowing look with Rachel. Joey hadn't eaten much yesterday, but it appeared his appetite had returned.

"So what's the plan for today?" Rachel asked.

"I'm not sure yet," he answered honestly. "I should check in with my boss again, see if he can give us anything further to go on."

She darted a glance at Joey and nodded. He sensed there was more she wanted to say but didn't feel she could talk freely in front of Joey.

When they were finished with breakfast, Rachel insisted on doing the dishes, so he took the opportunity to do a quick perimeter check. The only problem was that Joey wanted to come with him.

He glanced helplessly over at Rachel, silently pleading with her to help. As much as he liked spending time with the boy, he needed to make sure the area around the cabin was secure. And he didn't want Joey to come outside with him until he was convinced they were safe.

"Joey, I need you to dry the dishes for me, okay? There will be time later for you to play outside."

"That's women's work," Joey mumbled, lightly kicking at the chair.

"No, it's not," Nick corrected. "I did the dishes last night, so it's only fair you take your turn."

Joey's disgruntled expression faded as he considered Nick's words. "All right," he finally agreed, going over to pick up the dish towel.

Rachel ruefully rolled her eyes and he quickly ducked outside before he broke into a wide smile. Sometimes, it paid to be able to double-team kids.

The thought caused him to pause before heading soundlessly into the dense wood. As a single mother, Rachel didn't have anyone to count on when it came to raising Joey. She had to play the role of both parents.

Was it any wonder she was so protective?

He focused on the task at hand, moving slowly and methodically so he didn't miss any signs now that it was daylight. The day was overcast, denying him the sunlight he would have preferred. He stood in the clearing, imagining that the log cabin was the center of a large clock with the south side, straight ahead from the door, at the twelve-o'clock position. He began to make his way around the circle.

In the three-o'clock area, he found a tuft of brown fabric stuck to the tip of a branch that was roughly shoulder height. He stared at it for a long minute, trying to estimate how long it had been there.

He could check the internet for how long it had been since the last snowfall, but he figured, from the dusting on the ground, that it had been within the past day or two. But if the snowfall had been light, the tuft of fabric might have survived intact.

By December the gun deer-hunting season was over,

but bow-hunting season lasted until January. Was it possible that someone dressed in camouflage-colored clothing had been through here recently, bow hunting? Uncle Wally's land was posted, but considering no one had been up here lately, he figured the No Trespassing signs didn't mean much.

He wanted to believe there was a hunter in the woods rather than some other random person. Because if it wasn't a hunter, then he was forced to consider the fact that this cabin might not be as safe as he'd thought.

Rachel finished the dishes and then went over to straighten up the quilts on the bed. Near the end table, she found an old Bible. Opening the flap, she was surprised to discover it belonged to Nick's mother.

She carried the Bible back to the main living area, wondering if Nick's mother had left it here or if it belonged to Nick, himself? The book was clearly old and well used. The edges of the paper were gold and there were small cutouts for each of the Bible sections. In the center there was a place for family names and she discovered it had been filled in with neat handwriting stating the names of Nick and his two sisters.

She hadn't known about Nick's sisters. And she realized there were probably a lot of things she didn't know about Nick.

Curious, she opened the book and scanned the various chapters. It wasn't easy to decipher the meaning of the writing since, according to the title page, it was written in the Authorized King James Version.

"What are you reading?" Joey asked, coming over to sit next to her on the sofa.

She glanced down at her son, remembering the conversation he'd had with Nick before breakfast. It had nearly broken her heart to hear Joey describe how alone he'd felt in the dark room where Morales had kept him. She realized now that she'd done her son a disservice by not teaching him religion. "This is a Bible, which is a collection of God's words," she explained, hoping she was describing it right.

"Are there stories in there?" he queried, leaning over to see for himself.

"Yes, there are," she replied, although she wasn't sure exactly where they were. She vaguely remembered some Bible stories from her childhood, but how to find them in this huge book?

She opened the Bible to the New Testament, and the pages opened to the Gospel according to Saint John. "'In the beginning was the Word and the Word was with God and the Word was God,'" she read out loud. Joey leaned against her, seemingly content so she continued, "'The same was in the beginning with God. All things were made by him and without him was not any thing made that was made. In him was life; and the life was the light of men.'"

Soon, she got into the rhythm of the words, and the lyrical quality of the text helped her to relax. So intent was she on reading that she didn't hear Nick return.

When she glanced up, she saw him watching her, a gentle smile on his face. She stumbled over the next sentence and then stopped.

"You sound like you've been reading the Bible your entire life," he murmured, admiration reflected in his gaze.

She felt herself blush. "I hope it's okay that I'm reading

your mother's Bible," she said. "I found it on the bedside table in our room."

"She'd be thrilled," he assured her. "John's Gospel is one of my favorites. Although you also might try the book of Psalms—those are where I go when I need to reconnect with God. Or we might want to review the Gospel surrounding the birth of Jesus, as that's what Christmas is all about."

"All right," she agreed, thinking that this was the first time in her entire life that she'd had a conversation about the Bible with a man.

Actually, with anyone. Yet she found it wasn't the least bit awkward, at least with Nick.

Joey scrambled off the sofa and ran over to Nick. "Did you find any deer in the deer bed?" he asked, the Bible stories forgotten.

"Nope, didn't see any deer there today," he said with a wry smile.

She frowned and set the Bible aside. "What did you find?" she asked, sensing there was something bothering him.

He shrugged. "Could be nothing, but I think I'll call Jonah, just in case."

She did not like the sound of that. "Just in case what?"

He hesitated. "Just in case the bit of fabric I found outside doesn't belong to a hunter poaching on my uncle's land."

Nick tried Jonah several times before he connected with his friend. "I might need some backup," he said bluntly.

"What happened?" Jonah asked.

In the background he could hear Mallory's voice but

not exactly what she was saying. "I found some fabric stuck to a tree branch about fifty feet from the cabin. Can't be sure it's a random hunter or someone who could have followed us."

There was a moment of silence. "I want to help you, Nick, but Mallory has been having contractions. She says it's probably false labor, since she's not due until next week, but I'm not willing to take the chance."

"Hey, no problem," he hastened to assure his friend. "Stay with Mallory, I'm sure we'll be fine."

"Maybe you should call for backup? Or, find another place to stay," Jonah suggested.

"Yeah, maybe." Neither option thrilled him. He trusted his boss but didn't want to bring in anyone new. And if they left, he'd have to use his credit card, since he was almost out of cash. If the Mafia was involved, they likely had the ability to track them that way. Not to mention, he rather liked the coziness of the cabin. "Take care of Mallory, and call me if I'm going to be an honorary uncle."

"Nick, wait," Jonah said, before he could hang up. "I did find something interesting. I know you weren't keen on the Mafia angle, but guess who's back in Chicago?"

Nick rubbed his hand along the back of his neck. "Tell me you didn't find Frankie Caruso."

"Bing, bing, bing—you win the grand prize," Jonah joked.

Nick could barely drudge up a smile. "Where was he spotted?"

"That's what was so interesting. He was at a fundraiser put together by the mayor to raise money for diabetes research."

Diabetes research? "Are you sure?"

"I'm sure, but check it out online if you need more information."

Another coincidence. "Why does the Chicago mayor care about diabetes?"

"Because his wife was recently diagnosed with diabetes, and he thinks there should be more research into finding a cure."

"Okay, thanks for the heads-up," Nick said. After ending the call, he crossed over to the table and booted up the laptop.

He quickly pulled up a search engine and put in Caruso's name along with the word *fund-raiser*. Sure enough, there he was standing next to the mayor and his wife.

As he stared at the elder Caruso, he couldn't help thinking that Rachel may have been right all along. Caruso might have been the mastermind behind Joey's kidnapping. Seeing as he was such good friends with the mayor, it could be that Caruso wasn't happy about Rachel's failed diabetes medication. Could be that the mayor had a bone to pick with Rachel's company, too.

What better revenge than to kidnap her son, forcing her to sell off her shares of the company? And the added bonus? Making himself rich in the process.

TWELVE

Rachel could tell something was bothering Nick, but with Joey sitting right there, she was hesitant to ask too many questions about the investigation.

"Mom, can I work on my deer carving?" Joey asked from his favorite spot on the sofa.

"Deer carving?" she echoed with a raised brow. Nick's sheepish expression gave him away. "You taught him to do that?" she asked.

"Um, yeah. Hope you don't mind."

She should mind, but oddly she was touched that he'd taken the time. "Are you sure it's safe?"

"My uncle taught me how to carve when I was about his age, and I stressed the importance of being careful with the knife."

"All right, go ahead, Joey." At least carving would help keep her son occupied. She crossed the room to glance over Nick's shoulder at the computer screen. Only to be distracted by the scent of his shaving cream. It was strangely comforting and she had to fight not to put her arms around him.

Nick seemed impervious to her quandary. "Do you recognize anyone in the photograph?" he asked.

Forcing herself to concentrate, she narrowed her gaze on the photo. Suddenly, her stomach clenched with recognition. She pointed at the screen. "Frankie Caruso."

"Yeah, with the Chicago mayor and his wife," Nick murmured. "The mayor's wife was recently diagnosed with diabetes, and this was a fund-raiser to support research for a cure."

Another link to diabetes. "I'm sure Frankie is the one who hired Morales," she said. "It's the only thing that makes sense."

"Maybe." Nick jammed his fingers through his hair. "I need to go through the entire timeline from start to finish. There has to be something we're missing."

"I'll help," she offered. Her phone rang and she pulled it out of her sweatshirt pocket, surprised to see there was still one bar of battery left. Wincing, she saw the caller was Edith. It seemed like days since she'd spoken to her assistant. "Hi, Edith, how are you?"

"I'm putting in my notice," the woman said in a crisp tone. "You should have told me that you intended to sell off your shares of the company, Rachel. If I'd have known, I would have looked for somewhere else to work."

The reproach in the older woman's tone only sharpened her guilt. "I'm sorry, Edith, you're right—I should have told you. But why are you leaving? I'm sure Gerry could use all the support he can get."

"Gerry Ashton is not you, Rachel. Nor is he your father. I've been loyal to the both of you, but now that you're both gone, I see no need to stay on."

She was flabbergasted with Edith's decision. "Maybe you should take some time to reconsider," she said.

"Gerry has been with the company for seventeen years—I'm sure everything will be fine."

"I've made my decision." Edith's tone held an underlying note of steel. "And I'm telling you because you're the one I was working for."

Rachel sensed there was nothing she could say to talk her senior assistant out of resigning. "I'll make sure you get all your vacation pay, Edith," she said, even though technically she didn't own the company anymore. Surely the payroll staff would still listen to her. "And if you change your mind—"

"I won't. Goodbye, Rachel."

Rachel disconnected from the call just as her phone battery gave out.

"Edith resigned?" Nick asked with a dark frown.

"Apparently." She sank into the seat next to Nick, trying to grapple with the news. "I feel terrible about this. Edith has been with the company for thirty years."

"It's not as if you sold off your shares on purpose," Nick reminded her gently. "This isn't your fault."

Yes, it was her fault, but she couldn't deny that she'd do it all again in a heartbeat if it meant getting Joey back safely. Up until now, she'd convinced herself that her life was the only one impacted by her decision.

She took a deep breath and met Nick's sympathetic gaze. There was nothing she could do now but move forward. "Let's work on that timeline...."

Nick wanted nothing more than to reach over and pull Rachel close, to comfort her. She looked as if she'd lost her best friend, and maybe she had. He suspected Edith had been her rock, especially after her father passed away.

There wasn't anything he could say to her to make

her feel better, so he took her cue and agreed to work on the timeline.

"I need paper," he muttered. He'd prefer a large whiteboard or bulletin board, but paper would do in a pinch, far better than the computer.

"I think there was some in the bedroom, I'll be right back." Rachel returned a few minutes later with a tattered notebook. "Sorry, but this is all I could find," she said.

"Perfect," he said, taking the notebook from her hands. Their fingers brushed and he tried to ignore the tingling that radiated up his arm. This wasn't the time or the place to think about kissing Rachel again. He tore several sheets of paper out and set them side by side.

"We should probably start with the failed diabetes medication," Rachel said.

He nodded in agreement. "Do you remember the dates and times of the letters and phone calls?"

She reached over and took the pencil from his hand to write in the information. Her nearness was disconcerting. "And here's the date I called you," she added.

"And the same day, you took Joey to his basketball game," he said.

"Yes, that's the part that has bothered me." She scowled at the timeline. "I don't think I was followed, for sure not by the black truck."

Nick had to concur, since he'd followed her and had made sure no one had followed him. "It seemed the kidnappers were one step ahead of us for the first twenty-four hours—until we exchanged your cell phone."

"You thought they were tracking the GPS in my phone, right?"

"Was it a company phone?" he asked, slanting a sideways glance at her. "Or your personal phone?"

"It was a company phone, which also served my personal needs. I saw no reason to have two phones, and it's handy to have ready access to my work email at all times."

"Okay, so who would have access to the serial number for your company phone?" he asked.

Rachel shrugged. "Lots of people. Edith, for sure, and probably some of the staff in billing."

"Do you have an informatics department? Who takes care of interfacing your work email to your phone?"

"We contract with a small company, called Tech Support Inc., and they come in once a month for a day or two to update the computers, scan for problems, that kind of thing."

He'd never heard of Tech Support Inc. but a quick internet search didn't reveal anything alarming. "How long have you had a contract with them?"

"For several years," Rachel responded. "I hardly think they would give out private information like that."

"They might to someone within your company," Nick countered. "Say for instance, Karl Errol?"

"Maybe, but I doubt it. Karl is a researcher—wouldn't they see that as suspicious?"

"Not if he gave them a good reason. Or if he had someone else call, pretending to be you or Edith." He stared at the timeline for a moment. "I think it's clear that whoever tracked your cell phone was someone from inside your company, Rachel," he said slowly. "Not Frankie Caruso."

Rachel's emotions rolled up and down like a yo-yo, and Nick wasn't helping matters. First Frankie was involved, and then he wasn't. The kidnapping was related to her failed diabetes medication, and then it wasn't.

Her head ached and she pressed her fingertips to her temples, trying to ease the pressure. "I'm not sure what to think," she said finally. "Maybe we should go back to Chicago, see if we can talk to Karl."

Nick was still entering dates and times into their makeshift chart. "Josie's suicide is bothering me," he muttered half to himself. "Would make more sense if it was actually murder staged to look like a suicide."

That caught her attention. "Why?"

"Because suicide indicates she felt guilty about something," he explained. "If she was part of the cover-up related to the failed diabetes medication, then okay, I could buy that idea. But if she stumbled onto the truth and intended to come talk to you about it, then I'm more inclined to believe it was murder."

A chill snaked down Rachel's spine. "The meeting I was supposed to have with Karl and Josie the day I received the threatening letter and called you—it was set up by Josie. She told me that she had something important to discuss with me and insisted that Karl be there, too."

"That fits with my homicide theory," he said. "Do you think Edith knows anything more about what Josie wanted to discuss with you?"

"I doubt it. Edith was more concerned with fitting all the necessary meetings into my schedule. She wouldn't ask Josie why she wanted to talk to me. If Josie said it was important, then she'd find the time to make it happen."

Nick grimaced and then turned his attention back to the timeline. She found it hard to concentrate, though, too preoccupied by the idea of her employee possibly being murdered.

How Nick worked homicide cases on a regular basis

was beyond her comprehension. She admired his strength and his dedication, more than she should.

She glanced over to the sofa and frowned when she didn't see her son sitting there. For a moment panic set in. "Where's Joey?"

Nick glanced up in surprise. "He was there a few minutes ago."

She jumped up from her seat next to Nick. "Joey?" she called, her tone sharper than she intended.

Joey didn't answer but suddenly there was a loud crash from the direction of the bathroom. Without hesitation, she rushed over. "Joey?" She knocked on the bathroom door. "Are you okay in there?"

"The smell," she heard Joey whimper. Concerned, she opened the door, grateful there was no lock.

Joey was huddled on the floor, silent tears streaming down his cheeks. The medicine cabinet door was open and it took a minute for the harsh scent of aftershave to register, because she was focused on the smears of blood on the sink. "Joey, what happened?"

"Don't tell Nick," he whimpered.

She tried to figure out what happened. "Don't tell Nick what?"

"I cut myself with the knife," Joey managed to blurt out between sobs. "I didn't want to tell you because I didn't want Nick to be disappointed in me."

Her heart wrenched in her chest, and she knelt beside Joey and pulled him into her arms. "Nick won't be disappointed in you, sweetie. Let me see the cut."

He held out his hand, and she could see the slim cut along the pad of his thumb. There was a small bit of blood and she needed to examine the cut to make sure it wasn't so deep it needed stitches.

"Let's get that cleaned up, okay?" she suggested calmly.

"I don't like the smell," Joey said again.

She frowned and turned on the faucet, sticking his thumb beneath the gently running water. The broken bottle of stinky aftershave was lying on the floor, the liquid seeping into the wooden floor. "What happened, Joey?"

"I was looking for a Band-Aid," he said, sniffling back his tears. "And I accidently knocked it over."

"Is everything okay?" Nick asked from the doorway.

Joey's big green eyes once again filled with tears. "I'm sorry, Nick."

"Hey now, don't cry." Nick sent her a pleading look. "I don't care about that bottle of aftershave, it was old anyway."

But Joey shook his head. "No, I'm sorry about the knife," he said. "I was being careful like you said, but it slipped and I didn't want you to know I cut myself."

"I'm not mad at you, Joey, so don't worry about it, okay?" Nick flashed her son a reassuring smile.

Rachel was glad to see that the cut wasn't that deep, and she held Joey's hand under the warm water as she rummaged in the open medicine cabinet. "Do you have any tape and gauze I can use to keep it clean and dry?" she asked.

"We still have Jonah's first-aid kit in the kitchen," Nick assured her. She relaxed and nodded, remembering how she'd used it to change the dressing on Nick's wound.

"All right, let me put a towel or something around his thumb," she muttered. "Keep your hand in the water, okay?"

Joey nodded and did as she asked, while she searched for something to use. She found an old but clean hand towel in dark brown and figured the bloodstains wouldn't be too noticeable. "Okay, here, let's wrap this around your hand."

Joey sniffled again but allowed her to wrap the towel around his thumb. He turned toward the door, but his foot slipped in the slight puddle on the floor, making him wrinkle his nose in disgust.

She led the way into the kitchen, getting Joey settled in one of the kitchen chairs on the opposite side from where they'd been working on the timeline, while Nick brought over the first-aid kit.

"There's some triple antibiotic cream in here, too," he said, handing over the supplies.

"Good thing." She put a dollop of ointment over the cut and then carefully wrapped it in gauze and tapped it securely in place. "There, how's that?" she asked when she was finished.

Joey nodded. "Can you make the smell go away?" he asked.

She didn't quite understand why he was so upset about the smelly aftershave. It actually wasn't awful, the brand was well-known and obviously had remained popular over the years. She exchanged a perplexed glance at Nick. "Ah, sure, I'll clean up the bathroom floor, okay?"

"Are you hungry?" she heard Nick ask, as she walked down the hall to clean up the mess in the bathroom. "I can heat up some soup."

She filled the sink with soapy water and took yet another hand towel and did her best to clean up the spilled aftershave. But even after she finished, the scent still lingered.

There wasn't much she could do other than try to cut through the scent with a stronger cleaning agent.

She went back into the kitchen and found Nick heating up some chicken noodle soup for Joey. "Do you have any bleach or vinegar?" she asked in a low tone.

He grimaced. "I doubt it, but check in the pantry."

Calling the rough wooden open shelves a pantry was a bit of a misnomer, and she examined the contents but couldn't find anything she could use to help eliminate the odor.

"Don't worry," Nick said reassuringly. "I'm sure it will fade over time."

"No!" Joey shouted. "I don't like the smell! Make it go away!"

She rushed to Joey's side, wrapping her arms around her son. "Shh, sweetie, it's okay."

"Wait," Nick said, coming over to put a hand on her shoulder. "Does the smell remind you of something, Joey?" he asked.

Realization dawned slowly, and she pulled away just enough to look down at her son's face. Joey gazed up at her and then looked over at Nick. He didn't speak, but he slowly nodded his head yes.

Her heart clenched in her chest as the implication sank deep.

"What does the smell remind you of, Joey?" Nick asked gently. "Can you tell me?"

There was a long silence before Joey answered. "The bad man," he whispered.

"The bad man who put a hood over your head and carried you away after the crash?" Nick asked.

This time, her son shook his head no. "The other bad man. I didn't see him, but he spoke in a mean voice and he smelled bad. Like the bottle I accidently spilled in the bathroom."

The second bad man? For a moment Rachel couldn't move. Could barely comprehend what Joey meant.

Then she raised her head and locked gazes with Nick. And read the truth reflected in his eyes.

Forcing her to acknowledge that Joey had been somewhere near the man who'd arranged the kidnapping. Thinking back, she realized that their initial theory must have been correct. Morales had dumped the black truck shortly after the crash, catching a ride with someone else. The man who'd ordered the kidnapping in the first place.

Which meant her son might be able to recognize the voice of the man who'd masterminded the entire operation.

Once they found him.

THIRTEEN

Nick tore his gaze from Rachel's when he heard the soup boiling. He rushed to the stove to remove the saucepan from the electric burner. "Soup's ready," he said.

Rachel shook her head, as if there was no way she'd be able to eat, but he knew they had to try to keep things normal, for Joey's sake. He filled several bowls with the steaming soup and carried them over to the table in two trips.

"Try to eat something, Joey," he urged. "You don't have to think about the bad man anymore."

"But I can still smell him," Joey whined.

"Try the soup, and I'll clean the floor again," Rachel murmured.

"After you eat something," Nick said, gesturing to the empty seat. She put a hand over her stomach but sat next to her son. He gave Rachel credit for trying, when she leaned over her bowl. "Hmm, smells good."

Joey leaned over his own soup and took a tentative sniff. The aroma of chicken soup seemed to appease him enough to take a sip. "Tastes good," he admitted.

Rachel took a sip, too. "Yes, it does."

They hadn't prayed, so Nick said a quick, silent prayer

of thanks before taking a spoonful of his soup. The three of them sat in companionable silence as they enjoyed the simple meal. When Joey had finished, Rachel pushed away and carried her bowl to the sink. As soon as she'd rinsed her dishes, she returned to the bathroom.

Nick scrubbed a hand along the back of his neck, knowing that no matter how many times Rachel scrubbed the wooden floor, the scent of Wally's aftershave would linger.

In Joey's mind more so than in reality.

He quickly washed the dishes, while Joey went back to sit in front of the fire. The sad expression on the child's face made his heart ache. Sophie's life had been cut short by the car crash, but she'd always been a happy child. Loved school and had lots of friends. Both he and Becky had doted on their daughter. The thought of Sophie suffering the way Joey had made his chest hurt.

No matter how important this timeline was, he simply couldn't ignore Joey. Rachel returned to the room, looking dejected as she dropped onto the sofa beside her son.

"Hey, Joey, how would you like me to read the story of Christmas to you from the Bible?" he asked.

"The Bible has the story of Christmas in it?" Joey asked, his eyes wide with curiosity.

Rachel winced and he understood she was feeling guilty that Joey didn't know the real meaning of Christmas. "Yep, it sure does."

"Okay."

Nick picked up the Bible and settled onto the recliner. He opened his mother's Bible to the Gospel of Luke, Chapter 2 verse 7. "'And she brought forth her first-born son and wrapped him in swaddling clothes and laid him in a manger; because there was no room for them in the inn.

"'And there were in the same country shepherds abiding in the field keeping watch over their flock by night. And, lo, the angel of the Lord came upon them and the glory of the Lord shone round about them; and they were sore afraid. And the angel said unto them, Fear not: for, behold, I bring you good tidings of great joy, which shall be to all people. For unto you is born this day in the city of David a Saviour, which is Christ the Lord.'"

He continued through verse twenty and when he finished reading, he was humbled to realize that both Joey and Rachel were staring at him, as if hanging on every word.

"And that is the true meaning of Christmas," he murmured, encouraged that this would be another step for both of them in their journey to believe.

Rachel loved listening to Nick read from the Bible, but she also felt bad that she hadn't taught Joey about God and the story of Jesus before now.

"That was a nice story," Joey said with a wide yawn.

She kissed the top of his head. "It was a wonderful story, wasn't it? I want you to think about God whenever you feel afraid, okay?"

"I will," Joey's voice was soft and sleepy.

Nick set the Bible aside and returned to the kitchen table to continue working on the timeline.

She needed to help Nick, but she didn't want to leave her son. It wasn't until Joey's head tipped to the side, indicating he'd fallen asleep, that she eased away and went to sit beside Nick.

"I suppose you think I'm a terrible mother," she said softly.

He glanced at her in surprise. "Why would I think that?"

The shame was almost too much to bear, but she forced herself to get this out in the open. "Because I didn't teach Joey about God. Because I didn't raise him to believe."

"It's never too late to start, Rachel," Nick murmured. He reached up and tucked a strand of her hair behind her ear. "And no, I don't think you're a terrible mother at all. If you weren't raised to believe in God, then it's no wonder you raised your son the same way."

She was silent for a long moment, wishing she dared to ask him to hold her. She thought back to her childhood. "I think my parents believed in God—at least, I remember going to church when I was young. But by the time I was Joey's age, we suddenly stopped going to church... and I pretty much forgot most of what I learned."

"Do you know why your parents stopped attending church?" he asked. The way he took her hand and interlaced his fingers with hers gave her the strength she needed.

"My mother lost her parents when I was nine, and they died about six months apart. And then when I was in high school, she was diagnosed with breast cancer. She passed away my freshman year in college." The pain of losing her mother had been terrible, but she and her father had clung together to get through it. Easy to look back now and piece together what had happened. The deaths of her grandparents had hit her mother hard, and maybe for some reason she'd pulled away from God. Her father, too, especially after losing her mother.

"I've seen that happen sometimes, where a sudden death causes a loss of faith," Nick said, giving her hand a gentle squeeze. "But to be honest, Rachel, those are the times when you should lean on God the most. I know it's hard—I struggled to keep my faith after my Becky and Sophie died."

"I can't imagine how difficult that must have been for you."

He was quiet for a moment. "Becky and I were high-school sweethearts so when I lost her, I felt like I lost my best friend. But now, after all these months, sometimes I have trouble remembering exactly what she looked like."

"Oh, Nick," she murmured. No one had ever loved her the way Nick had loved his wife.

He forced a smile. "I guess that might be God's way of making me realize I have a different path to follow. I know it's not easy, but if you open your heart to the Lord, you will be rewarded."

Maybe he was right. Certainly she'd felt some sense of peace when she'd prayed for Joey's safety. She stared down at their entwined fingers for a moment, feeling connected to Nick in a way she'd never experienced with Anthony.

The thought scared her. She didn't want to have feelings for Nick. Didn't want to open herself up to the possibility of rejection. She trusted Nick to keep her and Joey safe, but to trust him with her heart? That was asking too much.

The expression in his eyes when he spoke of his wife made her realize that he might not be ready for a relationship, either.

She took a deep breath and forced a smile. "So, let's get back to that timeline, huh?" she suggested, releasing his hand and turning toward the notebook paper he'd left on the table. "Where did we leave off?"

There was a troubled look in his eyes as he stared at her for a long moment before he sighed and turned toward the timeline. "We left off at the time of Josie Gardner's suicide or possible murder," he said.

She nodded. Was she wrong about what Nick wanted? Maybe, but, somehow, it was easier to talk about who might have kidnapped her son than her tangled feelings toward Nick.

The rest of the day passed by quicker than she would have imagined. Dark clouds rolled in, bringing the threat of a storm, but while the wind kicked up a bit, no snowflakes fell.

Nick walked around outside again, and she was reassured by his diligence. He continued to work on the timeline long after they'd taken a break for dinner.

She bowed her head while Nick thanked God once again for providing the hot meal and shelter. There weren't many options for dinner, so they had to eat more of the canned beef stew again but no one complained.

"Are we going to be home in time for Christmas?" Joey asked.

"Christmas is three days away, I'm sure we'll be home by then," she assured him.

Nick looked as if he didn't necessarily agree. "We can celebrate Christmas here, too, if we have to," he pointed out.

She knew he was right. "If we have to, we will," she agreed. "But hopefully things will get back to normal soon."

After dinner, Nick continued to work on the timeline.

She found a game of checkers on the pantry shelf and played a few games with Joey to help keep him occupied. Soon Nick came over and asked if he could play the winner, and she was truly disappointed when Joey beat her.

As she watched Nick and Joey play, she was struck by how easy it was to feel they were a family. Had she been wrong to warn Nick to keep his distance? He was everything a role model should be: kind and considerate…strong yet gentle. What a wonderful husband and father he must have been. So different from her ex.

Joey won again, and he let out a whoop. She had to make sure her yearning for a family of her own wasn't visible on her face when she gave Joey a high five.

Several games later, after Joey had yawned for the fifth time in a row, she deemed it time for bed. "Say good-night to Nick," she reminded her son.

"Good night, Nick, you're the best dad ever," Joey said.

Her breath froze in her chest and she stared at her son in horror. Why had he said that? It was as if she'd somehow projected her secret wishes into her son.

"You're welcome, Joey," Nick said thickly. "Get some sleep, now, okay?"

"Come on, Joey," she mumbled, completely mortified by the turn of events. "Good night, Nick."

"Good night." Nick gave her a searching look, which she avoided meeting head-on—too afraid he'd see the same sentiment in her eyes. He picked up the Bible and as much as she was tempted to stay and listen while he read some more she had no choice but to go with her son, who was still afraid of the dark. Besides, she couldn't imagine trying to explain why Joey had called him the best dad ever.

She'd never been more acutely aware of how her son had been impacted by growing up without a father. Had he been looking for a surrogate father this whole time?

Was it any wonder he'd latched on to Nick?

She and Joey took turns in the bathroom, the scent of the aftershave far less obvious now, though still lingering in the air. Joey wrinkled his nose but otherwise seemed fine as he crawled under the pile of quilts on the bed.

Joey immediately fell asleep but, just like the night before, her mind refused to settle. She tried to remember some of the Bible phrases Nick had read but could only recall a line or two.

She kept replaying the moment that Joey had called Nick the best dad ever. She hoped Nick didn't put too much importance on what her son had said. The way she already had.

At some point she must have dozed, because a noise startled her awake. Another wild animal moving through the woods? She stayed perfectly still, straining to listen.

After several moments, she crawled from beneath the quilts and moved silently over to the window overlooking the back side of the cabin. There weren't any stars out as they were well hidden behind a blanket of clouds.

She heard it again, the same thunk that had woken her. Did animals make that kind of sound? Somehow she doubted it. She stuffed her feet into her athletic shoes and cautiously made her way down the hall to find Nick.

Nick shot upright when he felt a hand on his arm. "What?" he asked harshly, blinking the sleep from his eyes as he gazed up at Rachel.

"Get up, I think I heard something outside," she whispered.

His pulse kicked into triple digits and he swung around to put his feet on the floor. "Are you sure?" he asked in a low, raspy voice as he quickly slid his feet into his shoes and tied the laces.

"I don't think it was an animal," she said, her eyes wide with fear. "It was a thunking noise and I heard it twice."

Nick wrestled with guilt, knowing that he should have taken Jonah's advice and found a new place to stay. But it was too late for self-recriminations. He needed to get Rachel and Joey safely out of the cabin. "Wake up Joey and make sure he's wearing his winter jacket and his shoes, okay?"

"Okay." To her credit, Rachel didn't panic and went to do exactly as she was told.

He used the poker to break up the remains of the fire, and closed the iron doors on the fireplace, to help douse the flames and eliminate even that small bit of light. The room was plunged into darkness and it took him a minute for his eyes to adjust. He tucked his weapon in his shoulder harness and then went over to peer out the large picture window.

He couldn't see much, but that was okay, since it helped keep them hidden, as well. When Rachel and Joey returned, he crossed over to them. "Be as quiet as possible, okay? Follow me...we're going outside."

Rachel snagged his arm. "Aren't we safer in here?"

"No, we're boxed in. Try to trust me on this, Rachel."

He could barely see her in the darkness. "I do trust you, Nick."

Whether or not he deserved her trust remained to be seen. But they had to move, so he simply led the way over to the front door. As quietly as possible, he eased back the dead bolt, although the click was louder than he liked. Without wasting time, he opened the door and cast a quick glance around the clearing.

Joey and Rachel crowded behind him, waiting silently for his direction. He took a moment to pray for their safety, before guiding them out onto the front porch, keeping as close to the cabin as possible.

Rachel sent Joey first, and then followed from behind. He didn't have to tell her to make sure the door didn't slam shut as she softly closed it before making her way over to where they stood. The night was so cold they could see their breath in the air, and the frozen leaves and brush would make it far more difficult to move silently through the woods.

First, he needed to figure out which was the best direction to go. He waited for a long moment, listening to the sounds of the night. It was too cold for any insects, but at least the wind had died down.

As much as he wanted to use the car to escape, he couldn't deny the possibility that the intruder had already found it and disabled it. At least, that's what he would have done.

No, their best bet was to stay hidden in the woods for as long as possible. He didn't dare use his cell phone yet, as the light from the screen would only broadcast their position to whoever was out there.

The closest grouping of evergreen trees was to the left in the nine-o'clock position, so he bent down to whisper in Rachel's ear. "Follow me to the evergreens."

He could feel her head nod, her hair brushing his face. Satisfied, he inched across the porch, praying the boards wouldn't creak.

The trek to the group of evergreens seemed to take

forever, but the moment they reached them, he felt him-self relax. Thank goodness they were all wearing dark clothing, and, without the moon, he hoped their pale faces wouldn't attract too much attention.

"Stay here, I'm going to take a look around," he whis-pered again, right next to Rachel's ear.

"No, wait," she grabbed his arm in a tense grip. "I smell smoke."

He paused and tried to estimate how long the scent of smoke would linger in the air after he'd put out the fire inside the cabin.

"There!" Rachel whispered urgently, pointing to an area behind the cabin.

He saw what had captured her attention. Orange flames flickering in the darkness.

Fire!

FOURTEEN

Rachel stared at the small flickering flames in horror. The kidnapper must have found them. Who else would do such a thing? She knew Nick thought Morales had been ordered to kill her and Joey, but they'd managed to get away. The kidnapper must have come back to finish the job. And what if she hadn't woken up from the thunking noise? Would they have died inside the cabin? Had that been the kidnappers' plan all along?

Cold fear slid down her spine.

Thank You, Lord, for saving us!

"I think the outhouse might be on fire," Nick whispered. "And if that's the case, I'm afraid the fire will spread to the cabin." He paused, looking out over the trees. "Looks like the wind is blowing north. We'll need to head south so that we're heading in the opposite direction."

"Okay." She wasn't about to argue. Joey's hand was trembling inside of hers, from the cold or fear or both. She tightened her grip reassuringly, knowing she'd do whatever was necessary to keep him safe. "Lead the way."

Nick stayed between the trees, moving slowly and silently away from the cabin. She did her best to follow in his footsteps, but it seemed like twigs snapped loudly beneath her feet and her clothing brushed and snagged against the tree branches with every step. The cold night air blew sharp against her face, but she knew the fire was the bigger threat compared to the stinging cold.

Although both could be deadly.

They hadn't made it very far when a loud crack echoed through the night.

"Get down," Nick urged.

Someone was shooting at them! She instinctively dropped low, ducking behind a tree while covering Joey's body with hers, protecting him the best she could.

They waited motionless for what seemed like an hour but was likely only a few minutes. There was no further gunfire and she wasn't sure if that was good news or bad.

Was the kidnapper tracking them through the woods right now?

"We need to split up," Nick whispered, his mouth close to her ear.

"No! We need to stick together!" she whispered back.

"Listen to me." Nick's tone was harsh. "We need to get help. You and Joey are going to take my phone and head southeast. When you're far enough away, call 911."

"I don't even know where we are," she murmured anxiously.

"The address here is 472 and Highway MM."

She silently repeated it to herself, committing the address to memory.

"I'm going to draw the gunman away from you and Joey. So you need to get moving, now."

"I still think you should come with us," she whispered again. She couldn't help remembering the last time she'd tried to save her son by sending him out of the mangled wreck of their car only to watch him be captured and kidnapped. What if the same thing happened to Nick?

"Go!" he said, and he turned and fired in the direction from which the gunshot had originated. "I'll hold him off long enough for help to arrive."

She hesitated, torn between two impossible choices. She desperately wanted to get Joey to safety, but she also didn't want to leave Nick, unable to bear the thought of anything happening to him. Yet she knew her son was depending on her so she did as Nick asked, staying low and easing back into the cover of the trees, keeping Joey close to her side.

Joey must have understood the acute need for silence since he didn't say a word as they made their way through a particularly thick grove. When they'd gone about twenty yards, she crouched behind a large tree and took out Nick's phone. She unzipped her coat, using the edges of her jacket to help hide the unmistakable glow of the phone screen as she called 911. The operator seemed to take forever to answer, and when she finally did, she hoped she remembered everything correctly.

"Please send help," Rachel said urgently. "Someone is shooting at us and he's also started a fire. The address is 472 and Highway MM."

"Are you hurt?" the dispatcher asked.

"Not yet, but please hurry!" There was another loud crack followed by a cry of pain and she instinctively clutched Joey close, using her body as a shield to cover her son's.

Even though she'd dropped the phone, she could still hear the dispatcher's voice talking. She frantically searched the ground with her fingertips. The snow was cold, making her fingers numb, but she eventually found the phone and powered it off.

"Are you all right?" she asked Joey softly, fearing that the kidnapper had seen them despite her efforts to keep the screen hidden from view. "He didn't hit you, did he?"

"No, I'm not hurt," Joey whispered. "I'm scared."

Her heart ached for him. "I know, but remember what Nick taught us? God is watching over us. God will keep us safe."

Joey nodded solemnly. "I'm going to keep praying."

Tears pricked her eyes. "Me, too." She gave her son a quick hug and then glanced back over her shoulder searching for Nick. Panic swelled in the back of her throat when she couldn't see him. What if he'd been hit? The orange glow from the fire was brighter, indicating that it was beginning to spread.

Dear Lord, please keep Nick safe! Please keep us all safe!

"I smell the bad man," Joey whimpered.

Since all she could smell was smoke, she didn't necessarily believe him. But at that moment, a bright spotlight illuminated the woods, blinding her. The light was only forty feet away! She shoved Joey behind her and tried to edge closer behind an evergreen tree.

"Stay right where you are, Rachel!" a voice shouted. "If you move, I'll keep shooting."

She froze at the familiar voice. *Gerry?* Abruptly, all the puzzle pieces clicked into place. Gerry Ashton always wore strong aftershave, very similar to the kind Joey had spilled in the cabin. And now she clearly recognized his voice.

Her mind wrestled helplessly with the truth. The man she'd trusted more than anyone else in the company had been the one who'd hired Morales to kidnap Joey. Had Gerry also kept her son locked up in his basement? The thought made her furious. To think she'd played right into his hands by begging him to buy her shares of the company. Had he sent the letters, too, pretending to be part of the Mafia?

Gerry was one of the few who'd known about how her father had helped her escape Anthony. Maybe he'd used the Mafia link on purpose to scare her. She wasn't sure if he'd killed Josie Gardner, too, or if the researcher had really committed suicide, but it was clear he intended to kill her and Joey, right here, right now.

Everything suddenly made sense in a sick, horrible way.

How could she have been so blind? So stupid? How could she not have known? Edith must have suspected something wasn't right with Gerry, which was why she'd quit.

She should have asked her assistant for more information. But it was too late now. She forced herself to keep facing Gerry even as she whispered to her son. "Stay hidden behind the tree."

Joey soundlessly moved deeper into the branches. She lifted her arm to shield her eyes against the glare. "Don't shoot!" she shouted. "I'm not armed."

"No, but your boyfriend was." She tried not to react to Gerry's use of the past tense in reference to Nick. "You and Joey need to come back to the cabin, Rachel. Right now," Gerry demanded.

The cabin? Was he crazy? No way was she doing that. What was Gerry thinking to suggest she take her son anywhere near a burning building? If the cabin wasn't on fire yet, it soon would be. She'd rather take her chances getting lost in the woods. But how long could she hold him off? Gerry must know that she'd already called for help, especially if he caught a glimpse of the glow from Nick's cell phone.

And where was Nick?

"Why?" she asked, stalling for time. "Give me one good reason why I should make it easy for you to kill us?"

Another crack shattered the night and she gasped and ducked, half expecting to feel the searing pain from being hit by a bullet.

"That was just a warning shot," Gerry snarled. "Next time, I'll make that kid of yours an orphan."

She sucked in a harsh breath, feeling trapped. If they tried to run, Gerry could easily follow them with the light. She had no idea where Nick was, and she prayed he wasn't lying in the woods, bleeding to death. As the seconds stretched into a full minute, she wondered why Gerry didn't just shoot her and get it over with. What did he hope to gain in this weird cat-and-mouse game?

The glow of the fire burned bright behind Gerry, and suddenly it dawned on her that Gerry wanted them to burn inside the cabin. Maybe he thought that would make their deaths look like a tragic accident. Bullet wounds would be too obvious.

Grimly, she realized he had no intention of letting any of them live through this.

"Why are you doing this, Gerry? You have the money! And the company!" She thought it was best to keep him talking.

"Your father promised the company to me! That idiot Morales was supposed to kill you both. You're too smart for your own good, Rachel. I knew you'd figure out that I was the one behind this sooner or later."

She wasn't about to admit she hadn't realized that until right now. "Why did you decide to take over the company now? Why not back when my dad died?"

"Because Nancy was threatening to divorce me," Gerry said in a vicious tone. "I signed a prenup so I get nothing. I needed that company. And you were going to give all that money to settle the lawsuit!" He released a ragged breath. "You didn't deserve to keep it. But just taking over the company wasn't enough. Everyone kept asking about what it would take to bring you back. Leaving me no choice but to get rid of you both once and for all."

He was crazy, no doubt about it. How were they going to get away?

Another gunshot echoed, and this time she saw the spotlight waver, as if Gerry had ducked.

Nick! Nick was alive!

The next gunshot hit the spotlight dead on, shattering the bulb. But even with the spotlight off, there was too much light from the roaring fire that quickly engulfed the dry timber of the log cabin.

Rachel took the opportunity to move from their current location, urging Joey to stay shielded behind her as they darted around more trees. But then she froze when another crack of gunfire shattered the night.

She whipped around and, from the glow of the fire behind her, Rachel watched Gerry's dark shadow stagger and then finally go down.

She hesitated, torn by indecision. Was Gerry dead? Or at least hurt badly enough that he couldn't keep shooting?

And where was Nick?

She crouched beside her son for long, agonizing moments. She didn't want to risk Joey's life by taking him over to find Nick, but at the same time, she didn't want to leave him here, alone.

"Rachel?" Nick's voice was weak. "Are you and Joey all right?"

Her head shot over to the right, her eyes trying to pierce the darkness. "Yes, we're fine," she called back. "But where are you?"

"Over here." Nick's voice was definitely lacking strength—she could barely hear him over the roaring of the fire. "I've been hit."

Nick kept his eyes glued to where Gerry Ashton's body lay sprawled on the ground. If the man so much as twitched he'd shoot him again.

His eyes blurred and he blinked in an effort to bring the world back into focus. The smoke was getting thicker and he knew he couldn't stay too long. His left arm felt like it was on fire, and the loss of blood was making him dizzy. Figured he'd got hit in the same area as when they'd saved Joey during the money exchange.

Only this time, the injury was much worse. Propped against the tree, he tugged on the string from the hooded sweatshirt he wore, until it came free. Using the string like a tourniquet, he awkwardly wrapped it around his arm and used his teeth to tie it tight. He wanted to drag himself over to make sure Gerry was really dead, but on the off chance that the guy was only pretending in an effort to draw his prey closer, Nick decided it was safer to stay far away.

Where were the cops and the firefighters? He'd heard Rachel calling 911, so he knew reinforcements had to be on the way. Wally's cabin wasn't going to survive the fire, but he was more concerned about the fire spreading through the woods. Drought conditions had hit hard the previous summer, and despite the thin layer of snow covering the ground, he thought the trees were burning too fast.

As if on cue, a large pine tree to the right of the outhouse went up in flames, the tiny needles glowing red as they burned. Knowing they didn't have a lot of time left to get somewhere safe, he forced himself upright, using the tree for support.

"Nick!" He was caught off guard when Joey came running toward him. He opened his mouth to yell at the boy to stay down, when he realized that Gerry hadn't moved, not even an inch despite the fire growing closer.

Joey's second bad guy was finally dead.

"Hey, it's okay," he managed when Joey flung his arms around his waist, burying his face in his stomach. "I'm okay."

"I thought you were dead," the child sobbed.

Rachel looked upset at Joey's statement. "Where are you hit?" she asked.

"My left arm same as before, but never mind that, now. We need to get as far away from the fire as we can. It's been so dry up here that the fire will soon burn out of control."

"Lean on me," Rachel offered, slipping her shoulder beneath his injured arm and sliding her other hand around his waist.

He didn't like the fact that he was so weak that he had little choice but to allow her to help him. Surprisingly, Joey went around on the other side of him, and together they moved as quickly as possible away from the fire.

"Joey, can you find the gravel driveway?" he asked, since his vision was blurry again.

"I think so," Joey said. "This way!"

The three of them stumbled toward the direction of the driveway with a deep sense of urgency. Nick refused to look back over his shoulder, too afraid he'd see the fire nipping hotly at their heels.

There was another loud whooshing sound, and he knew another tree had gone up in flames. They had to get out of here, and fast!

When the gravel crunched beneath his feet, he let out a sigh of relief. Joey's sense of direction had been perfect. They continued moving as fast as they could, putting more distance between them and the raging fire. The smoke was still hanging thick between the trees.

He coughed and a spear of pain shot down his arm. He ignored it, more concerned when he heard Rachel and Joey coughing, too. How much time did they have before they succumbed to smoke inhalation?

Dear Lord, show us the way to safety.

"Come on, Nick, don't give up now!" Rachel urged in a raspy voice. Obviously the smoke was getting to her, too. And what about Joey? He was so young that Nick was afraid it wouldn't take long for the smoke to damage the boy's lungs.

He hadn't realized his steps were lagging behind, and he forced himself to move faster for both Rachel and Joey's sake. They deserved a chance to get out of here, alive.

Within five minutes, Nick practically fell over the hood of the car, and he slumped against the metal frame gratefully. For the first time in hours, he allowed himself a flash of hope. "Maybe we can drive out of here," he proposed, fumbling in his pockets for the keys. He found them and tugged them free. "Think you're up to it?"

"I'll try," Rachel said, jumping eagerly at his suggestion. She stepped forward to take the keys, and she opened the driver's door. But before she could slide inside, a man appeared out of the woods, holding a rifle.

"Don't move," he barked loudly.

"Karl!" Rachel exclaimed. Then, in a move that was so subtle Nick almost missed it, she pushed Joey behind her, probably intending for him to climb into the safety of the car. "What are you doing? Why do you have a gun?"

Karl? Nick stared in shocked surprise as he realized that the stranger was Dr. Karl Errol, the researcher he'd suspected was secretly working for Global Pharmaceuticals. His instincts must have been right on. The researcher must have purposefully set up Rachel's company to fail. But seeing him here, as if he'd teamed up with Gerry Ashton, didn't make much sense. Why would the researcher who'd tried to destroy Rachel's company work alongside Ashton, who clearly wanted to take over the company himself?

He didn't know for sure, but obviously Errol wasn't messing around. The way he held the rifle in his hands told Nick he wouldn't hesitate to kill them.

FIFTEEN

Nick gritted his teeth as Rachel tried to reason with Karl Errol. "Gerry is dead, Karl. You don't have to do this. Just let us go."

"I'm not working for Gerry," Errol said finally. "And my boss isn't going to accept failure."

Nick tried to think of a way out of this mess. But he couldn't come up with a safe option. Granted, he still had his weapon, but he didn't dare try to take Errol out while the guy held the rifle pointed directly at Rachel. Maybe if he was at full strength he could rush the guy, catching him off guard.

But he'd lost too much blood to risk it. He was far more likely to fall flat on his face before he reached Errol. He seriously felt as if a strong breeze would blow him over.

"Who's your boss, Karl? Why are you doing this?" Rachel asked, taking a step toward him. It was all Nick could do not to shout at her to stay back. "Have you really been working for Global Pharmaceuticals this whole time? Why? Why did you hate me so much you wanted to put me out of business?"

Errol shook his head, as if waging an inner war with

himself. "I didn't have a choice. I followed Ashton here and waited, hoping he'd take care of things for me. But he botched the job. Leaving me no choice."

Nick tried to take heart in knowing the guy hadn't shot them yet, even though he'd had time. Maybe there was a way to get through to him.

But how?

"There's no point in trying to reason with him, Rachel. He doesn't care about anyone but himself. I told you he killed Josie Gardener," Nick told her in a scathing tone. "She stumbled upon the truth and was going to let you know what she'd found out. So he killed her and set the whole thing up to look like a suicide."

"No!" Errol shouted. "I loved Josie! I would never hurt her. But she didn't love me."

A cold chill snaked down his spine. Now they were getting somewhere. "Who did she love, Karl?" he asked mildly.

"Ashton." Errol's tone reeked of loathing. "But that jerk didn't deserve her love. He had an affair with her even though he had no intention of leaving his rich wife."

"Ashton is dead. He won't hurt anyone ever again, Karl." Rachel's tone was soothing. She took another small step forward, holding her hand out. "Just put down the gun and we'll work this through, okay?"

"Stop!" he screamed. "You can't fix this. Don't you understand? I did it for Josie! I secretly worked for Global to make enough money to compete with Ashton. I told her I could afford to buy her nice things, and take her to fancy places. But she didn't care! She wanted to live in sin as Ashton's mistress rather than to give me the chance to make her happy."

Slowly the picture became clear. "Are you saying that Ashton killed Josie?" Rachel asked incredulously.

"Yes, because she was pressuring him to leave his wife. Maybe he was afraid she'd tell his wife about the affair. And if he divorced his wife he'd lose all the big bucks he'd gotten accustomed to spending. But none of that matters anymore." He blew out an angry breath. "I'm glad Ashton's dead. You saved me the trouble of killing him. But, unfortunately, I have no choice but to kill you, too." Errol tightened his grip on the gun.

"Wait! You do have a choice. What if I promise not to press charges against you?" Rachel asked in a desperate tone. "Then will you put the gun down? I promise I won't turn you in to the authorities. All I want is to go home with my son."

For a moment Nick thought she may have convinced Errol with her heartfelt plea. But then Karl slowly brought the rifle up to shoulder height and bent his head forward as if to take aim.

"No!" Joey came charging out from the back end of the car carrying a thick tree branch. His shout startled Karl enough that he jerked around toward Joey's direction, shooting wildly.

"Joey," Rachel shrieked.

The boy didn't stop. He must not have been hit by the wild shot, because he swung the tree branch with all his might, aiming at Karl's knees.

Nick made a split-second decision, gathering every ounce of his strength to propel himself across the small clearing toward Errol. As the guy fell down, howling in agony, Nick kicked the rifle up and out of the way and threw himself on top of the researcher.

Within moments, Rachel had the rifle safely in her hands. "Get out of the way," she shouted.

Nick rolled off Errol and she quickly brought the heavy stock down on Errol's head, knocking him unconscious.

The sound of sirens, hopefully from both ambulances and fire trucks, echoed through the night. Finally, there was hope that help was soon to arrive. He didn't have the strength to move, so he stayed right where he was.

"Joey, are you all right?" Rachel asked.

"Yes. I was afraid he was going to shoot you." Nick heard the boy's footsteps creeping forward. "Nick? Are you okay?"

He tried to crack a smile. "Fine, buddy. Just tired. I'm going to rest for a minute, okay?"

Rachel dropped to her knees beside him. "Come on, Nick," she pleaded. "You can't stay here—you need to get up! Karl isn't dead and we can't be here when he wakes up."

The panic in her tone pierced his soul, so he pushed himself upright with his good arm, biting back a groan of pain. He was still dizzy and knew he'd already lost too much blood. The artery in his arm must be nicked.

Somehow, with Rachel and Joey's help, he managed to get back on his feet. The three of them staggered toward the car and he leaned against the frame gratefully. There was no telling how long Errol would remain unconscious, so he knew they had to get out of there, and quickly. "Rachel, do you still have the car keys? Let's see if we can drive out of here."

"Good idea." Rachel slid behind the wheel and jammed the key into the ignition. He closed his eyes in despair when he heard a *click-click* as she attempted to start the car.

"I'm sorry, Nick," Rachel lamented, and got out of the car. "Either Karl or Gerry must have done something to the engine."

He opened his eyes and nodded wearily. "I shouldn't be surprised. Guess we'll have to try and make it to the highway by walking."

"Nick, you're bleeding!" Joey exclaimed.

He glanced down and winced when he saw the dark stain of blood smeared across the palm of Joey's hand. "Yeah, but it's just a scratch," he said, downplaying his injury. "I'll be fine as soon as the ambulance gets here."

Joey still looked horrified, and he hated knowing he was causing the child to be afraid again. Hadn't the poor kid been through enough? He'd never forget the way Joey went charging after Errol with the tree branch. The kid was a true hero. "Listen, Joey, can you hear the sirens? The police will be here soon. Everything's going to be all right."

"Let's go, Nick." Rachel slid her arm around his waist, putting her shoulder under his arm to help support him. He silently prayed for strength as they made their way down the rest of the gravel driveway. The hazy smoke made it difficult to see and to breathe. The three of them coughed as they walked. He could barely see a few feet in front of his face, so he had no way of knowing if they were anywhere close to the highway.

After about ten minutes, he could feel his strength waning, even with Rachel trying to take most of his weight. He stumbled on a large rock and knew he was going to fall. Instantly, he let go of both Rachel and Joey so he wouldn't take them down with him. He groaned loudly when he hit the ground, hard. For a moment everything went black and he stopped fighting, stopped struggling, welcoming the darkness.

"Nick! Are you all right?" From far away, he could feel someone shaking him and calling his name. Rachel? He didn't have the strength to reassure her.

Once he'd prayed for the Lord to take him so he could be with his wife and daughter again. But it hadn't been his time. Was God going to take him now? Just when he'd found Rachel? He didn't want to leave Rachel and Joey, but he didn't have the strength to fight anymore.

"Take me home, Lord," he whispered. "I'm ready to come home."

"Nick!" Rachel tried not to panic as she stripped away his coat so she could look at his arm. Not that she would be able to see much in the darkness.

"Is Nick going to die?" Joey asked, his voice trembling with fear.

"Not if I can help it," she muttered. Nick's jacket wouldn't come off and she soon realized he'd tied a string around the upper part of his left arm in an attempt to stop the bleeding.

"No, God wants me home...." he muttered, weakly pushing her hands away.

Rachel couldn't believe Nick was just going to give up. She remembered him mentioning his wife and daughter were up in heaven. Was he willing to give up his life in order to be with them again? Didn't she and Joey mean anything to him?

Maybe not, but that was too bad. She wasn't ready to let him go. She untied the string and yanked the jacket sleeve off. His blood-soaked sweatshirt confirmed her worst fears.

He was hit badly, far worse than he'd let on.

Working quickly, she felt for the worst part of the injury, trying not to wince when her fingers sank into the open wound. Once she'd found it, she retied the string around his arm above the injured area. What else could she use to stop the bleeding? She shrugged out of her coat, took off her sweatshirt and then put her coat back on. Using the sleeve of her sweatshirt, figuring it was cleaner than the hood, she balled it up and pressed it against the gouged area across Nick's biceps.

"Come on, Nick. Help me out here," she urged as she leaned all her weight against him, hoping to slow the blood loss. But Nick didn't move, didn't so much as flutter an eyelash.

"Wake up, Nick," Joey said, shaking Nick's other arm. "You have to wake up!"

The sounds of sirens grew louder. "Hang in there, Nick. The ambulance is almost here!"

Still, Nick didn't respond, not even when the ambulance and the firefighters arrived. Two paramedics came over to help Nick while the rest of the firefighters headed in with a huge water truck to the wooded area to douse the fire.

"He's lost a lot of blood," Rachel cautioned, when the two paramedics nudged her aside.

"Let's get an IV in, stat!" the female paramedic said curtly.

"I've got it," the younger man replied. "Fluids wide open until we can get the O neg blood flowing."

"His blood pressure is low—I'll get the packed red blood cells out of the ambulance," the woman continued.

She darted away and returned with a small cooler less than two minutes later. She quickly opened the cooler and took out what looked like packages of blood.

Rachel kept Joey close to her side as they watched the two paramedics work on Nick. Once they had the blood infusing into his veins, they brought over a gurney and began to strap him securely onto it.

"Could we go with you? Please?" Rachel asked, stepping forward. "Our car has been tampered with and we don't have a ride out of here. There's also a man who tried to kill us still back in the woods."

The two paramedics grimaced. "I'm sorry, but that's against the rules," the younger man said.

"Besides, the police will want to talk to you, especially if there's still a threat here in the area," the female paramedic added kindly. "We're taking him to Madison General Hospital and I'm sure one of the officers will give you a ride."

Her heart sank, but she also knew they were right. She had little choice but to stand there with her arm around Joey and watch as they bundled Nick into the ambulance.

"Do you think God will listen if we pray for Nick?" Joey asked, after the paramedic jumped into the driver's seat, started the engine and pulled out onto the highway.

She gathered him close and nodded. "Absolutely, Joey," she responded. "Dear Lord, we ask You to please keep Nick safe in Your care. Amen."

"Amen," Joey echoed.

Tears burned her eyes as she realized that no matter what happened moving forward, her son was going to be hurt by Nick's leaving. Because he already cared about Nick, already saw him as some sort of surrogate father.

And she couldn't blame him, because if she were

honest with herself, she'd admit she was falling for Nick, too. Maybe he didn't feel the same way, but she couldn't imagine a life without him.

Please, Lord, let him live!

"What do you mean you can't find Karl?" Rachel asked, her tone rising incredulously. With the smoke growing thicker in the woods despite the firefighters' attempt to douse the raging flames, the police officer had stashed her and Joey in the squad car while they went searching for the scientist. "He was lying on the ground about twenty feet away from the car. You found the car, right?"

"Yes, ma'am, we found the vehicle. And we looked all over but didn't find any sign of the research doctor or the weapon." The tall, dark-haired police officer had introduced himself as Sean McCarthy.

Rachel shivered and hugged Joey. The thought of Karl Errol being out on the loose in the woods with his rifle wasn't at all reassuring. She wished now that she had taken the gun with her. She glanced through the passenger-side window, hoping that Karl had taken the opportunity to escape rather than to seek revenge.

She could still barely comprehend that Gerry Ashton had decided to kill her and Joey as retaliation for her father giving her the company. And because he thought she was onto him. She felt sick to her stomach, thinking about how she'd been duped by the man she'd trusted.

Once again, her instincts had led her wrong.

"You say you believe Karl Errol was secretly working for Global Pharmaceuticals?" Officer McCarthy asked.

"That's what he admitted to. I'm still having trouble

understanding how two people hated me enough to try and kill me."

"Can't say that I have much experience with corporate espionage," McCarthy admitted.

"Me, either," she murmured. She didn't want to think about greed and corruption anymore. Right now, she wanted to see Nick. To make sure he was all right.

"Officer McCarthy, will you please take us to Madison General Hospital?" she asked, willing to beg if necessary. It seemed as if hours had passed since the ambulance had driven away with Nick. She wanted nothing more than to get far away from this place where Nick had almost died and where she and Joey had feared for their lives, too. "We've given you our statements. It's not like we can't discuss this in more detail later, right?"

Officer McCarthy hesitated but then nodded. "All right. We'll head over to the hospital. If Detective Butler is awake, I'll get his statement, as well."

Her shoulders slumped with relief. She didn't bother telling the officer that the likelihood of Nick answering any questions was slim to none. She wouldn't be at all surprised to find that Nick was already in surgery, having the injury to his arm repaired. If he survived long enough to get to surgery.

No, she refused to believe the worst. God was surely watching over Nick. He'd been a good Christian his entire life.

She didn't even want to consider the alternative. That God would take Nick home to be with his wife and daughter.

The ride to the hospital didn't take too long, although Joey was half asleep by the time they arrived. With Officer McCarthy as their escort, they made their way to the waiting area and were given a quick update about Nick's condition.

"Detective Butler is still in surgery," the woman behind the desk informed them. "But he should be out soon. Now tell me what relation are you to the patient?"

Rachel swallowed hard. "I— We're good friends. He, uh, has sisters, but I don't know how to get in touch with them." She knew he had parents, although she wasn't sure how to contact them, either. How was it that she was more familiar with the names of his dead wife and daughter than his living family members?

Maybe calling herself a friend was stretching the truth. She was just a woman who'd needed Nick's protection and his expertise. Nothing more, nothing less.

The kiss they'd shared didn't mean anything. And she'd be stupid to think it had.

She and Joey went to sit down, and soon Joey was snuggled against her, falling asleep. She tucked Officer McCarthy's business card in her pocket and let her head drop back against the wall.

As soon as they found Karl Errol, this nightmare would really be over. She and Joey could go back home to their normal lives. Granted there would still be some red tape before the money was returned her, but she was convinced it would all work out.

She wondered how long Nick would have to stay off duty as a result of his gunshot wound and hoped it wouldn't be too long. Grimly, she realized there was no way she'd ever be able to repay him for everything he'd done for her and for Joey.

He'd put his life and his career on the line for them. More than once. Without Nick's help she wouldn't have managed to get Joey back.

Not only had he kept them both safe, but he'd also taught them to believe in God.

Yet all she could offer in return was to pray for him to recover with the full use of his arm.

"Ms. Simon?" A hand shook her awake and she blinked, momentarily confused as to where she was. Then she recognized the unmistakable antiseptic smell of a hospital.

"What?" She winced when her neck muscles tightened painfully as she turned toward the hospital employee. "Nick? Is he out of surgery?"

"Yes. The doctor is on his way down to talk to you."

Joey was still asleep beside her and she tried not to wake him as she eased away. She rubbed her hands over her gritty eyes and was surprised to find that the sky outside was beginning to lighten.

A harried surgeon wearing green scrubs came into the room. "Ms. Simon? I'm Dr. Wagner. Detective Butler's surgery went well. We were able to save his arm, although it was touch and go for a while as his brachial artery was injured. He's just about finished in the recovery area and then will be sent to the ICU where they can watch him more closely." He smiled compassionately. "You'll be able to visit him in about forty-five minutes or so."

Her mind was spinning with all the information he'd told her. Although she was certainly relieved that Nick had made it through the surgery, she still couldn't help worrying. "Is there any way he could still lose his arm?" she asked.

For a moment hesitation shadowed the doctor's eyes. "We're going to keep a close eye on his circulation. If there's any change, we'll take him back to surgery. We'll know more after twenty-four hours or so."

Rachel nodded to indicate she understood. "Thank you," she whispered.

The doctor flashed a brief smile before he turned and left. Joey woke up, complaining that he was hungry. Unfortunately, Rachel didn't have any money on her, not even an ID. They'd left everything they had in the cabin, which was likely burned beyond repair by now.

"Here, these are meal passes for the cafeteria," the woman behind the desk said, offering up two small plastic cards. "They're worth about five dollars each."

"Thank you so much," Rachel murmured, taking them gratefully. Getting something to eat would help pass the time until she and Joey could visit Nick in the ICU.

It was closer to an hour later before the ICU called down for them. She held tightly on to Joey's hand as they went into the critical-care area. Nick's room was the second door on the left, so they cautiously approached.

"He looks bad, Mom," Joey choked out, his eyes filling with tears. "He looks like he's going to die."

"Joey, listen to me. The doctor said Nick is stable. He wouldn't lie to us. It's just that Nick is connected to lots of machines right now." She did her best to soothe her son, although she felt just as awful seeing Nick like this.

Rachel stepped forward and took Nick's uninjured hand in hers. "Nick, it's me, Rachel. Joey is here, too. The doctor said you're going to be fine. Do you hear me? You're going to be just fine."

Nick's eyelids fluttered for a moment and he looked directly at her. She smiled. "They said your arm should heal. I don't want you to worry about anything, okay?"

"Where am I?" he asked, his eyes full of confusion.

She tried not to let her fear show. "You're at the hospital in Madison. You just had surgery on your arm."

"But I—can't feel my arm," he whispered in agony.

"Your arm is right here." She patted the heavily bandaged limb gently. "The doctor said there's a good chance you'll make a full recovery." She made sure her tone was encouraging.

"I can't—" Nick stopped, closed his eyes, and turned his head away as if shutting her out.

Rejection seared her soul and she stepped back, keeping her expression neutral for Joey's sake. She didn't want to leave, but he'd made his feelings clear. Did he really think he was going to lose his arm? Where was his faith in God?

She didn't want to think that Nick preferred to be alone through this difficult time, but really, how much did she truly know about him? Maybe he only wanted his family here. Like his parents or his sisters.

She was just a woman he'd gone out of his way to help. Obviously, there was nothing more for her to do here.

She took a deep breath, trying to ease her heartache. This was why she'd avoided becoming emotionally involved. Only this time, she wasn't the only one who would be hurt.

Joey's heart would be broken, as well.

SIXTEEN

Nick fought the rising sense of despair. The doctor had told him that they'd saved his arm, but what was the point if he couldn't use it? His entire career would be over.

He shifted and groaned, and pain slashed through his left arm, robbing him of his breath. Was it a good thing to know he could feel pain? He forced his eyes open and stared at the heavily bandaged limb. His fingers were hugely swollen and no matter how much he tried, he couldn't move them. He concentrated on feeling them move, but no luck.

Nothing. He felt nothing.

With a disgusted sigh, he closed his eyes again, feeling guilty for the way he'd treated Rachel and Joey. They hadn't deserved his anger. He should be thanking God for saving his life, but instead he was focusing on the fact that his arm might never work right again.

Shame burned the back of his throat. He'd taught Rachel and Joey about having faith but couldn't manage to keep his own. Obviously, he owed them an apology.

But where had they gone? Now that he was awake, the pain in his arm throbbed in conjunction with the beat of his heart. His throat was still sore, no doubt from the smoke he'd inhaled out in the woods.

Abruptly, he wondered how Rachel and Joey were doing. After all, they'd inhaled a fair amount of smoke, too. Had they been checked out by a doctor? He shifted in the bed again, and a loud series of beeping noises brought a nurse running into his room.

"Relax, Mr. Butler, you need to calm down."

He almost corrected her—he was a detective, not a mister—but didn't want to waste his energy. "I need to know if Rachel and Joey Simon are both patients here, too," he croaked.

The nurse frowned down at him, as if she were worried about him. "They were here visiting you about twenty minutes ago, don't you remember?"

Twenty minutes? For some reason he thought it had been just a few minutes ago. "Are they still here?"

"I'll check for you, but you have to stay calm," the nurse said firmly. "The doctors spent a lot of time reconstructing the brachial artery in your arm. I can guarantee they won't appreciate having you damage their hard work by trying to get out of bed."

"Just find Rachel and Joey for me," he managed, not bothering to explain that he couldn't move his left arm if he tried.

The nurse left the room and it seemed like a long time before she came back carrying a small IV bag. "I have your antibiotic here," she said as she logged into the computer. "Just give me a few minutes here, okay?"

He did his best to give her the time she needed to scan his wristband and the medication, before she hung it on the IV pump. Only when she finished did he ask. "Rachel and Joey?"

"I'm sorry, but apparently they went home," she said, her tone full of sympathy.

Home? How? As far as he knew Rachel didn't have any money or a vehicle. Had she hitched a ride with someone? Borrowed money? What?

He stared at the four walls surrounding him, feeling totally helpless. He was in no condition to follow Rachel, to make sure she and Joey were still safe. Had the police arrested Errol? He certainly hoped so. No doubt they'd be here soon to get his statement about the events that had transpired outside of Uncle Wally's cabin.

Still, he couldn't believe Rachel and Joey had left without saying goodbye.

Exhaustion weighed heavily on Rachel's shoulders as she and her son made their way back down to the hospital waiting room. She needed to figure out a way to get home, no easy feat since Chicago was about three hours from Madison. A taxi was probably out of the question, which left a bus or a train.

When she asked the woman at the front desk about a train, she shook her head. "Sorry, there's bus service to Chicago, but no train."

Of course there wasn't a train. Why would anything be easy? She was about to ask about borrowing a phone, when the police officer who'd brought her and Joey to the hospital arrived. "Ms. Simon? Could we talk for a few minutes?"

Did she really have a choice? She forced a smile, knowing that her bad mood wasn't Officer McCarthy's fault. "Sure."

"Let's talk in the chapel across the hall," the policeman suggested. "There's more privacy."

She nodded and drew Joey along with her as they crossed over to the chapel. She sank into a wooden pew and gazed at the simple yet beautifully crafted stained glass cross over the mantel. She imagined this room was used by many family members praying for their loved ones to get better.

Unfortunately, Nick didn't want her anywhere near him while he was recovering. He'd rather face his unknown future on his own.

She forced herself to push away her painful thoughts. "What can I do for you?"

"I just want to go through the events one more time," Officer McCarthy explained. "We found the dead body of Gerald Ashton, as you mentioned before. But we still haven't found the man you referred to as Dr. Karl Errol. And I have to tell you, the vehicle that was parked there is gone, too."

She shivered, hoping Karl had taken the car to parts unknown. Although certainly they could trace the car's license plates? Officer McCarthy assured her they were looking for the vehicle. So she took a deep breath and began describing the events of the night before. Midway through, Sean McCarthy interrupted, asking her to start at the beginning.

With a sigh, she went back to the night Joey was kidnapped, explaining what they'd done. The officer's expression was grim by the time she finished. "I'm not sure if that cop of yours deserves a medal or a demotion," he said. "You're lucky things didn't turn out worse."

She thought Nick definitely deserved a medal, but she didn't say anything. "Look, Officer McCarthy, Joey and I need to figure out a way to get back to Chicago."

"I can give you a ride to the bus station, if that helps," he offered.

She smiled wanly and nodded. As much as it went against the grain to ask for handouts, they'd need money for bus tickets. "Would you loan me the money for tickets? I promise I'll pay you back."

There was the slightest hesitation before he nodded. "Sure, no problem."

Relief at having one problem solved was overwhelming. "Thank you so much," she whispered.

Officer McCarthy looked uncomfortable but gave a brief nod. "Okay, let's go then. I'll come back later to get Butler's statement. He's not going anywhere soon, and I'll probably get a more coherent story once he's feeling a little better."

Thinking of Nick made her sad all over again, but she tried to hide her feelings from Joey. They followed Officer McCarthy to where he'd left his car, parked right in front of the hospital in a clear no-parking zone. The traffic around Madison was crazy busy and the ride to the bus station seemed interminable. Staring out the window to calm her frayed nerves, the Christmas decorations reminded her that the holiday was only two days away.

Inside the bus station, Officer McCarthy used his credit card to pay for their tickets, and then he handed them some cash. "Get something for you and the boy to eat," he said roughly. "And I hope you have a merry Christmas."

Tears pricked her eyes at his kindness and she'd already made a note of how much money she owed him. "Thanks again, for everything," she said softly. "And I hope you have a merry Christmas with your family, as well."

He gave both of them a nod before making his way back outside. She sank into one of the hard plastic chairs inside the bus station since the next bus didn't leave until twelve-thirty in the afternoon. Thankfully, just a few hours more and they'd be on their way home.

Waiting was the worst, but finally they boarded the bus and settled into their seats. The bus was busy with what looked like college kids heading home to their families. The ride to Chicago took much longer than she'd anticipated, partially because of the frequent stops and then because of the heavy traffic the closer they came to the city.

While they were stuck in a snarling traffic jam, Rachel realized that she didn't have her house keys. She hadn't been home since the night of Joey's kidnapping. She'd left her mangled car with the keys in it at the scene of the crash as every ounce of energy had been focused on finding her son.

With a groan, she rested her forehead on the cold glass window and realized she'd have to take a taxi to her office to pick up her spare set of keys. Yet another delay before she and Joey would finally get home.

She could hardly wait.

Nick stared at Officer McCarthy in horror. "What do you mean you didn't find Errol? And now my car is missing? Are you telling me he's still out there on the loose?" The monitor above his head sounded an alarm and he took a deep breath, trying to calm his racing heart.

"Yes. That's exactly what I'm telling you. The only body we found was Gerald Ashton's. He died of a gunshot wound to his chest."

Nick momentarily closed his eyes, feeling bad that he'd taken a life. He'd been protecting Rachel and Joey after being wounded himself. But that didn't really make him feel better.

"Where's Rachel? And Joey? We need to keep them safe in case Errol decides to come after them."

"I took them to the bus station, bought them tickets to get home and gave them a little extra cash so they could get something to eat."

"You *what?*" Nick shouted, and this time, he didn't care about the beeping alarms. He tried to throw off the covers and make his way to the side of the bed, but it wasn't easy when his left arm was wrapped up tighter than a mummy. The doctors had explained the numbness was due to some sort of pain block they'd put in, which made him feel even more like an idiot for the way he'd acted toward Rachel.

But nothing was going to stop him from doing the right thing—now.

"Mr. Butler!" his nurse cried as she came running into the room. "What are you doing?"

"It's Detective Butler," he ground out between clenched teeth, trying to ignore the sweat that beaded on his brow. "And I'm getting out of here."

"You can't leave!" The nurse looked appalled and she crossed the room to push him back into bed even as she called out for help.

Frustrated to discover he didn't have the strength of a gnat, he threw a desperate glance at McCarthy. "Help me out, here. Don't you understand? Rachel and Joey are in danger as long as Karl Errol is still on the loose! The guy is working for Global Pharmaceuticals."

"I'm calling your doctor," the nurse threatened, acting as if she hadn't heard a word he said. Or maybe she just didn't care.

"Yeah, you do that," Nick said with a disgusted sigh. "Because I'm pretty sure I have the right to leave against medical advice."

"Only if you can make it out of here without passing out cold," the nurse said tersely, holding his gaze with bold determination.

"Now, just hold on a minute," McCarthy said, holding up his hand and trying to wedge himself between Nick and the nurse. "If you really think Ms. Simon and her son are in danger, I'll help you. No need to act like a lunatic."

Nick couldn't help feeling like a lunatic. He couldn't explain the bad feeling he had about the way Rachel and Joey had left him. Without saying goodbye. Without having Karl Errol in custody. That creep actually had his car!

"Fine," he bit out, knowing that he didn't have the strength to stay seated on the side of his bed for much longer. "What's the plan?"

"How about if I send some backup out to meet Ms. Simon and her son at the Chicago bus depot," McCarthy offered. "They can drive her home, stick around a bit to make sure everything's all right."

It was a start, but not good enough. "We need to get to Chicago, ASAP. I need you to help me get out of here," he said to McCarthy. "I'll need help since I can barely keep myself upright. We need to get to Rachel before Errol does."

"I don't know if that's a good idea," McCarthy hedged.

"I do. Trust me—I'll take full responsibility for my decision." Last year, Jonah had been in a similar situation, leaving the hospital against doctor's orders. And he'd been fine.

Nick had to believe everything would work out fine this time, too.

Dear Lord, please give me the strength I need to keep Rachel and Joey safe.

Rachel held on to Joey's hand tightly as they navigated the crowds at the bus depot. Without luggage, it was easy to push her way through the swarming mass of people to the door, and before long they found their way to the taxi stand. Now that they were back in Chicago, she couldn't wait to get home. But first a quick trip to her office building.

Her desperation must have shown as a taxi came barreling to a stop right in front of her. She thought she heard someone call her name but then figured she was imagining things. She urged Joey in first and climbed in after him.

"Where to?" the cabbie asked in a thick Middle Eastern accent.

"Simon Incorporated," she told him, rattling off the address. He nodded and pulled out into traffic, earning a loud protest from the guy behind him.

She almost closed her eyes, because the taxi drivers in Chicago were maniacs behind the wheel, and she always expected to get in a crash. But somehow, miraculously, they always managed to get to their destinations unscathed.

"Are we home yet?" Joey asked plaintively. She knew he was exhausted, and he'd truly taken everything in stride better than she could have expected.

"Almost. We're going to stop by my office first, so I can pay the taxi driver and get our house keys," she said in a hushed voice, hoping the driver didn't understand

English very well. She didn't think he'd have agreed to take her anywhere knowing that she didn't have anything more than ten dollars in her pocket, courtesy of Officer McCarthy's donation. She intended to get a check in the mail to him first thing in the morning, thanking him again for helping her out.

Joey sighed heavily but didn't whine or complain.

The traffic worked against them again, and she kept a wary eye on the time, hoping they'd get there before the office building shut down for the day. It was almost five o'clock in the evening and already pitch-black outside, except for the brightly lit buildings and the various Christmas decorations, of course.

She chewed her lower lip nervously. Hopefully, even if everyone was gone, the security guards would let her upstairs. Maybe Gerry hadn't had time to completely take over her company. Just the thought of explaining how Gerry had died was enough to overwhelm her.

It was five-fifteen when the taxi driver pulled up in front of her building. "Keep the meter running... I'll be right back."

"No! You pay first!" he protested.

"Look, I promise you I'll be back. We need to get home. I don't have a car."

He stared at her with eyes black as midnight but then he nodded. "If you not back soon, I come after you."

She breathed a tiny sigh of relief. "I will, I promise." Sliding out from the backseat, she waited for Joey to join her and headed inside.

Carrie, the perky receptionist, left promptly at five, but there was a security guard seated in her spot. Being inside the office building after being gone for so long seemed a little strange yet, at the same time, blessedly familiar. "George, how are you? How are the kids?"

"Great, Ms. Simon, just great. What are you doing here so late?"

"I forgot something up in my office. Would you mind letting me use the master key?" She hoped and prayed that Gerry hadn't told everyone to keep her out of the building.

"Sure, no problem." George held out a key. "Just bring it back when you leave."

"I will." She didn't hesitate, but went straight over to the bank of elevators. The doors opened immediately, taking them all the way to the tenth floor without a single stop.

She unlocked the door, noting that the entire office area was completely dark, as if everyone had gone home early. And considering it was nearly Christmas, she understood why. She flipped on lights as she walked down the hall to her office.

Her door stood open, which she thought was a little odd. Edith always kept the door closed and locked when Rachel wasn't there. Then again, the woman had given her notice. For all she knew, Edith hadn't even shown up for work today.

Hovering in the doorway, she reached inside to flip on the lights. She blinked for a moment so that her eyes could adjust before crossing the room to her desk and rummaging for cash and her keys. Joey plopped into her desk chair, spinning from side to side.

She was relieved to find her secret stash of bills was right where she'd left it. She grabbed the money and the spare set of keys.

"I've been waiting for you, Rachel."

The voice came from the hallway, and she swallowed a scream when she jerked her head up to see Karl Errol standing in the shadows. Her heart dropped to her stomach when she realized he'd traded the rifle for a small handgun, which he pointed directly at her. From this distance it would be hard for him to miss.

"Karl!" She faced him in the doorway, making sure to keep Joey behind her, hoping her son would figure out a way to slide down behind the desk. All the while, she kept her eyes locked on the research scientist. She couldn't believe Karl was here. How did he know that she'd stop by on her way home? Or had he planned to wait for her all night, surprising her in the morning? She swallowed hard, wishing she'd asked George to come up with her.

How long did she have to stall here before the cabbie came looking for his money? Or would he simply give up and drive away? She tried not to think the worst. "I'm so glad you're all right. We looked everywhere for you!"

"Yeah, right. You left me there to die, Rachel," he sneered with obvious reproach. "Good thing I still had the distributor cap for the car, hmm?"

"What do you want, Karl?" she asked, fed up with pandering to his ego. "What more could you possibly want from me?"

"I need to finish what I started," he said enigmatically. "I always finish the job."

"Why?" she asked helplessly, tired of the games. "Haven't you caused enough damage? You've ruined my company's reputation, and for what? Love? You don't have the faintest idea what true love is. Josie never would have accepted your love if she knew what you've done."

She couldn't help thinking of Nick. How she'd left

him in the hospital without even giving him a chance to explain what he'd gone through. Maybe he had shut her out, believing the worst about the damage to his arm, but sooner or later, he would have come around. If she'd learned anything about faith, it was that leaning on God's strength could help you through the darkest days. She was suddenly ashamed of her actions. She should have stayed. She should have given him a second chance.

Should have told him how she felt.

Now she could only hope and pray she wasn't too late.

"Do you honestly think that Detective Butler won't figure out that you're the one who killed me?" she continued, since Karl hadn't responded. "He's not stupid, Karl. I promise Nick won't rest until he finds you and makes sure that you spend the rest of your life behind bars."

"I have protection. My boss will protect me."

"Protection? From your boss? William Hanson, the CEO of Global? Or the Mafia?"

The way Karl reacted to William Hanson's name let her know she'd nailed it correctly. For once she didn't mind being wrong about the Mafia connection.

"You think William Hanson cares about you? I'm betting that as soon as you kill me, he'll do whatever it takes to get rid of you."

Karl scowled. "He won't kill me—I helped him out. He's already beaten you to market with a new diabetes drug. One that doesn't cause blood clots."

The thought of Karl purposefully ruining the new medication she'd put out to market made her seethe with anger. Not just because of her company's reputation, but because of the innocent people he'd hurt.

"So why kill me if Global has the new medication out?"

"My boss doesn't like loose ends. And since Ashton couldn't manage to do my dirty work for me, I have no choice but to finish this on my own."

Her heart leaped into her throat when he lifted the gun. "No matter what you do to me, Nick won't stop searching for you. I've already told the police about you, too. You'll never be safe, Karl."

Karl didn't answer; instead, he simply stared at her as if he hadn't heard a word she'd said. She had no way of knowing if she'd even gotten through to him.

She tried not to panic. Facing a crazy man with a gun was much harder when she didn't have Nick's reassuring presence nearby. But she'd left Nick back at the hospital in Madison.

She and Joey were on their own.

SEVENTEEN

Nick dozed during the long ride back to Chicago. Even with Sean McCarthy using flashing red lights and sirens, the trip took longer than he wanted. The doctor back in Madison had been really angry about him leaving, but he couldn't worry about his arm.

Rachel and Joey were far more important.

They swung by Rachel's house, which thankfully wasn't that far from her office building, but the place was locked up tight with no sign of anyone having been there. He told Sean to head over to the office building next, figuring that Rachel probably needed her keys.

When they reached the office complex, Sean parked behind a taxi with the "in service" light on. Nick managed to get out of the passenger seat under his own power, holding his left arm protectively against his body to minimize the pain as much as possible. Now that the numbing agent had worn off, he could feel his arm, but mostly all he felt was pain.

When they walked into the building there was a foreign taxi driver yelling at the security guard behind the desk. Nick couldn't understand half of what the guy was saying, but it became apparent that the taxi driver had brought Rachel and Joey here and wanted his money.

"Pay the man," he told Sean, before turning his attention back to the security guard who wore a name tag with the name George. He didn't know if that was a first name or a last name. "Are Rachel and Joey Simon upstairs in her office?" he asked.

"Yes, they went up about five minutes ago," the security guard said.

"Did anyone else go up either before or after her?" Sean asked, after paying the taxi driver.

"I've only been here about twenty minutes, but no one else went up while I was here." George cast a curious glance between Sean and Nick. "Is something wrong?"

"We don't know for sure," Nick said. "But we're heading up right now to make sure she's all right. If we don't come back down within ten minutes, call the police."

"Maybe I should go with you?" George offered.

"No, you need to stay here," Nick told him. "Make sure no one else goes up, do you understand?"

George nodded. "Got it."

Sean had already made his way over to the one of the six banks of elevators, and he was holding the door, waiting for Nick. He fought a wave of dizziness as he hurried in.

The ride to the tenth floor was quick and when the doors opened, the ding of the elevator seemed exceptionally loud. He hoped no one had overheard it.

"Stay back," Sean warned in a whisper, as he made his way into Rachel's office suite.

Nick had his weapon tucked into the waistband of his jeans but was hampered by the need to hold his left arm still, so he nodded, knowing that he would only be a liability if he didn't give Sean the room he needed.

The moment they opened the glass doors to the office area, Nick heard talking. And from the way Rachel was pleading with someone, he suspected Karl was there.

He couldn't see much with Sean in front of him, but the hint of desperation in her tone wrenched his heart. It was his fault she was here with Joey. If he'd responded differently in the hospital she probably would have stayed.

Especially if he'd had asked her to stay.

Please, Lord, keep Rachel and Joey safe!

Rachel saw something move behind Karl's right shoulder, but she did her best to keep her gaze trained on his so that he wouldn't figure it out.

"Karl, please. Give me the gun. I can tell you're not a cold-blooded killer," she said, stalling for time. She couldn't tell who was creeping up behind Karl, but just knowing she and Joey weren't alone was enough to give her hope and strength.

Besides, she was getting mighty tired of people pointing guns at her.

"Stay back or I'll shoot," Karl threatened, although the gun in his hand wavered just a bit.

"You want money, Karl?" she asked. "Because if that's the case then I'll double their fee if you'll put the gun down. I'll give you enough to change your name and leave town. Think about it—you'll get a fresh start."

Surprisingly, he seemed to consider her offer. But just as he was about to speak, an arm came around from behind and snatched the gun from his grasp.

"What the—" Karl's sentence was cut off when he

was slammed up against the wall, Sean McCarthy's arm planted firmly across his neck.

Rachel sagged against the edge of her desk in relief. She'd never been so happy to see a cop in her life. She didn't know how Sean had gotten here from Madison so fast, but she was thankful just the same.

"Karl Errol, you're under arrest for attempted murder and corporate espionage, and anything else that you've done that I haven't figured out yet," Sean McCarthy said, pulling out his handcuffs and clasping them firmly over Errol's wrists. The way the research scientist sagged against the door convinced her that he'd finally given up.

Thank You, Lord.

"Rachel? Are you and Joey all right?"

She straightened and looked past Sean into the hallway, tempted to pinch herself in the arm to make sure that she wasn't imagining Nick standing there. "Nick? Is that really you?"

After making sure Joey was okay, she found herself staring at Nick, unable to look away. He was propped against the wall, holding his left arm against him, his mouth bracketed with pain.

"Yeah. I had to make sure you and Joey were all right," he said.

She was so glad to see him, even though it was obvious he shouldn't be here. "What were you thinking?" she scolded as she rushed forward to meet him. "You should have stayed in the hospital. What if you lose the circulation in your arm?"

"It's nothing compared to the thought of losing you," he murmured, holding her gaze with his. "I'm sorry I hurt you, Rachel. I didn't mean to. I never should have allowed my faith to waver."

Her heart melted at his words, and she would have engulfed him in a huge hug if not for the fact that Nick looked as if he was hanging on by a thread. His brow was damp with sweat and his face was pale, two indications that he absolutely should not have left the hospital.

"Nick!" Joey cried as he ran forward, putting his arms around Nick's waist and hugging him hard. She caught the wince on Nick's features, but he didn't protest. "You're here!"

"Yeah, I'm here, buddy."

"Are you all better now?" Joey asked, tipping his head back to look up at Nick.

"Not exactly…" Nick said drily.

"Not at all," Rachel interjected with a deep frown. "You need to get back to Madison, Nick. The surgeon told me that the first twenty-four hours are critical. It's barely been twelve hours since surgery and a good portion of that had to be traveling here."

"Maybe you're right," he said, and the fact that he didn't try to argue with her was worrisome.

Before she could say anything more, he let go of Joey and slid down the wall to the floor.

"I told him to stay behind, but did he listen? No, he didn't." Sean's tone held disgust. "I guess we'd better call 911, the only way he's getting out of here is in an ambulance."

"I've already called 911," George said, coming down the hall toward them. "You made me nervous, and when you didn't come down right away, I decided to make the call. Good thing I did. The cops should be here any minute."

"Make sure there's an ambulance, too, would you, George?" she asked. She'd sat down on the floor beside

Nick, holding his head in her lap, unwilling to let him go, even for a minute.

"That surgeon is going to say 'I told you so,'" Sean joked, as he stared down at Nick's prone figure.

"Was worth it," Nick murmured in a voice so soft Rachel was sure she was the only one who could hear him.

"Rest now, Nick," she said, smoothing her fingers down his rough, bristly cheek. "We're safe now...."

There was a lot of commotion when the police arrived and soon after an ambulance crew showed up carrying a gurney.

She thought Nick was out cold, but suddenly his eyes opened and he reached for her hand. "Come with me to the hospital," he said hoarsely.

"I'll meet you there," she promised. "Just do what the doctor says this time, okay?"

Grimacing, he nodded his head. Then she slid out of the way, allowing the paramedics to lift Nick onto the gurney.

And for the second time in less than twenty-four hours, she stood with her arm around Joey, watching as the paramedics wheeled away the man she loved.

After Sean had handed Karl over to the Chicago authorities and she'd once again given her statement to the police, she convinced Sean to take her and Joey home.

Once there, she gave him the money she owed him, even though he kept trying to wave it away.

"Please take the money," she begged. "You've already done so much for me and my son. Please?"

Sean reluctantly took the cash. "Do you want me to drive you to the hospital before I head home?" he asked gruffly.

She hesitated but then shook her head. "No, we can take a cab or the subway. Getting around Chicago is much easier than trying to get around in Madison," she teased.

"Hey, I live out in the boondocks, so this is all new to me," the officer said with a wry grin. "We don't get this kind of big-city crime where I come from."

Her smile faded. "Be glad, Sean. Be very glad."

He slung his arm across her shoulder in a friendly hug. "Don't worry, this was enough excitement to last me quite a while."

After he left, she decided to take a shower before heading back to the hospital. She urged Joey to take one, too.

Freshly scrubbed and wearing clean clothing made her feel like a new person, although it was clear her son was still exhausted. She was tired, too, but she wanted to see Nick in the hospital, one more time, before they came home to sleep.

And even though she knew she could call a babysitter to stay home with Joey, she preferred to keep him with her, despite being certain the danger was finally over.

Besides, she figured Joey would feel better, knowing firsthand that Nick was going to be all right.

When they arrived at Chicago North Hospital, they found Nick was a patient in a regular room rather than being back in the ICU. They walked into his room just as a voice announced through the overhead speaker that visiting hours would be over in fifteen minutes.

"Hey, how are you feeling?" she asked, crossing over to Nick's bed. Joey stood at the foot of Nick's bed, regarding him thoughtfully.

"My ears are blistered from having the doctors yell

at me for fifteen minutes straight, but otherwise I'm good." His expression was more relaxed, and the brackets around his mouth had vanished, which she assumed meant he'd been given some pain medication.

"You look much better," she murmured. "And you deserve to have your ears blistered after that stunt you pulled."

"They wanted to transport me back to Madison General, but I guess the doctor there wasn't too interested in having me back." A hint of a smile played along the corner of his mouth. "Can't say that I blame him."

"How's the circulation in your arm?" she asked, glancing at the limb that was currently propped up on two pillows.

He moved his fingers and shrugged his right shoulder. "Pretty good, I guess. I can move my hand a bit more. No harm done, at least according to the surgeon here. I think that's one of the reasons he didn't push the issue of sending me back. Apparently, surgeons don't like to pick up other surgeon's leftovers."

She laughed, extremely relieved to hear that Nick wasn't any worse for wear.

"How long will you have to stay in the hospital, Nick?" Joey asked anxiously.

"Shouldn't be more than a day or two," Nick responded.

Joey's expression clouded. "But that means you'll be in here over Christmas."

"That's okay," Nick said quickly. "I don't mind."

There was another overhead announcement instructing all visitors to leave the building, so Rachel reached over and took Nick's good hand in hers, squeezing gently.

"We'd better get home. I promised Joey that he would be able to sleep in his own bed tonight."

"All right." Nick's eyes were at half-mast and she suspected that he'd be asleep before they made it out the front door.

"See you tomorrow," she promised, releasing his hand. "Come on, Joey. Let's go home."

"Bye, Nick." Joey flashed a grin before following her out of the room.

As they left the hospital to flag down a cab, she decided that since Nick was going to be in the hospital for Christmas, they would need to bring Christmas to him.

Nick hated being stuck in the hospital. The only bright spot in his day was that his arm seemed to be doing better. The doctors had taken down the bulky dressing to examine the incision and hadn't put it back on, making him feel ten pounds lighter.

"Looks better than it should," the surgeon told him grudgingly. "Considering you went several hours without your blood-thinning medicine, you're extremely lucky."

"I'm blessed," Nick corrected with a grin. "Truly blessed." He'd slept on and off during the night, waking up between pain medication doses, but he'd had plenty of time to think about what had happened up at the cabin. How much he'd wanted to live, when he'd managed to convince himself that he'd be happy for God to call him home. After missing his wife and daughter for so long, he realized that God meant for him to move on with his life. He wasn't sure what he'd done to deserve a second chance, but he couldn't deny the way Rachel and Joey had wiggled their way into his heart.

Now, if he could only find a way to convince Rachel to take a chance on him.

Outside his window, he noticed snow was beginning to fall. He wondered if that change in the weather was part of the reason that Rachel and Joey hadn't come in to visit him yet.

He couldn't bear to think that maybe they wouldn't show at all. Rachel had said she'd see him tomorrow. Surely she wouldn't have said that if she hadn't meant it.

But when the lunch hour came and went he began to lose hope. He exercised his fingers the way he was supposed to and wondered if he could convince Jonah or someone from the precinct to bust him out of here again.

If she didn't show up soon, he'd have no choice but to go to her.

"Knock-knock," a voice said from the doorway. Relief flooded him when he realized that Rachel and Joey had arrived.

"Come in," he called, struggling to sit farther up in his bed. He was tired of looking and feeling like an invalid.

The first thing he saw was a small pine tree about three feet tall covering most of Joey's face. His smile widened when he saw Rachel coming in behind the boy, lugging a large bag.

"Merry Christmas," she said as Joey set the small pine tree on the bedside table.

"Merry Christmas," he responded, unable to suppress his broad grin. It was after all, Christmas Eve.

"Close your eyes," she said, as she plunked the bag down on the guest chair. "We'll tell you when you can open them again."

He'd rather have gazed at Rachel all day but did as she requested. He could hear Joey giggling amidst the sounds of paper rustling. With his eyes closed, he could smell the refreshing scent of pine from the small tree.

It seemed like forever, but finally the rustling and the giggling stopped. "You can open your eyes now, Nick," Joey said excitedly.

He opened his eyes and gasped in surprise at the way they'd transformed his room. Not only was the tiny tree decorated with miniature lights, but there was a small nativity scene set out on display along with several strands of garland strung festively around the whiteboard on the wall.

"Beautiful," he murmured, and he wasn't talking about the Christmas decorations.

Rachel looked lovely, no doubt in part because she'd finally gotten a decent night's sleep. Her smile was shy and it took him a minute to realize she had what looked to be a brand-new Bible in her hands.

"I hope you don't mind, but I thought we could read the Christmas story again tonight," she said. "Or we could read the Psalms since I know you mentioned they're your favorite. I read Psalm 23 this morning and I can certainly understand why you like them so much. I feel blessed to have found God. And I owe it all to you."

His throat was tight with pent up emotion and he had to clear it before he could speak. "I'd like that," he managed, keeping his gaze centered on her. "Very much."

"I, um, didn't know how to get in touch with your family, so they don't know that you've been injured…."

"Rachel, come here," he said, holding out his good hand.

She approached him and put her hand in his. He was conscious of Joey watching them curiously so he couldn't say exactly what he wanted, but she needed to know the truth. "I'm happy just having you and Joey here, and I don't need anyone else."

Her gaze was uncertain. "Are you sure? Christmas is a time for families."

"I'm sure." He lifted her hand and kissed it, wishing that Joey wasn't there so he could kiss her properly. "You and Joey are all the family I need."

She blushed but didn't pull her hand away. "I'm glad," she murmured.

And it wasn't until much later, when Joey had fallen asleep in the chair, that he was able to tell Rachel how he felt.

"I'm falling in love with you, Rachel," he said softly.

She sucked in a quick breath. "How can you be so sure?"

He tried to think of a way to put his feelings into words. "I thought I was happy, living my life alone, doing my best to put the bad guys behind bars. But when you and Joey came into my life, I realized that I never felt as alive as I did with the both of you."

Her eyes glistened with tears. "I've been so afraid to get involved with anyone after Anthony. I told myself that I was protecting Joey, but I think in reality, I was protecting myself."

He took her hand and drew her closer. "Rachel, give me a chance to show you how much I love you. There's no rush, you can take all the time you need, if you'll just give me a chance."

"All right," she whispered.

"Is that a yes?" Nick asked, needing to hear her say the words.

She smiled and leaned over to kiss him, which was perfect since he wasn't able to get up and cross over to her thanks to the IV pumps keeping him tied to the bed. "That's a big yes, Nick. Because I've fallen in love with you, too."

He grinned, wishing she'd kiss him again, hardly able to believe his good fortune. Or rather, maybe he could.

For God had known the path he should take, all along.

EPILOGUE

Three months later...

Nick paused outside Rachel's doorway, patting the pocket that held the ring he'd purchased for her as he tried to quell his nerves.

He'd gone back to work last week, although he was still on desk duty thanks to his arm injury. He was grateful that each week his arm strength seemed to get a little better, so he didn't complain. Turns out there really wasn't any Mafia connection to Global Pharmaceuticals. Just a greedy CEO who'd hated Rachel's father. When Karl had implicated him in the espionage related to the defective diabetes drug, he'd crumpled like a house of cards.

Rachel and Joey's nightmare was truly over.

As glad as Nick was to know they were safe, getting back into the normal routine of doing investigations had cut into the time he'd been able to spend with Rachel and Joey.

Especially Rachel.

Last night, he'd picked up Joey after his last basketball game and had asked the boy's permission to marry his mom. Joey had been thrilled and Nick could only hope that the youngster had managed to keep his secret.

He pushed the doorbell, listening to the chimes echo through the house. He was pleasantly surprised when Rachel opened the door. "Hi, Nick."

"Hi, Rachel." He drew her in for a long kiss. "I've missed you," he murmured, gazing down at her upturned face.

"I missed you, too," she said with a smile. "Are you ready to go?"

"Sure. Is, uh, Joey around?"

"Yes, he's decided to have a friend sleep over tonight. Suzy, the babysitter, doesn't seem to mind."

Nick grinned. "Just give me a minute to say hello."

"All right," she agreed, standing back so he could come inside. The boys were sprawled in front of the television in the living room, playing some sort of basketball video game. Suzy was sitting with earbuds in place, listening to music.

"Hey, Joey, how are you?" Nick greeted him.

"Pause the game," Joey said to his friend, as he jumped off the sofa. "Hi, Nick!"

Nick bent his head down to Joey's. "Did you keep our secret?" he asked.

Joey's eyes gleamed as he nodded. "Yep."

"Good." He relaxed a bit. "Thanks, buddy. Now try not to interrupt us at dinner, okay?"

Joey rolled his eyes. "Why would I? Suzy is here. Besides, me and Ben are going to be busy playing our game, anyway."

"All right, see you later, then."

"Suzy, text me if you need anything," Rachel called out as he returned to her.

"Don't worry, we'll be fine," Suzy responded.

Nick drove Rachel to the small Italian restaurant where he'd reserved a private table in the corner. "How was work today?" he asked.

"The lawsuit has been settled and the new researchers seem to be doing all right so far." Rachel's smile dimmed. "The company will be on shaky financial ground for a while, but we'll make it."

"I know you will," Nick replied, admiring her determination. He pulled into the parking lot and handed his keys to the valet service before escorting Rachel inside.

"My favorite restaurant." Rachel beamed as they were seated. "I already know what I'm having."

"You should, since you have the menu memorized." He waited until the server had taken their order before reaching across the table to take her hand. "Rachel, these past few months with you have been wonderful."

She smiled and squeezed his hand. "For me, too, Nick."

The timing seemed right, so he took a deep breath and rose to his feet. Two steps brought him to Rachel's side and when he went down on one knee, her eyes rounded and her mouth formed a small O.

"Nick?" she whispered, looking a bit like she was in shock.

He smiled gently as he pulled the ring box out of his pocket and opened it. "Rachel, Joey has already given me his blessing. He told me he'd be thrilled to have me as his dad. So now it's up to you."

Her eyes filled with tears and for a moment he almost panicked, until he saw the tremulous smile bloom across her face. "I love you, Rachel. Will you please marry me?"

She barely looked at the ring, instead holding his gaze

with hers. "Yes, Nick. I'd love nothing more than to be your wife. And to have you be Joey's father. Of course, I'll marry you."

Yes! He did a mental fist pump but managed to draw her to her feet so that he could kiss her. He held her tight, wishing he never had to let her go.

The entire restaurant erupted into a round of applause.

He had to chuckle as he pulled away. "I love you, Rachel. And I promise to make you happy," he vowed.

She tilted her head to the side, her gaze solemn. "I love you, Nick, and I promise to make you happy, too."

He didn't doubt the sincerity in her tone for a moment and knew that he was doubly blessed to have found true love for the second time.

* * * * *

Dear Reader,

You may remember Detective Nick Butler from my story *Undercover Cowboy*. Once I finished writing Logan and Kate's romance, I decided I couldn't leave poor Nick hanging out there without a story of his own.

Rachel Simon is the CEO of Simon Inc., but when her nine-year-old son, Joey, is kidnapped right from under her nose, she's willing to give up everything she owns to get him back safely. Especially when she fears the Mafia might be the mastermind behind the kidnapping.

Detective Nick Butler lost his own wife and young daughter several years ago, so he understands the angst Rachel is going through. But while he's willing to do whatever is necessary to help her get Joey back, he's determined not to let anyone replace his wife and daughter in his heart.

Working together to stay safe, Rachel and Nick both slowly learn to trust each other. Can they also open their hearts and their minds to the possibility of love?

I hope you enjoy reading Rachel and Nick's story. I'm always thrilled and honored to hear from my readers and I can be reached through my website at *www.laurascottbooks.com*.

Yours in faith,

Laura Scott

IDENTITY CRISIS

All the prophets testify about Him,
that everyone who believes in Him
receives forgiveness of sins through His name.
—*Acts* 10:43

This book is dedicated to my wonderful in-laws,
Ted and Pat Iding, who welcomed me into their family
twenty-seven years ago and have loved me
like a daughter. Thanks for always being there.

ONE

Alyssa Roth pulled the hood of her sweatshirt up to cover her newly cropped blond hair as she cautiously approached her town house. She couldn't imagine why her twin sister might have come to her place, but she'd searched all Mallory's usual spots over the past few hours, without success. She'd called and left messages at Mallory's condo and on her cell. She was feeling desperate. She had to find her twin and warn her of the danger.

The hour was close to midnight, so there weren't many people out and about, but that didn't stop her from casting a worried glance over her shoulder. She'd taken a bus from a park-and-ride close to the motel and walked the rest of the way. Using her key, she opened the door and quickly crossed the threshold, locking the door behind her.

The interior was dark so if Mallory was there, she must be sleeping. She pulled a small penlight out of her pocket, unwilling to risk the overhead lights that would effectively broadcast her presence to anyone who might be watching.

Holding the light low at her side, she walked through the kitchen into the living room. She caught an unexpected flash of glitter, and relief washed over her as she realized Mallory's hair clip was on the table beside the sofa.

"Mallory," she whispered loudly as she headed down the hall toward her bedroom. "Wake up. You can't stay here! I'm in danger. I'm being followed and believe it or not, a cop actually tried to kill me!"

There was no response, and when she pushed open the door to her bedroom, her burst of hope faded when she saw the bed was empty. She took two steps into the room before she noticed the dark puddle staining the floor. She stared at it, slowly realizing it was blood.

Too much blood.

Dread sucked the oxygen from her lungs and she stumbled backward, hitting the door frame hard in her effort to get away. What had happened here? Every instinct she possessed screamed at her to run, but she forced herself to stay long enough to sweep her light over the room, half-afraid she'd find Mallory's body. She even went as far as to check the closet and under the bed. Nothing. The only item out of place was a bright yellow blouse, lying crumpled in the far corner, darkly stained with blood.

The hair clip and yellow blouse proved Mallory had been here recently. Alyssa swayed. Nausea threatened to erupt from her stomach in a violent heave. As a nurse, she knew there was too much blood to believe Mallory had escaped unscathed. She stared at the yellow blouse, a sinking realization making her knees weak.

The blouse wasn't Mallory's. It was the blouse she'd bought for herself last week. Her blouse. Her town house. Both full of blood.

She sagged against the door for support as her mind whirled with possibilities. The night before, Councilman

Schaefer had gripped her hand and whispered that he'd been stabbed by a hired thug working for Hugh Jefferson. Stunned, she'd gone straight to the authorities, but Officer Crane had brushed aside her concern.

She thought his response was odd, but one minute they were preparing Schaefer for surgery, the next he was dead. Later that night, after her shift at the hospital, a dark blue van tried to run her car off the road and she'd caught a glimpse of Officer Crane's ruddy face before she managed to avoid the crash.

Fearing for her life, she hadn't gone home. She'd checked into a run-down motel and spent the next twelve hours changing her appearance so she looked like Mallory, buying tight clothing and a gaudy purse. She went to the DMV for a new ID and obtained a fake tattoo above her collarbone to match her twin's.

Now she realized her efforts were in vain. She couldn't tear her gaze from the yellow blouse, feeling sick as she realized what must have transpired. Mallory probably had another fight with her ex and had come here to find Alyssa for support. Only, Crane or Jefferson must have been watching her town house and killed Mallory by mistake.

Alyssa was the one who knew how Jefferson had killed Schaefer. She was the one Crane had tried to run off the road. She was the one they wanted to silence.

Not Mallory.

Her fault. Her stomach twisted and she shoved a fist in her mouth to silence the scream building in her chest. This was all her fault. Mallory was the only family she had left in the world. And now her twin was gone. Likely dead. Brutally murdered.

Bands of self-reproach tightened around her throat,

squeezing tight. Sheer desperation had forced her to break her cardinal rule by borrowing Mallory's identity. But she shouldn't have rested until she found a way to warn Mallory.

Now it was too late.

Dear Lord, forgive me. Please forgive me!

A shrill whine of police sirens split the night air. Guilt surrendered to fear. She didn't know who had called the police, possibly a neighbor. Had they heard Mallory's scream? She didn't want to think about how her twin must have struggled, fighting for her life. With an effort, she focused on the present. She had to get out of there. Now. She couldn't trust anyone. Especially not the police.

Run! Run! One last glance over her shoulder at the blood-stained blouse ripped her heart in two. She didn't want to leave. But nothing good would come of staying here. She imagined if Mallory was here, her sister would be shouting at her to run. *Don't let them find you, Alyssa. Go! Run!*

Tears streamed down her face, blurring her vision. Galvanized by self-preservation, Alyssa clicked off the penlight and ran down the hall, through the open kitchen and living area, pausing only long enough to snatch the glittery hair clip from the table, stuffing it in her purse as she headed to the front door. Her hand clutched the doorknob. She paused, her heart thundering in her chest. The sirens grew louder. Closer. Too close. The back door?

Spinning on her heel, she retraced her steps, crossing the room toward the kitchen door. She stumbled against the table, unable to see. She swiped at her tears, finally finding the door. Sirens continued to echo outside. Did the police know she was here? Was Officer Crane right now trying to find her?

She left the town house, sprinting into the darkness. The windows in her neighbor's houses were dark—no one was up this late. So who'd called the police? Frantic, she stopped between buildings, trying to think. Indecision held her captive. Finally she ran to the right, through the darkness of her neighbor's backyard.

She ran as fast as she dared. Her heart thundered in her ears. Panic swelled, choking her. The need to move quietly battled a savage desperation to put as much distance between her and the bloody town house as possible.

Don't stop. Don't let them find you. Run!

Where should she go? What should she do? Whom should she trust?

Gage. She needed to find Gage. Her ex-fiancé hadn't believed her when she'd claimed Hugh Jefferson was dangerous. She didn't know why Jefferson had killed Schaefer, but she was convinced everything was related to the hotly contested condos Gage had been hired to build. After Schaefer's claims, she'd called Gage, warned him to stay away from Hugh Jefferson but he'd waved off her concerns. Surely Gage would believe her now. Besides, whom else could she trust?

No one. Only Gage.

She'd broken off their engagement because of Gage's lackluster faith and his overprotective ways. But right now, she longed for his protection, to feel the strength of his arms around her. To bury her face in the safe haven of his chest.

Her breath scissored from her lungs as she ran through alley after alley, backyard after backyard. Shadows in the normally innocuous Milwaukee suburb loomed ominously. She ducked beneath a low-hanging tree branch, its green leaves rustling in the summer night. The sirens went abruptly and eerily silent. Had they arrived at her town house? Did they discover they'd killed the wrong twin? Identical twins didn't have the same fingerprints, so it wouldn't be long before they discovered the truth. Were they out searching for her now? She was too scared to turn around and look.

Dear Lord, help me! Guide me! Keep me safe!

Her breath burned in her chest, threatening to give out for good. She ran for what seemed like forever, but what was probably only thirty to forty minutes. She was in a neighborhood she didn't recognize, but she was too afraid to slow down. The ground beneath her feet abruptly sloped downward. She missed a step. Her ankle twisted sharply under her weight. Pain knifed up her leg. She gasped and fell hard.

The world somersaulted as she rolled down the steep hill, momentum carrying her faster and faster until she smacked bottom. Her skull met the concrete sidewalk with a hard crack. Fireworks of pain exploded in her head.

A velvet shroud of darkness surrounded her.

"Alyssa? Are you there? Pick up the phone!" Gage Drummond scowled as he paused, then added in a calmer tone, "Alyssa, please, *please* call me as soon as you get this message." He flipped the phone shut, hating the feeling of helplessness.

Where was she? The hospital had called him to pick up Mallory because they couldn't reach Alyssa. One of Alyssa's coworkers had assumed he and Alyssa were still engaged and instead of correcting her, he'd agreed to come and get Mallory, hoping to get back into Alyssa's good graces.

Unfortunately, his good deed backfired, because he couldn't get in touch with Alyssa, either. He slipped his phone into his pocket and propped one shoulder against the dingy waiting room wall of Trinity Medical Center's emergency department.

Exhaustion weighed his eyelids. He considered borrowing a cup of the E.D.'s special coma coffee reserved for the graveyard shift. Strong enough to bring you out of a coma, or so Alyssa had claimed.

The memory hurt. He dug his thumbs into his eye sockets in an attempt to ease the pain. Bitter failure coated his tongue. He knew it was his fault she'd left him. But he didn't know how to fix their broken relationship.

Heaving a deep sigh, he opened his eyes and glanced around the waiting room. Surprisingly quiet for a Friday night, or rather early Saturday morning. A homeless man rocked in the corner, keeping a tight hold on his paper sack. One kid within a group of three—all looking like candidates for a Milwaukee gang with spiked hair dyed garish colors and rows of heavy silver chains encircling their necks—held a bloody bandage over his arm. An elderly woman coughed into a tissue and huddled in her seat, as far from the gang wannabes as she could get.

Gage ground his teeth together, detesting the idea of Alyssa working in this place every day. Shortly after she'd agreed to marry him, a junkie strung out on drugs had swung at her, knocking her to the ground and nearly breaking her jaw. He'd been appalled and angry—but even then, she'd refused to quit. Despite some serious arm-twisting on his part. He'd wanted her to stay home, to be safe. Or at the very least, to find a different type of nursing job. What was wrong with working in a nice clinic somewhere? His construction company was doing well enough that he could support both of them, but she wouldn't even discuss the possibility. She'd claimed she liked her job, even the part that required her to care for patients who threatened to harm her.

Gage willed the painful memories away. He was here because he needed to find a way to win Alyssa back. Getting up at two-thirty in the morning and picking up Mallory after her accident should win him some extra credit points, right?

"Gage?" Jennifer, the nurse who'd thought he and Alyssa were still engaged, poked her head into the waiting room. "You can see Mallory now."

Relieved to put the depressing sight of the waiting room behind him, he straightened and followed Jennifer into the arena, an open area surrounded by cubicles. His steel-toed construction boots clunked loudly against the shiny linoleum floor. A sweeping glance at the various employees clustered around the center workstation made him wonder if any of them knew where Alyssa might be. He frowned. He'd dialed her town house at least twenty times since the hospital called. Why hadn't she answered?

Another man? Gage stumbled, managing to catch himself even though his gut twisted painfully. Logically, he knew Alyssa's personal life wasn't any of his business, since she'd broken off their engagement two months ago. A spear of pain stabbed his heart. When she'd given him the ring back, Alyssa's reasons were that he was too overprotective and that he didn't have a close relationship with God. He couldn't figure out what she'd meant. After all, he'd done everything she'd asked of him.

He went to church with her, hadn't he? And he'd joined her Bible study group. It wasn't his fault that he had to work late, missing most of the sessions. He owned his own business and couldn't just switch shifts to get off work the way she did.

After she'd walked out, he'd wondered if maybe the basic truth was simply that Alyssa hadn't loved him. A possibility that had hurt, more than he'd ever imagined it could.

He scowled, pushing the pain aside, and walked into the doorway of the small cubicle. His gaze rested on his ex-fiancée's twin sister. He didn't particularly care for Mallory. She was so completely different from Alyssa. But since she was Alyssa's sister, he made an effort.

"Hey, Mallory," he greeted her with forced politeness. "What happened? How are you feeling?"

She opened her eyes and turned her head toward him. A square white bandage partially covered a large abrasion on her forehead. Gage sucked in a quick breath; the physical resemblance shouldn't have caught him off guard, but it did. Mallory's blond hair was shoulder length and wavy, whereas Alyssa wore hers much longer and straight. Blue eyes, identical to Alyssa's, stared suspiciously into his.

He'd subtly avoided his fiancée's twin because he hadn't appreciated the way Mallory had flirted with him before they'd gotten engaged. Alyssa had brushed it off as Mallory's way of protecting her twin, making sure he would be true to Alyssa, but he didn't buy that theory. He suspected Mallory either wanted to get rid of him, because she was jealous of his relationship with Alyssa, or that she'd wanted to steal him away for herself.

He could have saved her the trouble, because despite their broken engagement, his heart belonged to Alyssa.

Mallory was completely different from Alyssa in too

many ways to count. Alyssa upheld her Christian beliefs in everything she said and did, including her stubborn dedication to her career as a trauma nurse. Mallory, on the other hand, was outgoing, known to be the life of the party and an outrageous flirt.

Both women were beautiful on the outside, but in his opinion, only Alyssa had the same beauty deep within. Mallory's personality held a hard edge, whereas Alyssa's was softly inviting.

He missed Alyssa. Desperately. He tried not to dwell on the past, but it wasn't easy. Mallory wordlessly glared at him with distinct annoyance. The corner of her hospital gown slipped off to the side, providing him a distasteful glimpse of the rose and dagger tattoo she wore just below her collarbone.

He quickly averted his gaze, wishing he could just leave. But his job was to get Mallory home. Surely he could manage something so simple.

"Are you ready?" he asked with forced brightness. "I think you're about to be released, so let's bust out of here." There was no sign of the nurse, Jennifer. Where had she gone? To get the discharge paperwork, he hoped. Reluctantly, he tucked his hands in the back pockets of his jeans as he slowly approached Mallory's bedside.

She bolted upright like a shot, bringing up a hand as if to keep him at bay. "Hold it! Who are you? You don't work here." Her suspicious gaze sliced him. "Get out!"

Get out? Was she kidding? He ignored the tiny hairs on the back of his neck that rose in alarm. "Yeah. Very funny."

"This isn't one bit funny." She tugged her gown higher over her chest but thrust her chin in the direction of the door. "I told you to get out."

Gage held out his hands in mock surrender. "You're upset about being stuck with me? Well, too bad. They called me because you have a concussion and can't drive. If I leave, how are you going to get home?"

For a long moment she stared at him, as if he were an alien creature she needed to dissect with X-ray vision. "Home?"

"Yes. Home." He sighed, desperately seeking patience. "To your fancy downtown condo. The sooner I can drop you off, the sooner you'll be rid of me." And then his good deed for the day would be finished.

She reached up with one hand and massaged her temple. "I can't— Let's try this again." Dropping her hand, she leveled a look at him full of uncertainty. "Who are you?"

He stared at her in suspicious shock. Was this some sort of weird game? If so, he wasn't in the mood. He'd already spent his entire evening solving problems at three of his construction sites and had gotten less than four hours of sleep. No way was he doing this.

"Fine. You don't want me to take you home? Then I'm outta here." He spun on his heel but Jennifer walked into the room, blocking his escape route.

"Mallory?" The nurse glanced past him but didn't move from the door. "Dr. Anderson is writing your discharge note as we speak. Would you like to get dressed?"

"No. I want to know what's going on." The tone of her voice held a note of desperation. "Who is this guy? My head hurts. You're telling me to go home, but where is home? Why can't I remember anything?"

Dumbfounded, Gage swiveled toward her. Mallory's confused-yet-defiant gaze met his without an ounce of recognition. Doubt assailed him. Could she honestly be telling the truth?

The nurse was taken aback by Mallory's questions, too. "Since when can't you remember? You didn't say anything when Dr. Anderson examined you."

Mallory massaged her temple again, wincing beneath the pressure of her fingers. "I can't think straight with this headache." She frowned, picking at one corner of the blanket covering her. "It wasn't until this guy mentioned going home that I realized I couldn't remember."

Gage sighed and dropped heavily into a chair beside her bed. Thoughts of returning home for sleep anytime soon faded faster than an early-morning mist. What was going on? Was it possible Mallory really couldn't remember anything?

Jennifer clearly thought so. "I better find Dr. Anderson."

Unfortunately, the doctor didn't have any more advice to give them. He examined Mallory again, asking a barrage of questions. She knew which year it was and the president of the United States, but not anything personal about herself.

"What's your address?"

"I don't know." Mallory closed her eyes in frustration. Knuckles white, her fists clenched the sheets. She sucked in a loud breath. "I don't understand. What is wrong with me? How can I forget my address?"

"Do you remember any members of your family?" the doctor persisted.

"No." She lifted her shoulder in a shrug. "But I could be an only child."

Gage nearly laughed until he realized she was serious. An only child? Mallory and Alyssa were close, despite their completely different personalities. How could she forget her twin sister?

"Hmm." The doctor frowned and tabbed through the computer screens, reviewing parts of Mallory's electronic medical chart. "There aren't many details regarding your accident. You were found lying on a concrete sidewalk by a neighbor who was coming home after work. Your purse contained some cash and an ID, so we don't really believe this was a mugging. And certainly nothing to indicate a cause for amnesia."

"What do you mean nothing to indicate a cause for her amnesia?" Gage straightened—his interest piqued, in spite of himself.

The doctor shrugged. "Retrograde amnesia is often the result of a traumatic event combined with a head injury. Mallory has some short-term memory still intact, which even more strongly indicates a traumatic psychological event. However, without knowing what the source of the potential trauma could be, there really isn't anything we can do. We've already performed a CT scan of her head and didn't find any bleeding. When her brain can handle her memory, I'm sure it will return."

Gage rubbed a hand across the back of his neck. "So now what? Does she need to stay here? Get more tests?"

"No, that's not necessary. We've ruled out a head bleed. More tests aren't going to give any input into the source of her amnesia. I'd recommend she be released home, with instructions to follow up with her primary-care doctor in a week. But she really shouldn't be left alone. At least, not until her memory begins to return."

"I'm sure her sister will keep her company." Gage sighed again. Once he managed to find her.

He hoped, prayed, Alyssa hadn't found someone new.

Someone from her church, who went to every single Bible study group meeting no matter what. Someone who may have already replaced him in her heart.

"Good. We'll finish that discharge paperwork."

Gage fell silent after the doctor left the room. He was surprised to find he felt sorry for Mallory. In her current, injured state, he found her less irritating. Although the situation frustrated him to no end. Where was Alyssa?

"A sister? I have a sister?"

He lifted his gaze to meet her abruptly hopeful one. His annoyance faded a bit. "Yeah. Your parents are gone, but you do have a sister. Alyssa is your twin and she's an amazing person."

Mallory's gaze turned curious. "Wow. Sounds like you care about her."

"Yes, I do. Very much," he answered honestly.

"Alyssa." She repeated the name, wrinkling her forehead in concentration. "It's so *wrong* not to remember a twin sister. But the name seems right. Mallory and Alyssa. We're close?"

"Yes, you're close," Gage admitted, because it was true. Despite their differences, the twins always stood by each other no matter what.

"Where is she?" Mallory looked perplexed. "If we're close, why isn't she here?"

"Good question." He reached for his cell phone and redialed. After several long rings there was no answer. He didn't bother leaving another message. "We'll have to stop over there tomorrow. For now, we'll go back to your place. I'll sleep on the sofa."

"The sofa?" Her blue eyes, so much like Alyssa's, widened in horror. "I'd rather you slept in your car. What part of this don't you understand? I don't know you!"

Her barely restrained annoyance gave more credence to her story than anything else could have. She looked at him as if she detested the sight of him. And maybe she did. He couldn't figure Mallory out. Had never really wanted to.

With a frown, Gage stood. Mallory was more tolerable with amnesia, but he still longed to drop her off as soon as possible. Unfortunately, he was stuck with her until he could find her twin.

So where on earth was Alyssa?

TWO

Even after the hospital staff finally left her alone, she couldn't relax. Her pulse skipped erratically in her chest. Panic clawed up and over her back. Why couldn't she remember?

She fought for control against the invisible demons that snarled in her mind, holding her memory hostage. Logic told her she was in the hospital, but nothing looked familiar. The room was little more than a cubicle, three walls but no real door, just a privacy curtain drawn across the opening. She clutched the blanket tighter. She felt exposed. The flimsy curtain wouldn't protect her. Anyone could come in at any time. *Anyone.*

Like the tall, ruggedly handsome stranger waiting to take her home.

Run! Run! The urge to flee merged with panic. Something was wrong. Very, very, wrong. Certainty seeped into her bones, injecting her with the strength to move. She scrambled from the bed, wincing as her swollen and sprained ankle zinged when her foot hit the floor, and reached for her clothes. Maybe she didn't feel entirely safe around the large, sandy-haired man with the square jaw and golden-brown eyes, but she wasn't afraid of him, either. She grasped the slight distinction eagerly.

Her mind felt as if she were swimming through fog with no shore in sight. She pulled on her jeans, pausing when she noticed two small dark stains. Dried blood? From her head? She put a hand to the bruise above her forehead. No. Her throat closed and she gagged. From someone else. She wildly kicked the jeans off, chest heaving from the effort, pain searing her ankle. The denim landed halfway across the room. Frantic, she rifled through the linens on the cart next to the bed. What could she wear? Scrubs maybe?

"Are you ready?" The deep male voice from the other side of the curtain startled her. She stumbled against the bed, clumsily covering herself with the blanket from the bed.

"No! Stay out!" She stayed where she was until convinced he wasn't coming in. Closing her eyes, she took several deep breaths, fighting a wave of dizziness. *Come on, get a grip.* Steeling her resolve, she forced herself to limp across the room to fetch the dreaded clothes. With an effort she donned the midriff-baring T-shirt and hip-hugging jeans.

The name Mallory seemed right but the clothes felt foreign. Wearing such tightly fitting jeans and T-shirt was embarrassing. Why did she wear them? Didn't she care if others stared? Mallory gave her head a shake, and then winced as the pickax hammering in her head intensified.

This wasn't the time to worry about her clothes. Focus. She needed to focus. Urgency propelled her forward. With a suppressed shiver she pulled on the lightweight denim jacket. The bottom of the jacket barely met the waistband on her jeans. She tugged on it, as if she could will it longer, and then gave up. Close enough.

She picked up the huge, gaudy purse, slung it over her shoulder and yanked the curtain aside with a snap. "I'm ready. Let's go."

His gaze raked over her and she fought the urge to tug once more on the short hem of her T-shirt. His amber eyes held no clue to his thoughts. "Great."

He led the way through the emergency room, keeping his pace slow so she could keep up with her bum ankle. She swept a glance over the occupants of the waiting room, her attention snagged by a hacking cough. Despite her desire to leave as quickly as possible, her steps slowed to a stop.

An elderly woman sat huddled in a corner, her lips as blue as her hair. Mallory abruptly changed course, heading toward the woman, who held a crumpled, blood-stained tissue in the palm of her hand. The poor woman looked as if she was ready to take her last breath.

"Get a doctor over here, now!" Mallory called out to a passing nurse. "This woman's on the verge of respiratory arrest."

The harried nurse sputtered an argument but then noticed the same bluish tinge to the woman's lips that had drawn Mallory's attention. "I'll get an oxygen tank."

Seconds later, the nurse hurried over wheeling an oxygen tank. She cranked up the dial and placed an oxygen mask over the elderly woman's face. "Take a deep breath, Mrs. Sullivan. We're going to get you into a room right now." The nurse touched a button on a device hanging from a lanyard around her neck that must have functioned like some sort of intercom. "Steve, I need a wheelchair brought into the waiting room, stat."

Mallory watched as one of the orderlies brought over a wheelchair. Soon, the elderly woman was escorted back. Satisfied, she turned back toward the entrance.

Only to find the tall stranger staring at her in shocked surprise. "What was that about?"

"What do you mean?"

"How did you know she was going into respiratory arrest?" His gaze was suspicious and faintly accusing.

Good question. How had she known? "I'm not sure."

He stared at her again, seemingly at a loss for words. She couldn't understand his reaction, especially when he abruptly turned and continued walking through the door.

She quickened her gimpy pace, following him through the doors to the parking lot. "Wait! I can't move that fast!"

He spun around and came back toward her, his face pulled into a grimace. "Sorry," he muttered, although somehow she suspected that deep down he really wasn't.

Mallory didn't know why she annoyed him, but worse, she couldn't remember his name. Had he even told her? She couldn't remember. Her head hurt so badly she could barely concentrate.

And suddenly, the nearly invisible thread of control snapped. "Look, Mr. Whatever-Your-Name is, I don't know what your problem is and I don't care. Have you forgotten your promise to take me home? Or are you going to leave me stranded here without a ride?"

"I said I'm sorry. I shouldn't have snapped at you like that." He scrubbed a hand over his face, and she couldn't help noticing the deep grooves of fatigue bracketing the sides of his mouth. Maybe it wasn't personal. Maybe he was just tired. "Don't worry, I won't leave you stranded."

He seemed to be making an effort to remain calm,

adjusting his stride to meet hers, as they headed across the parking lot. He opened the door of a pickup truck and gestured for her to get in. Her tight jeans hindered her movement as she tried to jump into the truck seat.

"Do you need help?"

"No." Her cheeks burned with embarrassment as she struggled to leverage herself up and into the truck. He waited patiently then closed the door gently but firmly once she was safely inside.

She let out a tiny breath of relief when he climbed in beside her. She couldn't explain why she wanted to get away from the hospital, but the need to escape couldn't be ignored. She placed her palms on her thighs, trying to hide the bloodstains. If he saw them, he'd have questions, and unfortunately she didn't have any answers.

She wished more than anything that she didn't have to depend on him to take her home. His shoulders strained at the seams of his white cotton shirt as he started the truck and pulled out of the parking lot. The cuffs of his sleeves were rolled to his elbows. Dark hair sprinkled his skin. She fought the absurd urge to touch him.

"Gage."

She tore her glance from the mesmerizing strength of his arms. "Excuse me?"

"My name is Gage Drummond. Alyssa and I are—close friends."

Mallory lobbed the name through the spacious portion of her brain where her memory should have been. Gage was a nice name. "Yes. So you said."

He kept his eyes glued to the road. "Alyssa is a nurse. She works in the emergency department of Trinity Medical Center."

"I see." Mallory filed away that small tidbit of information. She had a twin sister who was a nurse and her boyfriend's name was Gage. Comforting, to a certain extent, to know she wasn't completely alone in the world. "Am I a nurse, too?"

"No." His response was terse. "You're an interior designer, working for a large architectural firm. You create color schemes for offices, hospitals, that sort of thing. So don't you think it's odd that you knew that woman was about to go into respiratory arrest?"

"Her lips were blue," she said, even though a blanket of unease settled over her, worse than the one she'd felt earlier when she'd woken up in the hospital with a fog-filled brain. The minute she'd noticed the elderly woman in the corner, she'd known something was wrong. Respiratory arrest was when someone stopped breathing. Despite Gage's claim she was a designer, she must have had some exposure to hospitals. Maybe she'd tried to follow her sister into nursing, but then dropped out? Why on earth couldn't she remember? Mallory licked suddenly dry lips and tried to shrug. "Everyone knows blue lips are a bad sign."

Gage's laugh didn't hold any mirth. "Yeah, maybe. Or this is part of some weird way of changing yourself into someone I'd like. Don't bother trying to flirt with me again. I happen to love Alyssa."

Mallory gaped at him in shock. "What are you talking about?" His comment floored her. Why would she try to flirt with him? Before he became involved with Alyssa? Or after? She felt a little sick that she might have treated her sister that way.

"Never mind," he said, as if he regretted bringing the subject up in the first place.

Ignoring the pounding in her head, she lifted her chin. "Rest assured I'm not interested in flirting with you."

"Good."

Silence hung heavy between them. Mallory shifted her attention to the scenery outside her window, at least the part she could see through the darkness. Arguing with the stranger had temporarily held fear at bay, but without something to occupy her brain, the sense of doom clung, lining her clothes, abrading her skin.

The night swallowed them, yet she felt safer inside the truck next to Gage than she had inside the busy, well-lit emergency department. Why? Why did she feel safer with a stranger? Peering through the window, she sought the source of her earlier apprehension. Was someone out there, looking for her? Whose blood stained her clothes?

Her blank memory didn't supply any answers. Outside, there was the faintest hue of light near the horizon, telling her dawn wasn't too far off. Yet dozens of stars still littered the sky. Leafy green trees and mild temperatures told her the season was summer. The seemingly calm and peaceful landscape was at odds with her inner angst.

Where, exactly, were they? Why wouldn't this haze over her mind go away? She focused on several street signs, seeking even one that seemed familiar. All the while, she was keenly aware of the stranger's disapproving presence beside her.

Not a stranger. Gage. Gage Drummond. She forced herself to use his name. They weren't strangers just because she couldn't remember him. He obviously knew her, at least enough to offer a ride in the middle of the night. But enough to protect her from harm? That she wasn't sure of. How could she have tried to flirt with him?

She risked a glance at him from beneath her lashes. There was no denying Gage was a very attractive man. Obviously, her sister was a very lucky woman. Her gaze clung to his hand, so strong, so capable on the steering wheel. His arms were firmly muscled and tan as if he spent a lot of time in the sun. She clenched her hands in her lap to keep from reaching out to touch him.

Gage and Alyssa were close, but where was Alyssa now? She found it odd how he didn't seem to have a clue where to find her. How often did a guy lose his girlfriend? Maybe he wasn't being entirely truthful. Maybe her sister's relationship with this man was on the rocks. Mallory swallowed hard. Harboring a secret attraction for her sister's boyfriend made her a horrible sister. She had to stop thinking about him, right now. So what if Gage exuded a confident strength she was drawn to? A strength she longed to lean upon?

Gage wasn't anything to her. She didn't even remember him. Rocky relationship or not, he belonged to Alyssa. Besides, he couldn't have made his feelings toward her more clear.

Forget about him. Even if Gage didn't know where her sister was, his feelings were obviously tangled into knots over it. And since she was dependent on him, she decided it was time to make amends. "I'm sorry."

"For what?"

"For whatever I did to put a wedge between you and Alyssa."

He was quiet for a long moment. "There is no wedge between me and Alyssa. And Mallory doesn't apologize. Ever."

She didn't need her memory to know she couldn't win this one. She threw her hand up then lightly tapped the side of her temple. "Silly me, I forgot." Sarcasm dripped from her words. "Consider my apology rescinded."

A few minutes later, Gage pulled up in front of a fancy-looking building in the heart of the city. She tensed and stared. Was this some sort of test? Did she really live here?

"Where are we?" She hated having to ask.

"Your place. Do you have your keys?" Gage asked, pausing in the act of opening his door.

"No. I meant what city?"

"Milwaukee, Wisconsin." He held out his hand patiently. "I need your keys."

Milwaukee didn't sound dangerous, but the sense of urgency wouldn't leave her alone. Mallory pulled open her large, gaudy purse and searched for the keys. She'd already gone through her wallet and found the pitiful amount of cash and her driver's license. There was also a package of tissues, a glittery hair clip, enough cosmetics to stock several counters at the department store and a hairbrush. No cell phone, which she thought odd. Why wouldn't she have a cell phone? Finally, her fingers closed around a ring of keys. Feeling relieved, she pulled them out and dangled them in front of him.

Gage grabbed them and jumped out of the truck. She slid out of the passenger side, favoring her ankle as she landed on the sidewalk. She followed him, moving at a much slower pace. The back of her neck tingled when she watched him use her key to gain access to the secured building. He held the door open for her, and Mallory felt admiration for his polite gestures. But before she crossed the threshold, she couldn't resist a furtive glance over her shoulder. No one lurked behind them. At least not that she could see.

But she kept wondering if someone was out there. Following her. Watching her.

Trying to control a flash of anxiety, she turned her attention to the building where she lived. The place was fancy, all chrome and glass with a decor that reeked of money. Had she designed the color scheme for this building? She guessed the condos inside were not of the traditional postage-stamp variety.

Gage waited, one strong arm holding open the elevator door for her. The elevator was surrounded by glass windows, providing a breathtaking view of the city lights. Yet she couldn't help feeling exposed, knowing that anyone outside could easily see them standing inside.

She tried to ignore the increasing paranoia. Was that a common reaction for people who had amnesia? Maybe.

When Gage reached over and pushed the button for the fifteenth floor, she was hit by a sense of familiarity. As if she'd done the same thing herself.

Her head ached with the strain of trying to remember. The sense of urgency grew stronger, and she tapped her foot as the elevator slid upward. The flashes of familiarity were encouraging. Maybe her memory would return after she'd gotten into more familiar surroundings. When the elevator doors opened on the fifteenth floor, she eagerly stepped out.

Oddly enough, there was only one door. Did she live in some sort of penthouse? Silently he used her key to gain access. Warily she stepped inside. The condo was huge, decorated with red furniture, black and red kitchen cabinets and white walls. Large windows lined one entire wall, giving her a breathtaking view of Lake Michigan.

"Wow." Drawn by the cool, calm water, where the sun was just beginning to creep up the horizon, she hobbled to the window. The lake was a balm to her frayed nerves. "I have spectacular taste," she murmured, impressed with the view.

Gage grunted, hovering in the entrance, as if uncomfortable in her private space. "You obviously like a lot of bold colors."

Bold colors were an understatement. She wasn't about to admit that the deep red, blue and black interior had almost made her wrinkle her nose in distaste. She must have liked the furnishings at some point in time. She swept a gaze over the room, noting a short hallway off to the left where she assumed her bedroom and bathroom were located.

"Have anything to drink around here?" Gage asked.

She glanced at him, raising a brow. "How would I know? I'll have to look."

When she limped in the direction of her kitchen, he frowned and glanced at her swollen ankle as if he could tell the pain was getting worse with each step. "Stay put, you should rest that ankle. I'll do it." He walked toward the fridge and opened the door. She paused, nearly shedding her jacket but then swiftly reconsidering, remembering the midriff-baring T-shirt. Better to stay covered up.

Feeling awkward in her own surroundings, she watched as Gage rummaged around and finally withdrew a jug of orange juice.

"Want some?" He held the container and two glasses. The expression on his face was carefully polite. His cinnamon-colored eyes looked directly into hers.

She dragged her gaze away with an effort. "Sure. I need to take the anti-inflammatory that the doctor prescribed." She pulled the pill bottle out of her purse. "He assured me it's only a sprain, but my ankle really hurts."

The inane conversation didn't bring the normalcy she desired. She was home, but something was wrong, she could feel it in her bones. There was nothing homey about this condo. Frankly, she couldn't imagine living there.

He poured her a glass of juice and she stepped closer, wary of invading his space. Silly, considering they were in her condo. She tossed the pills back and quickly took a sip of juice. The cool liquid soothed her parched throat.

"Anything look familiar?" Gage cocked an eyebrow over the rim of his glass.

"No." She downed the rest of the juice in a big gulp then set the glass down with a thud. The condo should be a safe haven, but a strong sense of disquiet kept her off balance. She fingered the bloodstains on her jeans and then wrapped her arms around her body, warding off a chill.

What would Gage say if she wrapped her arms around his lean waist, asking him to hold her? He was a stranger, but so far he was the only person who made her feel safe. The condo wasn't much better than the hospital. Would she ever feel safe again? She glanced at Gage, noted the restlessness in his eyes. She didn't want him to leave, yet he just as clearly didn't want to stick around.

For a moment panic surged at the thought of being left here alone. She reached out to touch his arm, a solid anchor for her shaky, trembling foundation. "Gage—"

A sizzle of awareness leaped between them. Gage jerked from her touch, sending a wave of juice sloshing to the floor.

Mallory snatched her hand away, her fingers tingling from the solid warmth of his skin.

"I have to go. I'll check on you later." Gage hastily set

his half-full glass down on the counter. Stepping over the mess, he gave her a wide berth as he headed for the door.

Mallory couldn't think of a single thing to say as he left the condo. She didn't understand the urge to beg him not to go. He might be a close *friend* of her twin, but he was still a stranger. Her knees gave way as she sank onto the nearest chair. Loneliness surrounded her, magnifying her dread.

She didn't want to stay here, but where could she go? What could she do? Run after Gage? Beg him to take her home with him? Throw herself into his arms?

She buried her face in her hands, full of self-loathing. What kind of person was she? And what sort of mess had she gotten herself into?

Gage's hands shook, making it difficult to slide the truck key into the ignition. Finally he jammed the metal home and started the truck with a twist of his wrist. He floored the accelerator, speeding away from Mallory's high-rise condo as if his life depended on putting distance between them.

His heart nearly hammered its way out of his chest. What was wrong with him? He must have accidently touched Mallory a dozen times in passing and never once experienced the jolt of electricity like the one that just zapped him. He rubbed a shaky hand over the stubble on his chin. He must be losing his mind. Alyssa was the twin he was attracted to. Not Mallory.

Calmer now, he realized he'd reacted that way only because he missed Alyssa. She'd broken things off, but he wanted to win her back. Somehow he'd transposed his feelings for Alyssa onto Mallory. Because Mallory with amnesia wasn't acting like Mallory. Twisted logic?

Maybe. But he couldn't come up with anything else that made sense.

For a moment he wondered if Alyssa and Mallory had switched places. Was it possible the woman he'd just dropped off was really Alyssa? His chest filled with hope, but then he slowly shook his head. No way. He refused to believe it. Alyssa told him she and Mallory had vowed to never switch identities. And Alyssa always told the truth.

He couldn't imagine any circumstance where Alyssa would agree to take Mallory's place. More likely, Mallory's strange actions arose from some identity crisis, a direct result of her amnesia. And why did he care? Mallory's amnesia wasn't his problem anymore. His good deed was finished.

She was Alyssa's problem now. He didn't head home but hooked a left turn toward Alyssa's town house. It was early, five-thirty in the morning, but that didn't stop him.

Shortly after their engagement, she'd given him a key to keep as a spare and he'd been remiss in returning it, hoping they'd get back together so he wouldn't need to. Since their split they'd spoken on occasion, civil conversations that had done nothing to fix the true problems between them.

On her front porch, he took a deep breath and lifted his hand to knock. She didn't answer, so he tried one more time to call her cell phone. Still no answer.

Steeling his resolve, he tried the door handle, oddly reassured to find the door locked. Alyssa always locked the door when she was gone. Using the key, he unlocked the door and pushed it open.

The heavy scent of pine cleaner layered with ammonia assaulted his senses. With a frown, he flipped on a switch, flooding the foyer with light. "Alyssa?" His voice reverberated loudly through the room. He stepped over the threshold, shutting the door behind him.

Her town house was always impeccably neat and clean, but the thick scent of the cleaner nearly choked him. It was as if the entire place had been doused in the stuff, which was odd, since Alyssa normally used vinegar to clean because it was better for the environment. He poked his head into the kitchen and living room, finding them both empty. The windows were all closed, but the air-conditioning wasn't turned on. Alyssa preferred fresh air from open windows, especially in the summer. Gage forced himself to walk down the hall, his footsteps echoing loudly on the hardwood floor. The pine scent mixed with ammonia grew impossibly stronger.

Her bedroom door hung partially open. Holding his breath, he pushed it the rest of the way until he could see her bed, neatly made. Discovering she wasn't home didn't sit well with him.

Where could she be? He knew Alyssa's Christian values wouldn't allow her to spend the night with a man. And if she wasn't with Mallory, or at work, where could she be?

The ammonia scent made his head hurt, so he opened the windows as he walked back through her town house. A sick feeling settled in his gut. Something wasn't right. Maybe he should call Jonah Stewart. His childhood friend was a detective with the Milwaukee police, and he had connections that would help in looking for Alyssa. But how long had she been gone?

She might not be missing at all. For all he knew, she was with some nursing friends from work. Or visiting a sick friend. He decided to wait here in the town house for her. Surely she'd come home sooner or later.

In the kitchen, the blinking light of the answering machine snagged his gaze. His messages to her would be on there, but what if there were others? A clue to her whereabouts?

Ignoring a flash of guilt, Gage rewound the tape and hit the play button. The first message came through almost immediately.

"Alyssa, this is Kristine from Trinity Medical Center. You requested a two-week personal leave of absence. You know the summer is our busiest time of the year because of increase in trauma patients, but since you sounded desperate, we've agreed to grant your leave."

Stunned, Gage hit the stop button on the machine. A two-week leave of absence? Why in the world would Alyssa desperately need two weeks off? The only family she had left was her sister, Mallory.

Maybe there really was a sick friend somewhere.

He hit the play button again. Aside from the messages he'd left, there were no other messages. Not even one from Mallory.

Gage turned away from the machine. Idly, he opened her fridge. The contents were spartan, no milk or anything that would spoil. Butter, ketchup and mustard, along with a jug of water, were left inside. He closed the door.

The house had been closed up tight and there was nothing to eat. Where had Alyssa gone? The last time he'd spoken to her was just two days ago when she'd called him from work, anxious to get together. Idiot that he was, he'd been thrilled by the idea that she'd wanted a chance to mend their relationship. Then she'd mentioned having grave concerns over his taking on the Jefferson condo project. She knew his construction company had been awarded the contract to build the new Riverside Luxury Condos owned by Hugh Jefferson. Condos that had been hotly debated within the city government for well over a year. She claimed there was something dangerous going on, and she begged him to cancel the contract.

He'd scoffed at her concern. First of all, he needed that contract. And besides, what could be so bad about building condos overlooking the Milwaukee River? The idea was ludicrous.

Until now. Alyssa's empty town house caused tension to slither like a snake through his belly. He didn't have any concrete reason to believe she was in danger, but the persistent worry wouldn't quit. Had something happened to her? Had he failed, again? The image of his dead mother swam in his mind and he shoved it away with effort.

Failure wasn't an option. Not this time. Because he knew his heart and soul wouldn't survive if he failed to find and protect Alyssa.

THREE

Since leaving wasn't an option, Mallory restlessly limped around her penthouse condo, searching for clues to jar her memory. Oddly, there wasn't an overabundance of personal items lying around. She discovered she had an eclectic taste in music ranging from rap to jazz. Several new-wave art prints were splashed on her walls. Nice, but she couldn't shake the awful feeling she was looking at her things through a stranger's eyes.

Bone-weary, she fought off an encroaching wave of fatigue. She blinked and forced her eyes to stay open. There had to be something here that could make her remember who she was. Or why she continued to feel an overwhelming sense of doom. Hoping to find more personal items, she headed down the hall, toward the bedroom.

On the dresser she found a framed snapshot of her and Alyssa. She picked up the photo, surprised to realize just how much they looked alike physically. Alyssa was easy to identify, since she was conservatively dressed and wore her long blond hair pulled back in a French braid. Alyssa's expression was full of joy, and she proudly wore a modest diamond on the third finger of her left hand.

In contrast, Mallory wore a slinky rose-colored dress,

and despite the bright smile on her face, there was a certain sadness reflected in her eyes.

Who'd taken their picture? A man? Gage?

Mallory set the photo down with a grimace. This unhealthy fascination with her sister's boyfriend had to stop. She needed to focus her attention on filling the cavernous blanks in her memory. On searching for the person whose blood stained her jeans.

Alyssa's boyfriend was definitely off-limits.

The huge bed was softly inviting, but she refused to simply go to sleep when she had no idea what was going on. Or why she might be sad in contrast to her sister's happiness.

Her control slipped and suddenly she couldn't stand wearing the uncomfortable and blood-splattered clothes another minute. She stripped everything off as quickly as humanly possible.

After a good hour in the bathroom, scrubbing her skin until it was almost raw, she felt much better. But finding something appropriate and comfortable to wear wasn't easy. She rooted through drawers, searching until she found a clean T-shirt that didn't fit too snuggly and a comfortable pair of yoga pants.

On the opposite side of the bed, a bundle of rose-colored silk on the floor caught her eye. Intrigued, she leaned down and picked up the garment, fingering the fabric thoughtfully. It was a gown, cut daringly low. She had no memory of wearing it, or of leaving it lying crumpled on the floor, as if she'd changed in a hurry. She lifted the dress and glanced around the otherwise neat room. From what she could tell, she wasn't normally a slob.

Had she worn the gown recently? She spread the rose silk on a nearby chair, wishing the simple item of clothing would spark some sort of memory. If not the gown, something else, then? She opened the closet door and rifled through the hanging garments. Only, nothing looked familiar. Her gaze landed on two boxes sitting on the closet floor.

Wincing against the swelling in her ankle, she kneeled beside the boxes and opened the flap of the top one. She found winter clothing, mainly turtlenecks and cashmere sweaters. She shoved that box aside and grabbed the second. This one held more clothes. Men's clothes.

The sick feeling in her stomach intensified as she stared at the contents of the box. Had she lived with someone? Been married? She wasn't wearing a ring. Divorced, then? And if so, from whom? She really should have asked Gage more questions.

Digging beneath the clothes, she found expensive dress shoes and a leather shaving case. Nothing else. Nothing to give a clue as to the identity of the owner.

Dazed, she stumbled to her feet. Limping over to the dresser, she opened every single drawer, relieved to find only female items of clothing. She couldn't explain why the thought that she may have actually lived with a man so bothersome. Except that it didn't seem like something she'd agree to do.

In the bottom drawer, beneath more sweaters—really, how many sweaters did one person need?—she found a buttery-soft, brown suede box.

Expecting to find jewelry, she was surprised to discover it empty except for a glossy photo lying inside. Hesitantly, she picked up the picture.

This time, she was dressed in yet another evening gown, this one in brilliant blue. But she wasn't alone. A man held her possessively in his arms. She swallowed hard, her stomach gurgling with tension as she studied the picture. The guy looked older than her, maybe in his mid- to late thirties, and was dressed in an expensive suit. His handsome face held a note of triumph, but she looked less than thrilled. A faint hint of distaste shadowed her gaze.

Who was he? The owner of the clothing she'd found in the box? Staring at the background behind them, she could see they were standing in some hotel, with linen-covered tables and an orchestra behind them. How many hotels were there in Milwaukee? Or even worse, how many hotels were in the entire United States? No way to know where the photo had been taken.

She put the glossy photo back inside the box, hoping, praying that the men's clothing belonged to some sort of ex-husband rather than just some guy she'd decided to live with. She didn't want to believe she was that sort of woman. But the slinky evening gowns and the revealing clothes, not to mention the rose and dagger tattoo she'd discovered just below her collarbone, told a different story.

She closed her eyes on a wave of helplessness.

Please, Lord, help me remember!

Loud pounding on her door startled her. She spun from the dresser, nearly falling on her face when her ankle screamed with pain. Her pulse jumped and, despite the T-shirt and yoga pants, she really wanted a robe or something to cover up with.

Since there didn't seem to be anything nearby, she yanked the blanket off the bed and wrapped it around her. Gripping the lower hem of the blanket so she wouldn't trip, she made her way down the hall toward the front door.

The banging grew insistently louder.

Nervously, she peered through the peephole. Gage's face, distorted by the glass, had her sighing in relief.

Not the guy in the photo or some other stranger. Gage. Gage had come back. A wave of pleasure swelled in her chest, and she quickly squelched it. What was wrong with her? He didn't belong to her, he belonged to Alyssa!

"Open up, Mallory," he called.

Hanging on to the blanket with one hand, she opened the door. "How did you get in? Isn't there security here?"

"I accidently kept your keys. And that's not important right now. Finding Alyssa is." He brushed past her, tossing the keys onto the kitchen counter. With a sigh, she closed the door behind him.

"I'm sorry, but I can't help you." The sheer agony on his face made her feel bad, as if she should be doing something more to help. "I'm afraid my memory hasn't returned."

He stared at her as if just noticing her for the first time. "What's with the blanket?"

She flushed and gripped the edges tighter. "I couldn't find a robe."

Gage gave her an odd look but didn't say anything. "Hurry up and get ready. Because we're heading out, together, to find Alyssa."

It was on the tip of her tongue to argue, but in the end, she didn't really want to stay here alone. Going out somewhere, anywhere, would be better than sitting around waiting for her memory to return. "All right, give me a couple of minutes."

"A couple of minutes?" The surprise in his tone made her glance back at him over her shoulder. "I'll hold you to that."

Once again, she tried to find clothing that she wouldn't

be embarrassed to wear in public. In the very back of the closet, she found a pair of slacks that weren't skintight, and she gratefully pulled them on. She found a long-sleeved, somewhat sheer blouse and pulled that over the plain T-shirt and buttoned it all the way up, not caring about the lack of fashion. Running shoes were harder to find, but she finally found a pair that looked almost brand-new in the back of the closet.

Odd, how there were parts of her that didn't seem quite right. Did amnesia make a person forget his or her personality? Or maybe a more likely answer was that she put on an act on the outside, hiding her true self within. But why would she put on an act for the public? Because she was afraid? Or because she had something to hide?

Her sister, Alyssa, was the one person who might know for sure. Mallory grimly realized that she needed to find her twin as much as Gage did, maybe more.

Gage seemed a little surprised when she returned to the living room in less than five minutes, but then he gestured to the answering machine in the corner. "You didn't listen to your messages?"

"No." She didn't want to admit the simple task hadn't occurred to her. "Why?"

He crossed over to press the button on the machine, which was located on the back wall of her kitchen. She followed more slowly, carefully stepping over the sticky orange juice mess she'd left on the floor. She felt foolish having avoided the kitchen after the scene with Gage.

"Mallory? This is Rick Meyer. We won the bid for the Jefferson project. I'd like to get started with some color schemes as soon as possible, so call me." Gage hit the button to stop the tape.

She stared at him. "Who's Rick Meyer?" Was it possible he was the older guy in the photo with her?

"Your boss. But I'm looking for a message from Alyssa." Gage rewound the tape and then replayed all the messages from the beginning.

"Mallory? Call me the second you get this message. It's urgent that we talk as soon as possible."

Gage stopped the machine. "That's her."

Mallory nodded. Her sister's voice sounded like an exact replica of her own. "I figured as much. But what does it mean? Why would it be so urgent that we talk?"

"I don't know." Gage spun away from the counter, his movements agitated. "Alyssa called me two days ago. She sounded paranoid, saying something about the Jefferson project being dangerous. She wanted me to drop the project and warned me to be careful."

Mallory suppressed a shiver. There was no denying the tense note of fear in her sister's tone. The laughing image of Alyssa standing beside her in the photograph mocked her. "What exactly is the Jefferson project?"

Gage dropped into a kitchen chair. "Hugh Jefferson is a wealthy businessman from Chicago. He bought several old warehouse properties along the Milwaukee River and apparently promised to bring in businesses, but then changed his mind and decided to build condos instead. The city government wasn't pleased and fought him tooth and nail, refusing to change the zoning permits. After a year-long debate, Jefferson finally got his permits and my company was awarded the construction contract. Despite the hassle of getting it approved, the project is nothing more than a real-estate endeavor. I can't see how there's anything dangerous about it."

Mallory frowned and sat at the kitchen table across

from Gage. She tried to make sense of the pieces, which frankly was easier than trying to remember. "I don't understand. What gave Alyssa the impression it might be dangerous?"

Gage scrubbed his hands over his face. "She worked the trauma room the night City Councilman Ray Schaefer was brought in. Apparently he was mugged and stabbed twice in the abdomen. According to Alyssa, before he died he told her a guy hired by Hugh Jefferson stabbed him."

"He died?" The blood-splattered clothes she'd been wearing flashed in her mind. Logically, she couldn't imagine she'd been anywhere near the councilman who'd died, but then again, the doctor did say that her amnesia was the result of a traumatic event. Watching a man being stabbed certainly would be traumatic. Had she really been there? Was Schaefer the guy standing with her in the photo? Her nausea deepened.

"Yeah, but according to a statement made by the chief of police, Councilman Schaefer was killed in a simple mugging, and they'd already caught the gang member who'd done the crime. The councilman was in the wrong place at the wrong time, and the kid had stabbed him as part of a gang-initiation dare."

So she hadn't been there. Her relief was quickly replaced with fear. "But what if the chief of police is wrong?"

Gage's face reflected his skepticism. "How could he be wrong? They caught the guy—it was all over the news."

"Yet Alyssa sounded frantic and claimed the project was dangerous." She tried to curb the rising panic.

"Thinking the worst isn't going to help." Gage's expression was one of sheer determination. "I have to be-lieve Alyssa is all right. And I have to trust that we're going to find her."

Arguing wouldn't help, so she let the matter drop. Think. She needed to think. "Okay, if Alyssa was wor-ried about something shady going on, what would she do?"

"She tried coming to me." Gage stared down at his hands for a long moment. Self-reproach shimmered from his cinnamon-colored eyes. Sympathy stirred deep in her heart. He really cared about her sister. And the radiant happiness reflected in Alyssa's eyes on the glossy photo was a strong indication she felt the same way about him.

The two of them deserved to find happiness together. She should be thrilled for them. So why did she feel depressed?

Gage raised anguished eyes to hers. "Since I refused to help, I'm not sure what she'd do. I left a message with a friend of mine who might be able to help find her. I checked her place, but she's not there. I even stopped at my house, but she wasn't there, either. All I know for sure is that she called you."

Mallory nearly apologized, before she caught herself. "Okay, obviously Alyssa's not here. Who are Alyssa's closest friends? People from work? Maybe she's staying with one of them because she was afraid to be alone?"

"Yeah. Maybe." Gage brightened, as if he hadn't con-sidered that option. "I think Paige Sanders and Emma Banks are her closest friends from work. We can start with them."

"And what if they're not home, or don't want to talk to us?" She watched as Gage swiftly paged through the phone book.

"We'll find a way to make them talk." He scowled darkly. "Because I'm not leaving until we have answers."

Gage slammed the phone book shut with a sense of frustration. He wasn't close to Alyssa's friends, another thing she'd complained about while they were engaged, and he soon realized he didn't know if either of the women were married, which meant they might not be listed under their own last name in the directory.

Finally he asked Mallory to call Trinity Medical Center, pretending to be Alyssa to request the numbers. He wasn't surprised when she was readily given the information. Mallory sounded more like Alyssa now that she had amnesia than she did before. He tried to put his finger on the difference. Maybe because the brittle edge had vanished from her tone.

Mallory acted more like Alyssa now, too. Not only was the sharp edge gone, but she didn't flirt the way she had before she'd hit her head. Even her clothes were more conservative than usual.

Thankfully, after that fiasco in the kitchen, she'd kept her distance from him. Which was a huge relief.

He felt bad for her. Having amnesia couldn't be easy. His memories of Alyssa were painful, but at least he had them. He couldn't imagine what his life would be like if he couldn't remember Alyssa.

"I have the phone numbers," Mallory said. He gratefully took the slip of paper and then used directory assistance to get addresses. At least they still had home phone numbers, because cell numbers would have been a dead end. Finally they were ready to leave. Hoping Jonah Stewart, his detective friend, would return his call soon, he waited, rather impatiently, while Mallory grabbed her massive purse and slung it over her shoulder.

She must not have noticed his impatience, because she grinned at him. "Okay. I'm ready, Freddie."

For a moment he stared at her in shock. *I'm ready, Freddie,* was a phrase Alyssa had often used, but had he ever heard Mallory say it? He tried to think back but couldn't honestly remember. She sounded too much like Alyssa, which made it harder to remember that he didn't like her. Normally Mallory was easy to dismiss. Especially since he'd already fallen for Alyssa.

He jerked the door open, and then paused to glance back at Mallory. Was it possible that Mallory was really more like Alyssa than he'd ever realized? She'd never acted anything like her twin, until now. "You're sure you don't remember anything?" he couldn't help asking.

"Oh, sure, I'm faking amnesia." She rolled her eyes with exasperation. "Of course I don't remember. Why would I bother to pretend?" Mallory truly looked perplexed.

To be more like Alyssa. To make me like you. Gage bit back the words before they could slip off his tongue. "Never mind. Let's go."

He closed and locked Mallory's door then headed for the glass elevator. He kept his gaze straight ahead. He wasn't particularly fond of heights. But he also refused to cave in to his fear. If anyone on a construction site knew he built tall buildings but was afraid of heights, he'd be the topic of endless jokes. Even on-site, he forced himself to manage every phase of a building project, even if that meant going up to the top.

He was glad when they reached the lobby level. Outside the sun was shining and puffy white clouds dotted the sky, the wind off the lake bringing a gust of cool air. A nice day, but he didn't care. Alyssa was missing and he was stuck with Mallory. He couldn't relax, not until he knew Alyssa was safe.

He glanced at Mallory, surprised when he saw her blue eyes filled with stark apprehension as she glanced around as if she'd never seen this part of the city before.

He'd wanted Mallory to come with him because he thought Alyssa's friends would respond better to her twin. He could only assume Alyssa had told her closest friends how they'd broken up. He and Alyssa had known each other for only about three months before getting engaged, and they'd tended to keep to themselves. He had no idea what reason Alyssa had given her friends for breaking off their engagement, but he suspected Alyssa confided that he was the problem.

Mallory stopped in the middle of the sidewalk, forcing another couple to step around her. Lost in thoughts of Alyssa, Gage followed too close and smacked his chin on her head.

"Ow." She rubbed the top of her head. He hastily backed up, putting at least a foot of space between them. "This is so frustrating. I'm walking along like I should know where we're going, but I don't."

"Over there." Gage nodded toward his truck, parked a few car lengths down the street. "The blue pickup."

"What about the rest of them?" She waited for several pedestrians to pass by before gesturing toward the scattered cars parked along the street. "Do you think my car is here somewhere?"

"You drive a three-year-old red Mustang convertible." He didn't see the car, and that was strange. Where would

Mallory have left it? Near the spot where the ambulance picked her up?

"Maybe someone stole it." Mallory scowled.

Gage didn't answer. An old-model beige Cadillac moved slowly down the street. Odd, how it didn't accelerate. Especially with no stop sign in sight. The clouds shifted from the sun and something glinted brightly from the partially open window of the backseat.

Long and narrow, he belatedly recognized the barrel of a gun.

"Get down!" Gage grabbed Mallory and shoved her down behind the parked cars. He dropped on top of her, protecting her body with his. Within seconds a storm of bullets showered the area around them.

FOUR

Glass shattered. People screamed. Debris spewed beneath a thunderous barrage of bullets. Squashed between the hard concrete and Gage's equally unyielding body, she listened to the violent assault, feeling helpless. The episode ended as quickly as it had started. After the roar of an engine and squealing tires echoed off the buildings, a stunned silence cloaked them.

"Are you okay?" Gage ran his hands urgently over her arms. "Say something, Mallory! Were you hit?"

"No. I'm okay." Her voice was barely a whisper. Yes, her body was bruised, but she was unharmed, thanks to Gage's quick reflexes. His unselfishness humbled her. He'd protected her with his life. Had anyone ever done that for her before? She had no way of knowing, but she somehow doubted it. She tried to raise her head to thank him.

"Stay down," Gage barked. Clearly he wasn't lulled into complacency because the hail of gunfire had ceased.

While she deeply appreciated his willingness to sacrifice himself, she couldn't breathe. Mallory tried to edge out from beneath Gage's suffocating weight. He must have figured out what was wrong, because he suddenly shifted to the right. She gulped in a huge breath of air, fighting a wave of dizziness.

Half of his body still shielded hers. Even in the desperate seriousness of the moment, she couldn't ignore her hyperawareness to his presence. Being held protectively by Gage was exciting yet familiar. Mallory kept her head low as she turned to see him, his face mere inches from hers. His eyes weren't the color of cinnamon anymore, but an intense chestnut-brown. His smooth jaw was clenched with anger, but his gaze was alert. For a guy, his sooty eyelashes were ridiculously long. His mouth was so close.

She had the insane urge to kiss him.

Their gazes locked, held. Mallory sucked in a quick breath. This was it. His eyes held the same awareness she was certain was in hers. Her heart quickened. Warm breath fanned her face. She stretched toward him—then froze when the distinct wail of police sirens filled the air.

Run! Run! Jerking her head toward the ominous sound, she sought a place to hide. Beneath one of the cars parked on the street? No. Too much glass carpeted the area between them. Around the building? Yes. There was time. They could make it. Wriggling against the weight of Gage's muscular limbs, she struggled to get free. He tightened his hold. She jammed her elbow in his ribs.

He grunted, his breath whooshing past her ear. "What's wrong with you? What are you doing?"

"Hurry!" she insisted. "We need to get out of here."

"Are you nuts? We can't leave. We're staying right here until the police arrive."

Before she could explain her unknown fears there were at least six or seven cops, covered from head to toe in full protective gear, surrounding them. Bile rose in her throat and she shrank against Gage's warmth, only this time he was the one who jerked away from the other's touch. The cops must have noticed their lack of weapons since they immediately fanned out, securing the area.

A tall officer with dark hair stayed behind. "I'm Officer Lowell. Are you okay? Anyone hurt?"

"We're fine." Gage swiftly rose to his feet. He hesitated for the barest fraction of a second before offering a hand to help her stand. "It's only a scratch."

A scratch? He was bleeding. Concern for Gage pushed past her irrational fear. She hastily stood, her gaze focusing on the ominous bloodstain oozing through his white shirt. "Why didn't you tell me you were hurt?"

"I'm fine." He avoided eye contact, rejecting her concern.

Mallory ignored him and took his arm. A thin rivulet of blood dripped from his elbow. The image of a bloodstained wall flashed in her mind, but she swallowed hard and shook off the faint memory. "This isn't fine. It's a bullet wound." She pushed the sleeve of his shirt out of the way to better see the injury.

"I have a first-aid kit." Another officer stepped forward carrying a square box. "And there's an ambulance on the way."

Mallory plucked white squares of gauze from the first-aid kid. Gage's muscular arm was tense beneath her fingertips. His skin radiated heat. "Thankfully the bullet only grazed you. God was definitely watching over us."

"God?" Gage echoed in surprise.

"Don't you believe in God?" she asked. He stared at her for a long moment before he gave a curt nod. Satisfied, she turned back to his wound, covering the bloody gash with gauze and then glancing up at the officer with the first-aid kit. "Do you have an elastic bandage?"

"Sure." The cop handed her the roll.

"Thanks." She wrapped the elastic bandage around Gage's arm, anchoring the gauze in place. "This will work until the ambulance gets here. You should go to the hospital, although I don't think the wound will need stitches."

Gage frowned at her. "How would you know?"

Mallory was taken aback at his tone. How did she know? A memory? No, the black mist still dipped and swirled. Then she frowned. Basic common sense, that's how. "The gash isn't deep."

With a scowl he pulled away. "I'm fine, no reason to go to the hospital." Turning away, he gave his attention to the police officers.

His dismissal hurt. Far more than it should have. Tears threatened, but she refused to succumb, blaming them on delayed shock. What was wrong with her? Gage was off-limits. He cared about her sister. Had she imagined that moment when it seemed he might kiss her? Probably.

She'd been stressed, traumatized by the gunfire, and had imagined the brief, emotional connection. And really, why did she care? She barely knew her own name, much less anything about Gage. He might have strong shoulders that came in handy when he was protecting her, but he belonged to Alyssa. Right now she needed to concentrate on getting her memory back.

Every muscle in her body tensed when she noticed a tall, burly police officer climb from his squad car. Unlike the others, he was dressed in uniform minus the protective gear, as if he'd heard about the situation on the radio and had come to investigate. In the middle of the sidewalk, he halted midstride and stared at her.

Mallory's stomach dropped to her knees. She sucked in a raw breath. In a flash she remembered the same ruddy-faced officer glaring at her impatiently. Then the brief memory vanished like a puff of smoke. The fog rolled in. She wanted to scream in frustration.

A long billy club swayed from his waist as he approached. On the other hip, he wore a gun. His hand hovered near the weapon, his fingers caressing the metal as if he were a gunslinger ready to draw. Forcing herself to breathe, she eased closer to Gage. Deep in conversation with Officer Lowell, Gage didn't notice how the ruddy-faced cop trained his gaze on her as he approached. When he stopped in front of her, fear coated her mouth like dust.

"What's your name?" he demanded.

She tried to swallow but couldn't. She wanted to run. To hide. But she was safe next to Gage, right? A spurt of anger at his blatant attempt to intimidate her caused her to jut her chin. "Mallory Roth. Why? What's yours?"

The grooves in his flushed face deepened. "Officer Aaron Crane. Do you have ID?"

Mallory nodded, tempted to ask for his as she reached for her purse. She found her driver's license and handed it to him.

Gage finished his conversation, and she grasped his arm to get his attention. He subtly pulled away, putting a good foot of distance between them, but he turned to face Crane. "Is there a problem, officer?"

"No. No problem." Crane stared at her license for a long moment before handing it back to her. He glanced at Gage. "I'll need to see your identification, as well."

Gage jerked a thumb over his shoulder. "These guys have the information. I already gave them my statement."

"Oh, okay. Good." Officer Crane nodded abruptly then turned and walked away. Mallory heard him ask his fellow officers, "What happened here?"

Ignoring Gage's questioning look, she eavesdropped on the exchange between the cops, unable to strip her gaze from the stocky policeman. She didn't like him. More than that, she feared him. Why? Although irrational, she feared Officer Crane would arrest her if given the chance.

The cops' discussion turned toward gang violence. One witness reported seeing a flash of green from the Caddy's window, a color known to be favored by the Skidds gang. Their conclusion sounded logical, but she couldn't shake her reaction to Officer Crane. After a long hour, they were allowed to leave. Amazingly, Gage's truck parked a few cars down the street hadn't been damaged in the shootout. She caught a glimpse of Officer Crane staring after them as they drove off.

Her hands began to shake. She clasped them together in an effort to make them stop. Silently, she swiveled in her seat to stare at the receding figure of Officer Crane.

"Are you sure you're okay?" Gage's concern was a life preserver she grabbed with both hands. Just knowing she wasn't alone was a huge relief. She forced a smile.

"I'm not the one who was shot," she pointed out, striving for a light tone. She settled in her seat, hanging on to the sense of normalcy. She desperately needed to keep her mind off creepy Officer Crane.

"I wasn't shot. I was nicked." Gage shook his head. "Never mind. We need to make a quick stop before we check out those addresses."

For a moment she was confused. What addresses? Then she remembered. Alyssa's friends. Of course. They were on a mission to find Alyssa.

"Where?" She didn't really care where they went, as long as it was far away from the scene outside her apartment.

"My place. I have a few calls to make. I also need the charger for my cell phone."

"What kind of calls?"

Gage shrugged but didn't answer. She tried to think of something to talk about. Anything to keep from focusing on the horror of someone trying to kill them. Was this related to Alyssa? Had someone mistaken her for Alyssa? By the time Gage pulled in front of a quaint two-story white house, her body was shaking in earnest. She locked her hands beneath opposite elbows to maintain the illusion of control and followed Gage inside.

An overwhelming sense of coming home fused her feet to the floor. Gage ignored her as he headed for the phone. Half-dazed, Mallory stood in the center of the kitchen. Cheerful green-and-white-checkered curtains fluttered over the windows. With an effort, she forced herself to walk through the kitchen, down the hallway and into the bathroom.

Closing the door behind her, she sank onto the commode and buried her face in her hands.

She'd lost her mind. That was the only explanation. It was impossible to feel more comfortable at Gage's house than her own condo. She couldn't have spent much time here. She lived in the fancy downtown condo. *He loved Alyssa.*

She had to stop thinking about Gage. There were bigger problems to consider. Such as who was the older man in the picture? Why did the sight of Officer Crane fill her with such fear and dread? Did she really remember him? Or was it only someone who looked similar to him? The danger had passed. She and Gage were safe now.

Weren't they?

Maybe. If the shooting really was gang related. Had they really been in the wrong place at the wrong time? And if so, why had Officer Crane looked at her so strangely?

The Jefferson project. Mallory shivered. Maybe Alyssa was right. Maybe everything really was related to the Jefferson project.

Dear Lord, help me. Keep us safe. Mallory took several slow, deep breaths. *In, count to ten, then out and count to ten. Now start over again. Breathe in...*

Wait a minute. Where had she learned that? The dark haze still hovered in her mind, but she could sense she was getting close to remembering. As she'd remembered Crane. He wasn't just some look-alike. Closing her eyes, she could clearly bring the memory back. His irritated features as he glared down at her. *She remembered him.*

"Mallory?" Gage tapped on the door. "Are you okay?"

The hovering image vanished. "I'll be out in a minute." She rubbed her aching temples and splashed water on her face, staring at her reflection in the mirror.

She needed to be strong. Between them, she and Gage would figure out what was going on. This was not the time to fall apart. Or become preoccupied with her sister's boyfriend. Alyssa was in danger, either from the Jefferson project or the gang members themselves. Amnesia or not, Alyssa was counting on her.

And she was determined to be the kind of sister her twin deserved.

* * *

"Dan, I need your help." Gage held the phone propped between his chin and his shoulder. His stomach rumbled so loudly, he suspected his chief project manager could hear it. "What do you know about Hugh Jefferson?"

"Aside from the fact we're building his condos? Not much," Dan admitted. "He's a businessman from Chicago, dabbles in various investments but prefers real estate. He's a mover and a shaker. Likes the finer things in life."

"Yeah, but why is he suddenly buying property in Milwaukee? There must be dozens of places to expand in Chicago. Why is he coming up here?"

"I don't know. Why? Is there a problem?"

Gage didn't want to go into too much detail over the phone. "I have some serious reservations about the project, that's all."

"Do you want me to see if I can find out more about him?" Dan asked.

"Yeah, that would be good." The police wanted them to believe the attack outside Mallory's apartment building was random. Gang activity was heating up, they'd claimed. The chief of police and the mayor had teamed up to form a special task force aimed at bringing gang activity under control. Today's shooting was a perfect example of why the task force was so important.

But Gage didn't buy it. He couldn't ignore the string of coincidences. First Ray Schaefer died of stab wounds. Now this attack outside Mallory's apartment. Alyssa seemingly missing.

He should have listened to Alyssa from the start, the night she'd called him from the E.D. He'd failed her. Again. The first time when he'd let her walk away, and the second when he hadn't believed her. Pushing back a wave of helpless regret, he struggled to think. Okay, say the Jefferson project was dangerous. Why? Who was involved? At what level?

"…meet me later?"

Gage belatedly realized Dan was waiting for a response. "Huh? Yeah, I know it's Saturday, but let's meet later. In the downtown office at six."

"Okay. I did find out something strange the other day, but let me look into things a bit and I'll fill you in later."

He was tempted to push Dan for more information, but just then Mallory entered the kitchen. "Fine. I'll see you later, Dan." Gage hung up the phone and slowly turned to face her.

"I remembered something."

Pale yet determined, Mallory stood in the center of his kitchen. Alyssa's kitchen. The one she'd taken such pleasure in helping him decorate. The green-and-white curtains had been her choice.

"Didn't you hear me?" she said again, impatiently. "I remembered something."

He blinked and straightened. "What did you remember?"

"The cop."

"Which cop?" As soon as he asked, he knew. The guy who'd approached and asked for her ID. He'd thought her reaction was strange at the time. Her fear of the officer had been palpable.

"Officer Aaron Crane."

"What about him? What exactly did you remember?" Gage held his breath, hoping and praying she would remember.

"Just his face, really. But I know I've seen him someplace before. I tapped his arm to get his attention and he glanced down at me with angry annoyance. That's all I remember."

She was right, it wasn't much. "Anything else? Where were you? Why were you talking to a cop? Were you with your twin? Maybe filling out a police report or something like that?"

Her brows pulled together in a deep frown. She rubbed the ache in her left temple then slowly shook her head. "I don't know. I'm sorry, I can't remember."

Her apology sounded so much like Alyssa. The way she'd mentioned how God had watched over them was also something Alyssa would say.

Not Mallory.

Alyssa had vowed not to take Mallory's identity ever again, but what if she thought her life was in danger? Would that be enough to cause her to forsake her vow?

Yes. Slowly realization dawned. Of course it would. "You're Alyssa."

"What?" She stared at him as if he were crazy. "My ID says otherwise."

He couldn't believe he hadn't figured it out sooner. The way she'd known the woman in the hospital waiting room was going into respiratory arrest—just the first of many clues. And he'd ignored them all. "You're not Mallory, you're Alyssa." He knew he was right. An overwhelming relief washed over him. He wanted to hold her.

"And you know this—how?"

The anger in her voice jerked him back to reality. "It's the only thing that makes sense. Earlier you asked me if I believed in God, and I do. So does Alyssa. But Mallory is not a churchgoer. Aly...*you* talked about it."

Slowly she shook her head. "I think you're just saying this to make yourself feel better."

"Feel better about what?" he demanded.

"About how close we came to kissing back there on the sidewalk."

He remembered that moment, when their faces had been close. Too close. "Nothing happened," he denied swiftly. "What's wrong with you? I thought you'd be glad to know your true identity."

"But I don't know my true identity, do I?" she countered. "Telling me I'm Alyssa or Mallory doesn't really change anything. I'm not anyone until I can remember for myself."

He didn't want to admit she was right. He knew she had to be Alyssa. Even from here he could see how her rose and dagger tattoo had faded. But while he might be convinced she really was Alyssa, the truth didn't change anything.

She still couldn't remember. Not her identity and not anything related to the danger they were in.

Danger. The realization hit him like a ton of bricks. If the Jefferson project was at the root of the danger, they couldn't stay in his house. Wouldn't that be the first place they'd look? He and Alyssa needed to get out of here, before his suburban neighborhood became the site of another supposed gang shoot-out.

"We can't stay here," he said, abruptly changing the subject. "We'll grab something to eat and then pack a couple of bags."

"Leave?" she frowned. "But we just got here."

"I know." He wished they could stay, because it was possible that being in familiar surroundings would help her memory to return. "We'll have to find a safe place to hide until we find out what's going on."

She didn't look convinced. "You really think we're in danger?"

"Yes, I do. But, Alyssa, you don't have to be afraid. I promise I'll protect you."

She scowled. "Don't call me Alyssa."

He was taken aback by her curt tone. "I have to call you something," he said, trying to sound reasonable. "Trust me, I know you're Alyssa."

"I do trust you to protect me," she said, her expression bleak. "But I can't be Alyssa or Mallory. I can't be anyone, not until my memory returns."

FIVE

Hugging herself, she turned her back on Gage, not wanting him to realize how close she was to completely breaking down. Why was he pursuing this? As much as Mallory's fancy condo didn't seem right, she couldn't simply accept his theory that she was really Alyssa.

This had to be some sort of defense mechanism on his part. A way for Gage to ease his guilt. He could deny it until the cows came home, but she knew they'd been close to kissing once they'd realized they were safe on the sidewalk. It hadn't been just her imagination. Obviously, he needed a way to excuse his behavior, by convincing himself she was Alyssa and not Mallory.

"Aly—look, I'm sorry. I know this is a lot for you to take in at one time. And I wish we could stay here until you do. We need to leave as soon as possible. Would you mind making sandwiches while I throw some things into a couple of duffel bags?"

Letting out her breath in a sigh, she reluctantly nodded. "Sure. I should be able to manage that."

"Thank you," he murmured softly, his gaze compassionate. His gratitude was almost too much to bear. It was easier when he acted as if he didn't like her. She'd convinced herself she had to keep her distance from him because he belonged to Alyssa.

But what if he really belonged to her? The mere thought made her heart race.

Now which one of them was taking the easy way out? Annoyed with herself, she waited until Gage left the kitchen before turning her attention to the task at hand. Now that he'd mentioned food, she realized she was terribly hungry. Sandwiches sounded good, so she crossed over to the bread box and found a loaf of light wheat bread, exactly the kind she liked. She found a butter knife in the silverware drawer and was opening the fridge before she realized she'd known exactly where the silverware was kept.

Could he be right? Was she really Alyssa?

Or could it be that Mallory had spent some time here, too, and also would have known where the silverware was kept? Actually, the more she thought about it, the more she realized the drawer, wider than the others, was the most logical place to keep silverware. The way she'd gone there first had nothing to do with having a buried memory.

And obviously, psychoanalyzing herself to death wouldn't help. The doctor had said her memory would return, and she had little choice but to believe him. She'd remembered Crane, right? The rest would come in time.

She found fresh turkey, lettuce, tomato and mayo for their sandwiches and quickly made several, figuring Gage would need at least two to keep him satisfied.

The first cupboard she opened didn't contain the paper bags, but she found them eventually and packed the sandwiches along with crisp green apples for their lunch.

"Are you ready?" Gage asked when he returned.

"Yes." She frowned when she saw the two duffel bags he had slung over his shoulder. "You have clothes for me in there, too?" she asked with dismay. She couldn't explain why the idea bothered her so much.

He flushed and shook his head. "No. But I have some sweatpants, T-shirts and sweatshirts for you to wear. We can't go back to Mallory's condo, it's not safe. Although, I suppose if you really want to wear your own clothes, we could stop at Alyssa's town house to pick up a few things."

A few hours ago, she would have jumped on the chance to get some different clothes, something comfortable to wear. Now, she sensed this was just another way for Gage to prove she was Alyssa. She shook her head, wincing at the flash of pain. Her headache still lingered in the recesses of her brain, no matter how much she tried to ignore it. "No, that's all right. Sweatpants and sweatshirts are fine with me. I'm always cold anyway."

"If you're sure," Gage said slowly. The way he looked at her with such an intent gaze made her uncomfortable. She could tell he was trying to figure out what was going on in her mind, especially since she didn't want to be called Alyssa. How could she explain what she didn't understand herself? "Let me know if you change your mind," he added. "If you're ready, let's get going. We can eat in the car on the way to visit Emma Banks and Paige Sanders."

"We're still going to question them, even though you think I'm Alyssa?" she challenged.

He looked surprised at her question. "You said yourself, you don't remember anything. And I guess I don't have proof, except for your faith. But it doesn't matter, really, because at this point, I need all the information they can give me."

She couldn't argue his logic, so she followed him outside, carrying the lunch bags. He'd changed into a short-sleeved knit shirt, and the muscles in his arms flexed as he tucked the bags safely behind the front seat of the truck. The elastic wrap was still covering the wound in his upper arm, and she made a mental note to change the dressing again later, to make sure the injury didn't get infected.

When the bullets had peppered the air around them, he'd covered her body with his, protecting her from harm. He'd never so much as muttered a complaint when he'd been hit. She was awed by his strength and protectiveness.

And she couldn't deny she was attracted to him. Still, she was determined not to act on her feelings until she'd regained her memories of him. Of their relationship. If there was a relationship to remember.

She climbed into the passenger seat beside him, fearing that telling herself to ignore the tumultuous feelings she had for Gage would prove far easier than actually doing it.

She watched warily as Gage's expression grew dark and grim as the day progressed. Checking with Paige and Emma proved futile. Both nurses denied seeing Alyssa other than the last time they'd worked together. Paige had been shocked at the news about Alyssa's leave of absence, and she couldn't offer any ideas about where Alyssa might have gone or whether or not she believed she was in danger.

Emma, on the other hand, had stared at her in shock when they met her at the door. To avoid confusion, she'd introduced herself as Mallory. After all, that was the name on her driver's license. "I thought you were sick," Emma said.

"What do you mean?" she asked with a frown.

"Alyssa told me she needed some time off because of her sister." Emma shrugged. "I guess I assumed you were sick."

"No. I'm not sick." She exchanged a long glance with Gage. Apparently Alyssa's time off work had been carefully planned. Had Mallory helped Alyssa with her plan? She wished she knew. "Did Alyssa say anything else?"

Emma shook her head. "'Fraid not."

She nodded and smiled. "Thanks for your help."

Gage fished a business card from his pocket and handed it to Emma. He'd given one to Paige, too. "If you hear from Alyssa, will you please call me? Doesn't matter if it's day or night, just call."

If he was putting on an act for Emma's benefit, he deserved to win an award. The anguish in his tone made clear his feelings for Alyssa. For her? Her heart surged with hope and she ruthlessly squashed it. She turned away, determined to keep her distance.

Neither of them spoke as they walked back to his truck. She forced herself to think about what they'd learned. Alyssa must have planned to disappear, which only lent credence to Gage's theory.

"You realize that if I'm Alyssa, Mallory is the one who's missing," she said after several long moments.

He shot her a quick glance. "Yeah, that thought occurred to me, too."

"So maybe we're going about this all wrong," she mused. "Maybe we need to be searching for Mallory. Rick Weber is her boss. Maybe he knows something."

Gage shrugged. "Seems to me Rick couldn't know much, since he left a message for Mallory about the Jefferson project. Besides, I don't get the impression Mallory is particularly close to her boss."

"Who is she close to?"

"You."

Her breath caught in her throat. "You mean—she's close to Alyssa."

He didn't answer for a minute, his attention on the road. Emma Banks lived outside the city, and the traffic on the freeway was particularly heavy, thanks to summer construction. He slowed to a crawl. "We're supposed to meet my project manager, Dan Kirkland, downtown in thirty minutes. At this rate, we're going to be late."

She let him change the subject, because really, why belabor the point? Deep down, she knew she'd rather be Alyssa than Mallory. Mallory lived a lifestyle she wasn't sure she liked. The condo was fancy, but not to her taste. But she also couldn't deny that there could be a very good reason for Mallory to hide her true nature beneath a facade. Maybe the older guy in the glossy photo had done something to hurt Mallory. Maybe that's why Mallory had looked sad standing next to a glowing Alyssa.

If she was really Mallory, then she'd accept herself for who she was. If she'd made mistakes in the past, then fine. She'd deal with that and move on.

God forgave all sins. Surely he'd forgive Mallory's sins. Whatever they were.

"I'm getting off the freeway," Gage muttered. "This traffic is ridiculous."

Her ankle throbbed and she opened her purse to find her pills, only to realize she left them on the kitchen counter. "Gage, do you think it's safe to go back to the condo for a few minutes?"

"What?" He looked over at her. "Why?"

"I forgot my pain medication," she admitted, worrying her lower lip with her teeth. "But if you think it's too dangerous, then I'll live without them."

Gage let out a sigh. "No one would expect us to go back, so it's probably fine. As long as we don't stay too long."

"Just enough to get my pills," she promised.

Gage drove past the high-rise condo once, looking over the area. The mess was mostly cleaned up and the police had left the area. He circled the block before pulling into an empty parking space a few blocks from the doorway. Even then, he hesitated for a long moment until he finally turned toward her.

"Will you wait here for me?" he asked. "No need for both of us to go in."

She shook her head. "Don't leave me outside alone, please, Gage. What if the gunman comes back? I'd rather be with you."

He hesitated and then nodded. "Okay, we need to be in and out in less than five minutes." His serious gaze met hers. "Ready?"

She pulled out her keys and then clutched her purse tightly. "Yes. I'm ready."

Gage took the keys and, moving swiftly, they both climbed out of his truck and headed into the building. The glass elevator was waiting for them on the ground floor and they hurried to step inside. The ride to the top floor took forever, and she couldn't help feeling completely exposed the way they were practically surrounded with glass. Once outside her door, Gage took her arm and moved her protectively behind him. He used her key to open the door and kicked it with his foot before daring to poke his head inside.

The red, blue and black condo appeared empty. The only real place to hide was in her bedroom. He led the way down the hall, making sure the room was clear before stepping back to allow her to enter the kitchen. The small pill bottle wasn't on the counter. In the bathroom? She hurried down the hall and into the bathroom, picking up the medication she'd left there.

Since she was right near the bedroom, she took a few minutes to stuff some underwear into her purse, too. She returned to the living room in less than two minutes. "I'm ready."

"Good. Let's go."

They rode the elevator down to the lobby. On the way out, she noticed, through the wide-envelope slot, that her mailbox was full. Glancing at her keys, she made a quick detour.

"What are you doing?" he asked.

"The mailbox is full, probably from yesterday's delivery. Don't you think it would be best to empty it out?"

"Good thinking." His approval made her smile. She simply shoved the mail into her purse, which was bulging by this point. They easily made it back out to Gage's truck well within their allotted time frame. He kept a hand under her elbow, herding her toward their vehicle. He gave her a boost up into the truck before skirting around to climb in beside her. Gage pulled away, and she sat back in relief as they left the fancy condo building behind.

"Your purse looks like it's going to explode," Gage teased.

She blushed, refusing to tell him she'd stuffed underwear in there, too. Sweatpants and T-shirts were fine, bu she needed underclothes, as well. "Where are we going to spend the night?"

"Good question." He kept his gaze on the road as he navigated several turns. "I'd like to talk to Dan first, and then figure out where to go from there."

She knew Gage was hoping Dan would have information for them. But what if he didn't? They needed answers, and her lack of memory certainly wasn't helping their situation.

She closed her eyes and focused on the brief recognition of Officer Crane. For a nanosecond, she could clearly see the taut lines of irritation on his ruddy face. When had she spoken to him? Where were they? At the police station perhaps? She had the impression of sterile-looking walls behind him. The feeling of doom persisted. And she couldn't help but wonder—would the return of her memory bring concrete reasons for the elusive sense of danger?

Gage tried to keep his eyes on the road, but he couldn't help sending quick sidelong glances over to Alyssa. He couldn't understand her reluctance to be called Alyssa, especially when he knew, deep down, that's who she really was.

It was the only thing that made sense.

Retrograde amnesia, the doctor had said. A temporary loss of memory around a specific, traumatic event. But amnesia wouldn't change someone's personality. And the woman sitting beside him acted and sounded like Alyssa.

But if she was Alyssa, then maybe they really should be searching for Mallory. Their parents had died a few years ago, leaving a modest inheritance for the twins. He knew Alyssa had put her half of the money into a savings account, planning to use some for their wedding.

But if Mallory needed it, she'd give it to her sister

without so much as a second thought. With cash, Mallory could be anywhere.

Gage pulled into the parking garage across the street from the high-rise building that housed Drummond Builders Inc. The parking attendant on duty greeted him cheerfully when he rolled down the window. "Good evening, Mr. Drummond."

"Good evening to you, too, Curtis." Gage pulled through the gate and parked in the first available space. After shutting off his truck, he got out and went around to open the passenger door for Alyssa. He knew she had a sore ankle, so he didn't say anything about how they were running late for their six o'clock meeting with Dan.

Alyssa's gaze swept the area, as if she'd never seen this part of the city before. Which he knew wasn't true, since she'd come to visit him here often. "Anything look familiar?" he asked casually.

"No, sorry." They walked together across the street and into the building. Alyssa continued to glance around as if seeing everything for the first time. Inside the chrome-and-glass office building, she waited for him to lead the way.

He tried not to show his disappointment. He'd really hoped Alyssa might remember his office building. They entered a quiet, conventional elevator and he pushed the button for the tenth floor.

"Only the tenth floor?" She cocked an eyebrow at him. "Not the penthouse suite? I'm shocked."

Her teasing made him smile. He and Alyssa had bantered like this a lot, before she'd broken off their engagement. "I'm lucky to afford downtown rent at all," he murmured. "The penthouse is out of my league."

"Can you afford to stay here, even without the Jefferson project?" she asked.

Slowly, he shook his head. "Probably not." He'd worked hard to grow the business over these past few years. His father had retired three years ago, yet their reputation for doing great work lived on. Branching out with something as big as the Jefferson project had been a risk, but one that had paid off. Or so he thought. Now, pulling out of the project would damage his reputation, and without other projects, he'd very likely have to downsize.

The idea that he might lose his business altogether made him feel sick. The subtle ding of the elevator brought him out of his grim thoughts. The doors silently slid open. The main office was closed for the weekend. Gage and his chief project manager were probably the only two who could be found working at odd hours, day or night, doing whatever it took to get the job done on time and under budget.

He unlocked the office door and stepped over the threshold. The summer sky poured in through the windows. Still, he flicked on the overhead lights so Dan would know they were here. He crossed the room, his footsteps muffled on the thick carpet.

"Nice place," Alyssa commented.

He nodded an acknowledgment but didn't answer. The message light on the office phone wasn't lit. He pulled out his cell phone, checking to see if he'd missed a message from Dan letting him know he'd be late.

No message, so he called Dan himself. But the call went directly to Dan's voice mail. Why wouldn't Dan have his phone on? Gage closed his phone with a snap. Where was he? Dan was rarely late.

"Problems?" Alyssa asked, sensing his mood.

"No. Dan will be here soon." He decided not to voice his concern. Alyssa had enough to worry about.

She arched her brow as if she didn't believe him, a gesture that keenly reminded him of Alyssa. "So, how about giving me the grand tour while we wait?" she suggested.

Gage couldn't think of a reason not to. Showing her around might spark her memory. And besides, anything was better than standing around staring at each other. He waved a hand at the office around him. "This is the main office. My assistant, Jane Hanson, sits here and generally manages to keep everything running smoothly."

He turned and walked toward the back of the room, where several other doors were located. "My office is through here." He unlocked the door farthest to the right and opened it. As owner of the business, he'd earned the corner office, complete with ceiling-to-floor windows. He didn't mention the attacks of vertigo that hit him when he stood too close to them. After flicking on the lights, he stepped back to allow Alyssa to enter.

She walked past him, brushing ever so slightly against him. She whistled softly under her breath when she saw the plush office complete with beautiful mahogany furniture. She headed straight for the windows. "Can you see Lake Michigan from here?"

"Uh—yeah. Sort of." He ventured farther into the room but didn't join her by the windows. He didn't like to stand so close, looking down. "To the right of the Art Museum you can make out the gleam of the lake."

"Oh, I see it now." She flashed him a warm smile over her shoulder. "Very nice. I really hope you don't have to give this up." Her eyes filled with concern.

"Me, either." It wouldn't be the first time he'd have to start from scratch. After his mother died, he and his father had lived hand-to-mouth, moving from one construction job to the next. Once he'd finished high school, their business had taken off to the point where they were financially secure. He'd thought it was a perfect time to get married, start a family.

Then things had fallen apart with Alyssa. And now the Jefferson project was surrounded in danger. Squashing the flash of helplessness, he stepped back so Alyssa could come back out. He closed and locked the door behind her.

"Whose offices are these?" She gestured to the remaining two doors.

"One is Dan's office. The other is actually a conference room. We run a pretty lean staff. I have several assistant project managers, but they stay on the job sites rather than camp out here. The most important part of our work isn't done within these walls."

"I can understand that. So the Jefferson project isn't the only one you're working on?" Alyssa reached out to try Dan's office door. The handle turned smoothly beneath the pressure of her hand and the door swung open.

"It's not locked," she said, stating the obvious.

Gage frowned and squeezed past her to enter the office, flipping on a light switch as he went. He could feel Alyssa following close behind him. Barely two steps into the room, he nearly tripped over the body lying on the floor.

Beside him, Alyssa cried out in horror. Grimly, he stared at the vacant, lifeless gaze of his chief project manager and the knife buried deep in his chest. Gage bit back a wave of impotent grief.

Dan hadn't been late for their meeting after all.

SIX

She stumbled backward, away from the dark stain on Dan Kirkland's chest. Blood. There was so much blood. She tried to close her eyes but the blood was everywhere, smeared on the walls and pooled on the floor. And in the far corner of the room, a bloody yellow blouse. She sobbed, overwhelmed with grief. *Mallory!*

"Alyssa!"

She blinked and the image faded. She was surprised to realize she was sitting on the floor, her back against the office wall and Gage looming over her. He had a worried expression as he knelt at her side. "Are you okay?"

She swallowed a wave of nausea and nodded. The image had been so real, but what did it mean? Where had she seen so much blood? She wanted to believe the bloody room was too horrible to be real, except for the bloodstains on her jeans. She gulped a huge breath of air and tried to swallow her panic. Dazed, she glanced around. How on earth had she gotten out of Dan's office, to the farthest side of the room, closest to the door?

"You shouted your sister's name." His gaze was full of compassionate concern. "Did you remember something? Something about your twin?"

The foggy haze was back and her temple ached. She was oddly reluctant to tell Gage about the blood and the yellow blouse. Was it really a memory? The sense of danger returned more forceful than ever. "I shouted Mallory's name?"

"Yes, when you saw Dan, and then you ran away." Gage sat back on his heels, scrubbing a hand over his face. "I don't blame you for being upset. I can't believe he's dead."

A real dead body was far worse than a bloody room. "How?" she whispered.

"A knife wound to the chest. His wallet is lying on the floor next to him, empty. Cash and credit cards are missing."

Alyssa started to tremble. "Robbery? You're saying this is a result of a simple mugging?"

"That's what they want us to believe, but there's no way this is anything simple." His hands shook, ever so slightly, and he closed them into fists. "We need to call the police."

"No!" her response was immediate. Intense. She grabbed his arm, hanging on tight. "Don't."

For a long minute Gage stared at her. Then he slowly stood, gently pulling her up onto her feet. "Alyssa, I have to. He was more than an employee, he was my friend. I can't leave him lying there. He has family, an ex-wife, parents. We have to call somebody. Especially when you and I know very well this isn't a random mugging."

Alyssa put a hand to her throat, the pressure in her chest so tight she could hardly breathe. "Let's get out of here first, and then call someone to investigate."

He frowned. "The police will want to talk to us, since we found the body."

She couldn't explain the deep fear twisting around inside. "Please, Gage? We can't stay here. We have to leave. Now." *Run! Run! Get as far from the blood and police as possible. Run!* She grabbed Gage's arm and tugged him toward the door. She'd drag him the whole way if necessary.

"Okay, okay, let me think." He hung back, halting her progress, and reached for his phone. "I left a message with Jonah earlier today. Jonah Stewart is a detective with the Milwaukee Police Department. He and I have been friends since high school. I'd trust him with my life. I'll call him for help."

The thought of going to the police terrified her, but surely they could trust Gage's high school friend. "We can call him once we're safely away from here. Please?" She couldn't explain the desperate need to escape. What if Crane was on his way here already? The guy had a knack for showing up at crime scenes.

The stark fear in her gaze must have gotten to him, because he finally relented. "Okay, let's go. I'll try him later."

She couldn't get out of the office suite fast enough. Gage walked over to the elevators and pushed the down button. Both cars were on the ground floor. "Let's take the stairs."

"Ten flights? Are you crazy?" he asked.

"Down is easy. Come on." She refused to take no for an answer. She headed into the stairwell, instinctively knowing Gage wouldn't let her go alone. She took the stairs down as quickly as she could manage on her ankle. The sounds of pounding feet intermingled with their heavy breathing. Alyssa didn't stop until they reached the ground floor.

She opened the door on the ground level with trepidation. Thankfully, the lobby of the office building was deserted. When they walked past the elevators, she noticed they were both on the tenth floor. Would both elevators be summoned at the push of a button? Or had someone ridden to the tenth floor to find them? Someone like Officer Crane?

She couldn't explain her paranoia, so she kept her wild thoughts to herself. Tugging on Gage's arm, she led the way outside and across the street to the parking garage where they'd left his truck. Dark apprehension clenched her belly and she couldn't relax, even when the parking lot attendant gave them a cheerful wave as they drove away.

Gage navigated the streets, his thoughts in turmoil. He still couldn't believe Dan Kirkland was dead. The image of Dan's vacant gaze and the bloody knife embedded deep in his chest haunted him. His grief was nearly overwhelming, but he held himself together with an effort, knowing Alyssa needed him to be strong. There would be time to mourn the passing of his friend later.

He darted a glance over to Alyssa. She was still pale, huddled in the seat as if chilled, although the temperature outside was warm. Her blue eyes were unnaturally bright, indicating she was still in shock.

She'd screamed when they'd all but stumbled across Dan's inert body and then had backed away, huddling against the opposite wall, sobbing and crying out her sister's name. He feared something terrible may have happened to Alyssa. Something traumatic that ultimately caused her amnesia.

And why was she so afraid of the police? Not just the

officer she'd remembered at the scene outside Mallory's condo, but apparently all police. Why would she be so frightened? What secret was hidden in her locked memory? He risked another sidelong glance, thankful to note her cheeks had regained a bit of color.

Hearing her call out Mallory's name had cemented his belief that she was Alyssa.

"Where are we going?" she asked in a low tone, as if feeling his gaze upon her.

"A small motel outside of town. A place called the Forty Winks motel. They'll take cash with no questions asked." Gage rubbed a hand over his eyes, fighting exhaustion. Although Alyssa looked far worse than he felt.

He wanted to hold her close, to offer comfort. But he forced himself to keep his distance. She didn't remember him, and for the first time, it occurred to him that when she did remember, she'd know exactly why she'd left him.

Gage forced himself to concentrate on their next steps. Once they arrived at the motel, he'd need to get in touch with Jonah to help take care of Dan. He couldn't help feeling guilty that they hadn't gotten to the office sooner. Maybe if they hadn't been late, Dan would still be alive. Had his project manager discovered something incriminating related to the Jefferson project? Was that why someone stabbed him? There were several homicides in Milwaukee every month. But there were now at least two deaths connected to the Jefferson project, and that wasn't a coincidence.

Gage gripped the steering wheel so tightly his knuckles turned white. There was a part of him that wanted to go back to the office building to go through whatever paperwork Dan might have reviewed. But Alyssa had been so upset, he hadn't had the heart to refuse her re-

quest. He had no choice but to believe the gunfire outside Mallory's condo had been a warning to stay away,
or worse, an attempt to kill them. Either way, he couldn't
take a chance with her life.

He'd do anything to keep her safe. And for the first
time in months, he silently prayed.

*Dear Lord, please give me the knowledge and strength
to keep Alyssa safe.*

The rooms in the Forty Winks motel were worse
than he remembered. Thankfully, they had two adjoining rooms. The two-story building had thirty rooms, all
facing outside. He'd requested rooms on the first floor
farthest from the office.

He unlocked the first door and crossed over to set the
duffel he'd packed for Alyssa on the bed. He unlocked
the connecting door between their rooms and then retraced his steps to the main door. "Alyssa, you need to
keep that connecting door open, okay?"

She stood uncertainly in the center of the room, looking fragile, as if a strong wind would blow her away.
"Sure."

Once again, he longed to take her into his arms to
offer comfort. Instead, he walked back outside and entered the second motel room. He opened his connecting door and noticed Alyssa had disappeared into the
bathroom.

His phone rang, and he was pleased to see the caller
was Jonah. "I'm so glad you called me back," he said
gratefully.

"You sounded desperate. What's up?"

"I have a big problem, Jonah. I really need your help."

"Lucky for you, I just finished up a case, so I have

some vacation time coming," Jonah said, his voice sharp with interest.

Gage hesitated. He'd known Jonah long before he'd become a homicide detective, but this wasn't the sort of bomb you dropped over the phone. "If you don't mind, I'd rather talk to you in person."

"No problem," Jonah agreed readily enough. "Where are you? I can leave right now."

Relieved, Gage gave his friend directions to their motel. If Jonah thought the Forty Winks was a strange meeting place, he didn't let on. After promising to be there soon, he hung up.

Gage immediately felt better. Jonah was a good detective, and he'd know what to do. There wasn't much to unpack, so he paced the length of his room, staying away from the connecting door but listening to the muffled thumps as Alyssa moved around.

Soon, she came over to stand in the open doorway between their rooms. Her hair was damp, and she'd changed her clothes, the neckline of his oversize T-shirt giving a glimpse of the rose and dagger tattoo just beneath her collarbone. The tattoo was more faded than ever.

"Did you get hold of your cop friend?" she asked.

"Uh, yeah." He sighed and scrubbed a hand over his face. "Jonah has met Alyssa before, so I'll have to explain about your amnesia."

She grimaced but nodded. "I understand."

There was a sharp knock at his motel door. Gage jumped up and crossed over, peering through the peephole to verify that Jonah was the one standing on the other side. Darkness had fallen, but the evenly spaced lights between the rooms were bright enough for him to easily recognize his friend.

He unlocked the chain and opened the door. "Jonah." He thumped his buddy on the back in greeting. "I can't tell you how glad I am to see you."

"Same here. I have to say, you piqued my curiosity." Jonah wore regular street clothes but the shoulder harness housing his gun was reassuring. "What's going on?"

Gage drew Jonah inside. "Jonah, you remember Alyssa, don't you?"

"Uh, yeah. Sure." Jonah studied her, looking uncomfortable. "Nice to see you again, Alyssa."

A faint smile touched her lips. "I'd say the same if I could remember you, Jonah," she murmured.

Jonah's jaw dropped in shock. "Alyssa hit her head and has amnesia," Gage hastily explained. He pulled up one of the two straight-back chairs. "Sit down, Jonah, and let me explain everything from the beginning."

Jonah sank into the seat, a dazed expression on his face. Alyssa sat on the bed, hugging her knees to her chest.

"I told you how I won the bid for the Jefferson project, right?" Gage asked. Jonah nodded. "Three days ago, City Councilman Ray Schaefer was brought into Trinity's E.D. after he was stabbed in the chest."

Jonah frowned. "Yeah, I heard he was the victim of a gang-initiation prank."

"Not true." Gage held Jonah's gaze with his. "Alyssa was working the trauma room that night. The councilman told her what really happened." Gage filled in the details.

Jonah's eyes widened, and he glanced over at Alyssa. "Did you talk to anyone else about this?"

"I don't know," Alyssa whispered. "I can't remember."

Jonah scowled, his expression clearly saying he didn't

believe her. "You can't remember anything? Are you sure?"

"Knock it off, Jonah. Her amnesia is real and you need to let me finish. I didn't take Alyssa's concerns seriously, and I think she must be in danger." He hated himself for letting Alyssa down. "And to make matters worse, Mallory is missing."

"We should file a missing person's report, right away." Jonah leaned forward, in full cop mode.

"There's more," Gage cautioned. "Earlier today, when Alyssa and I were leaving Mallory's condo, someone opened fire on us, shooting from the back window of a rusty beige Cadillac. When the police arrived, they told us we were victims of gang violence."

"Yeah, there have been reports of increasing gang violence in the form of random shootings," Jonah admitted.

"Both Ray Schaefer and us?" Gage raised his eyebrows in disbelief. "I don't think so, because the problems don't stop there. I called my chief project manager, Dan Kirkland. I told him I had serious reservations about the Jefferson project. I explained how Alyssa was convinced it was dangerous. He mentioned he'd found something odd, but he wanted to verify it first. We made arrangements to meet at six o'clock this evening. But we were late. We thought he wasn't there, but then we stumbled upon his dead body." His voice turned husky with grief. He cleared his throat and forced himself to continue. "Dan had been stabbed in the chest, his wallet lying empty beside him."

"Two people associated with the project dead and one attempt on your life." Jonah slowly summarized the key events, his expression grim. "I don't like it. I don't like it at all."

Relief washed over him. He and Alyssa weren't alone, not anymore. "Exactly my point. And Schaefer was stabbed, too, just like Dan."

"Okay, but why call me?" Jonah asked, perplexed. "Why not call the police?"

"Jonah, you're the only cop I know on a personal level, and to be honest we don't know who to trust. The Jefferson project was hotly contested and there's a lot of money on the line. For all we know, anyone could be involved in this."

Jonah raised his brow. "You mean like the mayor?"

"Possibly. Why not?" He shrugged. "Expensive, luxury condos mean a nice increase in city taxes. Eric Holden has only been the interim mayor for a few weeks, since Mayor Flynn's unexpected death from a massive heart attack. They're holding a special election on Tuesday to make things official, aren't they? The timing is suspicious. Could be someone who works for Holden. Or the city. There could be cops involved."

"Creepy Crane," Alyssa said suddenly.

"Who?" Jonah turned in his seat to face her.

"Aaron Crane. He's a cop."

Jonah frowned. "And you don't like him?"

Alyssa slowly shook her head. "I don't trust him. He was one of the cops who came to the scene outside the condo. The way he stared at me—I can't describe it."

"You're a beautiful woman, Alyssa." Jonah shrugged diplomatically. "Can't arrest a guy for being interested in a beautiful woman."

"No, it wasn't that." Alyssa waved a hand in annoyance. "He stared at me as if he'd seen a ghost. He wanted to know my name and asked to see my ID."

"We always check IDs at the scene of a crime," Jonah said in exasperation. "So what?"

"They checked mine, too, remember," Gage added, supporting his friend.

"It was almost as if he knew me," Alyssa persisted. "And now that I think about it, I gave him Mallory's ID. Maybe that's the only reason he let me go."

Gage was glad she'd seemed to accept she really was Alyssa, but now that she mentioned how Crane looked at her ID, he found he was glad she'd borrowed Mallory's identity. Especially if it kept her safe.

Jonah sighed heavily. "I have to admit, I never liked Crane. He's far too arrogant for his own good. But that doesn't mean he's involved in this. We need facts, not gut feelings." Jonah turned toward Gage. "I don't suppose you've notified the police about finding Dan Kirkland's body in your office?"

The expression on Gage's face must have told the whole story.

"Great, just great." Jonah pushed his fingers through his sun-streaked hair. "I have to call this in, and it's going to look suspicious that you came here first."

"Alyssa was upset, shaking. I had to get her out of there," Gage said slowly. "But you have to tell them she's Mallory and that we left because we didn't know if the killer was lurking around somewhere."

"Okay, that works," Jonah agreed. "As a homicide detective, I can investigate his death, but that means I need to get over there right away."

"Thanks, Jonah. I owe you one," Gage said gratefully.

"Yeah." Jonah stood. "But hey, what are friends for? Just don't go anywhere, because after I examine the crime scene I'll have to officially interview both of you. We need to follow the book as close as possible on this."

"We're not going anywhere." Gage kept his gaze from straying to where Alyssa still sat on the bed. Her hair had dried and now waved softly around her face.

"Okay, then. Give me a couple of hours to get everything I need from the crime scene." Jonah didn't appear to mind the prospect of a long night ahead of him. His eyes were bright with interest. Gage knew his buddy loved nothing more than solving a good puzzle.

"Like I said, we'll be here." Gage followed him to the door. When he left, Gage called out, "Jonah?" His friend glanced over his shoulder questioningly. "Be careful. If Dan's death is related to the Jefferson project, you could be in danger, too. Especially if the danger is from inside."

"Don't worry, I know how to handle this." Confident as ever, Jonah raised a hand as he left.

Gage watched him leave, the gnawing in his gut worsening with every step. Jonah was a good cop. One of the best. He could take care of himself. Gage let out a heavy sigh and shut the door, flipping the dead bolt and then looping the chain lock for added security. Both locks were relatively useless against the kind of hit that occurred outside Mallory's condo, but whoever the bad guys were, they'd have to find them first.

"He's going to help us," Alyssa murmured. "He seems like a good man."

"Yeah. We can trust him to do what's right." He looked anywhere but directly at her. "Why don't you try and get some rest?"

"I will if you will," Alyssa said softly.

"Shouldn't be a problem, I'm going on less than four hours of sleep. I'll be fine."

She looked at him oddly for a long moment before slipping off the bed and retreating through the open connecting door. "Good night, Gage."

"Good night." Gage closed the door between their rooms, but didn't lock it. He headed for the bathroom, the hot water helping to relax the knotted muscles in his shoulders. He tried not to think of Dan's lifeless eyes staring at him from the office floor, but the image haunted him.

He must have dozed, because an odd noise had him jerking upright in surprise. He held his breath, his heart hammering in his chest. Was someone trying to break in?

Then he heard the noise again, from Alyssa's room. He softly padded to the connecting door and hesitantly opened it, waiting for his eyes to grow accustomed to the dim light. He was horrified to find Alyssa standing in front of her motel room door, struggling to unlock it as she mumbled under her breath.

He froze, trying to make sense of what he was seeing. Was she sleepwalking? "Alyssa? Where are you going?"

She didn't seem to hear him. "Blood—there's too much blood."

That was the same thing she'd said in the office after he'd stumbled over Dan's body. Was she dreaming about it now?

"Alyssa." He raised his voice and crossed over to place a hand on her shoulder. He gently tried to pry her away from the door. "Wake up. You're having a bad dream."

Either his voice or his touch must have gotten through to her, because she stopped struggling. She stood stock-still before turning to glance at him.

"Gage? What happened?"

The expression in her eyes made his heart thunder

in his chest. She was looking up at him as if she recognized him. Did she finally remember? The way he'd proposed marriage? And the way she'd broken up with him? He reined in his emotions with an effort. "I'm here," he murmured soothingly, brushing a strand of hair away from her damp cheek. "Come away from the door. You're safe, Alyssa."

"I don't remember getting up," she confessed softly. She shivered and he put a supporting arm around her shoulders. He wasn't prepared for her to cling to him, burying her face in the hollow of his chest.

"Alyssa," he murmured helplessly, running a soothing hand down her back. When she lifted her head and glanced up at him, he couldn't stop himself from capturing her mouth in a sweet kiss.

SEVEN

Her mouth was warm, pliant beneath his. Kissing Alyssa reminded him of the good times they'd had together and how much he cared about her. But as much as he wanted to crush her close and deepen the kiss, he forced himself to ease away.

Alyssa stared up at him, her eyes dazed. "You shouldn't have done that," she whispered, lifting a hand to her mouth.

"I'm sorry," he said, accepting full responsibility for his actions. She was right—he shouldn't have kissed her like that. As if they were still a couple, when he knew full well they weren't.

"You don't even know for sure I'm Alyssa!" Her voice held a note of panic.

"I know you're Alyssa," he said soothingly. "But if you don't believe me, take a look in the mirror. Half your rose and dagger tattoo is missing."

"It is?" She scrambled from the bed, apparently anxious to see for herself. She spent what seemed like an inordinate amount of time in the bathroom before she returned. "You're right. This tattoo is fake. I guess I must be Alyssa."

He nodded and stood, giving her plenty of room to get back into bed. "I'm glad you finally know who you are."

"I already told you that knowing isn't remembering. I don't remember who I am, and I don't remember you, Gage," she said in a low anguished tone. "I wish I did, but I don't."

"I know." He tried to smile reassuringly, realizing that by kissing her he'd just ruined the perfect opportunity to start their relationship over. "I didn't mean to take advantage of the situation, Alyssa. I only came over because you were having a nightmare."

"Yes. I remember dreaming about blood." She shivered and clenched her hands together tightly as if to keep them from shaking. "Lots of blood."

"Don't force your memory," he advised, wishing he could do something to ease her torment. "The doctor told you it would return when you're ready."

"I think I'm a little afraid to remember," she admitted in a low whisper. "What if the blood from my dream is real? What if I saw something horrible?"

His heart twisted at the stark anguish in her eyes. "Don't think about your dream any more tonight. For now, I want you to rest. You're safe, Alyssa. I won't let anything happen to you."

"Thanks, Gage." She offered a faint smile. "I'm sorry I woke you. I'm sure I'll be fine now. Good night."

"Good night, Alyssa." He didn't think she'd really be able to go back to sleep, but he sensed she needed to be alone. Thanks to his impatience, she needed space.

Time and distance far away from him.

Alyssa could hear Gage moving softly around in his connecting room. Ridiculous to feel a sense of loss, considering he was right next door.

Her lips still tingled from his kiss. And if she were honest with herself, she'd admit that Gage's kiss had felt a little familiar, almost like coming home. She closed her eyes, willing her evasive memories to return. But there was only the infernal swirling mist.

If she was really Alyssa, then it was no wonder she was so attracted to Gage. But it wasn't just that he was handsome, in a rugged sort of way. She liked what she knew about him so far. He believed in God, which was important to her. He was also polite, considerate and protective. All very positive and admirable qualities. So why couldn't she remember him?

Her head began to throb, so she closed her eyes and concentrated on breathing. Maybe she didn't have specific and distinct memories about Gage, but she instinctively trusted him. She believed he'd protect her. Hadn't she felt safe with him the first time she met him? Back at the hospital, when everyone thought she was Mallory?

The danger surrounding them was all too real. The bullets that had rained around them had been real. Dan's dead body with the knife protruding from his chest had been real. She was convinced her fear of Officer Crane was real, too.

She felt so helpless. Useless. How could she help Gage if she couldn't remember what she was so afraid of? Instinctively, a Bible verse from 2 Samuel flashed in her mind, so clearly it was as if she could see the words on the page. *It is God who arms me with strength and keeps my way secure.*

Alyssa closed her eyes and opened her heart to prayer. *Dear Lord, please give me strength. Guide me and help me to remember. Amen.*

Gage tossed and turned, unable to get comfortable. He still felt guilty for kissing Alyssa. No matter how she'd turned to him when she was afraid, the last thing she needed was for him to crowd her.

Patience, an admirable quality, had always been difficult for him. Alyssa had told him to pray to God for patience. He didn't have the heart to tell her he doubted praying to God would change his basic personality.

But he could believe that God was testing him. And finding him less than worthy. Guilt, his new constant companion, tightened his chest. He should have told Alyssa the truth about their broken engagement. In the beginning, when he'd thought that she was Mallory, he'd alluded to a relationship between them. He hadn't come out and claimed to be Alyssa's boyfriend, but he also hadn't corrected her obvious assumption.

Now their relationship, or lack thereof, was like a giant elephant in the room. He decided to tell her first thing in the morning. Alyssa should know the truth.

Clearly, Alyssa had been right all along. Hidden land mines of danger surrounded the Jefferson project. But he couldn't comprehend why. Who else, besides Hugh Jefferson, would benefit from building the Riverside Luxury Condos? And why kill City Councilman Ray Schaefer? Had the councilman's death been a necessary evil, as Dan's must have been? A way to silence them so they couldn't betray the truth?

The truth about *what?*

Gage tried to ignore the endless fountain of questions. But no matter how hard he tried, he couldn't seem to push them aside long enough to fall asleep.

Loud, insistent pounding startled him from his thought. Gage staggered to his feet and headed for the door. Peering through the peephole, he recognized Jonah. The light outside their room must have burned out. He could barely make out his friend's grim features in the early-dawn light.

"Gage?" Alyssa's voice called out from behind the door to her room. She must not have been sleeping, either.

"It's Jonah." Gage undid the locks and opened the door, glancing at his watch. Not quite six yet. He stifled a yawn. "Hey, thanks for coming back. Did you find out anything?"

"Yeah." Jonah shouldered past him and quickly shut the door. A sharp tingle of fear slithered down Gage's spine when Jonah shot the dead bolt home and rechained the lock on the door. Jonah wasn't afraid of anything, but he certainly wasn't taking any chances now.

"What is it?" Gage didn't like the grim expression on Jonah's face. Jonah snagged the chair he'd used earlier, and Alyssa reclaimed her spot on the bed, hugging her knees, her gaze darting between the two of them.

"It's bad." Jonah ran a hand over his haggard features. "Worse than I'd expected." Jonah looked as if he hadn't slept a wink, and Gage immediately felt bad for sending his friend out to face Dan's death alone. But he couldn't have left Alyssa, either.

"You'd better tell me," Gage said, mentally bracing himself as he dropped into the vacant chair.

"The cops were already at your office building when I arrived."

Gage blinked and straightened. "What? How could they know about Dan? We didn't report his death. We didn't call anyone but you."

Jonah lifted red-rimmed eyes to meet his. "I'm telling you, they were already there. Gave me some baloney about how they'd gotten an anonymous tip that they'd felt compelled to follow up on. They wanted to know why I was there."

Fear churned in his gut. The situation was getting worse by the minute. "What did you tell them?"

"That you and I are friends and that you'd called me because you hadn't heard from your project manager. That I'd promised to do a little digging to see if I could find the guy on my own time."

A dizzy wave of relief washed over him. "So they bought your story."

"Possibly, but I wouldn't bank on it. Your pal, Officer Crane, was there." Jonah glanced at Alyssa.

"He's part of this. I knew it," she whispered.

Gage noticed that this time, Jonah didn't argue. "They'd just started to record the crime scene when I arrived. I tried to claim the case as my own, but Crane told me that the case already belonged to Detective Sean Foley. I hung around until they were finished." He sighed heavily. "They want to talk to you, Gage. I promised to bring you in."

No way. He wasn't going anywhere. This is exactly what they wanted. To tie him up in red tape until he was rendered helpless, so they could get to Alyssa. He refused to leave her alone and vulnerable.

"After finishing up at the crime scene, I went back to my office," Jonah continued. "I thought I'd try to look into the Jefferson project. You know, review the problems they had getting it approved."

"And?" Gage held his breath.

"And nothing. I hit a brick wall." Jonah frowned and dragged his gaze up to meet Gage's. "You know computers are my thing. Remember when we were seventeen and I hacked into the government system?"

Gage nodded.

"Not this time. I can't tell you how many layers of security I went through. There's something odd about this Jefferson guy." Jonah scowled. "Why would the roots of a condo project be buried in security deeper than Fort Knox?"

Gage shook his head, unable to speak. Whatever the secret was, he knew that people had died because of it.

And Alyssa's memory held the key.

Alyssa couldn't get warm. She'd cranked the heat unit in the corner of the dingy motel room, yet she couldn't manage to get warm.

Your pal, Officer Crane, was there. The words echoed in her mind. She shivered and rubbed her arms. If the police were somehow part of the danger surrounding the Jefferson project, how high did the deception go? To the shift supervisor over Creepy Crane? To the chief of police? The mayor?

Her gaze settled on Jonah. He and Gage shared an easy camaraderie, but what if the detective wasn't entirely innocent? He was a cop. And he'd promised to bring Gage in for questioning. A shiver racked her body. Maybe Jonah was a good cop doing his job. She prayed Gage's instincts were right. They couldn't fight the entire Milwaukee Police Department or the myriad of city government officials on their own.

"We need to get out of town." She hadn't realized she'd spoken out loud until Gage and Jonah swung their gazes in her direction. Determination made her raise her chin. "You can't take Gage in—they'll try to pin Dan's death on him. At least long enough to distract us from the Jefferson project."

"Don't worry, I'm not going anywhere. I won't leave you alone." Gage's tone was lined with velvet steel. Overwhelming relief filled her heart. No matter what may have transpired between them, he still cared. Which was good, because heaven knew, she cared about him, too.

"If you take off, you'll look guilty," Jonah warned. "They can't pin this on you—the scene was set up to look like a robbery."

"Unless my prints are conveniently found on the knife," Gage argued.

"Too obvious. And since you found him, your prints could be explained." Jonah didn't relent.

"But they don't know I was there. I left the scene."

Jonah shrugged. "You had a hysterical female on your hands, what else could you do?"

Alyssa's cheeks burned and she hid her face against her knees. As much as she wanted to protest, she really had been one step away from hysteria. How could she explain the sense of danger that haunted her? Had the police gotten there right after they left? What if she and Gage had still been there? Would there have been three bodies lying on the office floor? She shivered again. The image of Dan's body was still embedded in her mind.

"They're not going to buy that, and even if they did I don't care. I'm not leaving Alyssa alone. Not for a second." Gage's voice jerked her thoughts away from the morbid.

"Okay, okay. Let me think for a minute." Jonah scowled and nearly swayed in his seat. "If they're really trying to set you up, then we need to take your statement sooner than later. But in a controlled way. Maybe you need a lawyer."

A lawyer? Alyssa's stomach tightened and fear threatened to choke her. They were in serious trouble if Jonah was recommending a lawyer.

"Maybe we need to find Mallory," Gage said.

"Mallory?" Jonah's head snapped up. "Why?"

Gage shifted restlessly in his seat. "Alyssa left a message on Mallory's answering machine saying it was urgent they talk. Alyssa sounded afraid, but we don't know what happened after that. But what if she had a brief conversation with Mallory? Could be Mallory knows something that will help steer us in the right direction."

"Any idea where to look for her?" Jonah asked.

Gage sighed and shook his head. "I went to Alyssa's town house, but she wasn't there. And the place was completely empty, as if Alyssa had closed the place down before she left. And Mallory wasn't at her condo, either."

"I wouldn't have put Mallory in danger," Alyssa spoke up, causing both men to look at her. "If I was in danger, I would warn Mallory to be careful. To get away and hide. I doubt she knows anything that can help us."

The blunt comment left a strained silence among the group. Finally Jonah rose to his feet. "I really should force you to come in for questioning."

Gage tensed, hands balled into fists at his sides. Alyssa knew he wasn't going anywhere. "You can try."

Jonah let out a disgusted sigh. "Forget it. You're right. This whole thing reeks of an inside job. I don't blame you for wanting to take off. But you need to stay in touch with me, Gage. I mean it. I can't work this thing in the dark."

Alyssa breathed easier when Jonah relented. She was so glad he wasn't going to force Gage to go in. But where did that leave them? What should they do next?

"Jonah, maybe you shouldn't work this thing at all." Gage's voice was soft, and her heart squeezed at the flash of concern reflected in his eyes. "I don't want any more of my friends turning up dead. Maybe you should just turn and walk away. Pretend you never found me."

"Are you going to leave it alone?" Jonah countered. "Are you going to turn around and walk away?"

"No." There was no hesitation in Gage's tone. "But I don't have a choice. Alyssa's life is in danger."

She stared at him in exasperation. "Your life is in danger now, too, Gage."

"She's right, you're both in danger." Jonah grimaced. "And you know me well enough to know I won't walk away, either. God will watch over us. Just be sure to stay in touch, understand?"

"Yeah, I hear you." Gage stood and followed Jonah toward the door and then held out his hand. "I owe you again, Jonah. More than I'll ever be able to repay."

"You don't owe me anything," Jonah corrected softly. "This is what friends are for." He took Gage's out-stretched hand and shook it firmly. "Keep me informed if you stumble across any new information." He dropped Gage's hand then shot a sidelong glance at Alyssa. "Or if Alyssa's memory returns."

"I'd like to go back to my office. See if Dan left anything in his notes that might clue us in as to what he might have found."

Jonah shook his head. "Don't bother. The cops took all of the paperwork in as evidence. I'm sure you won't find anything left that's any use to you."

Paperwork? Evidence of a robbery? That didn't make any sense. Her stomach tightened with dread. The cops were one step ahead of them every time. Jonah was right. If Creepy Crane was involved in this, there wouldn't be a shred of evidence left behind. He would have made sure of it.

"Dan was more than my chief project manager, he was my friend," Gage argued.

"Trust me, I'm not about to let a dirty cop tarnish my

badge." Jonah was no less fierce. "But we need to tread carefully. Don't do anything until you hear from me."

Gage let out a deep, frustrated sigh. "Okay, I'll wait to hear from you."

"Good. You should probably find a new place to stay tonight, just to be on the safe side. I'm using my private car and made sure I wasn't followed, but it doesn't hurt to be extra careful. Especially since we know someone on the inside is involved in this."

"Sounds like a good plan," Alyssa said, getting up and walking over to stand beside Gage. The fog still clouded her memory, but the sense of urgency was back in full force. She had the distinct impression there was something important she needed to do. But what?

Jonah opened the door, but then paused and turned back to Gage. "Call my cell when you get settled in your new digs."

"I will."

Jonah left, closing the door behind him. She turned back to find her duffel bag. They needed to find a safe haven.

If such a thing even existed.

Gage disappeared into his room, no doubt to collect his own things. There was an abrupt pounding on the motel door, and her heart leaped into her throat.

"Wait!" Gage was there in an instant. He moved toward the doorway and took a moment to peer through the peephole. "Jonah?" He quickly opened the door. "What's wrong?"

"You need to get out of here! A Milwaukee squad car just pulled in and I have a bad feeling they're looking for you."

EIGHT

Gage didn't question Jonah's instincts, because he suspected the same thing. And even if they weren't looking for them, he wasn't about to take a chance, not with Alyssa's life. He took her duffel along with his and tossed them over his shoulder. Clutching Alyssa's hand firmly, he followed Jonah outside.

Red and blue flashing lights pinpointed the squad car located half a dozen parking slots away from his truck. There was no sign of the officers. Were they inside grilling the clerk? How had they found him so quickly? By putting an APB out on his truck tag?

"Take my wheels." Jonah must have had the same thought as he shoved a set of keys into Gage's hand. "It's the green Bronco at the end of the row."

Gage quickly palmed the keys and tossed his set to Jonah. They didn't have much time. The officers could come out of the tiny lobby at any moment. Keeping close to the wall, Gage jogged toward the Bronco with Alyssa right beside him. Just as he opened the door, he heard a shout.

"Stop! Police!"

"Hurry!" Gage tossed the bags inside and jumped

behind the wheel. He jammed the key into the ignition and started the vehicle as Alyssa scrambled into the seat beside him. She managed to pull the passenger door closed when he threw the Bronco into Reverse and floored it. A brief glance toward the motel confirmed the cops were hightailing it back to their squad car. He didn't doubt they intended to give chase.

"They're following." Alyssa voiced his thoughts. "Step on it, Gage."

He didn't argue. The Bronco roared beneath his touch. As he maneuvered the city streets he shifted through his options. Where could they go? The cops on their tail had no doubt called for backup. With no thought beyond getting out of the city, he took a wild turn and headed for the interstate. "Buckle your seat belt."

"You, too," she pointed out as she fastened hers then twisted in her seat to peer out the back window.

Gage kept his eyes glued to the road as he tried to fasten his seat belt one-handed. She reached across his chest to help him. "Keep your head down," he ordered. Wrestling with the steering wheel, he took another sharp turn. A few more blocks and they'd be on the interstate. "For all we know they're trigger-happy."

Alyssa ignored him, turning again in her seat to stare behind them. "They lost some ground on that last turn."

What was she doing? He didn't want a play-by-play from her. He needed Alyssa to stay safe. That's all he'd ever wanted, to protect her from the seedy side of life. In spite of all his efforts, though, they were hip-deep in sludge now. To throw the cops off, he drove over the median to the wrong side of the street then made a quick turn. Thankfully the traffic wasn't too bad at this hour on a Sunday morning, although several cars honked at him in warning. If he remembered correctly, there was another on-ramp for the interstate a few blocks down.

"Come on," he muttered as he swerved around a slow-moving vehicle. "Almost there."

"Hey, now they're really far back." Alyssa sounded relieved.

"How far?" Despite his need to keep his eyes on the road, he risked a glance in the rearview mirror. The squad behind him had picked up a second squad, and he was glad to see they'd dropped farther behind.

"Keep going, Gage. We're going to make it," she said encouragingly.

Alyssa's positive attitude shocked him. He'd expected her to fall apart, but instead she was supporting him. Even though they were breaking the law.

"Look out!" Alyssa cried.

He swerved sharply, just in time to avoid a truck that had pulled out in front of him. His heart leaped into his throat. Focus. He needed to focus. And to pray.

Dear God, help us. Keep us safe!

"Hang on." Gage sped up the on-ramp. "And keep your head down!" One of the cars started to move forward and he took a path around it, effectively cutting it off. The driver laid on the horn in annoyance.

Once on the freeway, he quickly sliced through three lanes of traffic to reach the far-left lane. Gage knew they couldn't stay on the interstate for long. There would be new cops on their tail in no time. He was certain every cop within a fifty-mile radius had been alerted to search for Jonah's Bronco.

Still, he waited until they'd gone a good couple of miles before he swerved onto the narrow left shoulder and slammed on the brakes.

Alyssa squealed and hung on to the dashboard. "What are you doing?"

Gage wrenched the wheel into an illegal U-turn in the middle of the interstate. Once he'd gained enough speed, he cut across the three lanes of traffic and took the first exit. At the end of the ramp he turned right, then at the next street he hung another quick left, all the while heading south.

"You did it, Gage." Alyssa's voice was full of awed relief. "You lost them."

Adrenaline surged through his bloodstream even though he knew they weren't safe. Not yet. He glanced at Alyssa. "I'm sorry if I scared you."

She actually smiled. "Yeah, I wouldn't recommend running from the police often, but I'd rather be safe."

"And we are. For now." He was impressed she'd taken his stunt-driving so well. "But we have to ditch the car."

She paled. "You're not going to steal one, are you?"

"No. Don't worry, that's not part of the plan."

She visibly relaxed. "But you do have a plan, right?"

He wished he did. Somehow, they needed to lose themselves in the city. Milwaukee was a big place. Shouldn't be too difficult to hide. He pulled into a well-known shopping mall parking lot and threw the vehicle into Park. "Sort of a plan. One that starts with leaving Jonah's Bronco here and going forward on foot."

Alyssa did her best to keep up with Gage, and the adrenaline from their wild car ride had sustained her for a while. But after two hours of walking, her legs felt as if each limb weighed a hundred pounds. Her head and ankle throbbed in unison and her throat was parched. She'd give anything for a long, cold drink of water.

With both their bags slung over his shoulder, Gage led the way through another parking lot, around a building and then through a back alley. She didn't voice a single complaint. Gage seemed to know what he was doing. He'd lost the cops on their tail and stayed off the main streets where they could easily be picked up.

"There's a bus stop ahead," Gage murmured close to her ear. "We'll hop the bus for a few blocks then try to head farther south."

"Where are we going?" She didn't like feeling as if they were stumbling around in the dark. Nothing about their surroundings seemed familiar. The street signs were a meaningless blur. She tried to remain calm, in spite of the mist that continued to swirl in her mind. Clouds obliterated the sun from overhead. Despite the warm air and her exhaustion, she shivered. Danger could be anywhere, around the next corner, over the next hill. How would she know?

"We're only a few miles from the Jefferson construction site."

"What?" She stumbled. Gage grabbed her elbow to prevent her from falling forward. She pushed away a blond curl that stuck to her sweaty cheek. "Tell me you're not serious."

"I'm very serious." He tugged her to the right. She forced her confused and exhausted feet to follow. Her ankle screamed in protest. Belatedly she noticed the blue bus stop sign.

"Don't you think that's the first place they'll look?" She couldn't quite grasp his logic.

"Maybe. But it's also where Dan was when I called him to ask about the Jefferson project." Gage sat on the bus stop bench and Alyssa dropped gratefully beside him.

"So?"

"So if there's anything left at the site that might indicate what's going on, I want to find it before the police do." Gage's gaze was grim.

"I see." He was right. They wouldn't get to the bottom of this mess unless they had something to go on. Swallowing her apprehension, she stretched out her legs, gently moving her sore ankle.

Gage picked up a newspaper someone had left on the bench and held it up to shield their faces.

"Are you okay?" Gage asked in a low voice, as if sensing her bone-weary exhaustion.

"Fine," she murmured. She stared at the small newspaper print directly in front of her face. Would reading the news trigger her memory? She scanned a few articles.

A story about the new mayoral candidate caught her eye and she shifted a bit so she could read it easier. There'd been a benefit the night before last, and a large picture of two men shaking hands at the Pfister Hotel was splashed on the front page. She quickly bypassed the picture in her haste to read the article. The reporter reiterated how the incumbent Mayor Flynn had suffered an unexpected heart attack and died several weeks ago. Eric Holden was the Common Council president who'd stepped up to the role as interim mayor. Holden was also the favorite candidate to date. Early polls showed him in a wide lead over former City Councilman Gerald Maas.

She thought the name Holden seemed a little familiar. Their bus pulled up. "Let's go," Gage said, setting the newspaper aside.

Alyssa took the newspaper and folded it, keeping it so she could look at the article again later. Interesting how she didn't remember her family or her friends, but a stranger's name stirred a shadow in the misty fog of her brain.

Gage stayed back, allowing her to step into the bus first. She slid onto a cracked vinyl seat, scooting over to the window to make room for Gage. Once they were seated, the bus lumbered down the street.

"You're sure about going to the building site?" she asked. "You don't think the police will be there waiting for you?"

"It's possible they think they have whatever they need from my office building." Gage glanced at her, concern in his eyes. "But I can always get a room at a motel first, and you can wait for me there."

"No. I'm going with you." Despite the warmth, she was cold, inside and out. She was afraid of going to the Jefferson condo building site, but she was even more afraid of Gage going off without her. What if something happened to him? Then she'd really be all alone.

"Okay, if you're sure."

"I'm sure." They needed to stick together, now more than ever. She'd do whatever was necessary to prevent Gage from ending up like Dan Kirkland.

Dead.

"Gage? Have I been here before?" she whispered from their crouched position beside the trailer office site. The newspaper worked its way out of her bag, and she tucked it firmly inside, so it wouldn't blow away in the breeze, giving away their position.

"No, we only just started building here within the past month or so." Gage swept the area with his gaze, presumably to make sure the police hadn't beat them to the scene.

She found that bit of information strange. Why wouldn't she have come here? Wouldn't she have been interested in what her boyfriend was doing?

"Stay here," Gage murmured. "I'm heading inside."

She grabbed his arm before he could make his move. "Without me?"

"Alyssa, I need you to stay here, to keep an eye out for the police." His gaze pleaded with her to understand. "I promise I won't be long."

She wanted to protest. To make him listen. But he was right in that someone needed to keep watch. Besides, in the bright light of day, carrying two duffel bags holding their meager belongings, they were too noticeable together. Her stomach clenched but she forced herself to release his arm.

"Okay, but if you're not back in fifteen minutes, I'm coming to find you," she threatened.

His cinnamon-colored eyes widened with alarm. "Fifteen minutes isn't much time. Just be patient and keep watch. If you see anything suspicious get somewhere safe, okay?"

She frowned. Did Gage really think she'd leave him to face the danger alone? If so, he didn't know her very well. She'd appreciated his protectiveness, but now it seemed he was carrying it a bit too far. "Come back out here in fifteen minutes to let me know how it's going. Don't shut me out, Gage. We're in this together."

He stared at her for a long moment but then gave a curt nod. "Okay, fifteen minutes." Before she could say anything more, he disappeared around the corner of the trailer.

She let her breath out in a soundless sigh. Once they were safe, she needed to have a little heart-to-heart with

Gage. They couldn't argue like this every time they faced some sort of danger. Though her memory was a temporary blank, she could still function as part of the team. Even with her hurt ankle, she hadn't complained or slowed them down so far, had she?

Steadily, she inched forward until she could see around the corner of the trailer. Gage was nowhere in sight, so she assumed he was already inside. Would he find the evidence they so desperately needed? She prayed he would.

With a glance at her watch, she settled on top of the duffel bags to wait. There was no way she was going to give him a second longer than the time frame they'd agreed upon. She stared at her watch, as if she could will the hands to move faster.

Fourteen minutes, thirty-five seconds and counting.

Gage used his master key to open the door to the trailer/office and stepped inside. Luckily, it was Sunday, and as he'd expected, there wasn't anyone inside working. He moved toward the desk he or Dan would use whenever they were on-site. There was a tall, old beat-up file cabinet next to the desk. He opened drawers and began looking through paperwork, hoping he'd recognize the clue when he found it.

What information could Dan have stumbled on? Most of the files were neatly organized, except in the last drawer he found one sticking up, as if it had been hastily returned.

The original bid on the Jefferson project.

Gage didn't hesitate to pull the fat file out and lay it on the desk. He scanned the information inside. His signature stared up at him from the original quotes, but then he saw there were additional notes scribbled in the margins. Examining them closer, he realized the handwriting was Dan's.

"MaKay Builders, Conrath Construction Company, Jacobson and Sons." He read the names of his largest competitors out loud. There were numbers written alongside the names. It took him a minute to realize they were quotes.

Two of the three quotes were a little lower than his winning bid.

For a moment he could only stare at the information with a sense of disbelief. That couldn't be right. Why would Jefferson give the deal to a small construction company like Drummond Builders if it hadn't won the lowest bid? He stared at the scribbled notes in the margin. Had he read them wrong? Were the numbers something other than dollar amounts? At the bottom of the notations was a strange reference to Northwestern University.

Before he could make sense out of that, the wail of sirens split the air. Reacting instinctively, he slammed the folder shut and jumped from the chair. Tucking the folder under his arm, he peered out the closest window. The knot in his gut tightened.

He couldn't see Alyssa from this angle, but the police seemed as if they were definitely headed this way. He never should have left her alone outside without a cell phone. She was vulnerable, more so with the void in her memory. He was responsible for her. If he didn't move fast, they'd be trapped.

Fifty-two seconds to go. What was taking Gage so long? Had he found something that would help them? A full minute had passed since the guy had wandered too close to the construction site for her peace of mind. The stranger was a big guy, dressed in baggy jeans and faded T-shirt, and she'd watched in horror as he'd paused barely two feet from her hiding place to light a cigarette. Was he someone from Jefferson's payroll sent to find her and Gage? Frightened beyond belief, she stayed motionless. And when her nose had twitched at the scent of smoke, she'd pinched her nostrils, fighting the urge to sneeze. He'd stood smoking for agonizingly long moments then flicked his partially finished butt into a drum that functioned as a garbage can. Luckily, he'd wandered away, back toward the other side of the construction site.

Thirty seconds. Tired of waiting, she crept from her hiding place and then froze when she heard sirens, her heart hammering in her throat. Almost instantly, she saw the red and blue flashing lights in the distance that seemed to be headed straight for them.

No! The police had found them!

NINE

As Gage eased out from the trailer, he was assaulted by the acrid scent of smoke. He couldn't see what was burning, but a small cloud of smoke drifted over from the other side of the trailer. Keeping flat against the aluminum siding so the police couldn't see him, he went around to the back, where he'd left Alyssa.

She wasn't there. His heart leaped into his throat as he scanned the area searching for her. Where was she? Had she run because of the police cars? He found himself hoping she had.

Ka-boom!

The ground shook and he stumbled over the duffel bags near his feet, nearly falling flat on his face. Where in the world was Alyssa? He peered around the corner toward the front of the trailer, horrified to see a squad car was pulling up into the driveway in front of the trailer. Two cops jumped out, but instead of going inside the trailer, they ran off toward the source of the smoke.

"Gage? Let's go!"

Shocked, he spun around to see Alyssa crouched behind him. The pungent scent of gasoline and smoke permeated her clothes. "Are you okay? Did you start a fire?"

She flushed and nodded guiltily. "I'm pretty sure the pickup truck was abandoned. It was rusted through and all four tires were flat. Let's go, we have to hurry!"

He wasn't going to argue, since the two officers were preoccupied by the fire. "This way," he whispered. He grabbed the two duffel bags and urged her to go first so he could protect her from behind.

They left the shelter of the trailer and, staying low, crept behind the police cars to get away from the construction site. Crossing the street was their biggest risk, and when Alyssa veered to the right, toward the parking structure about a block down, he followed her lead.

Her choice was a stroke of genius. Soon they were hidden within the dim interior of the structure, shielded by the myriad of parked cars. Silently, they wove through the rows to the other side. Alyssa didn't hesitate but climbed up and over the waist-high wall, landing with a muffled grunt on her feet on the other side. Gage couldn't help but grin with admiration. She was smart, constantly thinking even when running for their lives. He tossed the duffels over the low wall and then followed her to the other side. Although she'd taken twenty years off his life back there, he couldn't deny her idea for a diversion saved them.

Still, from here on out, he wasn't going to keep exposing her to danger. He wasn't a cop like Jonah, but all those years on the move with his dad had taught him how to fend for himself. He'd wanted to protect Alyssa from the seedy side of life. She was a nurse, not a private investigator.

They kept moving, cutting through streets and taking alleys whenever possible. Gage tried to focus on his surroundings. They needed a plan. They couldn't keep running around the city on foot. "Take a left here," he said.

"There's a college campus just a few blocks down, with lots of students hanging around. We need to be someplace where we'll blend in."

She arched a brow. "Are you saying I look like a college student?"

He flashed a tired smile. "The way we're dressed, we both could pass for students." He paused to glance at her gas-stained sweatpants. "Did you really blow up a truck?"

"I wasn't trying to blow it up," Alyssa defended herself. "I was trying to set the seats on fire, but that didn't work. I wasn't even sure there was any gas in the tank, but I stuck the oily rag with the cigarette butt into the opening and ran. I was just as surprised as anyone when the thing exploded."

A flash of fear gripped his chest. "You're lucky you weren't killed," he said, unable to keep his voice from rising. "You should have stayed put like I told you to!"

She frowned and tucked a stray curl behind her ear. "You know, Gage, you're not giving me enough credit. I helped save us back there. The least you could do is to thank me, rather than giving me a lecture."

He was taken aback by her tone. "I wasn't giving you a lecture. Don't you understand? I need to know you're safe."

"Neither of us is safe," she argued heatedly. "The way you want to protect me is sweet, but we're in this together. You need to treat me as an equal partner, Gage, instead of a liability."

Equal partner? She had to be joking. She couldn't remember her name, much less anything that might lead them to the source of danger. His job was to keep her safe. End of discussion. "You're not a liability," he said, trying to smooth things over. He absolutely didn't want her to feel bad. This was his fault for not listening to her in the first place. Clearly time to change the subject. "Let's go down this street here. There's a pub called Rickey's where we can sit for a while and get something to eat."

As it was the end of August, the impending fall semester had brought many students back to campus. Rickey's wasn't overly crowded, but there were enough people that they could fade into the crowd. Gage pushed through the students gathered at the bar to watch the baseball game on the dual televisions mounted overhead. He was grateful to find a small table in the back corner.

Alyssa dropped into the chair with a low moan. "My aching feet," she murmured.

During their months together, Alyssa would often come home after a long shift in the E.R. complaining about her sore feet. He'd always offered to give her foot massages to relieve the pressure and pain. He missed those days they'd spent together. Going out for brunch after church on the weekends she had off work. Spending Saturday evenings down at Jazz in the Park near the lakefront. They'd spent a lot of time together. What had gone so wrong?

A waitress came over to their table to ask if they'd like something to drink. "Would you mind bringing a pitcher of ice water and a couple of glasses?" Alyssa asked. "I'm really thirsty."

The waitress narrowed her gaze, as if perturbed at the lack of a sale. Gage spoke up hastily. "Would you also bring menus? We'd like to order something to eat."

Her scowl eased and the waitress nodded. "I'll be right back."

"How much cash do you have?" Alyssa asked in a low voice. "I'm hungry, but maybe we should limit our meals."

"We're fine," he assured her. In reality he had only a couple of hundred in cash, but he didn't want her to worry. If nothing else, he could use an ATM machine, but he was sure that the MPD would be trying to track them by watching their transactions, so he'd have to use one on the opposite end of the city. Not an easy feat without a set of wheels.

"If you're sure," Alyssa murmured, taking the glossy menu from the waitress. "Ooh, grilled chicken sounds wonderful."

He had to smile, because she always ordered grilled chicken. He used to tease her about it.

He remembered everything about Alyssa. The way she brushed and braided her long hair, the way she smelled like lilacs after the rain, the way she used to smile at him, as if they'd shared a deep secret. And then the day she'd given him back his ring, stating she couldn't marry him.

"Gage?" she called, breaking into his thoughts. "What do you want to eat?"

"Oh, uh, a medium burger with fries," he said quickly, barely glancing at the menu. Rickey's always had great burgers. "Thanks."

The waitress took their menus and hurried off. He took a long drink of his water while glancing at Alyssa. She looked tired, but her blue eyes sparkled. "So where do we go from here?" she asked.

Good question. "We need to find another cheap motel, but offhand I don't know of any and I don't want to be wandering around where we can be easily spotted."

She grimaced. "Well, I'm no help."

"Don't worry, I'll come up with something. Would be nice to have access to a computer so I could do a search."

"Maybe the university library is open," Alyssa suggested.

"Good idea," he murmured. Why hadn't he thought of that? "We'll head over there after we finish eating."

Their food arrived a few minutes later, and they both busied themselves with eating. They ate relatively quickly, since they hadn't eaten since the day before. On the television closest to them, he caught a glimpse of the Jefferson building site. With a frown, he stared at the screen. Alyssa must have noticed because she glanced over to see what had caught his attention.

Breaking News: Fire at Jefferson Construction Site was the main headline across the bottom of the screen. A TV reporter stood back as the cameraman panned the scene, and Gage noticed several fire trucks parked alongside the police cars.

"Here's a police officer now," the reporter said. "Officer, do you have any idea how this fire started?"

"We're still investigating, but we have reason to believe the cause is arson." The officer wasn't Aaron Crane, but Gage thought he caught a glimpse of the cop in the background. Didn't the guy ever sleep? Why was he at every single accident scene?

"Arson? This condo project was a source of contention in the recent mayoral debate between Maas and Holden. Maas has vocalized concerns related to the project. Do you think one of Maas's supporters is responsible for this?"

"We're not ruling anything out just yet, but we are looking for help in finding Gage Drummond and Mallory Roth. They are both persons of interest in regards to this fire and the unfortunate slaying of Daniel Kirkland. If anyone sees either of these people—" their pictures in full color were splashed on the screen "—please call our anonymous hotline as soon as possible."

He heard Alyssa suck in a harsh breath, and the burger curdled in his stomach. "Persons of interest" in his mind was akin to being set up to take the fall. All because someone thought they'd gotten too close to the truth behind the Jefferson project. Whatever the truth was.

"Let's go," he murmured, pulling out cash and leaving more than enough on the table to cover their tab. He reached for the duffel bags. "We need to get out of here."

Luckily she'd finished her grilled chicken. She spared a few minutes to finish her water before following Gage. What would they do now? Keep moving, obviously, but for how long? Thanks to this news story, the whole city would be looking for them. They'd have to stay out of public places. How could they figure out what was going on if they were constantly on the run?

Her ankle protested sharply when she matched her stride to keep up with Gage. Stubbornly, she ignored the pain. She suspected the injured tendons wouldn't heal very well unless she stayed off her foot, which wasn't going to happen anytime soon. No point in whining about what couldn't be changed.

She followed Gage to the back door of the bar. He seemed to know his way around, and they slipped outside without anyone stopping them. All they needed was a head start. "Are we still going to the library?" she asked.

"Yeah." He led the way across the street to the large university buildings. There was a group of kids standing out on the corner, and Gage asked them for directions to the library. They pointed them in the right direction.

The library was a large building, and Alyssa immediately felt safe among the stacks of books. She realized she loved libraries. Another memory? She glanced around, willing something to come to her, but no luck. She just knew she loved books.

As Gage used a computer to access the internet, she sat beside him, wondering once again about their relationship. Didn't she mind that he constantly tried to keep her safe? His protective attitude was nice and flattering, but at times she wanted to claw free of his cloak.

Gage was ruggedly attractive, but even more so, she was drawn to his musky, woodsy scent. She stared at his strong, square jaw and tried to remember being with him. She imagined her laughing expression from the photograph on Mallory's dresser. Had she felt happy with him? For a brief moment, she caught a flash of the two of them on a horse-and-buggy ride. A memory? Or just wishful thinking?

She wished she knew for sure.

"Okay, I found a place for us," Gage said. "It's about ten miles away, on the other side of town. Do you think you can make it that far?"

"Of course," she responded, although she wanted to wince. Ten miles? It would take hours to walk that far, unless Gage allowed them to take a bus part of the way. Risky to take the bus, although there weren't TVs in the city buses, so they might go undetected. Regardless, it wasn't as if they had much of a choice. She wished they could stay longer in the sanctuary of the library. "I wonder if Mallory sent me an email."

Gage swiveled to look at her. "Good idea. You have

a Yahoo email account. Do you remember your password?" he asked eagerly.

"I can try a few that seem logical," she offered. Gage pulled up the Yahoo home page and typed in her email address. She took over at the keyboard, trying to think logically. What would she use as a password? Something with her nursing background? Gage's name? Mallory's?

She tried a few variations, but none of them worked. "I'm sorry, Gage." She hated feeling so helpless. Useless. If only she could remember.

"Don't worry—we can always try again later." He didn't show any sign of impatience. "But you gave me an idea. I'll check my email messages, too. Maybe Dan sent me something."

She leaned forward to read over his shoulder. "Did he?"

"No. Just a message from my dad, asking me to call him when I have time." Gage shut down the email program and turned to her. "Are you ready?"

"Sure." She stood, hiding a wince, and walked with Gage out of the library, back into the bright sunlight. From there, Gage took the lead, weaving a path on smaller, less traveled streets until he felt safe jumping on a bus.

Ten miles was a lot farther than what it sounded like, especially when they didn't take the direct route. And Gage had vetoed the bus idea. After what seemed like forever, but was really a few hours, they approached the motel.

"I need you to stay hidden until I've rented a room," Gage directed in a hushed tone. "I don't want them to see you, in case they're watching the news."

She wasn't sure she liked that idea. "What if they recognize you and call the police?" she asked.

"I'm going to use an assumed name and offer cash. Hopefully they won't insist on seeing an ID. I'll ask for adjoining rooms." Gage glanced at her and shrugged. "Let's hope they don't ask any questions."

She swallowed hard and nodded. She could only hope and pray they didn't. "Okay. But hurry."

His expression softened. "I will."

The minutes went by agonizingly slowly, but soon she saw Gage come out of the motel office and walk down to a room on the end of the row. He unlocked the door and then gestured for her to come join him.

Inside, she saw he'd already opened the doors between the rooms. Almost immediately, Gage's phone rang. The noise made her jump. "It's Jonah," he said before answering. He listened for a minute and then said, "Yeah, we saw the news."

Listening to Gage's one-sided conversation left some gaps, but she caught the gist. "We didn't start the fire on purpose," he explained to Jonah. "The cops were coming and we used it as a diversion to get away. Don't shout— we had to go to the construction site, because I needed to know what Dan discovered. And I did find something interesting. My bid for the project wasn't the lowest one. There were two others that were slightly lower than mine. Granted, not by much, but it makes me think Jefferson specifically targeted Drummond Builders."

She glanced at him sharply. He hadn't said a word to her about his discovery. Was he keeping secrets on purpose? To protect her? She'd tried to get him to understand they were in this together, but clearly, Gage preferred keeping her in the dark, a fact she didn't appreciate one bit.

Had Hugh Jefferson really targeted Drummond Builders? And if so, why?

"I know it doesn't make sense," Gage continued. "But I found Dan's notes written in the margin. It could be the odd discovery he'd mentioned to me over the phone."

Once Gage was doing more listening than talking, she crossed over to her duffel and took out the part of the newspaper she'd kept. She'd used a good chunk of it to start the fire in the old abandoned truck, but she'd kept the section with the article related to the mayoral debate.

The name Eric Holden still bothered her. Why did it sound so familiar? Smoothing the newspaper on the small round table, she found the article and went back to the front page, where it started. There was a large photo, with two men standing and shaking hands. She stared intently at them, trying to see the details of their facial features. She estimated Eric Holden was in his early forties, a handsome man with perfectly groomed dark hair with just the barest hint of gray at his temples. Holden was noticeably taller and younger than the man standing across from him.

Her gaze dropped to the caption beneath the photo, and her heart lurched when she realized that the other man in the photo was the infamous Hugh Jefferson. She stared at the grainy photo of Jefferson. He didn't look at all familiar, and she was immensely relieved that he wasn't the same man who was standing next to Mallory in the glossy photo she'd found in Mallory's dresser.

The sign on the podium identified the location of the photo as the Pfister Hotel. Parts of her memory were intact. She knew the Pfister was a luxurious hotel in the heart of Milwaukee. For a moment she thought of the rose-colored evening gown she'd found in Mallory's condo. Had Mallory worn the gown to this benefit? The timing was certainly right. Had she been escorted by the man in the glossy photo? Or had she gone alone?

Gage finished up on the phone and came over to where she was intently studying the newspaper. "Did you find something?"

"Did you?" she countered, glancing up at him. "I heard you and Jonah talking about what you found in Dan's notes. Something about not being the lowest bid for the project?"

"Yes, that's correct." Gage was watching her warily, as if sensing her discordant mood. "I guess I forgot to mention that when we were at Rickey's."

Maybe, or maybe he was trying to protect her again. She tried not to dwell on it. "Surely there are other reasons to choose a builder besides money. Maybe he liked your company's reputation?"

"Maybe," he said with a shrug. "But my company is so much smaller than the others that I can't believe my reputation is that much better. And there was a strange notation, too, about Northwestern University. I'm assuming Jefferson went there, but I haven't figured out why Dan thought it was significant. So what did you find?"

She tapped the glossy photo with a fingertip. "This is Eric Holden and Hugh Jefferson. According to the article, Jefferson is a huge supporter of Holden's campaign."

"That doesn't exactly surprise me," Gage admitted. "The two look very chummy in that picture."

"I found a rose-colored evening gown in Mallory's condo," she went on. "And look at this woman here, off to the side. All you can see is her back, but she has short blond hair and she's wearing a rose-colored gown. Do you think she could be Mallory? Do you think Mallory was actually at this benefit?" The moment she asked the question, an awful thought occurred to her.

What if the woman in the photo was really her, Alyssa, dressed as Mallory? She'd taken Mallory's identity, and all along, they'd assumed she'd taken it to hide from danger. But what if she'd really taken Mallory's identity as a way to get information regarding Councilman Schaefer's death?

TEN

Gage stared at the photo, wishing he could see more than the woman's back. "This could be Mallory," he admitted. The pieces of the puzzle still didn't make much sense. Whether Mallory attended the benefit or not didn't help them much. He glanced at Alyssa and belatedly realized she'd gone pale. "What is it?" he asked in alarm. "Is something wrong?"

She slowly shook her head but didn't meet his gaze. "No, I'm fine."

He didn't believe her and found it agonizing to realize she didn't trust him enough to let him know what was going on in her mind. Was her lack of trust partially because he hadn't told her what he'd found inside the construction trailer? He hadn't been holding back on purpose. Truthfully, his priority had been to get Alyssa safely out of there. And then out of Rickey's when he saw their pictures splashed all over the news. He'd dragged her from one end of the city to the other, in spite of her sore ankle. It wasn't until he'd spoken to Jonah that he'd remembered what he'd found.

"Alyssa, I'm sorry."

She glanced up at him in surprise. "For what?"

He sank into a chair and spread his hands wide. "For making you feel bad. I'm not trying to keep information from you. We've been on the run since this morning, and when I see how exhausted you are, I can't help feeling guilty. This entire situation is mostly my fault. I would give anything to keep you safe."

Her smile was brittle. "Gage, I'm not going to break. I told you before, we're in this together. Rehashing what we could have done or should have done isn't going to help. We need to be focused on working through this, together. Through the good times and the bad."

She was asking too much of him. He didn't think he could survive if something happened to her. Didn't she understand they were in this mess only because he hadn't believed her? He stared down at his hands for a moment. "I promise to try," he said doubtfully.

There was a long moment of silence. "Do you mind if I ask you a question?"

"Anything," he answered readily.

"What kind of relationship did we have?" His stomach clenched when her blue gaze captured his. "I mean, have we been dating for a long time? Were we serious?"

He'd figured she'd ask this question sooner rather than later. And he couldn't lie to her. "My feelings for you were serious," he admitted. "But you told me I didn't have a close enough relationship with God and that I was too overprotective."

"The overprotective part is easy to believe," she murmured dryly. "But I thought you told me you were a believer."

How could he explain what he didn't fully understand himself? "I do believe in God," he affirmed. "But I'm not as religious as you."

A small pucker furrowed her brow. "You don't pray?"

He thought about the few times over the past thirty-six hours he had prayed. For strength. For Alyssa's safety. To thank God for bringing her back into his life. He couldn't deny praying made him feel stronger. "Sometimes, yes. But probably not often enough. It's something I'm working on."

She tipped her head to the side. "Are you working on your faith for me or for yourself?"

He sucked in a quick breath, a lightbulb snapping on in the middle of his brain. When he'd met Alyssa, he'd renewed his faith for her sake, going to church, going to Bible study because that's what she'd wanted. But he hadn't taken his relationship with God to heart. Not as something he'd needed to do for himself. How could he have been such an idiot? "Yes, I won't lie to you. I was renewing my faith for you at first, but I've now realized I need to work on my faith for my own sake. And I really do want a closer relationship with God."

A small smile tugged on her mouth. "I'm glad. And if you need help, I'm here for you, Gage."

He wished he could hug her close, even kiss her. But he forced himself to keep his distance. He forced himself to look back at the newspaper photo. He wasn't a big fan of politics, but he sensed that Jefferson knew how to use them to his advantage. "We know there was discord among the city councilmen about Jefferson's condo project. Schaefer was against it, and so was the former mayor, but then he had a heart attack, and with Holden's help, the city approved Jefferson's permits. We started construction almost two weeks ago, so there has to be some reason Jefferson wanted to silence Schaefer, if we believe his claim he was stabbed by one of Jefferson's men."

"I'm with you so far," Alyssa urged.

Gage slowly shook his head. "I think Schaefer must have found something out about Jefferson. Jefferson must be involved in something illegal. It's the only thing that makes sense."

"And Jefferson has cops working for him, and the mayor on his side, to help cover up whatever illegal activity he's involved in," Alyssa added. "Could it have something to do with drugs?"

"I don't think so," he murmured. "Drugs don't fit. Has to be something related to the condo project. And the only thing I can think of is money laundering."

Alyssa gasped. "Gage! What if he's paying you to build his condos with dirty money?"

"I know." The very thought made him feel sick. "And that would explain why he wanted my company to do the work, even though we weren't the lowest bid. Could be he figured a smaller company wouldn't ask as many questions, or look too deeply into the source of his financing." And like a fool, he'd walked right into Jefferson's trap.

Alyssa grasped his hands in hers. "It's not too late, Gage. You can still get out of it."

He wished he had her confidence. "It's not going to be easy to break the contract. Not without losing my entire business. Besides, I have a feeling Jefferson is used to getting his way. He's not going to let me out of the contract easily. What we need is to find some sort of proof that we can use to go to the authorities."

"Going to the local police isn't going to help," she pointed out. "Not if Jefferson has them in his pocket."

He raised his grim gaze to meet hers. There had to be a way out of this mess. "Then I'll have no choice but to go to the FBI with whatever proof we find."

* * *

Alyssa yawned, trying to keep her eyes open. After being up so early and walking for so long, she could barely stay upright. She stretched out on top of the bed in her room while Gage made notes about their theory so far.

"Hi, Margaret, is Dad around?" she heard Gage ask. His voice was low, but she could hear through the open connecting doors.

She forced one eyelid open, glancing over to where Gage was using his cell phone to call his dad. Was Margaret his stepmother? She wished she knew more about Gage's past.

"He's golfing? Okay, just let him know I called. Thanks."

"Who's Margaret?" she asked.

"My dad's wife. I've met her a few times, she seems nice enough. She obviously cares about my dad." She noticed he avoided mentioning anything about his mother. "I'm going to head out to get some dinner for us. There's a fast-food restaurant a few blocks down the street."

She struggled to sit up. "I'll go with you."

"There's no need," he hastily assured her. "Why don't you stay here and take a nap?"

The idea of a nap had far too much appeal. But she refused to be treated like an invalid. "No way. Where you go, I go."

"Alyssa, please. Wait for me here. We're too noticeable together."

Here he went again, with his overprotective attitude. "Anyone can easily recognize you from your photo. We're both in danger, remember?"

"I look different with my stubbly face," he said, rubbing a hand over his beard. "And I don't think they'll look at me twice if I'm alone."

She put a hand up to her light hair. "Maybe I should get some hair dye?"

He stared at her, as if seriously considering her offer. "Might not be a bad idea," he admitted. "I'll look for a grocery store on the way. But please stay here, Alyssa. I gave Jonah our room number and he might try to swing by. I'd hate for him to come when neither of us is here."

She narrowed her gaze, hating how he'd boxed her in a corner. She didn't want Jonah to come here while they were both gone, either. "Okay, I'll wait here. But I expect you to be back in less than twenty minutes. I mean it, Gage, no going off on your own without me."

"I promise I'll be back in less than twenty minutes." He rose to his feet and strode toward the door. Then he stopped and glanced back over his shoulder. "What do you think of becoming a redhead?"

She hid her wince and nodded. "Sounds like a plan."

Gage flashed a quick grin and then eased out of the motel room door.

She must have dozed because when she woke up, Gage was sitting at the small table, munching a French fry. "I didn't want to wake you," he said by way of apology. "You looked as if you needed sleep more than food."

She grimaced and pushed her hair away from her face. "I suppose, but cold fries don't taste very good."

"I wrapped them in tinfoil to help keep them warm." He took out a burger and the foil-wrapped fries and handed them to her.

Burgers weren't on her list of top favorite foods, but right now she was so hungry she didn't care about the high fat content. Eagerly, she dug in. Even the lukewarm fries weren't too bad. "Have you heard from Jonah?" she asked between bites.

Gage nodded. "He texted me. He wants me to meet him at the fountain in Rainbow Park at nine."

"Nine? Tonight?" She glanced at her watch, surprised to see it was already seven-thirty. She'd slept later than she'd realized. "Why not come here?"

"He's afraid he'll be followed. He's already in trouble with his boss because we managed to escape from the motel earlier this morning. He doesn't want to let on that he's helping us."

The burger and fries she'd eaten congealed into a hard lump in the pit of her stomach. "Did he get arrested?"

"No, but apparently they threatened to. They took him off duty and placed him on administrative leave until we're caught."

"Poor Jonah," she murmured. "I hope he doesn't resent helping us."

"Jonah is a good friend. He's angry, but not with us." Gage finished his food and balled up the wrappers. "He takes his oath to serve and protect very seriously. There were some problems with his uncle who used to be on the force, which is why he doesn't appreciate anyone attempting to tarnish his badge."

"Still, I feel bad he's put his career on the line for us."

Gage stared at her, then quirked a brow. "Sounds like you admire him."

She frowned at the slight edge in his tone. "I do admire him. It wasn't easy for me to trust the police, but I trust Jonah."

The muscles in Gage's jaw tightened. "Jonah goes to church regularly. He's very religious."

And Gage was telling her this—why? "I imagine a

man who puts his life on the line every day has a good reason to have a close relationship with God."

"Maybe once this is over, you and Jonah can go out sometime."

"What? Are you crazy?" She couldn't believe he was trying to set her up with his friend. "I'm not interested in Jonah."

Gage avoided her gaze. "He's more your type than I am."

For several long moments she could only stare at him in shock. "Gage, what are you trying to say? I know I lost my memory, but I thought we were a couple. I wouldn't date another man if I'm already involved with you."

"What if you weren't involved with me?" he countered. "What if you broke up with me over a month ago? Would you be interested in Jonah then?"

"Broke up?" She could hardly comprehend what he was saying. "Are you really telling me we broke up?"

"I care about you, Alyssa. More than you could possibly know. I didn't lie about that. When we both thought you were Mallory, you assumed we were together, and I didn't correct you. But it's time you knew the truth." He paused, took a deep breath and met her gaze head-on. "You broke up with me, for the reasons I mentioned earlier."

She remembered he'd claimed she wasn't happy about the way he was so overprotective and that he didn't have a close enough relationship with God. Still, it didn't seem right that she would have broken up with him. Not when she was still so attracted to him. "I did?"

"Yes. You did." His mouth formed a grim line. "I don't blame you, but I want you to know, I have changed. I'm working on the overprotective part, and I've already learned the value of prayer."

His words thrilled her. "I'm happy for you, Gage."

"Thanks." He cleared his throat loudly. "I'm relieved to hear you're not interested in Jonah, because that means I can ask you to give me a second chance."

Gage held his breath, waiting for Alyssa's response. He'd tried to give her an out, knowing Jonah was far better suited for her than he was, but she declined and now he wasn't about to give her up. Not without a fight.

He ignored the tiny voice in his brain that warned him against getting too emotionally involved. When Alyssa's memory returned, she'd likely remember she didn't care about him in the same way anymore.

But he'd needed to lay his cards on the table, to make sure she understood how much he still cared.

"Gage, it wouldn't be fair for me to give you an answer now, when I still don't have my memory back."

His flicker of hope died. "I understand. And I didn't mean you had to give me a second chance right now, but once your memory has returned and we're safe, I hope you'll consider my request."

"Do you think my memory will return?" she asked with a troubled gaze. "What if it doesn't?"

"It will," he responded confidently. "The doctor seemed to think your memory will return, so we just have to think positive."

"Right." She gave a tight nod. "Think positive."

"Are you finished?" he asked. She'd finished her burger but still had half her fries left. When she nodded, he quickly took care of the mess. "We have to get ready to meet Jonah. Are you sure your ankle is up for another long walk?"

She grimaced but nodded. "I'll be fine."

He didn't believe her. "Have you been taking those meds the doctor prescribed?"

"Of course." She hesitated and then frowned. "Most of the time."

He wished she'd stay here, safe in the motel, but knew she wouldn't. He didn't push the issue. Hadn't he just claimed he was trying to change? Ignoring his screaming instincts, he waited for her to dig a dark sweatshirt out of their bag before opening the motel room door.

The sky wasn't nearly dark enough to suit him, although the dark clouds moving in helped a bit. At the fast-food restaurant several people were talking about the storm they were supposed to get later tonight. He hoped the rain would hold off until after their meeting with Jonah.

Rainbow Park wasn't that far, but he set a zigzag course, taking them well out of their way, just to be on the safe side.

Alyssa stumbled once and he quickly grabbed her arm before she could fall. "Lean on me," he offered.

She obliged him by putting her arm around his waist, allowing him to help support her. He knew her ankle must be causing her a lot of pain, and he swallowed a wave of frustrated helplessness.

Alyssa should be back at the motel, sleeping, with her injured ankle elevated on pillows, not being dragged through the dark city streets.

He slowed his pace to accommodate her needs. He didn't mind having her lean on him for support. In fact, he wished he had the right to hold her in his arms. Glancing at his watch, he realized he'd have to take the direct route from here if they were going to make the meeting on time.

"I'm slowing you down," Alyssa murmured.

"Don't worry, we're fine. We have almost fifteen minutes yet, and the park isn't that far from here."

She didn't say anything else as they made their way down one street and then took a left. He sensed her relax when she saw the sign for Rainbow Park.

The fountain was in the center of the park, and he swept a sharp gaze over their surroundings as they made their way along the well-lit path. He was glad the sun had gone down completely now. The darkness was their friend.

The fountain was up ahead and he slowed his pace, scanning the area for any sign of Jonah.

"Where is he?" Alyssa asked in a hushed whisper. "We're not early."

No, they weren't early. "I don't know," he admitted.

"Should we split up and search for him?"

"No, we're not splitting up." Not now, not ever as far as he was concerned. The park seemed deserted, but they couldn't afford to take chances. The back of his neck itched and his instincts were telling him that something was wrong. "Let's walk around to the other side," he instructed softly. Could be that Jonah was hiding in the shadows until they arrived.

She tightened her grip on his waist and he tucked his cheek against her hair. He'd bought the red dye, but she hadn't taken the time to use it yet. He couldn't deny he'd miss her soft blond curls. Although he preferred her hair longer, the way it used to be.

The lights in the park were brighter than he remembered. Staying as close to the shadows as he could, he made his way off to a small patch of trees on the other side of the fountain. If Jonah was afraid he'd been followed, he wouldn't stand out underneath a streetlamp.

Once they reached the trees, he paused to give his eyes a chance to adjust to the complete darkness. "Jonah?" he whispered.

Nothing.

He took a few more steps and then stumbled against something soft. Was there something dark on the ground?

"Oh, no, Jonah?" He heard Alyssa's horrified gasp.

No. Not Jonah, too. Not after losing Dan. His heart pounded with dread as he dropped to his knees and felt for Jonah's wrist. A pulse. He wasn't dead. They weren't too late. His friend was still alive.

For a moment overwhelming relief washed over him. *Thank You, Lord! Thank You for sparing Jonah's life.*

"Call 911," he said tersely, handing Alyssa his cell phone and then ripping off his shirt to hold pressure over Jonah's bleeding abdominal wound. "Tell them to hurry!"

ELEVEN

Alyssa peered through the darkness, barely making out Jonah's ashen features. A wave of helplessness hit hard. When would this nightmare end? As soon as the thought formed, she was ashamed of herself. She needed to trust God's plan. Her fingers shook as she quickly dialed 911 on Gage's cell phone. After giving the dispatcher their location, she snapped the phone shut. She shoved aside a wave of hopelessness and knelt beside Gage. "Let me see how bad he's hurt."

"It's too dark to see much," Gage said, his voice terse. "I think he may have been stabbed in the side."

She kept her fingers on his pulse, reassured by the faint beat. "Is the weapon still in the wound?"

"No. But I'm assuming this is another knife wound, similar to Dan's, but lower and to the side, as if Jonah sensed his attacker behind him and turned at the last minute."

"Here, use this." She shrugged off her hoodie and handed it to him. "You'll need to use your body weight for pressure to stop the bleeding. If the knife wound nicked the liver he'll be in danger of losing lots of blood." As Gage followed her instructions, she ran her hands along Jonah's arms, legs and the rest of his body, blindly searching for other injuries. A large lump on the back of his head was the only additional injury she found.

"I feel like we're sitting ducks out here," Gage murmured. "I hope this isn't a trap."

She sucked in a harsh breath, glancing around fearfully. She sensed Gage moving and she quickly grabbed his arm. "Don't leave me."

"I won't," he assured her. "We need to move him closer to the streetlights," he said thoughtfully. "The police will come with the ambulance. Officer Crane could have done this himself, and is right now waiting for the call to come across his radio."

The mere thought of Officer Crane showing up made her pulse kick into triple digits. Once again, she glanced around, feeling as if there was a large bull's-eye painted on her back. "He'll arrest us for sure this time."

"We're not going to let that happen," Gage said grimly. The wail of sirens filled the air. "Come on, help me move him."

She gripped Jonah's legs, while Gage moved up to his heavier upper torso. Together, they managed to shift Jonah closer to the fountain and the bright overhead streetlights. When Gage stepped back and reached for her hand, she shook her head. "No, we can't leave yet. Not until we find a rock or something heavy to place over his wound."

They both began searching even as the sounds of sirens grew louder, indicating they were close.

"Here's one." Gage lifted a large rock and put it on top of her hoodie. The sirens grew louder and she couldn't help glancing fearfully over her shoulder. "Let's go."

"I can't leave," she whispered. Leaving Jonah here,

alone and injured, went against every fiber of her being. Even though she felt certain this was a trap set by Crane. Even if Crane wasn't the one who responded, there were likely warrants issued for their arrest. "Wait for me behind the trees," she urged.

"I'm not leaving you alone," he argued.

"You have to—we'll attract too much attention otherwise." She caught a glimpse of the red lights from the ambulance, and the police car wasn't far behind. "Hurry!"

Gage finally moved back into the shadows, just when the ambulance pulled up. Two men jumped out and grabbed their supplies out of the back before hurrying over.

"What do we have here?" the first paramedic asked, as he kneeled beside her.

"Deep penetrating flank wound on the right. May have nicked his spleen. He has a pulse, but I'm afraid he's been down for a few minutes."

"What happened?" the second paramedic asked as the first one quickly started a large-bore IV in Jonah's right arm.

"I—don't know. I was just walking through the park on my way home and found him like this." The police car pulled up, and she knew she had just seconds to leave. "Excuse me, I think I'm going to be sick."

She bolted away, lunging for the protection of the trees. Gage grasped her hand and she followed his lead as he melted into the darkness, moving quickly but quietly.

Lord, please keep Jonah safe in Your care, Amen.

Gage's heart was pounding so loudly, he feared the police could hear it. He should have insisted they leave before the paramedics arrived, but it was too late now.

There were some trees providing coverage, but then there was a wide-open area they had to cross before they could seek shelter in the thicker grove of trees.

"Stay low and run toward those trees as fast as you can," he said, his mouth close to her ear. "I'll be right behind you."

She didn't argue, and she managed to sprint faster than he'd given her credit for as she made her way toward the sanctuary of the trees. He stayed right behind her, protecting her in the only way he could, expecting to feel the hot streak of a bullet hitting him in the back.

Alyssa reached the trees and he followed two seconds later. He thought he may have heard a shout, but he didn't bother to look back. The trees offered protection as they weaved their way in a diagonal pattern toward the northeast side of the park.

"This way," he said, tugging on Alyssa's arm. She stumbled, and he reached out to grab her before she could fall. All this running had to be excruciating for her injured ankle. "Are you okay?"

"I'm fine." She obviously wasn't the type to wallow in self-pity.

He risked a quick glance behind them but didn't see anything other than trees. So far so good. Turning forward, he tried to envision where the road was. Following his instincts, he changed their direction slightly, and soon they found the road. There were houses on the other side, across from the park, and he led the way toward two that didn't have any lights on in the windows. Ducking between them, he ran through the backyards to the next street down, praying they didn't stumble across any dogs.

He could hear Alyssa's heavy breathing and tried to slow down, for her sake. But he kept cutting through

people's backyards to confuse anyone who might be trying to follow them.

Fifteen minutes later, Alyssa slowed to a stop, bending over and putting her hands on her knees. "Break,"
she croaked. "I need to rest."

They weren't far enough from Rainbow Park to relax
their guard, but he could see Alyssa was at the end of her
strength. She'd kept up with him admirably. He glanced
around, trying to get his bearings, wishing they were
closer to the motel.

There used to be a small all-night diner just a couple
of blocks away. "Can you manage just a little longer?"
He anchored her arm around his waist, encouraging her
to lean on him. "Two more blocks then you can rest for
a bit."

She nodded wearily and he half carried her to the
diner. It was a public place, but he didn't know what else
to do or where to go. His only trusted police contact was
right now on his way to the hospital, fighting for his life.
Jonah couldn't help them anymore.

They were on their own.

Gage grit his teeth and held on to Alyssa as he crossed
the street and approached the diner. He could only pray
no one inside would recognize them from the earlier
newscast.

The place was surprisingly crowded and ancient tunes
blared from an equally ancient jukebox. Gage was grateful for the crowd of people as he made his way to the
back, where the restrooms were located. A few of the
customers glanced at them curiously, but most ignored
them.

"Oh, no," Alyssa whispered in a horrified tone.

"What's wrong?"

"We're covered in Jonah's blood." Her voice was brittle, as if she might collapse at any moment. In the dim light of the diner, he could see she was right. Both of their hands were streaked with blood and there were dark smears on their clothes, as well. Luckily, those stains were not as obvious, since they were both wearing dark colors to blend in with the night.

"Here's the bathroom. Do your best to wash up, okay?"

Alyssa stumbled into the ladies' room, closing the door behind her. He grasped the door frame for a moment, grappling with the need to keep her in sight at all times. Finally he turned to follow his own advice, washing off the evidence of Jonah's blood.

His buddy was a good cop. One of the best. The only person he could imagine getting past Jonah was another cop. Crane? Or someone else? He wished he could be sure. Without Jonah's help and support, he felt as if they were stranded at sea in a canoe without paddles. What they needed was a plan.

Too bad his exhausted brain couldn't seem to come up with anything feasible.

Alyssa scrubbed her hands and arms until the pink-tinged water ran clear. She tried her best to soak the bloodstains from her clothes, without much success.

Bracing her weight on the porcelain sink, she closed her eyes. Fatigue oozed from every pore. Running on foot from the police was getting old. Yet the only person who'd believed their story was Jonah. Poor Jonah, who'd been stabbed because he'd tried to help them.

She sighed and tried to pull herself together. Jonah would be fine. He'd had a decent pulse and the paramedics had arrived quickly. He stood a very good chance of recovering. She'd have to call Trinity later to see if Diana was working in the ICU. Diana would let her know if he made it through surgery.

Abruptly she straightened and stared at her reflection in the chipped mirror. Diana? The image of a petite woman with delicate facial features and chin-length dark hair filled her mind. A memory?

She tried to remember more, but the blurred image wouldn't give any hint as to where she and Diana may have been. Likely the hospital, but her brain didn't even give her that much. Still, the surge of excitement was enough to banish her fatigue. Tiny flashes of memory were coming more and more frequently, usually when she least expected them.

Squaring her shoulders with renewed determination, Alyssa cupped her hands and splashed cold water on her face. Maybe she and Gage had suffered a setback tonight, but they weren't beaten yet.

Together, with God's help, they'd find a way to get through this.

She huddled next to Gage at a small table in the back of the diner, gratefully sipping a large, cold glass of water. "I remembered something," she said in a low tone.

Gage's eyes brightened eagerly. "You did? What?"

She felt bad for getting his hopes up. "Nothing that will help us, really, but as I was washing up in the restroom I thought about Jonah, and a colleague's face and name flashed in my mind. Diana White is a friend of mine who works in the ICU at Trinity."

"That's great, Alyssa," Gage said. "The fact that you're starting to remember is a good thing. Maybe if you can get one night of decent sleep, you'll remember more."

"Maybe," she acknowledged. They hadn't been given any time to rest since they'd discovered her true identity. "Anyway, I was thinking I could use your phone to call Trinity Medical Center, see if they have any news about Jonah."

Gage nodded thoughtfully. "You could, but it's still early. Only about thirty minutes since we ran from the park."

"They'd rush him to the hospital and he could already be in surgery by now." She leaned forward. "Gage, I really need to know if he's at least made it that far."

With obvious reluctance, he handed over his phone. She dialed the number and put her free hand over her ear to drown out the noise from the wailing jukebox. There was a loud beeping in her ear but then she heard ringing. When the operator answered, she requested to be put through to the trauma ICU.

"Trauma ICU, may I help you?"

"Is Diana White working tonight?"

"Yes, just a minute please." The elevator music returned for several long seconds, until a female voice came over the line. "This is Diana. May I help you?"

"Diana, this is Alyssa Roth."

"Alyssa?" Diana's voice rose dramatically. "Where are you? Did you know the cops were here looking for you? What's going on?"

The police had shown up at Trinity? Her stomach clenched at the news. The police had put the name Mallory Roth out as being a person of interest, but obviously they'd thought she'd give them information regarding her sister. "I don't have time to explain, but I need to know if you received a new patient, a cop by the name of Jonah Stewart?"

Diana gasped on the other end of the line. "How did you know? You didn't stab him, did you?"

"Of course not!" How could Diana even ask that question? Unless the police were spreading that rumor? The lump in her stomach congealed and sank. Soon, there wouldn't be anyplace left to hide. "He was hurt helping me. Is he all right?"

"He's in surgery. And you know hospital privacy rules prevent me from telling you any details. I can tell you he's in surgery because that's already been on the news and there are cops swarming the place. Alyssa, who stabbed him? What's going on? If you're in trouble—"

"Look, Diana, I don't know anything about who stabbed Jonah, and if you care about me at all, you won't tell the police I called. Goodbye." She snapped the phone shut before Diana could ask anything more. She handed the phone to Gage. "I heard something beeping in your phone. Is it low on batteries?"

"Could be." Gage took the phone. "I have some battery life yet, but there's a message. I don't remember the phone ringing."

She watched him punch in the code needed to listen to his voice mail. "Who is it?"

"Jonah. He must have left the message before he got hurt. He discovered there was a police response to your town house late Friday night, early Saturday morning."

She frowned. "Really? The same night I ended up in the emergency department? What time did you come and pick me up?"

"About three in the morning. They called me at two-thirty."

"Maybe I called the police, before I lost my memory?" She was trying to reason through the possible scenarios, but it wasn't easy without a memory.

"No, that's what Jonah found so odd. There wasn't a record of any calls to the dispatcher or to the 911 operator referring anyone to your address. In fact, there wasn't a record of the police response to your town house that night."

What? That didn't make any sense. "Then how does he know there was a police response?"

"He said he had a conversation with a rookie who mentioned a response that was abruptly called off. The rookie thought it was weird, especially when he was told not to record it."

"A cover-up," she whispered. A bloody room flashed in her mind. Was it possibly at her town house? Or somewhere else?

"Exactly." Gage scrubbed his hands over his face. "I'm sure they covered up some crime, but what, I don't know."

"Murder." The word popped out of her mouth with conviction. The bloody room had to be a memory fragment.

"Without a body?" Gage sighed and shook his head. "Although maybe there is a body. Maybe one in the morgue as a John or Jane Doe."

The thought of Mallory possibly being dead made goose bumps ripple across her skin. She didn't remember her twin sister, but she didn't want to lose her, either. "I doubt there would be a record of the body." At his puzzled expression, she continued, "Don't you see? If there's no paper trail recording the police response to my address, there can't be a body turning up at the morgue. You can't have one without the other."

"Are you ready to walk back to the motel?" he asked when Alyssa finished her water.

He thought she winced, but she gamely nodded and slid out of her seat. "As ready as I'll ever be."

They slipped outside, leaving the anonymity of the crowded diner. Immediately, he felt more conspicuous out on the road. The shrill ringing of his phone startled him. Apprehensively, he pulled it out, relieved to notice the call was from his dad.

Arizona was in a different time zone. His father was calling at eight at night, his time. "Hi, Dad," he greeted his father. "How are you?"

"Hugh Jefferson called me."

The blood drained to the soles of his feet. "What? When?"

"Just now. He said I needed to arrange a meeting for the three of us, and I had the impression that it wouldn't be healthy to refuse his request."

His dad's voice sounded far away, as if he were on the other end of a long tunnel. It took a moment to realize his hearing was obstructed by the high-pitched buzz of pure fury. How dare Jefferson use his father to get to him? His father was innocent—he had no part in Jefferson's sick game. This time, Jefferson had gone too far.

And then it hit him. Northwestern University. The place where his dad had gone to college all those years ago. The same place Gage had gone. The same place Hugh Jefferson had gone?

No wonder Jefferson had targeted Drummond Builders. He'd purposefully used someone he knew he could threaten and blackmail to do what he wanted.

"You need to get out of there, Dad. Right now." He clenched the phone so hard, his fingers hurt. "Take Margaret on a trip. Use a rental car. Don't tell anyone where you're going, not even me."

"What's going on, Gage?"

"I'm sorry, Dad. Jefferson is trying to use you to get to me." Jefferson had found his Achilles' heel and made no qualms about using it to his advantage.

There was a long silence. "Why?"

To make me finish his condos. As soon as the thought formed in his mind, he knew it was true. Jefferson knew that Gage would want to pull out of the contract, and he was threatening his father's life to get him to keep working for him. The bleak realization weighed heavily on his shoulders. He'd failed to protect his mother all those years ago, when her second husband started beating her, but this was worse. Much worse. He couldn't protect both his father and Alyssa at the same time.

"I'm working on a project for him, but we're not in agreement as to how things should be done." The biggest understatement of the year. "Don't worry, I'll take care of things here. But I need you to be safe, Dad. I'm begging you to get out of there. Right now. Take a trip with Margaret."

"You think we're in danger."

"Yes. Leave the house and don't come back until you hear from me."

"Okay, then, we'll go. One of the advantages of early retirement is that we can pretty much do whatever we want. I'll take Margaret out of here, but I want you to keep in touch, Gage. I'm worried about you, too."

"Don't worry, I'll stay in touch. Take care, Dad." He paused, before adding, "I love you."

"Right back at you, son."

Gage closed his eyes and snapped his phone shut. He stared at the cell phone for a minute, fighting a wave of fury.

"Gage?" Alyssa gently touched his arm. "Are you all right?"

"No. Jefferson has dragged my father into this with an implied threat. Either I do what he wants or he'll hurt my father. I've asked him to leave town, but it's very possible Jefferson has criminals working for him in Arizona. I hope it's not too late." For a moment he was tempted to give in, to do whatever Jefferson wanted in order to protect the ones he loved. Never had he felt so helpless, not since he was ten years old and watching his mother suffer his stepfather's big meaty fist.

Ruthlessly, he shoved those memories aside. Failure wasn't an option. Somehow, he needed to figure out how to get out of this mess. Giving in to Jefferson's demands would be signing his own death warrant—once the project was complete, anyway.

No. Somehow, some way, he needed to keep Alyssa and his father safe.

TWELVE

Alyssa listened with horror to Gage's blunt assessment of Jefferson's latest stunt. Was there anything Hugh Jefferson couldn't do? Did he have people working for him everywhere? Gage was afraid his father wasn't safe, even all the way across the country in Arizona. And she understood why. What she didn't know was how to stop Jefferson's evil plan.

Please, Lord, help me remember!

"Is there anything I can do to help?" she asked when they'd walked a few blocks in silence.

"No." She didn't think she'd ever heard Gage sound so defeated.

Suddenly, his dejected tone made her mad. "Listen, Gage, we can do this. We're smart and resourceful. We've dodged Jefferson and Crane so far. And don't forget, we have God supporting and guiding us."

He glanced at her but didn't respond. She didn't want to push, or preach, but surely he'd feel better if he shared his burden with God?

She could feel Gage tense when the headlights of a car approached, but they kept walking and soon the car passed them by. "How much farther until we reach the motel?" she asked, half dreading the answer.

"Not that far, especially if we take a few shortcuts."

Unfortunately, Gage's shortcuts meant sneaking through more backyards. A dog started barking loudly from the yard next to them, making Alyssa jump out of her skin. By the time they arrived back at the motel, she wanted nothing more than to shower and climb into bed.

As they approached the motel, she noticed a convenience store nearby. She glanced at Gage. "Do you have a couple of dollars? I want to buy another newspaper."

He glanced at her as if she were crazy. "Why?"

She shrugged. "So far, we learned a lot from the paper that was left on the bus, but it was Friday's paper. I thought a more recent newspaper might give us more information."

Gage nodded thoughtfully. "Can't hurt. Wait here, I'll get it."

She wanted to protest but honestly didn't have the energy. Times like this, she didn't mind Gage's protective attitude so much. If only he'd learn to strike a balance. She rested against the building, relieved they were nearly at the motel. Her ankle was throbbing like mad.

Gage returned quickly with the newspaper tucked under his arm. She sensed his nervousness as they hurried across the street.

"What's wrong?" she asked.

"Nothing, probably just my overactive imagination," he muttered.

Her gut clenched. More possible danger? Would she ever be able to relax again? "Tell me."

"It seemed like the clerk was staring at me," Gage admitted slowly. "I have a bad feeling he recognized me from the news."

* * *

Despite her physical exhaustion, Alyssa spent a restless night. Between the pain in her ankle and being afraid the police were going to come arrest them, she woke up every hour on the hour.

At seven, she gave up hope of getting more sleep. There was a tiny coffeepot on the dresser and she brewed a pot as she dyed her hair. Putting the red coloring over her blond curls wasn't easy, but she had to admit, the end result wasn't too bad. She certainly looked different.

Her blue eyes were still pretty distinctive, though, and the only way she could think to disguise them was to buy cheap clear glasses, since she didn't wear contacts and wasn't about to start now.

There was a brief knock at the connecting door between them and she glanced over to find Gage standing in the doorway. "Good morning. How did you sleep?"

"Terrible." Gage was staring at her red hair in shock. "I didn't think you'd actually use it."

She rolled her eyes. "You bought it for me to use, right? I don't have the option of growing a beard."

He scratched at his dark jaw with a grimace. "It itches."

She flashed a grin. "Don't look at me for sympathy."

"Okay, Red."

"That's the oldest nickname on the planet," she said with a groan. She liked this feeling of camaraderie that seemed to have sprung between them. Did their relationship before her memory loss have that same closeness? Somehow, she didn't think so, not if she broke up with him. She gestured to the tiny pot. "Want to share my coffee?"

"Yeah, and I bought breakfast." He set the bagels and

cream cheese on the small table. "Figured with all the walking we've been doing, we could use a few extra carbs."

No argument there. She ripped a bagel in half and spread a thin layer of cheese over it before taking a huge bite. She chewed thoughtfully for a moment. "We need a game plan."

"Did you read the newspaper?" he asked.

She shook her head. "Not yet."

"I skimmed it this morning, and there was a huge article about the special mayoral election being held tomorrow."

"Tomorrow?" She nearly choked on her bagel and then remembered Jonah had mentioned something about that the previous night, when they were at the first motel room. "I forgot it was Election Tuesday." Her memory hadn't suddenly returned when she woke up this morning, but even so, she sensed she wasn't big into politics. "Obviously Eric Holden is the main candidate, since he's the interim mayor, but who's the other candidate?"

"A Hispanic guy by the name of Gerald Maas. Interestingly he's a former city councilman himself." Gage took a deep sip of his coffee, capturing her gaze over the rim. "I figure anyone opposing Eric Holden is a friend of ours. My plan is to find Gerald Maas and see what, if anything, he knows about all this."

She had to admit, it was a good plan. They finished their breakfast and she found it difficult to tear her gaze from Gage's face. Even with the scruffy growth of his beard, he was very attractive. He'd asked for a second chance, and right now, she was willing to give him one. Would she feel differently when her memory returned? It was hard to imagine.

When they left the motel on foot, Alyssa wanted to weep at the pain that zinged up her leg. She ground her teeth together, determined to tough it out. Gage had enough to worry about without her adding to it by whining.

"Dan's truck!" he said abruptly, snapping his fingers. "Why didn't I think of that sooner?"

"Dan's truck?" Maybe it was lack of sleep combined with only one cup of coffee, but she wasn't following him. "What about Dan's truck?"

"I have a key." Gage dug into his jeans pocket and pulled out his wallet. "I'm sure Dan's truck is parked down by our offices."

Since Gage's office building was on the other side of town, she didn't consider this revelation particularly good news. "It will take all day to walk there," she protested. "We have to figure out some way to find Gerald Maas."

Gage sent her a sidelong glance. "And you think I don't have faith?" he asked dryly. "The newspaper listed his campaign headquarters, and since the election is tomorrow, I'm sure someone will be there, maybe even Gerald himself."

She blushed and realized he was right. She was tired, crabby and in pain, but that was no excuse to lose faith. "Brilliant idea, Gage. Although I'm almost afraid to ask where the campaign office is located."

"Not to worry. We can take the number ten bus downtown, pick up Dan's truck and then go to the campaign office. Piece of cake."

Gage's good mood was contagious. She admired him for putting his fear for his father aside, at least on the surface. She found herself thinking she was very lucky to have Gage at her side during all this. She couldn't imagine what she'd have done without him.

Cautiously, they made their way past the convenience store without incident. "Guess the clerk didn't recognize you after all," she murmured.

"I hope not, but regardless, once we have Dan's truck, I think we'll come back here, get our stuff and find a new place to stay for the night." Gage's expression turned grim. "No sense in pushing our luck."

She had to agree. They found the bus stop and had to wait only a few minutes for the bus to arrive. With her red hair and Gage's darkly shadowed jaw, she didn't think they'd look too much like the photos on the news. But she kept her head down and avoided direct eye contact with other passengers as she slid into a seat in the back of the bus.

The ride downtown took longer than she expected, as the bus stopped many times along the way. But once they reached the end of the line, she was grateful they weren't far from the parking garage. "Where do you think he parked?" she asked.

"He has a white truck. There, it's the third one from the end."

The thought of actually driving from point A to point B was enough to pick up her mood. She'd never been so happy to see a vehicle in her life. Gage slid behind the wheel and started up the truck with a twist of the key.

Riding to Gerald Maas's campaign headquarters took less than ten minutes to cover a distance that would have taken at least an hour or more to walk.

Inside, the place was busy with people picking up fliers for one last campaign push. "Can I help you?" a

Identity Crisis

harried, rather buxom woman with blond-streaked hair asked when she saw them standing there.

She noticed Gage put on his most charming smile. "Good morning, ma'am. We're both huge supporters of Gerald Maas. Would you happen to know where he is?"

"Supporters?" her brown eyes gleamed. "How would you like to canvass some neighborhoods for us?"

"We'd love to!" Alyssa blinked when Gage readily took a handful of Maas for Mayor fliers. "But we really need to talk to Gerald, first. Is he swinging by here soon?"

"No. If I know Gerald he's down on the river, fixing up that old railroad property of his."

"Railroad property?" she echoed, glancing over at Gage. He shrugged, indicating he had no idea what the woman meant.

"You know where the old Milwaukee railroad used to cross the river?" When Gage shook his head no, she went on, "Right across the street from the south end of the Summerfest grounds. The old brick building used to be the control tower for the railroad bridge. It's not in use now, of course, but the building is still there. Would make a nice little place for a restaurant or deli. Any property on the water is worth something these days."

Yeah, like Jefferson's condos overlooking the river. "Oh, yes, of course," Gage said. "I know exactly where it is. Thanks so much."

Back out in the truck, she glanced at him. "How did you know where she was talking about?" she asked.

"Because I know the downtown area pretty well." He pulled out into traffic, and once again she was thrilled not to be walking. "It's actually not far from here."

Five minutes later he pulled off and parked the white truck. As they approached, she noticed the two-story narrow brick building with large windows on three of the four sides overlooking the Milwaukee River. It was cute, too small for condos, but as the woman mentioned, perfect for a small restaurant or deli.

"There he is," Gage murmured.

She followed his gaze. There was a small concrete patio in the back of the control tower building, overlooking the water. Two plastic chairs were back there, and a middle-aged man, with black hair liberally sprinkled with gray, sat pensively looking out over the water.

As they closed the distance, he spoke without turning around. "Nice day for fishing isn't it?"

"Uh, yes sir." Gage took the lead, coming up to stand beside the former councilman. "My name is Gage Drummond and this is Alyssa Roth. We'd like to ask you a few questions, if you don't mind."

Gerald narrowed his gaze suspiciously. "You reporters?"

"No!" she exclaimed. "We're not Eric Holden fans, and we're concerned about what will happen to the city if he wins this election."

The older man looked between them and then nodded slowly. "All right, then, please sit down." He indicated the plastic chair next to him.

She glanced at Gage, silently asking where they should start. He cleared his throat and turned toward the former councilman. "Mr. Maas, we know that Hugh Jefferson is financially supporting Eric Holden's election, and that greatly concerns us. We have reason to believe Jefferson is dangerous."

Maas slowly nodded. "Councilman Schaefer said the same thing to me about a couple of weeks ago. And now he's dead."

She sucked in a harsh breath. "Why?"

Maas lifted one shoulder. "Schaefer took the lead in voting against giving him a permit. But in the end, the rest of the group was swayed in favor of granting the permit because of the additional tax revenue, ignoring Jefferson's shady business deals. And you're right, Holden will likely win this election. I'm trying my best, but I don't have the clout that Jefferson has."

"We need to stop him," she urged, leaning forward. "Help us stop him."

Maas lifted tired brown eyes to hers. "Unfortunately, there isn't much I can do. No one is listening to me. If you have any sort of proof regarding Jefferson, you should take it directly to the police."

"We can't," she protested softly. "He has officers, at least one for sure that we know of, working for him."

"If we had concrete proof, we could take it to the FBI," Gage offered. "Do you know anything that can help us?"

Maas was silent for a moment. "I have my suspicions of course, just like others do. But I couldn't find any proof to support my theory."

She frowned and exchanged a look with Gage. "What theory?"

"That the previous mayor, Tony Flynn, was murdered."

Flynn murdered? Stunned, Gage stared at Maas. "I thought the autopsy proved he died of a heart attack?"

Maas's tone was bitter. "Pretty convenient heart attack, if you ask me. I don't believe it. Flynn was disgustingly healthy, ran marathons on a regular basis. He didn't have a family history of heart trouble. And he was found crumpled over his desk after a late meeting with Holden."

"Anyone can have sudden death from a heart attack," Alyssa protested. "Even a marathon runner."

Maas waved a finger at her. "I know what you're saying, missy, but I still don't believe it. Mayor Flynn wasn't one to fold under pressure. Are you really going to sit there and tell me that there isn't something that can be given to a person that mimics a heart attack, even on autopsy?"

"The only thing I know of is potassium chloride," she whispered, looking stricken. "An injection of potassium chloride would mimic a heart attack, and the higher levels of potassium in the bloodstream would be associated with the actual event itself."

Gage was shocked. "But it can't be easy to get your hands on potassium chloride," he protested.

"Not easy," Alyssa acknowledged. "Every hospital in the country keeps the stuff secured in the pharmacy. No vials are allowed up on the nursing units. But still, nothing is impossible."

Maas grimaced. "So now you know why I can't help you with proof. They're too good at covering their tracks."

Gage hated to admit failure, but after asking a few more questions, he realized Maas couldn't help them any further. "Thanks for your time, sir. And I hope you win this election."

"I hope so, too." Gerald Maas set down his fishing pole to stand and shake their hands. "Good luck."

"Thanks." He cupped Alyssa's elbow in his hand, offering her support as they made their way back to Dan's truck. He could tell by the way she was walking that her ankle still bothered her. He wished he had thought about Dan's truck sooner.

"So now what?" she asked when they reached the truck. "Maas didn't help much, except to reinforce our suspicions."

"I know, but somehow it makes me feel better to know

we have at least one ally." Gage drummed his fingers on the edge of the steering wheel. "Let's run back to the motel, pick up our stuff and find a new place to stay for tonight."

"Sounds good." She sat back against the seat with a sigh. "Thanks, Gage."

He lifted his eyebrows in surprise. "For what?"

A small smile tugged the corner of her mouth. "For being here with me through all this. I'm so glad to have your support."

He was humbled by her words. He didn't deserve her gratitude—he still felt responsible for her current state. Still, she was right in that they had a lot to be thankful for. "You're welcome, but you need to know, the feeling is mutual."

She reached over and put her hand on his. He clasped her small hand in his, wishing he had the right to pull her into his arms and kiss her. He tried to keep his concentration on the road, but he was all too aware of Alyssa beside him.

"Um, Gage?" The underlying fear in her voice cut through his thoughts. "There's a squad car behind us."

He glanced up at the rearview mirror, and his gut tightened with fear. Almost instantly, the red and blue lights went on, and the squad car came up right behind them, practically touching their rear bumper, indicating they needed to pull over. "Can you tell if the driver is Crane?"

"I don't know. I can't see past the sun glare." She twisted in her seat and then glanced at him. "There's too much traffic. We'll never be able to lose him."

"We'll get arrested if we pull over." He swept a frantic glance over the area. To the right there was a road, relatively free of cars, that wound beneath the interstate.

"Hang on," he said as he yanked the steering wheel, making a sharp right.

Unfortunately, the police car followed, red and blue lights still flashing.

"Gage!" Alyssa shouted. "Look out, he has a gun!"

Desperately, he swerved again, but too late. The bullet hit its mark and their rear tire blew, sending the truck sliding out of control. He wrestled with the steering wheel, slamming on the brakes to try to avoid the concrete pillar. He managed to slow the vehicle down, but the front end of the truck still smashed into the pillar with enough force to cause the air bags to deploy.

Instantly, he was pinned in his seat, listening to the shattering glass of the windshield.

"Gage?" The air bags began to deflate, and he felt Alyssa's hand gripping his arm. "Are you all right?"

"Yeah, but we have to get out of here." He shoved his door open, but a strong hand stopped the door from opening all the way. The ruddy face of Officer Crane loomed before him, a cruel smile twisting his thin lips. The gun he'd used to shoot out their tire was leveled at Gage's chest.

"Well, well, well. This must be my lucky day." The deep, mocking drawl made him clench his fingers on the steering wheel in anger. Especially when Crane leaned over to leer at Alyssa. "Did you really think the red hair would fool me?" he asked snidely. "Get out. You're both under arrest for the murder of Dan Kirkland."

Gage wanted nothing more than to wipe the satisfied smirk off Crane's face, but the gun held him immobile. They were trapped. There was no way out of this one. He didn't doubt that Crane would shoot them both if they tried to run. He couldn't bear to look at Alyssa as he slid out of the driver's seat. He couldn't face how he'd failed her yet again.

"Up against the car, both of you. Hands behind your back."

Cage stood helplessly against the truck, and Alyssa soon joined him. Crane snapped plastic ties around his wrists, locking them together. From the corner of his eye, he watched Crane place the same type of plastic ties around Alyssa's wrists.

"This way." Crane kept the gun in one hand, using it to urge them both to the back of his squad car. He opened the back door and waved the gun, gesturing for them to get in. Gage waited for Alyssa to scoot in first, then slid in beside her. Crane slammed the door behind them.

Crane slid into the driver's seat, picked up the radio and began speaking. "Dispatch, I'm reporting an abandoned vehicle, a white Chevy pickup, license 555 ERP, registered to a Daniel J. Kirkland, deceased. It's located under the Marquette interchange. No sign of the driver or any passengers at this time. Send a tow truck to the scene, over."

"Ten-four," the radio squawked.

Crane replaced his radio, started the car and then eased into traffic. Dread curled in Gage's gut. "You're not taking us to the police station, are you?" he asked.

Crane let out a mirthless laugh. "Ooh, you're so smart, Drummond. No, we're not going to the police station."

Beside him, he heard Alyssa's sharp gasp.

Defiantly, he met Crane's gaze through the rear-view mirror, refusing to show the man any trace of fear. Crane's eyes were bright with triumph. "Jefferson has other plans for the two of you." His evil gaze shifted to include Alyssa. "I can hardly wait for both of you to get what you deserve."

THIRTEEN

Red dots of fury swam before Gage's eyes. He strained against the ties binding his wrists, ignoring the increasing pain in his arms. He had to protect Alyssa. To keep Crane from laying one slimy finger on her.

His fault. Once again, this mess was his fault. Why on earth had he picked up Dan's truck? His stupidity had gotten them captured. For a moment, a wave of helplessness washed over him.

Lord, please help us! Guide us and give us strength to escape Crane!

The silent prayer helped to steady his racing heart.

"Where are you taking us?" Alyssa's voice held a fine tremor, although the stubborn tilt to her chin was reassuring. Her show of bravery made him even more determined to find a way to escape Crane.

"Anxious to be alone with me, babe?" Crane taunted. The way his leering gaze lingered on Alyssa caused Gage to grit his teeth in frustration. "Maybe we can have a little fun together after I get rid of your boyfriend."

Gage kept his expression impassive, refusing to let Crane know how much his taunts were getting to him. He forced the red haze of fury away and he stared out the window, making mental notes of which streets Crane took. The only advantage they had at this point was that Crane hadn't checked their pockets prior to slapping the plastic cuff ties around their wrists. Gage carried a small Boy Scout knife in the front pocket of his jeans, a gift from his father many years ago. With his hands behind his back, the knife wouldn't be easy to reach, but at least they weren't completely helpless.

He refused to believe there wouldn't be a chance to escape. Alyssa told him he needed to put his faith in God, so he would. *Help me, Lord. Help me find a way out!*

Crane headed west, the opposite direction than Gage had expected. Crane turned on National Avenue and then turned right again, heading under the 35th Street viaduct to a section of the city that once housed many manufacturing plants. Now only old, dilapidated warehouses remained. With a sinking feeling, Gage quickly realized the area looked deserted.

The police car slowed to a stop in front of an old warehouse at the end of a dead-end street. Crane pulled a keyring out of his uniform pocket and unlocked the heavy padlock on the door. After raising the garage door, he got back in the squad car and pulled the vehicle inside the warehouse. Crane closed the garage door with a loud bang.

Darkness enveloped them. After a minute, Gage's eyes adjusted to the dim light. There were windows high on the walls of the warehouse, practically covered in grime. His heart sank as he realized the windows were a good ten feet off the ground. The rest of the warehouse was mostly empty, except for a few crates and boxes lining one wall, many appearing to be rotted or broken.

Crane abruptly opened the door closest to Alyssa. "Hey, babe," he greeted her, as if she happened to be voluntarily spending time with him instead of being kidnapped. Crane grasped Alyssa's arm and pulled her out of the squad car, still holding the gun in his right hand. Gage edged across the seat to scramble out after her, as if his presence alone might keep her safe. "You're a real looker, aren't you?" Crane said, using the barrel of the gun to trace a line from her neck down toward the open collar of her shirt.

Alyssa held her head high, as if she wasn't afraid of being mauled or worse, although fear and loathing shone from her blue eyes.

"You think you have your bases covered?" Gage asked sharply, desperate to divert Crane's attention from Alyssa. "We just talked to Gerald Maas. He knows you murdered Flynn, Schaefer and Dan Kirkland. Don't you think the body count is a bit steep? I mean, really, how many deaths can you blame on gang members?"

Crane swung his head around to scowl at Gage, although his gun hand never wavered. Then he widened his eyes with feigned innocence. "Me? I didn't kill anyone. You're the one who murdered Kirkland. And we have plenty of evidence to prove it."

"Like what?" Gage needed to keep him talking, both to keep him from getting too close to Alyssa and to know exactly what they were dealing with.

Crane stepped closer to Alyssa, the tip of his gun brushing her skin, and she automatically took a step backward. One step, two steps, three. Gage subtly eased along with them, trying not to let Crane get between him and Alyssa.

"Your fingerprints on the knife in his chest. Documents that show Kirkland stole money from Drummond Builders to pay off gambling debts," Crane bragged. "Let's see, I believe that's both motive and opportunity."

"Fabricated evidence," Gage summarized bitterly. Dan hadn't been a gambler, although he didn't doubt Crane's ability to plant anything he wanted to support his false claim.

"Enough evidence for the D.A. to file charges." Crane abruptly laughed. "If you refuse to cooperate with us, that is. We have to keep you alive long enough to finish the condo project."

Alyssa was still moving backward, away from Crane's gun, when her heel caught on the stack of crates behind her. She stumbled and fell backward against the wooden crates.

Just when Gage feared the worst, that Crane would actually attack Alyssa right before his eyes, the radio blared from inside the squad. "Unit 19, are you there? Unit 19 come in, please."

For a moment, Gage wondered if Crane would ignore the summons. The ruddy-faced cop was staring intently at Alyssa as if he'd never been this close to a woman before. Finally, after what seemed like an eternity, he gestured toward Gage with the gun. "Get over there next to her."

Gage gladly complied, coming over to crouch next to where Alyssa was still sprawled against the crates. With her arms bound behind her back and her bum ankle, she struggled to get back on her feet.

"Don't move," Crane warned as he backed up to the squad car. He opened the front passenger door and reached across for the radio. "Unit 19 responding, over."

"Unit 19, the chief wants you to report to his office, pronto."

The chief? As in the chief of police? Gage couldn't tell if Crane was upset by this new directive or not. Was it possible the chief of police was on to Crane? Or was he also a party to Jefferson's illegal activities?

"Ten-four, I'll be there in fifteen." Crane put the radio back, his teeth gleaming in a feral grin. "Duty calls, but don't worry, I'll be back shortly."

Gage estimated they were a good twenty feet from the garage door. Maybe when Crane opened it to get the squad car out, could they run through the opening?

Almost as soon as the thought formed in his mind, Crane came toward them. "Get to the farthest corner of the warehouse and sit down on the floor. Now."

Since Crane still held the gun on them, they had little choice but to obey his curt command. Alyssa managed to use one of the crates for leverage to get back on her feet. Gage stayed right beside her as they walked to the farthest corner of the warehouse.

"Jefferson wants you alive, but if you try to run, I'll be forced to shoot you in the leg," Crane told them in a flat, emotionless tone. "I earned expert status in marksmanship, so don't doubt my ability to hit what I'm aiming at. Understand?"

Gage nodded, understanding only too well as he slid down the wall next to Alyssa. Right now, he was willing to wait for Crane to leave before trying anything further. He sat as close to Alyssa as possible, his arm pressed against hers in an attempt to give her strength and support.

Crane backed up to the garage door, opened it up and then returned to back the squad car out. He left the car idling while he shut the door with a definite thud.

Alyssa closed her eyes in relief when Crane left. The man's lewd stare made her feel sick to her stomach. She knew he'd intended to touch her, or worse.

Thank You, Lord, for sparing me.

"Alyssa, get back up on your feet," Gage hissed in an urgent whisper, cutting into her silent prayer. "We don't have a lot of time."

Her ankle was throbbing worse than before, from tripping and falling against the crates, but she resolutely inched up the wall behind them.

"Can you reach into my front pocket?" Gage asked, positioning himself behind her.

She felt for the edge of his front pocket with her fingers, but Crane had put her wrists together so tightly, there wasn't much room to maneuver. "I can feel the top edge of your pocket," she confirmed.

"Scoot down and try to slide your fingers in. See if you can get hold of the pocketknife," he directed.

Gage had a pocketknife? For the first time since she saw the cop car behind them, she believed they might actually have a chance to escape Crane. She crouched down a bit and worked her fingers into the front pocket of Gage's jeans. She could feel the smooth plastic of the pocketknife, but grasping it and pulling it up seemed nearly impossible.

"Take your time," Gage murmured encouragingly.

The plastic ties cut sharply into her wrists, but after several failed attempts, she finally managed to get the knife gripped between her first and second fingers. Drawing it carefully upward, she finally pulled the small pocketknife free and folded it into her palm. "Got it," she cried.

"Great! Now hand it to me." Gage turned around so they were back-to-back, enabling her to pass the knife. Opening the knife wasn't too difficult, and he finally ran his thumb across the sharp edge of the blade.

He tried to maneuver the sharp edge against his own plastic ties, but he couldn't get enough leverage. After several tries, and several cuts to his hands and wrists, he gave up. "Alyssa, you need to take the knife handle and use the blade to cut through the plastic."

"I can't see what I'm doing. What if I hurt you?" she asked. "Maybe you should cut through mine instead."

"No!" his abrupt refusal startled her. "Don't worry about cutting me. You can do this, Alyssa. We need our hands free in order to find a way out of here."

Alyssa bit her lip and took the smooth handle of the knife in her fingertips. "Okay, I have the knife. But I can't tell where the tip of the blade is."

"Leave that part to me," he assured her. "Just make sure you don't lose your grip on the knife, okay?"

Easier said than done, as the plastic coating felt slippery from sweat. She held the knife as firmly as possible as Gage moved closer. There was pressure on the other end of the knife, and she heard Gage suck in a harsh breath. Had she cut him? "Are you all right?"

"Fine," he said through gritted teeth. She could feel him pushing against the knife as he worked to get it into position. Something warm and slippery trickled over her fingertips, and she knew he must be bleeding. "There, the blade is right under the plastic cuff. I'm going to push my wrists down while you keep the pressure with the knife steady, okay?"

"Okay." She did as he asked, and after a few attempts the plastic tie broke free.

Gage dropped his arms to his sides and then turned to take the knife from her fingers. "Hold still," he murmured as he used the knife to cut through the plastic ties binding her wrists. "You're free."

"Oh Gage!" she spun around and threw herself into his arms. He clasped her close, crushing her tight. She buried her face against his chest. "I was so scared," she confessed in a muffled tone.

"Shh, I know. It's okay." She could feel his cheek resting against her hair.

She wanted to stay in Gage's arms forever, but obviously, getting their wrists free from the plastic ties was only the first step in escaping. They were still locked in the warehouse. With effort, she pulled away and glanced around. "Do you think we can get through those windows up there?"

"We're going to try," Gage said grimly. He crossed over to the pile of broken crates and gingerly picked up one and set it on the other.

Bright red blood dripped from his fingertips. "Gage, you're bleeding. Did I cut you?"

"Just a nick, I'm sure." He ignored his injury and continued to pile one crate on top of another under the window with the least amount of grime.

"Wait a minute," she demanded when blood continued to flow down his wrist. "That cut is way too deep. I need to put a pressure dressing over it."

Reluctantly, he paused long enough for her to take the elastic bandage from his earlier injury and apply it to his wrist instead. The cut in his wrist looked far too deep for comfort. But there wasn't much she could do without first-aid supplies, so she wrapped it up as tightly as she dared before joining him in piling the crates on top of each other.

"We have to hurry. Crane could come back here at any moment." Gage tested his weight on the crates, causing them to shake and groan.

"I should go up. I'm lighter," she pointed out.

"I'm taller." Since she couldn't argue that, she did her best to hold the wobbly crates still as Gage climbed up to reach the window. "It's stuck shut. Hand me a piece of wood. I'll break it open."

She did as he asked, ducking her head when pieces of glass fell to the floor around them. Gage took his time, making sure there were no shards of glass left in the frame. He was high enough that he could easily lever himself out of the window, and she had to bite her tongue to stop from begging him not to leave her here alone.

"Stand back, I'm coming down."

"What? Why?" Despite her initial fear, she knew that Gage needed to get out of the window to bring help of some kind.

He shot her an exasperated glance. "You're going through first."

She shook her head as he dropped down beside her. "I don't know if I can do it, Gage."

"Sure you can. I'm not leaving you in here alone. You have to shimmy through the window. It's large enough that you should be able to pull yourself up, swing your leg through and then drop over the other side."

She stared at the rectangle-shaped window dubiously. "I don't know, Gage. Maybe you should go and get help."

"Leaving you here isn't an option, Alyssa." His determination and support was heartwarming. "Either you go or neither of us gets out of here."

She let out a heavy sigh and then cautiously began climbing up the pile of crates. They didn't shake as much under her weight, and she reached the top in no time. She grasped the bottom of the window frame and tried to pull herself upward, but she didn't have enough arm strength.

"I'm coming," Gage said. The tower of crates swayed dangerously and she clung to the window frame, holding her breath, praying the rickety crates would hold their combined weight. "Okay, I've got you." With Gage pushing her up from below, she was able to get her torso through the window and balance on the edge long enough to get her leg up and over. From there, it wasn't nearly as hard to get her other leg over the window frame. She hung there for a moment, wishing she knew how far the drop would be, and soon decided it didn't matter. One way or another, she was going down.

Give me strength, Lord, she prayed and then let go. Her feet hit the ground hard and a sharp, stabbing pain shot through her ankle as she fell backward on her bottom. She managed just barely to keep her head from hitting the ground, too.

She looked up and saw Gage was already making his way through the broken window. She scooted out of the way just in time for him to land on the ground beside her.

"Alyssa? Are you all right?" He knelt at her side.

"I need help to get up," she told him. He gave her a hand and she kept all her weight on her good leg as he slowly pulled her upright. "I don't know if I can walk," she confided, fighting tears of frustration.

"Lean on me," Gage encouraged.

She did as he asked, but even with his support, she couldn't put any weight on her ankle. "I can't do it, Gage. I can't walk." Close. They were so close to escaping. Panic clawed up her throat, choking her. "Gage, how are we going to get out of here?"

Gage could tell Alyssa was close to losing it. He battled a wave of dizziness as he glanced around, looking for something for her to use as a cane. The elastic bandage she'd wrapped around his wrist was already bright with blood, and the way the wound wouldn't stop bleeding, he suspected she'd hit an artery when she'd cut away the plastic cuffs.

"Here, see if you can use this for support." He picked up a hunk of pipe that happened to be lying on the side of the warehouse. If she could manage to walk with the pipe, he hoped they could get out of sight.

Yet it wouldn't be easy to hide in broad daylight, especially now that they were both injured. He refused to give up hope, though. They'd gotten this far, hadn't they? God had already given them the strength to escape the warehouse. Surely they could lose themselves in the anonymity of the city.

He was proud of the way Alyssa grasped the waist-high length of pipe and leaned on it as if it was a cane. Deep lines of pain bracketed her mouth, but she took a few wobbly steps and then glanced at him. "This will work for a while, so let's go."

Gage glanced around, trying to pick the best escape route. Too bad there weren't a lot of options. "We'll have to avoid the main road, since we know Crane is heading back this way. Let's go behind the warehouses and see where that takes us."

Alyssa nodded gamely but didn't say much as she slowly moved beside him, leaning heavily on her makeshift cane. As they rounded a third warehouse, they came across an old, rusted bicycle with tires that were low on air but not completely flat.

"Can you get up on the seat?" he asked, holding the frame steady.

"Yes, but how are we both going to fit?" she asked skeptically.

"I'm going to stand and pedal while you hang on to my waist." Pedaling on low-pressure tires took a lot of strength and effort, but he refused to give up. At least not until they managed to get somewhere safe.

Riding double was awkward, but he made decent time, especially when they could coast downhill for a few blocks. Each yard he was able to put between them and their warehouse prison made it easier to breathe.

Gage tried to think of a place to go, but he didn't know of any other motels that would take cash without asking too many questions. Not to mention the stream of blood oozing down his arm.

Alyssa must have noticed too, because she tightened her grip around his waist. "Gage, we need to find some first-aid supplies." She was balancing precariously on the seat, with her legs outstretched so they wouldn't interfere with his pedaling. "You're losing too much blood."

He didn't answer, because he knew she was right. If he didn't find a place to rest and get off the bike soon, he might very well fall off. And where was he supposed to find first-aid supplies? Their duffel bags were probably still in the back of Dan's truck, which meant he had only the money in his wallet and nothing more.

Wait a minute—Alyssa had a first-aid kit in her town house. As a nurse, she'd prided herself on having the best first-aid supplies. He'd avoided her town house until now, because he'd considered it too dangerous to go back.

But their options were severely limited by their respective injuries. They wouldn't stay overnight, but they could at least pick up the first-aid kit, and maybe a change of clothing. And best of all, her town house was only a few miles away.

With a firm destination in mind, he pushed himself

to pedal harder and faster. Cautiously, he first rode past the town house, making sure there was no one staked out there, before heading around the block.

"Where are we?" Alyssa asked hesitantly as he pulled up in front of the cheery white building.

He'd almost forgotten her amnesia. "At your town house," he murmured, rolling the bike to a stop. He put his foot down on the ground and then held the bike steady for Alyssa. "I have a key."

"You do?" She looked horrified by the thought.

"Don't worry—I promise I didn't stay here with you, Alyssa. You only asked me to keep it as a spare. You gave a key to your sister, too." He bypassed the front door, preferring to use the less conspicuous side door. He quickly unlocked it, pushed the door open and then held out his arm so that Alyssa could lean on him to hobble inside.

She took several steps, looking around curiously. He was relieved the place looked the same way as it did a few days ago, when he'd come here to look for Alyssa the morning after he'd picked her up from the hospital. He'd left the windows open, so the pine scent wasn't as overwhelming as it had been before.

Alyssa leaned against the wall, favoring her sore ankle as she worked her way down the hall to the bedrooms. Were the surroundings familiar to her at all? Curious to see her reaction, he followed close behind. When she reached the master bedroom, she froze.

"What is it?" he asked, putting his arm around her. Her shoulders were shaking, and he knew she was crying. She stayed there for so long, he began to get worried. "Alyssa? You're scaring me. What's wrong?"

"I remember," she finally whispered in a low, agonized tone. "Gage, I remember!"

FOURTEEN

In a rush, memories tumbled through her mind, falling into place like dominoes. Councilman Schaefer bleeding on a stretcher, telling her Jefferson's thug stabbed him. Officer Crane refusing to believe her, and then later trying to run her off the road. Hiding in a flea-ridden motel and borrowing her twin sister's identity. Searching for Mallory. A glittery hair clip on the living room table. Blood pooled on her bedroom floor. A blood-stained yellow blouse crumpled in the corner.

Mallory!

She gripped her stomach as pain sliced deep. Her fault. Her twin had been killed because someone had mistaken Mallory for her! Guilt rolled over her, beating her down like tidal waves, threatening to send her crashing to the floor. Slowly, she sank to her knees, covering her face with her hands. *Lord, help me. Please, help me. If Mallory is dead, please bring her home to You.*

"Alyssa? What is it? What do you remember?"

Gage's deeply concerned voice and his strong hand on her shoulder finally penetrated her inner turmoil. She remembered how he'd proposed marriage while on a horse-and-carriage ride. And she remembered breaking off their engagement, because he'd suffocated her with his protectiveness and he hadn't embraced his faith. But she still cared about him. More than she'd admitted before. With an effort, she tried to pull herself together.

"Mallory," she whispered in a hoarse voice. "I remember my twin. She died because of me."

She heard Gage suck in a deep breath. "She died? You actually found Mallory's body?" His tone was incredulous as he glanced around as if trying to picture what she'd seen.

"No." She could barely get the word past a throat tight with grief. "I found her hair clip on the table in the living room, so I knew Mallory had been here. When I walked into my bedroom, there was blood and a stained yellow blouse over there. In that corner." She gestured with her right hand. "There was so much blood—I can't see how she could have survived. Don't you see? I was in danger—Crane followed me and tried to run me off the road. Mallory came here, and they must have killed her by mistake!"

Gage's grip on her shoulder tightened. "I'm not surprised that Crane tried to kill you. But, Alyssa, you don't know for sure that Mallory is dead. Isn't it possible the blood wasn't hers? Maybe she fought off her attacker and somehow managed to escape?"

She stared at him in shock. She'd been so certain Mallory was dead, but maybe, just maybe, Gage was right. Was it possible Mallory had escaped a horrible attack? Fragile hope bloomed in her heart. With all the blood, she'd honestly expected to find a dead body, but she hadn't. She wanted very badly to believe Gage was right. "But if Mallory is still alive, where is she? Why wouldn't she call me or try to find me? Why wasn't she at home in her condo?"

"I'm not sure," Gage allowed. "But remember, you haven't been home for a while. I stopped by here a few days ago, and the pine cleaner scent was overpowering. I knew something was wrong because you always use vinegar to clean. Now I believe Crane or Jefferson had this place cleaned to hide the scene of a crime. That's why the pine cleaner scent was so overpowering. Maybe they deleted a message from Mallory. Or maybe Mallory thought for some reason she was the one in danger, and that by leaving she'd protect you from harm."

Alyssa knew the latter was a very strong possibility. Her twin was extremely protective, to the point of doing outrageous things, like flirting with Gage to make sure he truly cared for Alyssa. If Mallory for some reason thought she herself was the target, then absolutely, Mallory would take off to protect her.

She lost her cell phone, which was another reason Mallory couldn't have gotten in touch with her, even if she'd wanted to. "If only I hadn't lost my cell phone, there might be a message from Mallory on there," she murmured, remembering her mad dash through her neighbors' backyards as she'd run for her life. Until she'd fallen, rolling down the hill. "We have to find her, Gage. If there's any chance Mallory is alive, we have to find her."

"We will," he assured her. "Once we're safe, we'll look for your sister until we find her."

Alyssa felt something warm dripping on her arm, and her gaze settled on the blood-soaked bandage around his wrist. "I'd almost forgotten why we came here. That cut is really deep—your wrist shouldn't still be bleeding like that."

He grimaced. "I know. I think the artery might be nicked."

She scrambled to her feet, ignoring the shaft of pain that shot up from her ankle. "An artery?" she echoed, appalled with herself. What kind of nurse was she? Knowing that Gage needed immediate medical attention made it easier to push her grief and worry for Mallory aside. "Sit down in the kitchen and hold pressure while I get the first-aid kit from the bathroom." She remembered exactly where she'd stored her first-aid kit and was relieved the infernal fog was lifted from her mind.

Thank You, Lord, for the return of my memory. And please, keep Mallory safe in Your care.

She grabbed the first-aid kit from the bathroom closet and hobbled into the kitchen. Gage was sitting on the table, holding pressure on his injured wrist. He looked pale, and she suspected he'd already lost too much blood. She opened the kit, took out her supplies and then went over to the kitchen sink to get soap, water and towels.

She gently cleaned his wrist. The gash in his skin was much larger and deeper than she'd realized. Her guilt must have shone on her face, because he quickly spoke up. "Not your fault," he said firmly. "You couldn't see what you were doing, and neither could I. We were lucky to escape with only minor injuries, so don't make this worse than it is. I'm sure a pressure dressing will work just fine."

"I don't think so," she murmured, not at all happy with the way blood constantly oozed out of the cut. "This is too deep. The artery needs to be stitched closed. We need to get you to a doctor."

"No hospital, no doctor," he curtly refused. "You're a nurse, Alyssa. If it needs a suture, do it yourself."

She stared at him in horror. He didn't understand what he was asking. "If the arterial blood flow to your hand is damaged, you could lose circulation to your fingers," she argued. With two fingers, she pressed hard on the area just above the open cut and the blood flow stopped. She held it for a full minute, hoping the collateral circulation would work. She tested his fingers, making sure they stayed pink and warm.

"We don't have a choice, Alyssa," he told her. "You're strong and I know you have the skill and ability to do this. But you have to hurry—we aren't safe here for long. I'm sure once Crane discovers we've escaped from the warehouse, he'll think to check here at some point."

He was right. As much as she hated the thought of hurting Gage, or possibly causing irreversible damage to the circulation in his hand, they didn't have time to waste. His wrist needed immediate care. "Okay, hold pressure right here." She indicated the area she wanted him to press. "I'll need to find a needle and thread."

Gage nodded and did as she asked. She stood and bit back a cry of pain when her sore ankle took her weight. After she took care of Gage's wound, she planned on wrapping her ankle with an Ace bandage.

She found her sewing kit without problem and took it back into the kitchen. She gathered her small scissors, gauze, tape and antibiotic ointment. She found a small box of matches in her kitchen junk drawer and lit one to sterilize the needle.

After she had everything she needed, she returned to the kitchen table. "Are you ready?" she asked, feeling sick to her stomach. She hadn't sutured anyone up while they were wide-awake and able to feel what she was doing. "This is going to hurt."

"I know. Just do what you need to do."

She wished she didn't have to do anything, but his calm acceptance helped steady her. She carefully examined the wound. The area she needed to stitch wasn't on the surface, but down inside the cut. His arm jerked when she gently inserted the needle. "I'm sorry," she murmured, blinking the tears from her eyes so she could see what she needed to do. Caring for strangers in the emergency department was far easier than sticking Gage with a needle. She felt every flinch as deeply as if she were poking a needle into her own skin. "I'm sorry," she repeated, helplessly.

Sweat beaded on her forehead and rolled down the side of her temple as she concentrated on the task at hand. Six long, agonizing stitches later, she dropped the needle with relief. "There. I'm finished." She washed the remaining blood away, and then liberally spread a layer of antibiotic ointment over her rather-uneven stitches before wrapping gauze loosely around his wrist. She felt dizzy, as if she'd been the one stitched up. She was amazed that Gage had been able to take the pain so well.

"Thanks, Alyssa," he murmured, his lips forming a faint smile. He lifted his uninjured hand to cup her face, his thumb lightly tracing the curve of her cheek. "I probably don't tell you often enough, but I think you're amazing."

Her breath caught, tangled in her throat. She gazed into his cinnamon-colored eyes and remembered how much she'd admired him when they'd first met. Gage had accompanied a crew member who'd gotten hurt on one of his construction sites. His caring and compassion for his employee, despite the accident being mostly the man's own fault for not wearing the proper safety gear, had immediately drawn her to him. He'd asked her out, and uncharacteristically, she'd agreed.

They'd gotten engaged within a few months. Too quickly, she realized now. Returning his ring and walking away was the hardest thing she'd ever done. But she couldn't marry a man who didn't celebrate his faith. And deep down, she knew Gage had just been going through the motions because she'd asked him to. Not because he wanted to.

"Alyssa," he whispered her name, drawing her close. "I know you're remembering all the reasons you left me, but please give me another chance to show you how much I've changed. I finally understand what you wanted for me, so don't write me off as hopeless. Please?"

She leaned into his embrace, wanting to do as he asked. Certainly, he wasn't hopeless. She managed to nod, mere moments before his mouth captured hers in a poignant kiss.

His mouth was sweet, gentle, yet insistent as it captured hers, sweeping away any lingering doubts. She reveled in his embrace, wishing she could stay in his arms forever.

Gage buried his face in Alyssa's hair, drawing deep breaths to steady his racing heart. He couldn't regret kissing her, even though he knew they needed to leave. Now. He fully expected Crane to show up at any moment. Reluctantly, he pulled away and forced a smile. "Let's find some clean clothes and then get out of here."

Alyssa sank into a kitchen chair. "I have to wrap my

ankle, or there's no way I'll be able to walk even with a cane."

"Let me," he said, and quickly dropped to his knees. When he saw her darkly bruised and swollen ankle, he felt awful. How could he ask her to walk? A surge of helplessness gripped him by the throat. She'd been so worried about the cut on his wrist, yet her ankle was just as bad, if not worse. It had to be broken. For sure, they'd have to continue using the bike. Gently, he took the Ace bandage and wrapped her ankle, providing some support, although not nearly enough in his opinion.

She loosened the laces on her running shoe and then slid it back on her foot. "Gage, I left my car in a park-and-ride not too far from here. That night, when I found the blood, I'd taken a bus, because I was worried Crane would try to follow me."

"You did?" He'd been dreading the return of her memory, knowing she'd remember why she'd left him, but now he realized her memory could be a tremendous help. "That's perfect. We can borrow your bike from the garage, and with both of us biking, we'll make decent time to the park-and-ride."

"Okay." Relief relaxed her facial features.

It took several precious moments to find and change into clean clothes, but he knew they couldn't easily rent a motel room wearing blood-stained apparel. Thankfully, Alyssa had a backpack and they stored some essentials, mainly granola bars and medical supplies for his wrist, and then they were once again ready to go.

Alyssa was pedaling slowly, as if even that much pressure on her ankle hurt. He was tempted to force her to ride double again, but he knew they'd look far more conspicuous if he did that.

The park-and-ride wasn't far, but it took them the better part of a half hour to get there. His heart sank when he didn't see her familiar car.

Alyssa scowled. "Where is it? Gage, I know I left my car right here," she gestured to the now-empty parking space.

"Let's look around, maybe with everything that's happened, you're not remembering it clearly."

But even though he circled the entire park-and-ride twice on his bike, he knew she was right. She'd no doubt left her car there, but it was gone now.

"Crane," she muttered under her breath. "I bet that lowlife probably had it towed, because he knew there was evidence of the crash on the driver's side, where he tried to sideswipe me off the road."

Gage nodded grimly. "I'm sure you're right. But let's look on the bright side—we have four wheels between us." His attempt at humor fell flat.

The shrill ring of his phone nearly sent him crashing off his bike. Hoping, praying it was his father, he quickly checked the number and saw it was Jonah's. But Jonah was in the hospital. "Hello?" he answered cautiously. Was this another trap? Had Crane gotten hold of Jonah's cell phone?"

"Gage? Where are you?" Although it was weak, he clearly recognized Jonah's voice.

"Jonah? How are you? Is everything okay?"

"I'm out of the hospital, but don't dare go back home." Jonah's voice was faint, and Gage had to strain to hear him. "I think we need to stick together."

He was all in favor of sticking together, but was Jonah stable enough to leave the hospital? He'd been stabbed just last night. He tightened his grip on the phone. "We're at the park-and-ride by Watertown Plank Road, and we can certainly meet you. I can't believe your doctor discharged you from the hospital."

"The doctor didn't discharge me, I left against medical advice. But only because someone tried to sneak into my room to finish off the job they started at the park. I'm better off taking my chances out here with you than being a sitting duck in my hospital room."

He reeled from the news. "We'd pick you up, but we don't have a car," Gage said to Jonah. Was it possible Crane or Jefferson had a nurse working for them? A nurse who'd sneaked into Jonah's room to try to finish him off? The same nurse who'd gotten hold of potassium chloride to kill Mayor Flynn?

"My buddy loaned me a car. I'll meet you along Underwood Creek Parkway in five minutes. I'm driving a black Ford Taurus."

"Alyssa and I are on bicycles and we'll head over that way right now." He snapped his cell phone shut. "We're meeting Jonah at the parkway."

"He shouldn't have left the hospital," Alyssa murmured as she turned her bike toward the north end of the park-and-ride. "He just had surgery yesterday."

"He claims someone tried to sneak into his room to finish him off," he said, relaying Jonah's story. "Claims his odds are better out here than stuck in his room."

"Maybe," she said, her tone betraying her doubt. "If he doesn't pass out from pain or infection. Good thing we packed the first-aid supplies. We're the three injured musketeers," she joked weakly.

He flashed a reassuring grin. "Yes, and we're just as resilient," he agreed.

The smile she flashed over her shoulder gave him hope that they might find a way out of this mess yet. Within a few minutes, they reached the parkway. This early in the evening, in the warm summer air, there were a lot of cars parked and many people running or riding bikes. They fit right in.

He spied a black car parked at the side of the road, isolated from most of the others. When they approached, the headlights flashed twice. "That's Jonah," Gage said in relief as he closed the distance, with Alyssa following close behind.

Jonah rolled down his driver's-side window as they approached. "You'll need to leave your bikes here. There isn't enough room for them in this dinky car. Hide them in the trees over there," he said, indicating the small patch of trees.

"Okay, but unlock the door, Alyssa needs to sit down. I'll ditch the bikes."

"Fine," Jonah said, unlocking the doors. "But hurry, I'm starting to get light-headed. One of you is going to have to drive."

Gage tossed both bikes in the deep thicket along the edge of the creek, and then hurried back over to the car. He wasn't at all reassured to find Jonah slumped over the steering wheel.

"His pulse is faint but steady," Alyssa said from the passenger seat beside him. Her worried gaze met his. "But you need to get us someplace safe soon, because Jonah needs fluids, antibiotics and rest—stat."

FIFTEEN

Alyssa kept her fingers on Jonah's pulse the entire ride to the motel. Thanks to a car with a full tank of gas, Gage was able to take them outside the city limits, off the main highway.

She was worried about Jonah. He'd obviously left the hospital too early. She could probably give him enough fluids and force him to rest, but antibiotics? They couldn't get a prescription for antibiotics without a doctor's order.

Gage pulled up to the motel and glanced at her in the rearview mirror. "I know you're tired and your ankle hurts, but it would be best if you could go in to rent the room. The red hair might throw them off."

His plan made sense, and with their limited reserves, she knew they couldn't afford two rooms anyway. She slid out of the car and took the money he handed her. Her ankle screamed in pain, but she resolutely ignored it and forced herself to walk into the motel lobby.

"I need a room for the night," she said, flashing the heavyset older man standing behind the counter a bright smile. "I hope you'll take cash, though, since I had to cut up my credit cards." She leaned forward and lowered her voice, as if sharing a dark secret. "I was addicted to QVC."

The old man smiled as she'd hoped he would and handed over an actual, old-fashioned key. "Sixty-two per night is the cash rate, Ms. er—?" He looked at her expectantly.

"Anderson, but please call me Amy." Sixty-two sounded like a lot, but she handed over the money and snatched the key off the counter. "Thanks so much."

"You're in room seven, at the end of the row. And checkout time is eleven o'clock," he added as she turned away from the counter. She gave him a tiny wave to show she heard him and left the lobby, leaning heavily against the wall to rest her ankle as soon as she was out of his line of vision.

The distance back to the Ford Taurus where Gage and Jonah waited seemed like ten miles instead of ten yards. Gathering every bit of strength she possessed, she pushed away from the wall to head back toward the vehicle, but she halted when she noticed the vending machine. She fed two dollars into the machine and pressed the button for a bottle of Gatorade. The stuff didn't taste very good in her opinion, but the electrolytes and sugar would help Jonah's dehydration faster than plain water.

"We're in room seven. Just give me a minute to unlock the door," she said to Gage through the open driver's window.

"I'll get Jonah. You rest your ankle."

As much as she wanted to do that, she didn't think Gage would be able to get Jonah's muscular frame inside without help. But she needn't have worried, because Gage and Jonah staggered in while she was still searching for something heavy to prop the door open. She was relieved to see Jonah was awake and walking somewhat on his own.

"Thanks," Jonah grunted when Gage helped lower him to the edge of the closest bed.

"I need to check your wound," she said, moving to his side.

"It's not that bad," Jonah protested wearily. "After surgery they told me I was lucky because my ribs deflected the tip of the knife away from my diaphragm."

She agreed with the doctor's assessment. A paralyzed diaphragm took away a person's ability to breathe on his or her own. "Did you lose the lower lobe of your lung?" she asked as she looked at his dressing. Thankfully, there was no sign of bleeding.

"Yeah. How did you know?" Jonah asked.

"Alyssa is a trauma nurse, remember?" Gage spoke up. "And that means you need to listen to her advice."

"Yes, starting with drinking this entire bottle of Gatorade," she informed him. "Honestly, Jonah, you shouldn't have left the hospital. Without antibiotics, your wound is likely to get infected."

"I have the bottle of antibiotics they gave me," he offered, pulling them out of his pocket. "And they were talking about sending me home in a day or two anyway, so what's the difference?"

She eagerly scooped up the bottle of antibiotics. *Thank You, Lord!* With God's help, she knew they could get Jonah back on his feet very soon. "Here, you're due for a dose now, and you can wash it down with the Gatorade."

Jonah did as she asked. "Gage, I know where to find Hugh Jefferson," he said, after he finished off the entire bottle of Gatorade.

"Where?" Gage demanded.

"I did some searching and discovered he has a boat slip down at the marina. The name of his private yacht is *Lucky Lady*."

Food, hydration and rest worked wonders for Jonah. Alyssa was relieved and reassured when after twenty-four hours, he claimed he felt one hundred percent better.

"We need to plan our next steps," Gage said over breakfast from a local fast-food restaurant. He'd slept on the floor without complaint. "We can't just keep hiding out at motels. We have an ally in Gerald Maas, but I'm not sure how much weight his opinion will carry, since he didn't win the election last night."

Eric Holden's landslide victory had been all over the news. She couldn't help feeling guilty that they hadn't been able to do more to help the best man win.

"I think we need to go down to the marina, to stake out Jefferson's yacht," Jonah murmured. "Maybe we'll catch something incriminating with my camera phone."

"I doubt he'll be so careless," she felt compelled to point out.

"He's arrogant enough to think he's above the law," Gage countered. "I agree with Jonah. He and I should head down to the marina. It's the only clue we have."

She froze, staring at Gage in shock. "You and Jonah?" she slowly repeated. "What about me?"

Gage avoided her gaze. "You should stay here and rest that ankle. We'll be back soon enough."

She couldn't believe that he was so willing to leave her here. What about being partners? What about being in this together? "I can't stay here. Checkout time is eleven o'clock. I'm going with you."

"No, you're not." Gage slapped some more money on

the small table. "You're going to ask to stay another night, and then you're going to wait here for us, where you'll be safe." The sharp edge to his tone ripped her heart.

So much for his claim that he'd changed. Maybe he'd made strides with his faith, but he still refused to treat her as an equal partner. "Gage, I'll be safer with you and Jonah than staying here alone."

"No, that's where you're wrong, Alyssa." Gage rose to his feet, and this time, when he finally met her gaze, she could see he'd already made up his mind. "I've done nothing but drag you into danger, over and over again. You're staying here, end of discussion."

"End of discussion?" she echoed in horror. Gage was showing his true nature, and she wasn't sure she liked it at all. How dare he talk to her like this? Especially after everything they'd been through.

"Yes. And don't bother arguing. There's nothing you can say or do to make me change my mind."

Gage almost caved at the stark, wounded expression in Alyssa's blue eyes. But he knew how awful her ankle looked—rest was what she needed more than anything. Besides, what was wrong with keeping her safe? Being safe wasn't a bad thing, it was a good thing. He'd failed her when Crane had captured them, and it was only through a little luck and a lot of faith that they managed to escape. He couldn't stand the thought of failing her again.

"Don't do this, Gage," she implored him. "You told me you changed, that we were partners. I thought you trusted me. Trusted the Lord to watch over us."

"I do, but logically, there's no reason to put you in

danger, Alyssa. We're going on a fact-finding mission, nothing more."

Jonah rose to his feet and edged toward the door. "I'll wait in the car while you two fight this one out," he murmured.

"There's nothing to fight about." He tore his gaze away from Alyssa's and followed Jonah to the door. "We'll be back before you know it," he shot over his shoulder before closing the motel room door behind him.

"Whew," Jonah whistled under his breath as they walked across the asphalt parking lot. "She's not happy with you, man."

Gage shrugged, knowing Jonah's words were a gross understatement. For a moment he hesitated, but then steeled his resolve and opened the driver's-side door to slide behind the wheel. "I'd rather she was safe and mad than in danger."

"I know what you mean," Jonah admitted. "But she was right about having faith, Gage. I don't think I'd be here today if not for God's love and support."

He glanced at his friend in surprise. He knew Jonah was religious, but his buddy had never said anything like this before. "Really?"

Jonah nodded. "I accepted Christ years ago when my partner took a bullet meant for me. I almost quit the force, but it was only through church and renewing my faith that I was able to return to my job."

Gage remembered when Jonah's partner had died, but he didn't realize how traumatized his friend had been at the time. Now he felt guilty for his ignorance. "I'm sorry, Jonah. I didn't know."

His buddy shrugged. "I knew you were busy trying to keep your business afloat."

Yes, he had been, but his business shouldn't have been put ahead of his best friend. As he drove, he realized Alyssa had felt the same way, when he'd used work as an excuse not to attend her Bible study group. His business had claimed a lot of his attention, and that wasn't necessarily a bad thing. Except when it got in the way of his relationships. "I'm sorry, Jonah," he repeated. "I'm sorry I wasn't there for you."

Jonah raised a brow. "I'm not the one you should be apologizing to," he pointed out. "Alyssa is the one you just left behind."

"Only to keep her safe," he added. "You're injured. It's not as if we're going to take any chances here. For all we know, Jefferson's yacht isn't even in port." He glanced at the dashboard clock. "We'll be back at the motel in a couple of hours."

Alyssa made her way back to the motel office, with Gage's money clutched in her hand. She wasted fifteen minutes crying, grieving for something she'd never have, before she'd pulled herself together.

First she needed to secure the room for a second night. Then she needed to find some way to contribute to the investigation. She'd already used the phone book in the room to find Gerald Maas's phone number. Maybe the former mayoral candidate wouldn't mind coming out to the motel to pick her up.

The older man from yesterday wasn't behind the counter. A younger woman who might have been his daughter glanced at her curiously when she walked in. "May I help you, miss?"

Alyssa's smile was strained. "Yes, I'd like to keep the

room for another night." She set the cash on the counter and pushed it toward the clerk.

The younger woman frowned a bit when she saw the money, and then her sharp gaze returned to Alyssa's face. For a moment, she wondered if the young woman recognized her. She resisted the urge to fluff her red hair as she returned the clerk's gaze. "Oh, you're the Amy Anderson in room seven, aren't you?" she asked. "My dad mentioned you didn't have a credit card."

Tension eased from her shoulders. "Yes, that's correct. Being addicted to QVC didn't help my credit rating, let me tell you. But I'm slowly paying off my debt, month by month."

"Hmm. I see." The young woman slowly took the money, counting the cash. "What brings you to the area?" she idly asked.

Alyssa tried to think of a plausible explanation. "Oh, I'm just passing through," she said vaguely, slowly backing away from the counter. "Thanks again for letting me stay," she said as she pushed through the door.

She could feel the young woman's gaze burning into her back, and she tried to walk normally down the sidewalk to her room. Her heart pounded in her chest and sweat gathered along the back of her neck. Probably just her overactive imagination, thinking the clerk may have recognized her from the news. Hadn't Gage thought the same thing the night before? And they'd been safe, hadn't they?

Inside her motel room, she used the phone to call Gerald Maas, but when there was no answer, she was forced to leave a message. Now what? The minutes seemed to pass by with excruciating slowness.

She stretched out on the bed and closed her eyes to

pray. *Dear Lord, please keep Jonah and Gage safe in Your care. And please grant us the strength and wisdom to find the evidence we need to put Jefferson and Crane behind bars. Amen.*

A sense of peace settled over her and she must have dozed a bit, because her mind was still groggy when she heard a sharp rap at her door. "Housekeeping!"

She swung her legs off the bed and crossed over to the door. Remembering her earlier paranoia about the clerk recognizing her, she took a minute to peer through the peephole. She could see a small, gray-haired woman standing there alongside her cleaning cart. Relieved, she opened the door. "I don't need anything except a few extra towels," she began, only to stop abruptly when Crane jumped out from behind the cart.

"No!" she cried, trying to slam the door in his face. But he was too quick, and he slapped a hand on the door, shoving it so hard she stumbled back.

"Well, well, well," he drawled, his evil grin leering at her from above. Horrified, she struggled to get back on her feet. "If it isn't Ms. Roth, once again."

"Help me," she cried out to the maid, but the woman shook her head and backed away, taking her cart with her. She was trapped. The only way out was through the door where Crane stood.

"No one is going to help you," Officer Crane said, reaching down to drag her roughly to her feet. She could feel his hot breath against her cheek, and she struggled not to scream. "Where's your boyfriend?"

She shook her head, unwilling to say anything about Gage. When he ruthlessly snapped metal cuffs around her wrists, she couldn't do anything but pray.

Help me, Lord! Save me from this horrible, evil man and protect Gage and Jonah.

"Not talking, huh? Oh, you will soon enough, once Jefferson gets hold of you." His evil grin made her feel sick to her stomach. He dragged her toward his squad car. Out of the corner of her eye she could see the maid huddled against the wall. "Ms. Roth, you're officially under arrest for the murder of Dan Kirkland."

Gage had to park a few blocks from the marina, and as he and Jonah walked he told himself it was a good thing he'd left Alyssa behind, since walking would have been difficult for her.

But then again, he knew she'd walked much farther distances without complaining.

Had he made the wrong decision to leave her behind? He hadn't thought so, but now he wasn't so sure.

"Okay, we're looking for slip number thirty-one," Jonah said in a low tone. "And keep your eyes peeled for someplace to sit and watch without attracting attention."

He nodded and carefully looked at each boat as they approached the marina. The place was busy even midmorning on a Wednesday, although he saw many smaller boats, not bigger yachts like the one registered to Hugh Jefferson.

"Look over there." Jonah nudged him and gestured to the right. "See those bigger boats? I think one of those must belong to Jefferson."

Gage saw the area he meant. "Yeah, I see them. I can't read the names on the boats, though."

"We have to get closer." Jonah led the way along the pier as if he came down to the marina often. "There it is," he said excitedly. "The one on the end, see it? *Lucky Lady*."

"I see it." Gage was intimidated by the sheer size of the boat. Had to be a good eighty feet long. "And there's a small sailboat on this side that's almost directly across from it. I think we should sit in that boat and keep watch."

"Okay," Jonah agreed. "But you'd better pray the owner isn't going to come down anytime soon."

"Don't worry, I will pray." Gage had never talked about prayer and faith like this with anyone except Alyssa before. But knowing that Jonah believed somehow made it easier to be open and honest with his friend.

As soon as they returned to the motel, he vowed to make amends with Alyssa. And the next time they went out on a fact-finding mission, he was going to bring her along. Truthfully, leaving her behind hadn't helped his concentration any. In fact, his thoughts were torn between wondering how she was doing and the job at hand.

He and Jonah slipped into the sailboat and hunkered down so they were partially hidden by the mast. From their angle, they could see clearly into the back of the boat.

"No sign of Jefferson," Jonah murmured beside him. "But with a yacht that big, he could easily be down below in the cabin."

Gage made himself comfortable on a boat cushion, sensing they were going to be here for a long time. Although it occurred to him that if Jefferson wanted to escape on the boat, there wasn't anything they could do to stop him. They didn't even have a boat to use in pursuit. "The Coast Guard," he said suddenly.

Jonah glanced at him with admiration. "You're right,

Gage, we should have thought of that earlier. The Coasties have the right to board any boat they want, for any reason."

That was an interesting fact Gage hadn't known. "I don't suppose you know anyone enlisted in the guard?" he asked.

"Actually, I do," Jonah responded slowly. "A guy by the name of Rafe DeSilva. He's stationed up at Sturgeon Bay, but they make their way all around the Great Lakes."

"Try calling him," Gage urged. "If he doesn't answer, then leave a message."

Jonah looked uncertain. "Gage, what am I going to tell him? That we suspect Jefferson is a crook and they should board his boat? What if they don't find anything?"

Gage let out his breath in a heavy sigh. "I guess you have a point," he murmured. "We should wait until we have a good reason to call."

Suddenly, Jonah gripped his arm, hard. "I think we have our reason, Gage. Look! Isn't that Crane walking down the pier with Alyssa?"

Gage's heart leaped into this throat when he saw Crane walking alongside Alyssa, heading directly toward Jefferson's yacht. Her wrists were free, but he could tell by the way Crane held her close to his side that the dirty cop had a gun pressed against her. "Call the Coast Guard, now," he urged Jonah. "Before it's too late!"

Jonah already had his phone out to make the call. Gage watched helplessly as Crane urged Alyssa onto the boat. He shouldn't have left her alone. And he wouldn't leave her alone now. Without saying anything to Jonah, he stood, rocking the small sailboat, and dove into the water.

Jefferson's yacht wasn't leaving without him.

SIXTEEN

"Step into the boat," Crane growled into her ear. Shaking with fear, she did as he commanded. The moment she was on board the engine rumbled to life beneath her feet. Crane kept the gun aimed at her as he quickly unmoored the boat from the slip and then jumped on board. Within seconds the boat slowly drifted away from the pier.

"Welcome aboard the *Lucky Lady,* my dear," a gravelly male voice said from behind her. "It's a beautiful day for a boat ride, wouldn't you agree?"

Alyssa slowly turned to face Hugh Jefferson. He was dressed impeccably in a white shirt and white slacks, as if they were truly headed out for a simple pleasure cruise. He flicked a piece of lint from his sleeve and then gestured to the inner cabin behind him. "Ladies first."

She swept a quick glance around, frantically hoping to catch some onlooker's gaze, but no one seemed to pay them the least bit of attention as the boat slowly backed away from the pier. The sun was out and seagulls swooped and dived over the water, searching for food. The scent of fish was strong, making her feel sick. For a moment she was tempted to dash forward and throw herself in the water, but she held herself back.

She needed to have faith in God. Not to mention, faith in both Gage and Jonah. Surely they were close by and would sound the alarm. Who was piloting the boat? She didn't know and was afraid to ask. Reluctantly, she moved forward, brushing past Jefferson as she went down the short hall to the private sitting area of the yacht.

He followed right behind, too close, as she could feel his hot breath on the back of her neck. "I've been waiting for this moment for a long time, *Alyssa*," he hissed.

The sound of her name instead of Mallory's caused her heart to drop like a stone. Jefferson knew her real identity? She walked forward, across a plush carpet lining a ridiculously extravagant sitting room. Stubbornly, she lifted her chin. "Really, Hugh, I'm appalled you've mistaken me for my twin sister," she bluffed.

"Alyssa, you underestimate me," Jefferson drawled. He pushed her in the small of her back, making her stumble forward, pain zinging up her injured ankle. She grasped the edge of what looked to be a well-stocked bar and then slowly turned to face him, her stomach twisting with dread. "Did you really think your poor dye job and pathetic attempt to evade me actually worked? I've always known your true identity." His gaze narrowed dangerously. "Now, if you want to live, you'll tell me where to find both your sister, Mallory, and your boyfriend, Gage Drummond."

Hearing his name caused Gage to flatten himself along the side of the luxurious yacht, his heart pounding so loud he could barely concentrate. Slowly, he inched along the wall, edging as close as he dared. Hopefully, Jonah would soon send the Coast Guard after them, because now that he was on board, he wasn't sure what he could do to help.

He just knew he couldn't leave Alyssa to face Hugh Jefferson and Creepy Crane alone.

"Would you like something to drink, my dear?" Jefferson asked as if he were entertaining guests. "I'm sure you must be parched. I have an excellent selection of wines or single-malt Scotch, if you prefer something smooth."

"No, thank you," Alyssa responded politely.

Gage could hear the distinct sound of ice clinking against glass, and he assumed Jefferson was pouring himself a drink. "Have a seat," Jefferson encouraged. "You won't be getting off this boat anytime soon, so you may as well get comfortable."

"If you knew who I was all along, why attack Mallory?" she boldly asked. "Why not keep coming after me?"

"Yes, I must admit, your sister's escape was not part of the plan," Jefferson said, his voice taking a hard edge. "In fact, I was most displeased with the man who failed me. He deserved to die."

Gage swallowed a lump of fear. Jefferson obviously didn't care how many lives he took, as long as he got what he wanted.

"You should have let me take care of her, boss," Crane said in a bragging tone. "She wouldn't have gotten away from me."

"You?" Jefferson's voice was dangerously soft. "Have you forgotten how you let Alyssa escape not just once, after your pathetic attempt to run her off the road, but a second time, when you had both of them locked in the warehouse?"

Another long pause. Gage couldn't help a sense of satisfaction at how easily Jefferson knocked Crane down a few pegs.

"Wasn't my fault I was summoned by the chief because he wanted an update for his press conference," Crane argued hotly. "You need me, Jefferson, and don't forget it."

"You think so?" Jefferson said softly. "I wouldn't be so sure."

Gage held his breath, hoping the two men would keep fighting. He continued to edge along the side of the boat, scanning the water for any sign of the Coast Guard.

There was another long silence, and Gage went still. Had he inadvertently done something to attract attention?

"Now what?" Alyssa demanded loudly, so loudly she was nearly shouting. What in the world was she doing? "Are you going to kill me? Toss me overboard? What?"

She was trying to warn him. Gage started to back up, but seconds too late. Crane stepped around the edge of the boat, his gun pointing straight at Gage's chest. Belatedly, he realized the water dripping off him had made a small trickle that had rolled down, alerting Jefferson and Crane to his presence.

"Good timing, Drummond," Crane said, flashing his evil smile. He waved the gun, motioning Gage forward. "You're just in time to join the party."

Alyssa was horrified when Gage entered the room, followed closely by Crane holding the gun. The moment she'd noticed the steady stream of water, she'd suspected Gage was on board, but unfortunately, being trained as a police officer, Crane had noticed it, too.

The creep had been desperate to get back into Jefferson's good graces. Capturing Gage on Jefferson's boat hadn't hurt.

"Let's kill them both now," Crane said, his gaze darting nervously between Alyssa and Gage. If she didn't know better, she'd think the cop was actually intimidated by Gage. "We can dump their bodies overboard and they'll be fish bait before they're ever found."

"Excuse me, who put you in charge?" Jefferson asked softly. The softer his tone, the more nervous Crane appeared. Jefferson turned toward Gage, inclining his head regally. "Drummond, so glad you could join us."

"Stop it!" Crane shouted, his hand starting to shake. "We have them both, and Holden won the election by a mile. What do we need them for? You can find some other builder to use as a front for your money laundering. We need to shut them up, permanently!"

"For once, I agree with Aaron," a third voice said. Alyssa couldn't believe it when Eric Holden stepped into the room. She glanced at Gage, a mirroring dismay clearly reflected in his eyes. She knew exactly what he was thinking. Their odds were dwindling fast. How many others did Jefferson have stashed on his massive yacht?

"Holden, I told you to stay below." Jefferson's face turned red. Alyssa edged closer to Gage, seeking reassurance.

"I don't follow your orders," Holden snapped. "I'm the one with the power now, remember? Without me, you'll never get additional building permits. Besides, our boss is the one who calls the shots, not you."

Jefferson seemed to wrestle his temper under control, staring at Holden with frank disdain. "We'll do this my way," Jefferson reminded him. "No one can stop us now."

Without warning, Holden turned and shot Crane pointblank in the chest. Alyssa bit back a scream and turned away from the horrific sight.

"Easy," Gage murmured, so close she could feel his

arm brushing against hers. Bile rose in her throat and she fought the urge to be sick.

"Idiot," Jefferson growled. "We're not far enough from shore to dump the body."

"He'll keep," Holden said, as if he hadn't just murdered a man in cold blood. "You know as well as I do, his boss was starting to get suspicious with all the hours Crane put in. Better to get rid of him now, before he could take any of us down with him."

"You still should have waited until we were farther out," Jefferson admonished him. "We can't afford to have bodies floating around too soon."

Alyssa knew, in that moment, that she and Gage would be next. A strange sense of calm came over her. She believed in God and if she died this afternoon, she knew she'd ultimately end up in a better place. And so would Gage. They'd be together in heaven.

Gage's warm hand touched hers, and she grasped it as if it were a lifeline. He'd come for her, just as she'd known he would. He might be stubborn and overprotective, but she wished now she'd told him how much she loved him.

She shifted slightly and saw the bottle of Scotch Jefferson had opened sitting on top of the bar. Gage met her gaze and gave a nearly imperceptible nod as he slid his hand into his pocket. He still had the pocketknife. A hysterical laugh threatened to bubble up from her chest. A half-empty bottle of Scotch and a pocketknife to defend themselves against two men with guns? What were they thinking? But then again, they also had faith and God on their side.

"So what do you think? They're too young to use the fake heart attack ploy," Holden was saying. "But maybe alcohol? They came on board to celebrate my win, drank too much and fell overboard?"

"Your army medic training is very handy," Jefferson mused in admiration. "Sure, why not? We'll claim we tried to find them but, alas, we couldn't."

Alyssa lifted her chin, refusing to let either Jefferson or Holden see any trace of fear. As sick and far-fetched as their plan was, she knew there were plenty of people willing to believe anything, especially the word of someone with money and prestige. Unfortunately, Jefferson and Holden had both.

How many lives had the two men taken? How many more before they were caught?

Gage's fingers brushed hers again, and he darted a glance out the side window, which was partially covered with horizontal blinds. Through the narrow slats, she saw lights from an approaching boat. Help on the way? By the way Gage's fingers pressed against hers, she thought for sure it was.

She glanced at him and easily read Gage's intention. Now was the time to make their move, especially since Holden had given Jefferson the gun so he could prepare a needle and syringe.

In a swift motion, she swept the bottle of Scotch off the bar and swung it at Holden's head, since he was closest to her. Thick glass met his even thicker skull, knocking the newly elected mayor off balance. Spinning around, she followed up with another well-aimed blow, knocking him to the floor. Alcohol spewed from the open end of the bottle, spraying over the walls and soaking into the soft carpet.

At the exact same moment, Gage rushed Jefferson, leading with the pocketknife but also going for the gun. A wild shot rang out and Alyssa ducked as pieces of the fancy chandelier overhead crashed down on them.

Sparks flew from the bulbs, and then flames sprouted like tiny, lethal fairies dancing madly along the alcohol-soaked carpet. Alyssa had knocked Holden unconscious, but she watched in horror as Gage and Jefferson wrestled for control of the gun.

Smoke gathered in the room, making her eyes water and obscuring her vision. She needed to help Gage, but how? The bottle she'd used on Holden rolled away, and she spent precious moments searching for it. But then she spied the silver blade of the knife. She grabbed it, gasping in pain as the heat from the metal burned her skin.

She wrapped part of her shirt around the knife handle and looked over to where Gage and Jefferson were rolling along the floor. Gage was on top of Jefferson, but they were dangerously close to the burning area of the carpeting. "Look out!" she cried. In a heartbeat, Jefferson rolled over on top of Gage, taking them farther from the fire.

What could she do to help Gage? The cord hanging off the horizontal blinds caught her eye and she used the knife to hack off a good-size section. Turning back to Jefferson and Gage, she was appalled to see Jefferson was on top of Gage, his hands around Gage's throat.

Moving fast, she darted forward and looped the string over Jefferson's head, pulling backward across his neck.

"Accckkkk," he gurgled, loosening his grip on Gage to grasp at his throat. Gage wrestled the gun out of the other man's grip and shot him.

Alyssa dropped the cord, watching in horror as Jefferson crumpled to the floor. The greedy flames had crawled up the walls, feeding off the interior of the yacht like a starving beast. They were almost completely surrounded by fire when she heard Gage shouting at her.

"Come on, let's go!" He grabbed her hand and dragged

her through the narrow opening leading to the back of the yacht. Soon, they reached the small deck on the back of the boat.

The oncoming rescue boat was close, but not close enough. She heard a garbled sound behind them and glanced back in time to see a figure running toward them, waving his arms, clothes and hair on fire.

"Jump!" Gage shouted.

She jumped.

Shockingly cold water closed over his head. For a few moments he floated in the muffled silence, stunned at how fast the sharp, cold temperature numbed his limbs.

Alyssa! He struggled to kick his legs, propelling himself up to the surface. His strength faded fast, his movements sluggish. He had no idea how cold the water in Lake Michigan actually was, except to know it was too cold to stay immersed for long.

His head broke free, the air amazingly warm on his face. Gasping for breath, he looked frantically for Alyssa. The Coast Guard cutter moved steadily toward them, but where was Alyssa?

Panic swelled, making it harder to breathe. He knew she could swim, but where was she? Desperately, he turned in a circle, searching for a sign of her. He couldn't lose her now. He couldn't!

Not without telling her how much he loved her.

A flash of pink near the surface off to his right caught his eye and he forced his limbs into action, swimming as fast as he could.

"Alyssa!" he grabbed her supine body, dragging her face out of the water. With herculean strength, he flipped her over on her back.

She wasn't breathing!

"Gage! Alyssa!" He heard Jonah shouting at them from the Coast Guard cutter, but he couldn't respond. Alyssa was limp in his arms, and he cradled her head in the crook of his arm, bending over at an awkward angle to administer mouth-to-mouth breathing.

Again and again, he blew life-giving oxygen into her lungs, hoping, praying his feeble attempt would work. The Coast Guard boat came closer, and he willed her to hang on long enough to be rescued.

"Life preserver!" someone shouted from the side of the boat.

The circular life preserver at the end of a long line dropped beside him with a splash. He gave Alyssa one last, big breath before grabbing on.

She coughed and immediately threw up a lungful of lake water.

Thank You, Lord! Thank You!

"Ready!" Gage shouted. Within seconds, the Coast Guard drew them to safety, pulling Alyssa up first and then reaching down for him.

Several crew members must have noticed them shivering, because they were quickly wrapped in blankets.

"Jefferson?" Jonah asked, kneeling beside them.

He slowly shook his head. "I'm not sure if he's still on board or if he jumped into the water."

"He didn't jump," Jonah said with certainty. "We kept an eye on him, because if he had gotten overboard, we would have tried to save him. But he collapsed on the back deck and didn't move. They're going to try putting the fire out before taking the risk to board the boat."

Gage didn't blame them. He closed his eyes, silently begging God's forgiveness. He hadn't wanted to kill the guy. All he wanted was to escape long enough to get Alyssa out of there.

"Gage?" Alyssa's voice pulled him from his thoughts.

He glanced over at her and then reached out to pull her into his arms. Jonah backed off to give them privacy. "I'm sorry, Alyssa. I'm so sorry I left you alone at the motel."

"Shh, it's okay." She clung to him, burrowing close. "It's over. We're finally safe."

"Do you think God will forgive me?" he asked in a low, agonized tone. "I wasn't trying to kill him. I aimed the gun low, hoping to wound him. But then the fire…" He couldn't finish. The vision of the burning man would haunt him forever.

"Yes, Gage, I'm sure God will forgive both of us. God forgives all sins." She glanced back to where the burning boat still bobbed on the water. "Even theirs," she whispered.

"I never should have left you alone," he said again. "You were right, Alyssa. I'm sorry I've been so overprotective."

She pulled away to meet his gaze. "Why, Gage? What made you so overprotective?"

She'd never asked that before, and humbly he realized he should have talked about his past sooner. "My mother divorced my father when I was young, and she married a man who liked to use his fists. One night, their fighting woke me up and he was beating her, bad. I tried to stop him, but I was only ten and skinny as a rail. He leveled me with one blow. I dragged myself up and out of the house to get help, but I was too late. My mother suffered severe brain damage. She went into a coma and never woke up. She died three weeks later."

"Oh Gage," Alyssa murmured, wrapping her arms around him. "You should have told me."

She was right. There were so many things he should have done differently. Most important, he should have done a better job of embracing his faith. "I don't blame you for breaking off our engagement," he admitted. "I didn't take my relationship with God seriously, the way I should have. Now I can see that part of the reason was that I was still angry with Him, for taking my mother's life. In hindsight, I can see how I rationalized my need to work as more important than attending your study group." Suddenly, his less than stellar actions were crystal clear. "I only hope you'll let me attend your Bible study group again moving forward, so I can learn how to better serve God." He forced a smile. "Maybe once I graduate, you'll consider giving our relationship a second chance."

"Oh Gage," she murmured. "Of course I will." Before she could say anything more, Jonah returned.

"Sorry to interrupt, but the Coast Guard managed to put out the fire on Jefferson's yacht. Unfortunately, the only survivor was the guy driving the boat, who claims he doesn't know anything. Jefferson, Holden and Crane are all dead."

Guilt lodged in the back of his throat. If only he'd listened to Alyssa and taken her along. "I'm sorry."

Jonah's grim expression didn't help ease his guilt. "Unfortunately, we can't question them, to find out who they were working for."

Alyssa shifted in his arms, gaping at Jonah in shock. "You're right! Holden mentioned a boss. How did you know Jefferson wasn't the top guy?"

Jonah shrugged. "When I saw Crane dragging you onto the boat, I called my boss, who confided that they've suspected there were a couple of leaks in the department." He scowled, clearly upset with the thought of other dirty cops. "And then Rafe DeSilva mentioned they've been watching Jefferson's yacht for a long time, especially since he used the yacht often to go between Chicago and Milwaukee. They've seen Jefferson with several other men, one in particular who seemed to be the one in charge. Based on these two new pieces of information, they really wanted to take these guys alive."

"That's it!" Alyssa gripped Gage's arm. "Mallory isn't dead! Jefferson tried to get me to tell him where she was, so he obviously doesn't have her stashed away somewhere. Remember what you said, about Mallory taking off and hiding if she thought she was the target? I think you're right. She might have information about the guy in charge. We have to find her."

"Don't worry, finding Mallory has just risen to the top of my priority list," Jonah said, his tone lined with steely conviction. "My boss has given me the okay to continue working this case. For now, we're going to head back to shore."

When Jonah moved away, Gage glanced down at Alyssa. "I'll help find her, too," he vowed. "No matter what it takes, we'll bring her back, safe and sound."

"I know." When she smiled at him, his heart filled with joy. "I love you, Gage. I'm so thankful God watched over us and protected us."

He was humbled by her declaration, one he wasn't even sure he deserved. "I love you, too, Alyssa. More than you'll ever know. And I promise this time, I'll make you happy."

She hugged him hard and kissed him. *Thank You, Lord!* He silently rejoiced, knowing that accepting his faith had brought Alyssa home to him.

EPILOGUE

Alyssa used her new crutches to walk into Gage's house, where Jonah had already set up a satellite office. She was exhausted after spending the past few hours in the emergency department at Trinity Medical Center. Her face still burned with embarrassment at being poked and prodded by her colleagues. Using the crutches had also given her a new appreciation for the importance of upper-arm strength.

"Well?" Jonah asked, glancing up from his laptop computer. "I see they didn't keep you overnight."

"No, but she's going to have to come back," Gage said. "The orthopedic surgeon told her to stay off it for the next four to five days and then return for an MRI. He also told her he'd likely have to do surgery to repair the damage to her tendons and ligaments."

"But other than my ankle, I'm fine," she reminded him. "You saved my life, Gage. Minor repairs to my ankle are nothing in the big scheme of things." Gage had hovered over her gurney during the entire E.R. visit, and she knew he was still wrestling with guilt. She crutch-walked over to the sofa, and before she could even lift her foot off the floor, Gage was there to do it for her, putting her injured ankle up on a pillow. "Thanks," she murmured. She captured his hand in hers, gazing up at him, letting him see the love reflected in her eyes.

"Alyssa, who is Henry Stein?" Jonah asked abruptly. "Not Mallory's boyfriend, I hope."

She tore her gaze from Gage, belatedly remembering the glossy photo of Mallory and a strange man she'd found in the condo. Now that she had her memory, she vaguely remembered her twin was dating some guy named Anthony. "Don't be silly. Henry Stein is Uncle Henry. Well, actually, he's technically not our uncle; he's my mother's cousin. He must be in his late sixties or early seventies by now. Why are you asking about Uncle Henry?"

"Did you know he has a small lake cabin in Crystal Lake, Wisconsin?" Jonah asked.

"Oh, yeah, I guess now that you mention it, I do remember that," she mused. "Mallory and I went there a couple of times as kids. But I doubt Uncle Henry gets up there much anymore, though. He had a minor stroke last year and his left side is a little weaker than his right."

"So Mallory knew about the cabin."

"Yes." She smacked herself on the forehead. "I should have thought of the cabin sooner. Although to be honest, the cabin doesn't have the comforts of a hotel. It's a bit rough. And Mallory isn't the roughing-it kind of girl."

"Maybe not, but it's a lead I intend to follow up on," Jonah said as he shut down the computer. "I'm going to head up there tonight. If I find anything, I'll get in touch with you."

She glanced questioningly at Gage, who nodded. "Alyssa, you need to stay off that foot and get some rest. You trust Jonah, don't you?"

"Yes. Of course I trust Jonah." She smiled at Gage's best friend. "But promise me you'll call as soon as you know anything."

"I will. Take care, Alyssa. Gage." Jonah didn't waste any time. He slid the laptop into its carrying case and then headed for the door. Gage followed him out and then disappeared into the bedroom for several long minutes.

The house seemed eerily silent after Jonah left. Alyssa relaxed against the sofa cushions, reveling in the feeling of being safe at last. Gage returned about ten minutes later and came over to sit beside her on the sofa.

"Alyssa, did you mean what you said back on the boat?" he asked hesitantly.

"Yes, Gage." She knew exactly what he was trying to say. "I love you. And I believe you've deepened your relationship with God."

"I have, Alyssa. And I love you, too." He opened his palm and she saw her old engagement ring. "I can buy you a different one if you'd rather," he said quickly, when all she could do was stare in shock. "Will you do me the honor of being my wife?"

"Oh Gage," she murmured, holding out her left hand so he could slide her ring back on her finger, where it belonged. "Of course I'll marry you."

"I love you, Alyssa. More than I can ever say."

The modest diamond winked on her hand, and when Gage drew her carefully into his embrace, she knew this time, with the power of God's love, they'd make their relationship work.

* * * * *

Dear Reader,

I've always been fascinated by twins, especially identical twins. I've seen TV documentaries about twins separated at birth who have the same careers, the same medical problems, even the same hobbies. But what if you had identical twins with completely different personalities? This sparked the idea for my next two stories.

Alyssa and Mallory are twins, but due to a traumatic event when Mallory was younger, they lead very different lifestyles—until danger forces them to take each other's personalities.

Gage Drummond was engaged to Alyssa Roth, but after a few short months, she gave him his ring back because he was overprotective and didn't have a close relationship with God. But when Alyssa is in danger, he's willing to risk his life to save hers.

Reunited love is the theme of *Identity Crisis* in Alyssa and Gage's story. I'm always thrilled to hear from my readers, and I can be reached through my website at www.laurascottbooks.com.

Yours in faith,
Laura Scott

We hope you enjoyed reading
this special collection.

If you liked reading these stories, then you
will love **Love Inspired® Suspense** books!

You enjoy a dash of danger.
Love Inspired Suspense stories feature
strong heroes and heroines whose faith is
central in solving mysteries and saving lives.

Enjoy six new stories from
Love Inspired Suspense every month!

Available wherever books and
ebooks are sold.

Love Inspired®
SUSPENSE
RIVETING INSPIRATIONAL ROMANCE

**Suspenseful romances
of danger and faith.**

Find us on Facebook at
www.Facebook.com/LoveInspiredBooks

Get 2 Free Books,

Plus 2 Free Gifts—

just for trying the Reader Service!

LIS17R2

Looking for inspiration in tales
of hope, faith and heartfelt romance?

Check out **Love Inspired**®,
Love Inspired® **Suspense** and
Love Inspired® **Historical** books!

New books available every month!

CONNECT WITH US AT:

www.LoveInspired.com

Harlequin.com/Community

 Facebook.com/LoveInspiredBooks

 Twitter.com/LoveInspiredBooks

www.ReaderService.com

Love Inspired®

LIGENRE20

Reward the book lover in you!

Earn points from all your Harlequin book purchases from wherever you shop.

Turn your points into *FREE BOOKS* of your choice
OR
EXCLUSIVE GIFTS from your favorite authors or series.

Join for FREE today at
www.HarlequinMyRewards.com.

Harlequin My Rewards is a free program (no fees) without any commitments or obligations.

MYR17

Love Inspired®

Inspirational Romance to Warm Your Heart and Soul

Join our social communities to connect with other readers who share your love!

Sign up for the Love Inspired newsletter at **www.LoveInspired.com** to be the first to find out about upcoming titles, special promotions and exclusive content.

CONNECT WITH US AT:

Harlequin.com/Community

 Facebook.com/LoveInspiredBooks

 Twitter.com/LoveInspiredBks

LISOCIAL2017